Still
Life

BY JOY FIELDING

Still Life

A Novel

Joy Fielding

ANCHOR CANADA

Library and Archives Canada Cataloguing in Publication data
is available upon request.

ISBN 978-0-385-68959-5
eBook ISBN 978-0-385-67206-1

Cover design: Adapted from an original by Jae Song
Cover image: Stuart McClymont/Stone+/Getty Images

Printed and bound in the USA

Published in Canada by Anchor Canada,
a division of Penguin Random House Canada Limited
A Penguin Random House Company

www.penguinrandomhouse.ca

10 9 8 7 6 5 4 3 2 1

Penguin
Random House
ANCHOR CANADA

To all the truly wonderful women in my life

ACKNOWLEDGMENTS

There are a lot of people to thank this time around. As always, thanks to Larry Mirkin and Beverley Slopen, who read my early drafts with critical eyes and kind hearts. Their advice is invaluable. Thanks also to Judith Curr, Emily Bestler, Sarah Branham, Laura Stern, Louise Burke, David Brown, and everyone else at Atria Books, who work so hard to make my books a success in the United States, and to John Neale, Brad Martin, Maya Mavjee, Kristin Cochrane, Val Gow, Lesley Horlick, Adria Iwasutiak, and the staff at Doubleday Canada, a division of Random House of Canada. My humble thanks to all my publishers, editors, and translators throughout the world. I'm so grateful to you all. To Corinne Assayag of worldexposure.com, who has done such a superb job with my website. And to Tracy Fisher and her assistant, Elizabeth Reed, at the William Morris Agency. You had a hard act to follow, Tracy, and I'm sure Owen is very proud of the job you're doing. I know I am.

People often ask how much research I do on my books, and I'm always forced to admit that I hate doing research, preferring to "make up my facts." But there are times when real research is necessary, and I couldn't have written *Still Life* without the help of the following: Dr. Alan Marcus, who provided me with hours' worth of notes about what can happen to a person who has been struck by a car, including the various hospital tests, operations, and procedures that might follow; Dr. Keith Meloff, who detailed what happens to the brain of someone in a coma, and the kinds of tests that might be performed; and Dr. Terry Bates, who answered many of my more casual questions. These three gentlemen couldn't have been more gracious or helpful, and I thank you again.

Special thanks to Dr. Eddy Slotnick and his wife, Vicki, who provided me with lots of information about Philadelphia and its suburbs. I referred often to the notes I took from our many conversations, and hope I got the details right.

And thanks, of course—as well as hugs and kisses—go to my husband and daughters. Extra thanks to Shannon for her assistance with regard to my e-mail. And to Aurora, for making my life easier and for making sure I'm well fed. And lastly, to you, the readers. Your support, as well as your letters of encouragement, are a constant source of joy and satisfaction. You keep reading, and I'll keep writing.

Still
Life

1

LESS THAN AN HOUR before the car slammed into her at a speed of almost fifty miles an hour, throwing her ten feet into the air, breaking nearly every bone in her body and cracking her head against the hard concrete, Casey Marshall was sitting in the elegant, narrow dining room of Southwark, one of South Philadelphia's more popular white-tablecloth restaurants, finishing lunch with her two closest friends and stealing glances at the beautiful, secluded courtyard behind their heads. She was wondering how long the unnaturally warm March weather was going to last, whether she'd have time to go for a run before her next appointment, and whether she should tell Janine the truth about what she really thought of her latest haircut. She'd already lied and said she liked it. Casey smiled at the thought of an early spring and allowed her gaze to drift over her right shoulder, past the luminous still-life painting of a bouquet of enormous pink peonies by Tony Scherman, and toward the magnificent mahogany bar that was the centerpiece of the restaurant's front room.

"You hate it, don't you?" she heard Janine say.

"The painting?" Casey asked, although she doubted Janine had even noticed it. Janine regularly boasted she was oblivious to her surroundings. Having said that, she always seemed to select only the finest, most expensive places for them to have lunch. "I think it's fabulous."

"My hair. You think it's awful."

"I don't think it's awful."

"You think it's too severe."

Casey looked directly into Janine's intense blue eyes, several shades darker than her own. "A little, yes," she agreed, thinking that the sharp, geometric angles of the blunt cut that hugged Janine's long, thin face put too much emphasis on the already exaggerated point of her chin, especially when combined with the almost blue-black tint of her hair.

"I was just so tired of the same old thing all the time," Janine explained, looking to their mutual friend, Gail, for confirmation.

Gail, sitting beside Janine and across from Casey at the small, square table, nodded obligingly. "A change is as good as a rest," she said half a beat behind Janine, so their sentences overlapped, like a song being sung in rounds.

"I mean, we're not in college anymore," Janine continued. "We're over thirty. It's important to keep current. . . ."

"Always good to keep current," Gail echoed.

"It was just time to do away with the Alice in Wonderland hairdo." Janine's eyes settled pointedly on the naturally blond hair that fell softly across Casey's shoulders.

"I liked your hair long," Casey demurred.

"So did I," Gail agreed, tucking a few frizzy brown curls behind her right ear. Gail never had a problem with her hair. It always looked as if she'd just stepped on an electrical current. "Although I like it this way, too," she added.

"Yeah, well, it was time to move on. That's what you always

say, isn't it?" The question was accompanied by such a sweet smile that it was difficult to know whether or not to take offense. What wasn't difficult for Casey to figure out was that they were no longer talking about hair.

"Time for more coffee," Gail announced, signaling the waiter.

Casey decided to ignore the deeper implications of Janine's remark. What was the point in reopening old wounds? Instead, she offered up her gold-rimmed white china cup to the handsome, dark-haired waiter, watching as the hot brown liquid cascaded artfully from the spout of the silver coffeepot. While Casey knew Janine had never quite gotten over Casey's decision to leave the legal placement service they'd cofounded fresh out of college to start her own business in the totally unrelated field of interior design, she'd talked herself into believing that after almost a year, Janine had at least made peace with it. What complicated things was the fact that Casey's new business had taken off running, while Janine's had ground to a halt. And who wouldn't resent that? "It's amazing how everything you touch turns to gold," Janine regularly observed, always with the dazzling smile that accompanied the vaguely unpleasant undertone in her voice, making Casey question the validity of her instincts. It's probably just my guilty conscience, Casey thought now, not sure what she should feel guilty for.

She took a long sip of her black coffee, feeling it burn the back of her throat. She and Janine had been friends since their sophomore year at Brown. Janine had just made the switch from prelaw to honors English; Casey was double-majoring in English and psychology. Despite the obvious differences in their personalities— Casey generally the softer, more flexible of the two, Janine the more brittle and outgoing; Casey the more conciliatory, Janine the more confrontational—they'd clicked immediately. Perhaps it was a case of opposites attracting, of one woman sensing something in the other that was lacking in herself. Casey had never tried too hard to analyze the forces that had brought them together, or why their friendship had endured a decade past graduation, despite the myriad changes those ten years had brought, changes that included the dissolution of their business partnership and Casey's recent marriage to a man Janine described—complete with dazzling smile—as "fucking perfect, of course." Casey chose to be grateful instead.

Just as she was grateful for her other close friend, Gail, a young woman much less complicated than either Casey or Janine in virtually every respect. Casey had known Gail since grade school, and although more than twenty years had passed, Gail was essentially the same guileless, open-faced girl she'd always been. With Gail, what you saw was what you got. And what you got was a thirty-two-year-old woman who, despite much hardship, still ended almost every sentence with a giggle, like a shy teenage girl, eager to be liked. Sometimes she even giggled in the middle of a sentence, or even *while* she was speaking, a habit that was as disconcerting as it was endearing. Casey considered it the auditory equivalent of a puppy offering up its stomach to be stroked.

Unlike Janine, there were no pretenses where Gail was concerned, no hidden agendas, no particularly deep thoughts. She generally waited until she knew how you felt about something before offering up an opinion of her own. Occasionally Janine grumbled about Gail's naïveté and "unrelenting optimism," but even she'd been forced to agree that Gail was such a pleasant person, it made you feel good just to be around her. And Casey admired the skill involved in being able to listen to both sides of an argument and make each party believe you were on her side. It was probably what made her such a good saleswoman.

"Everything okay?" Casey asked, turning her attention back to Janine and praying for a simple yes in response.

"Everything's fine. Why?"

"I don't know. You just seem a little . . . I don't know."

"Of course you do. You know everything."

"You see—that's exactly what I mean."

"What do you mean?"

"What do *you* mean?"

"Am I missing something here?" Gail asked, large brown eyes darting nervously between the two women.

"Are you angry at me?" Casey asked Janine directly.

"Why would I be angry at you?"

"I don't know."

"I honestly don't know what you're talking about." Janine touched the gold locket at her throat and adjusted the collar of her crisp white Valentino blouse. Casey knew it was Valentino because she'd seen it on a recent cover of *Vogue*. She also knew that Janine couldn't afford to pay almost two thousand dollars for a blouse, but then, Janine had been dressing beyond her means for as long as Casey could remember. "It's very important to wear nice clothes," Janine had said when Casey questioned one of her more exorbitant purchases. Followed by: "I may not have been born with a silver spoon in my mouth, but I know the importance of dressing well."

"Okay," Casey said now, picking up the silver spoon next to her coffee cup and turning it over in her hand before letting it drop. "That's good."

"So maybe I *am* a little irritated," Janine conceded with a shake of her newly geometrically cut hair. Several straight black strands caught the side of her generous mouth, and she impatiently brushed them aside. "Not at you," she added quickly.

"What's the problem?" Casey pressed the instant-replay button in her mind, quickly reviewing the last sixty minutes. The women had enjoyed their various salads and glasses of white wine; they'd gossiped and caught up on everything that had happened in the two weeks since their last meeting. Everything had seemed fine. Unless Janine was still obsessing about her hair. . . .

"It's just that little twerp, Richard Mooney—you remember him?" Janine asked Casey.

"The guy we set up at Haskins, Farber?"

"The one and only. Jerk finishes in the bottom third of his graduating class," she explained to Gail. "Has zero social skills. Can't get a job to save his life. Nobody, but nobody wants to hire him. He comes to us. I tell Casey he's a loser, we shouldn't take him on, but she feels sorry for him, says we should give him a shot. Sure. Why not? She's leaving soon anyway, as it turns out."

"Whoa," Casey exclaimed, raising her palms in protest.

Janine dismissed Casey's objection with a megawatt smile and a wave of her long, French-manicured fingernails. "I'm just teasing you. Besides, we *did* take him on, and a few months later you *were* gone. Isn't that true?"

"Well, yes, but . . ."

"So that's all I'm saying."

Casey was having a hard time figuring out exactly *what* Janine was saying. She would have made a great lawyer, Casey was thinking, wondering why they were talking about Richard Mooney at all.

"So back to Richard Mooney," Janine said, as if Casey had voiced her confusion out loud. She returned her attention to Gail. "Sure enough, we were actually able to do something for that little twerp. Turned out one of the partners at Haskins had a soft spot for Casey. She batted her eyelashes at him a few extra times and he agreed to give Mooney a try."

"That was hardly the reason," Casey interjected.

"Anyway, Mooney goes to work at Haskins, lasts barely a year, then gets canned. Of course, by now, Casey's in her new role as decorator to the stars. And who's left to deal with the fallout?"

"What fallout?" Gail asked.

"What stars?" asked Casey.

"Well, I can't imagine Haskins, Farber is too happy," Janine said. "I can't see them beating down my door in the near future, looking for a replacement. But guess who *does* show up at my door first thing this morning? The little twerp himself! He wants a job, says we screwed up the first time in sending him to Haskins, we should have known it would be a bad fit, and that it's up to me to find him a more suitable position. When I suggested he go elsewhere, he got quite upset, demanded to know where the person in charge was. That person, I assume, being you." Janine nodded toward Casey. An oblong chunk of blue-black hair fell across her left eye. "He raised quite a ruckus. I almost had to call security."

"That's awful," Gail said.

"I'm so sorry," Casey apologized. Janine was right—it *had* been her idea to take Richard Mooney on; she *had* felt sorry for him; maybe she *had* batted her eyelashes at Sid Haskins a few extra times. "I'm sorry," she said again, although she knew this wasn't the only time a lawyer they'd recommended to a particular firm hadn't worked out. Janine herself had been responsible for at least two pairings that had proved less than ideal. It was like Internet dating: People who seemed well suited on paper often proved anything but. You could never predict chemistry. Casey understood— as did Janine—that these things happened. However, she didn't think this was the appropriate time to point that out.

"It's not your fault," Janine conceded. "I don't know why I let him get to me. I must be PMS-ing."

"Speaking of which . . . well, no, not exactly," Casey said, stopping to debate with herself whether or not to continue, then plunging ahead. "Warren and I have been talking about having a baby."

"You're kidding," said Janine, thin lips opening, long chin dropping toward the table.

"I can't believe you waited until the end of the meal to tell us such exciting news," said Gail, punctuating her sentence with a laugh.

"Well, it's just been talk up until now."

"And now it isn't?" Janine asked.

"I'm going to stop taking the pill at the end of the month."

"That's fantastic!" Gail said.

"Are you sure this is the best timing?" Janine questioned. "I mean, you haven't been married all that long, and you've just started a new business."

"The business is doing great, my marriage couldn't be better, and as you pointed out earlier, we're not in college anymore. I'm going to be thirty-three on my next birthday. Which should be just about when the baby would be born. If things go according to plan, that is."

"And when haven't they?" Janine asked with a smile.

"Good for you." Gail reached across the table to pat the back of Casey's hand. "I think it's great. You'll be a terrific mom."

"You really think so? I didn't have a very good example."

"You practically raised your sister," Gail pointed out.

"Yeah, and look how well that turned out." Casey glanced back at the still-life painting over her shoulder and took a deep breath, as if trying to inhale the scent of the blush-pink peonies.

"How *is* Drew anyway?" Janine asked, although the tone of her voice indicated she already knew the answer.

"Haven't heard from her in weeks. She doesn't phone, doesn't return my messages."

"Typical."

"She'll call," Gail said. This time no soft giggle accompanied her words.

Janine signaled the waiter for the bill by wiggling her fingers in the air, as if she was already signing the check. "Sure you want to give up that perfect body?" she asked Casey as the young man brought the bill to the table. "It'll never be the same, you know."

"That's all right. It's . . ."

". . . time to move on?" Janine quipped.

"Your boobs will get bigger," Gail said.

"That'll be nice," Casey said as Janine divided the amount.

"Fifty-five apiece, including tip," Janine announced after several seconds. "Why don't you give me the money and I'll put it on my credit card to speed things up?"

Casey knew Janine's request had nothing to do with saving time and everything to do with writing off today's lunch as a business expense. "So, what are you up to this weekend?" she asked, handing Janine the appropriate amount of cash.

"I have a date with that banker I went out with last week." Janine's blue eyes were already growing opaque with boredom.

"That's nice," Gail said. "Isn't it?"

"Not really. But he has tickets for *Jersey Boys,* and you know how hard it is to get tickets, so how could I refuse?"

"Oh, you'll love it," Casey said. "It's fabulous. I saw the original on Broadway a few years ago."

"Of course you did." Janine smiled as she pushed herself off her chair and to her feet. "And this week you'll be with your fabulous husband, making fabulous babies together. I'm sorry," she said in the same breath. "I'm being a real bitch. For sure I'm PMS-ing."

"Where are you off to now?" Gail asked Casey as they retrieved their coats from the maître d'.

"Think I'll just stick around here. I was debating going for a run, but I don't think I have enough time before my next appointment." Casey checked her watch. It was a gold Cartier, a gift from her husband on their second anniversary last month.

"Save your energy for tonight," Janine advised now, leaning

forward to kiss Casey on the cheek. "Come on, Gail, I'll give you a ride back to work."

Casey watched her two friends walk down South Street arm in arm, thinking them an interesting study in contrasts: Janine tall and contained, Gail shorter and spilling out in all directions at once; Janine an expensive glass of champagne, Gail a mug of draft beer.

Which made her—what? Casey wondered. Maybe she *should* try a more current hairstyle. Although when had long blond hair ever really gone out of fashion? And it suited the soft oval of her face, her fair complexion and delicate features. "Don't even try to tell me you weren't prom queen," Janine had said shortly after they met, and Casey had laughed and kept silent. What could she say, after all? She *had* been prom queen. She'd also been captain of the debating and swim teams, and scored near perfect on her SATs, but people were always less interested in that than in how she looked and how much she was worth. "Someone just told me your old man is worth gazillions," Janine had remarked on another occasion. Again Casey had remained silent. Yes, it was true her family was almost obscenely wealthy. It was also true that her father had been a notorious ladies' man, her mother a self-absorbed alcoholic, and her younger sister a drug-fueled party girl on her way to becoming a total screwup. Four years after Casey graduated college, her parents were killed when their private jet crashed into Chesapeake Bay during inclement weather, officially making her sister a total screwup.

It was these thoughts that were absorbing Casey's attention as she walked along South Street, Philadelphia's answer to Greenwich Village, with its collection of pungent smells, seedy tattoo parlors, funky leather shops, and avant-garde galleries. Truly a world unto itself, she was thinking as she crossed into South Philly and headed toward the large indoor parking garage on

Washington Avenue. That was the problem with having lunch in this area—it was almost impossible to find a place to park, and once you got away from South Street, the dividing line between Center City and South Philadelphia, you were pretty much in *Rocky* territory.

Casey entered the parking garage and took the elevator up to the fifth floor, retrieving her car keys from her oversize black leather bag as she walked toward her white Lexus sports car at the far end of the platform. She heard the gunning of an engine in the distance and looked over her shoulder, but she saw nothing. Aside from the rows of multicolored automobiles, the place was deserted.

She didn't hear the car until it was almost on top of her. She was approaching her Lexus, right arm extended, thumb on the button of the remote to unlock the driver's door, when a silver-colored SUV came careening around the corner toward her. She didn't have time to register the driver's face, to ascertain whether a man or woman was behind the wheel. She had no time to get out of the way. One minute she was walking toward her car, the next she was being propelled through the air, her arms and legs shooting into four different directions at once. Seconds later, she came crashing down, a limp repository of broken bones, her head slamming against the hard pavement.

Shortly after that, the SUV disappeared into the streets of South Philadelphia, and Casey Marshall slipped into oblivion.

2

SHE OPENED HER EYES to darkness.

And not just ordinary darkness, Casey thought, straining to catch even a glimmer of light. It was the blackest black she'd ever seen, a wall of impenetrable density she couldn't see over or around, affording not even a hint of shading or shadow. As if she'd fallen into a deep underground cave. As if she'd accidentally stumbled into the black hole of the universe.

Where was she? Why was it so dark?

"Hello? Is anybody there?"

Was she alone? Could anybody hear her?

There was no answer. Casey felt a tiny bubble of panic materialize inside her chest and tried to control its growth with a series of measured, deep breaths. There had to be a logical explanation, she assured herself, refusing to give in to her fear, knowing that if she did, it would expand until there was no room for anything else, and then the now monstrous bubble would burst, spreading its poison throughout her veins and circulating to every part of her body.

"Hello? Can anybody hear me?"

She opened her eyes wider, then squinted, hearing Janine's reprimand in the back of her head, reminding her that squinting causes wrinkles. "Janine," Casey whispered, vaguely recalling their lunch together. . . . When? How long ago?

Not long, Casey decided. Hadn't she just left her? Yes, that was right. She'd had lunch with Janine and Gail on South Street— she'd had a delicious warm chicken and papaya salad and a glass of pinot grigio—and then headed over to Washington Street to retrieve her car. And then what?

And then . . . nothing.

Casey pictured herself walking up the sloping concrete of the old parking garage toward her car, heard the heels of her black Ferragamo pumps clicking along the uneven pavement, and then another sound, a rumble, like distant thunder. Coming closer. What was it? Why couldn't she remember?

What was happening?

It was at that precise moment Casey realized she couldn't move. "What . . . ?" she began, and then stopped, the bubble in her chest instantly metastasizing into her throat, robbing her of her voice. Why couldn't she move? Was she tied down?

She tried to lift her hands but she couldn't feel them. She tried kicking her feet, but she couldn't locate them either. It was as if they didn't exist, as if she was a head without a torso, a body without limbs. If only there was some light. If only she could see something. Anything that would give her a clue as to her predicament. She didn't even know if she was lying down or sitting up, she realized, trying to turn her head; when that failed, she strained to lift it.

I've been kidnapped, she thought, still trying to make sense of her situation. Some lunatic had snatched her from the parking garage and buried her alive in his backyard. Hadn't she seen a movie like that a long time ago? It starred Keifer Sutherland as the hero and Jeff Bridges as the villain, and hadn't Sandra Bullock played the small part of Keifer's girlfriend, the poor unfortunate who was chloroformed at a gasoline station and came to in an underground coffin?

Oh, God, oh, God. Had some lunatic seen that movie and decided to play copycat? Stay calm. Stay calm. Stay calm.

Casey fought to regain control of her now ragged breathing. If she *had* been kidnapped, if she *was* lying in a coffin beneath the cold ground, that meant her supply of air was limited, and it was imperative she not waste it. Although she didn't feel a lack of air, she realized. Nor did she feel cold. Or hot. Or anything.

She felt nothing at all.

"Okay, okay," she whispered, straining to see traces of her breath in the darkness. But again there was nothing. Casey closed her eyes, counting silently to ten before reopening them.

Nothing.

Nothing but deep, unending blackness.

Was she dead?

"This can't be happening. It can't be."

Of course it wasn't happening, she realized with a sudden rush of relief. It was a dream. A nightmare. What was the matter with her? Why hadn't she realized this before? She could have spared herself a lot of needless grief and wasted energy. She should have known all along she was dreaming.

Now all she had to do was wake herself up. *Come on, silly. You can do it. Wake up, damn you. Wake up.*

Except she couldn't remember having gone to bed.

"But I must have. I must have." Obviously, the whole day had been a dream. She hadn't met with Rhonda Miller at nine o'clock this morning to discuss her ideas for decorating the Millers' new riverside condominium. She hadn't spent a couple of hours checking out the wide assortment of materials on Fabric Row. She hadn't met her friends for lunch at Southwark. They hadn't talked about Janine's hair or her unpleasant encounter with Richard Mooney. The little twerp, Janine had called him.

Since when had she ever been able to recall her dreams in such vivid detail? Casey wondered. Especially while she was still dreaming them. What kind of nightmare was this? Why couldn't she wake up?

Wake up, she urged. Then again, aloud, "Wake up." And then, louder still. "Wake up!" She'd read somewhere that you could sometimes jolt yourself awake with a loud scream, a scream that would literally push you from one level of consciousness to another. *"Wake up!"* she screamed at the top of her lungs, hoping that she wouldn't frighten Warren, who was undoubtedly sleeping peacefully beside her in their king-size bed, his arms wrapped loosely around her.

Maybe that was why she couldn't move. Maybe Warren had fallen asleep with his body draped across her side, or maybe their down-filled comforter had twisted itself around her, like a cocoon, preventing her from moving or feeling her arms and legs. Except Casey knew even as she was thinking these thoughts that they weren't right. She'd always been able to sense when her husband was close by. Now she had no sense of anything.

Warren Marshall was almost six feet tall and 185 pounds of well-toned muscle, thanks to thrice-weekly workouts at the small boutique gym in the upscale Main Line suburb of Rosemont, where they lived. Casey could detect no hint of his presence, no whiff of his clean, masculine smell.

No, she realized, as a new bubble of fear took root in her belly. Warren wasn't here. Nobody was here. She was all alone.

And she wasn't dreaming.

"Somebody," she cried. "Somebody, please help me."

Her words echoed in her ears, causing only a few ripples in the overwhelming silence that surrounded her. Casey lay in her black hole, waiting in vain for her eyes to adjust to the darkness, and cried into the void.

She fell asleep and dreamed she was a child playing golf with her father. She was only ten the first time he'd taken her to Merion Golf Club, the exclusive private course where he was a member, and he'd spent hours on the range with her, patiently working with her to perfect her swing, proudly proclaiming to anyone within earshot that she was a natural. She was twelve the first time she broke a hundred, fifteen the first time she broke ninety, twenty when she got the first of her two hole-in-ones. She remembered offering to help her younger sister with her game, but Drew had turned her down flat, preferring to flail around helplessly, throwing her clubs to the ground, and then storming off the course in a snit. "Let her go," she could hear her father say. "*You're* the athlete in the family, Casey." Hadn't he named her after Casey Stengel? he reminded her. "So, all right, I picked the wrong sport," he'd say, laughing, and her mother would roll her pale blue eyes and turn aside to stifle a yawn, having heard the anecdote too many times to find it even vaguely amusing anymore. If indeed she ever had.

"Okay, can somebody bring me up-to-date, please?" Casey heard her father say now.

Casey felt the air around her head begin to swirl, as if someone were shaking a tambourine near her face.

"Yes, Dr. Peabody," her father said.

Who was Dr. Peabody? Dr. Marcus was their family physician, and had been ever since she could remember. So who was this Dr. Peabody? And what was he doing in her dream?

It was then that Casey realized she was no longer asleep, and that the voice she'd been hearing belonged not to her deceased father but to someone who was alive and well and standing not very far away. She opened her eyes. It was still pitch-black, so she couldn't see anybody. But at least she wasn't alone, she realized gratefully. And the voices were definitely close at hand. Surely sooner or later, somebody would stumble across her. All she had to do was use her own voice to guide them.

"I'm over here," she shouted.

"The patient," someone answered, ignoring her outburst, "is a thirty-two-year-old woman who was the victim of a hit-and-run accident approximately three weeks ago. March twenty-sixth, to be exact."

"Hey, you," Casey called out. "Dr. Peabody, I presume! I'm over here."

"She's on life support, having suffered multiple traumas, including multiple fractures of the pelvis, legs, and arms, all of which required extensive surgeries," the doctor continued. "The external fixators in her bones will be in place for at least another month, as will the casts on her arms. More seriously, there was massive bleeding to the abdomen, which led to bleeding into the abdominal cavity. Doctors did an exploratory laparotomy and discovered a ruptured spleen. A splenectomy was then performed."

What the hell was he talking about? Casey wondered. *Who* was he talking about? And why did his voice keep going in and out, strong one minute, and then weak the next? Was it even a man's voice? she wondered. And why did it sound so heavy, as if it were covered in a thick coat of molasses? Were they underwater? "Hey," she called out. "Do you think you could talk about this later? I'd really like to get out of here."

"Luckily, an MRI determined that there wasn't any spinal fracture of the neck or back, which could have led to lower-extremity paralysis. . . ."

"'Luck' being an odd choice of words in this case, wouldn't

you say, Dr. Peabody?" the first voice interrupted. "Considering the fact the patient might be in a coma for the rest of her life."

What patient? Casey wondered. Who were these people? Was she in the basement tunnel of a hospital? Was that why it was so dark? How had she gotten here? And why couldn't anybody hear her? Were they farther away than she'd first assumed?

"Yes, sir. I didn't mean to suggest—"

"Dr. Benson, would you like to continue?"

Dr. Benson? Who was Dr. Benson?

"The patient was found to have a subdural hemorrhage," another voice continued, although it was getting hard to distinguish one voice from the next, "and Dr. Jarvis drilled a burr hole into the skull to remove the blood from just beneath the skull bone, in order to let it drain out."

"And the prognosis?"

"Generally good in most cases, especially when the patient is young and in as good physical condition as Mrs. Marshall. . . ."

Mrs. Marshall? *Mrs. Marshall?* "Excuse me, but that's *my* name." Who were they talking about? Was there another Mrs. Marshall? Or was this some sort of elaborate hoax cooked up by Janine? "Okay, guys. You've had your fun. Enough is enough. Would somebody please just tell me what's going on?"

". . . But the patient also sustained a major concussion to the brain, which led to a coma. We've performed several MRIs over the last three weeks, which show the subdural hemorrhaging is dissolving and clearing up, but the shock to the brain continues, so it's too early to know whether the damage is permanent or not."

"So, tell me, Dr. Rekai," the doctor in charge said. "What's the ultimate prognosis?"

"It's impossible to know for sure at this time," came the reply. "The patient's brain has been rocked, as they say."

"Who says that?" Casey demanded, indignant at the casual brutality of the assessment. Some poor woman was in a coma and they were being insensitive and glib about her condition.

"How long do you estimate she'll remain on life support?" someone asked.

"Her family is very unlikely to consider taking her off life support at this time. Nor would the hospital approve any attempt to do so. The patient has a strong heart, and her body is functioning, so we know her brain is functioning, albeit at a decreased level of activity. Casey Marshall could be on the ventilator for years, or she could wake up tomorrow."

"Casey Marshall?" Casey repeated incredulously. What was he talking about? The likelihood of there being more than one Casey Marshall . . .

"Is the fact she opened her eyes yesterday of any significance?" somebody asked.

"Unfortunately not," came the immediate answer. "It's not unusual for a comatose patient to open her eyes. As you know, it's an involuntary action, as is blinking. She can't see anything, despite the fact her pupils are reacting to light."

Again Casey felt movement around her, although she couldn't process what it was. What light were they talking about?

"And the trach tube?"

"We'll be performing a tracheostomy tomorrow afternoon."

"A tracheostomy?" Casey demanded. "What the hell is that?"

"Dr. Benson, would you care to tell us about what's involved in a tracheostomy?"

"You heard me?" A wave of exhilaration washed over Casey. "You actually heard my question! Thank God. Oh, thank God. I'm not the woman you're talking about, that poor woman in a coma. You had me so worried."

"A tracheostomy is normally performed on a patient after

they've been on a trach tube for more than a few weeks," Dr. Benson replied. "If the patient isn't suffering from respiratory distress and is relatively comfortable, as this patient seems to be, then a tracheostomy should be performed or the tube will erode the trachea."

"And what exactly is involved in this procedure, Dr. Zarb?"

Dr. Zarb? Dr. Rekai? Dr. Benson? Dr. Peabody? How many doctors were there? Why couldn't she see any of them? And why did they continue to ignore her? She wasn't the woman they were talking about, this poor unfortunate in a coma. Possibly for years. *No, it couldn't be.* Possibly for the rest of her life. *Dear God, no! It can't be.* It was too awful to even think about. *I have to get out of here. I have to get out of here right now.*

"We do an ostium, an incision in the neck," Dr. Zarb explained without further prompting, "whereby a trach is inserted directly into the neck, instead of through the mouth. If the patient is later able to breathe without the assistance of the ventilator, then we remove the trach tube and let the trach close up on its own."

"Is there much chance of that happening in this case, Dr. Ein?"

"Impossible to say at this point. The patient has several things going for her: Casey Marshall is young. She's very fit. Her heart is working perfectly. . . ."

No. I won't listen to this. It can't be true. It simply can't be. I'm not the woman you're discussing. I'm not in a coma. I'm not. I'm not. Please, God. Get me out of here.

". . . And don't forget she's Ronald Lerner's daughter."

I can hear you! How can I be in a coma if I can hear you?

"For those of you too young to remember, Ronald Lerner was a businessman of dubious moral character who made a killing in the stock market, then died in a plane crash a number of years back. He left the bulk of his very sizable estate to the young woman you see lying comatose before you, proving not only that money can*not* buy happiness but that it's no protection against the vagaries of fate.

Although at least Casey Marshall will be able to afford the best in private medical care once she's released from the hospital."

This isn't happening. It isn't happening.

"Any more questions?" someone asked. Casey thought it might be Dr. Ein, but the voices were getting increasingly difficult to distinguish from one another.

"When can the peg tube come out?" she thought she heard someone—Dr. Peabody? Dr. Zarb?—ask. *What the hell's a peg tube?* she wondered frantically.

"Not until the patient can eat on her own," came the response, so Casey concluded there must be some kind of feeding tube connected to her stomach.

I want to go home. Please, just let me go home.

"And the antibiotic drip?"

"Not for at least another week. The patient is very susceptible to infection because of all the procedures she's had. Hopefully we can get her started on some physical therapy once all the casts come off. Okay? Any other questions before we move on?"

Yes! You have to start over from the very beginning. Explain everything that happened: the accident, how I got here, what's going to happen to me now. You can't just leave me alone in the dark. You can't walk away and pretend I don't exist. You have to come back. I can hear you! Doesn't that count for something?

"Doctor Ein," someone said.

"Yes, Dr. Benson."

"The patient seems to be in some sort of distress. She's grimacing and her heart rate is going up."

What's happening?

"It's possible she's experiencing some pain. We'll increase the Dilaudid, Demerol, and Ativan she's getting."

No, I don't need drugs. I'm not in pain. What I need is for you to listen to me. Please, somebody, listen to me!

"That should make you more comfortable, Casey," the doctor said.

No. I'm not comfortable. I'm not comfortable at all.

"All right, let's move on."

No. Wait—don't go. Please, don't go. There's been a huge mistake. I can't be the woman you're talking about. I can't be. None of this is happening. You have to come back. I have to make you understand that I'm not in a coma. God, please. You have to make these people understand that I can hear them. If you do that, I promise I'll be a better person. I'll be a better wife, a better friend, a better sister. Please. You have to help me. I'm so afraid. I don't want to spend the rest of my life lying here, not being able to see, or move, or speak. I want to hold my husband in my arms again, and laugh with my friends. I want to make things right with Drew. Please. Don't let this be happening. It can't be happening. It can't be.

Casey felt her thoughts begin to wobble and disperse. She was suddenly very woozy. Dilaudid, Demerol, Ativan, she was thinking as she felt her eyes close.

Seconds later, she was asleep.

3

"CASEY," SHE HEARD SOMEONE say softly. And then again, more forcefully. "Casey. Wake up, sweetheart."

Reluctantly, Casey felt herself being dragged into consciousness by her husband's voice. She opened her eyes, saw Warren looming over her, his handsome features distorted by the proximity of his face to hers, so that he appeared bloated and gargoyle-like. "What's going on?" she asked, trying to clear her mind of the strange dream she'd been having, and noting that the clock radio beside their king-size bed said 3:00 a.m.

"There's someone in the house," Warren whispered, casting a worried glance over his left shoulder.

Casey followed his gaze through the darkness, her pulse quickening as she sat up.

"I think someone might have gotten in through a basement window," he continued. "I tried calling 911, but the lines are dead."

"Oh, God."

"It's all right. I have the gun." He held it up, its barrel glistening in the reflection of the half moon outside their window.

Casey nodded, recalling the argument they'd had over his insistence to keep a gun in the house. "For our protection," he'd said, and now it seemed he'd been right. "What do we do?" she asked.

"We hide in the closet and lock the door. If anyone opens it, I shoot first and ask questions later."

"God, that's awful," Casey said, using Gail's voice. "Does anybody really talk like that?"

"They do on TV," Warren answered.

What? What's going on? What TV?

"I don't think I saw this one," Gail said.

What is Gail doing in our bedroom? Why has she broken into our house?

"I don't think anybody did. Looks like one of those straight-to-video numbers. But the doctors seem to think keeping the TV on might help stimulate Casey's brain, and frankly, it helps pass the time."

"How long have you been here?" Gail asked.

"Since about eight o'clock."

"It's almost one now. Have you had any lunch?"

"One of the nurses brought me a cup of coffee about an hour ago."

"That's all?"

"I'm not very hungry."

"You have to eat something, Warren. You have to keep up your strength."

"I'm fine, Gail. Really. I don't want anything."

"They're getting closer. I hear them on the stairs. We don't have time."

What are you talking about? Who's on the stairs? What's happening?

"Get under the bed. Hurry."

"I'm not going anywhere without you."

Who are these people?

"Enough of that crap," Warren said.

A clicking sound. Then silence.

What was happening? Casey wondered, startled to realize she didn't know whether her eyes were open or closed. Had she been asleep? For how long? Had she been dreaming? Why couldn't she distinguish between what was real and what wasn't? Were these people *her* Warren, *her* Gail? Where was she?

"Her color's better," Gail remarked. "Has there been any change?"

"Not really. Except that her heart rate has been fluctuating more than usual. . . ."

"Is that good or bad?"

"The doctors don't know."

"They don't seem to know much about anything, do they?"

"They think she might be experiencing more pain—"

"Which isn't necessarily a bad thing," Gail interrupted. "I mean, it might signal she's coming back to us."

"Patients in deep comas can still experience pain," Warren said, his voice flat. "How fair is that?" he added.

Casey could almost see him shaking his head. This was definitely *her* Warren, she thought, recognizing the familiar rhythms of his voice, the gentle cadence of his tone. *Oh, Warren. You've found me. I knew you would. I knew you wouldn't let me stay in this awful, dark place.*

"I can't believe this is Casey," Gail was saying. "The last time I saw her, she looked so beautiful, so full of life."

"She still looks beautiful," Warren said, and Casey detected a hint of defensiveness in his voice. "The most beautiful girl in the world," he said, his voice drifting away.

Casey pictured his eyes filling with tears and knew he was

fighting to keep them from falling. If only she could wipe away those tears, she thought. If only she could kiss him and make everything better.

"What'd you girls talk about that day anyway?" he asked. "You never told me much about your lunch."

"There wasn't much to tell," Gail said, a little laugh bracketing each end of her short response. "To tell you the truth, I don't really remember what we talked about. The usual, I guess." She laughed again, although the soft sound was more sad than joyful. "I didn't realize I should be attaching any more weight to it than normal. I didn't realize it might be our last time together. Oh, God." A loud sob cut through the air, like a sudden thunderclap.

Oh, Gail. Please don't cry. It'll be all right. I'm going to get better. I promise.

"I'm sorry. I keep forgetting," Warren was saying. "This must bring back painful memories."

Casey pictured Gail lifting both shoulders in a gentle shrug, then tucking a few wayward curls behind her right ear. "Mike was in a hospice for two months before he died," Gail said, talking about the husband she'd lost to leukemia five years earlier. "There wasn't anything anybody could do but watch him fade away. But at least we had a few years to prepare," she continued. "Although you're never really prepared," she added in the next breath. "Not when the person is so young."

"Casey isn't going to die," Warren insisted.

He's right. The doctors have misdiagnosed my condition. This whole thing is a big mistake.

"I won't even consider taking her off life support."

"Taking her off life support?" This time it was Gail who asked the question. "When did the doctors suggest taking her off life support?"

"They haven't. They agree it's way too early to be thinking that way."

"Of course it is. Then who?"

"Who do you think?"

"Oh," said Gail. "I didn't realize Drew had been here lately."

My sister's been here?

"Are you kidding? She hasn't been here since right after the accident. Says she can't bear seeing her sister in this condition."

"Sounds like Drew," Gail said.

"She called last night for an update," Warren continued. "When I told her there'd been no change, she demanded to know how long I was going to let Casey suffer this way. She said she'd known her a lot longer than I have, and that there's no way her sister would want to be a vegetable for the rest of her life . . ."

A vegetable? No, the doctors have made an unfortunate mistake. They've upset everyone unnecessarily.

". . . kept alive by a bunch of tubes and ventilators."

"That's only until she starts breathing again on her own," Gail said forcefully. It had been a long time since Casey had heard her friend sound so intense. "Casey will get through this. The broken bones will mend. Her body will repair itself. She'll regain consciousness. You'll see. Casey will be as good as she always was. This coma is just her body's way of healing itself. We should be grateful that she's not awake, that she doesn't know what's going on. . . ."

Except she did know, Casey was forced to acknowledge, as the direness of her predicament suddenly reasserted itself, spreading through the dark space around her like a nasty stain.

The patient is a thirty-two-year-old woman who was the victim of a hit-and-run accident approximately three weeks ago. . . . She's on life support . . . multiple traumas . . . extensive surgeries . . . external fixators . . . massive bleeding to the abdomen . . . A splenectomy was then performed. . . . the patient might be in a coma for the rest of her life.

A coma for the rest of her life.

"No! No! No!" Casey shouted, unable to block out the truth any longer. No amount of denials, no amount of rationalizations, no amount of pretending her doctors might be mistaken could hold back the horrifying truth of her condition—that she was a thirty-two-year-old woman trapped in a possibly irreversible coma, a coma that cruelly enabled her to hear but not see, to think but not communicate, to exist but not act. Hell, she couldn't even breathe without the help of a machine. This was worse than being lost in some dank underground cave, worse than being buried alive. Worse than death. Was she doomed to spend the rest of her days in this dark, free-floating limbo, unable to distinguish between what was actually happening and what was merely imagined? How long could this go on?

Subdural hemorrhage . . . burr hole into the skull to remove the blood . . . major concussion to the brain . . . Casey Marshall could be on the ventilator for years, or she could wake up tomorrow.

How many hours, days, weeks could she lie here, suspended in blackness, hearing a succession of voices float about her head like passing clouds? How many weeks, months, years—God forbid, years!—could she survive, not being able to reach out to those she loved?

The patient's brain has been rocked.

For that matter, how long would it be before her friends stopped visiting her, before even her husband moved on? Gail rarely talked about Mike anymore. And Warren was only thirty-seven. He might hover over her for a few more months, maybe even a year or two, but eventually he'd be coaxed into someone else's all-too-eager arms. The others would follow, lulled back into their everyday lives. Soon everyone would be gone. Even the doctors would eventually lose interest. She'd be carted off to some rehab facility, abandoned in a distant corner of a stale-smelling corridor, propped up in a wheelchair, and left to listen to a succession of lost feet shuffle by. How long before she went mad from frustration and rage, from the sheer boredom and predictability of it all?

Or she could wake up tomorrow.

"I could wake up tomorrow," Casey repeated, trying to draw comfort from the thought. Judging by what she'd heard, the accident had happened three weeks ago. So maybe Gail's optimism wasn't entirely unfounded. Maybe the fact she could now hear was a good sign, a sign that she was on the road to recovery. Her hearing had returned. Her eyes had opened. Maybe tomorrow the darkness would lift, and she'd be able to see. Maybe once the tube was out of her mouth—Was it out already? Had the doctors already performed the tracheostomy they'd been talking about . . . when? How long ago?—she'd regain the use of her vocal chords. She was already getting better at being able to distinguish between outside voices. They no longer all blended together or sounded as if they were coming to her from the far side of a thick wall. Maybe tomorrow it would be better still. She might even be able to blink in response to any questions they might pose. She might find a way to show everyone she was alert and cognizant of what was being said.

Maybe she was getting better.

Or maybe this was as good as it was ever going to get, she realized, feeling her spirits suddenly deflate, like air whooshing out of a child's half-blown balloon. In which case, her sister was right.

She'd rather be dead.

"Do the police have any new leads?" she heard Gail ask.

"Not that I know of," Warren said. "None of the auto-body shops in the Philadelphia area have reported any vehicles being brought in with the kind of extensive damage you'd expect in an accident of this nature. No witnesses have come forward, despite all the publicity. It seems the car that hit her has vanished into thin air."

"How could somebody do something so awful?" Gail asked. "I mean, it was bad enough he hit her, but then to just leave her there like that . . ."

Casey imagined Warren shaking his head. She saw his soft brown hair fall across his forehead and into his darker brown eyes. "Maybe the driver had been drinking. Probably he panicked," Warren theorized. "Who knows what goes on in people's minds?"

"You'd think his guilty conscience would have gotten the better of him by now," Gail said.

"You'd think," Warren agreed.

Another silence.

"Oh," Gail exclaimed suddenly.

"What?"

"I just remembered something we talked about at lunch," she elaborated, her voice tinged with sadness.

"What was that?"

"Casey said the two of you had been talking about having a baby, that she was going to stop taking the pill at the end of the month."

Casey felt a twinge of guilt. That was supposed to have been a secret, she remembered. She'd promised Warren she wouldn't say anything to anyone until it was a fait accompli. "Do you want everyone to keep asking how it's going every month?" he'd argued gently, and she'd agreed. Would he be disappointed, maybe even angry, she hadn't kept her word?

"Yeah," she heard him say now. "She was all excited. A little nervous, too, of course. I guess because of her mother."

"Yes, her mother was quite something."

"That's right. I forgot. You knew her, didn't you?"

"I don't think anybody really knew Alana Lerner," Gail said.

"Casey almost never talks about her."

"There wasn't much to say. She was the kind of woman who never should have had children."

"And yet she had two," Warren observed.

"Only because Mr. Lerner wanted a boy. She didn't have much to do with them once she popped them out. They were pretty much raised by nannies."

"Nannies who were constantly being fired, from what I understand."

"Because Mrs. Lerner was convinced her husband was sleeping with them. Which he probably was. He certainly made no secret of his affairs."

"Some family."

"It's a wonder Casey turned out so well," Gail said, and then started to cry. "I'm sorry."

"Don't be. I know how much you love her."

"Did you know she was my maid of honor?" Gail asked, continuing before Warren could respond. "I married Mike right out of high school, if you can believe it. I was eighteen. Eighteen, for God's sake. A baby. Mike was ten years older, and he'd just been diagnosed with leukemia. Everybody told me I was gonna ruin my life, that I was crazy to marry him. Everybody except Casey. She said, 'Go for it.' " Again, Gail's voice was lost in a series of soft sobs.

"She's going to get better, Gail."

"You promise?" Gail asked, echoing Casey's silent question.

But before Warren could answer, there was a sudden flurry of activity. Casey heard the pushing open of a door, the approach of several pairs of sturdy shoes, multiple voices. "I'm afraid we're going to have to ask you to leave for a few minutes," a female voice announced. "We have to give the patient a sponge bath, adjust her position so she doesn't get bedsores."

"We shouldn't be more than ten, fifteen minutes," a second, higher-pitched voice added.

"Why don't we go get something to eat in the cafeteria," Gail suggested.

"All right," Warren agreed.

Casey heard the reluctance in his voice even as she felt him being drawn from the room.

"Don't worry, Mr. Marshall," the first nurse told him. "Patsy and I will take good care of your wife."

"I'll be back soon, Casey," Warren said.

Casey thought she felt him move close, lean in, maybe even pat her hand under the bedsheet. Was she just imagining it?

"Now, that is one lovely man," Patsy proclaimed, her voice dropping half an octave as the door shut behind them. "My heart really goes out to him."

"Yeah. I sure wouldn't want to be in his shoes," the other nurse said. "Speaking of which, did you happen to check hers out?"

"What? No, Donna. I can't say that I did."

"Very classy. Very expensive."

"I didn't notice. Okay, Mrs. Marshall," Patsy said, returning her attention to Casey. "Let's get you all cleaned up for that handsome husband of yours."

Casey heard the rustle of sheets, and although she felt nothing, she'd never felt more exposed. Was she wearing a hospital gown or a nightgown from her own closet? Was she wearing anything at all? Were they touching her? Where exactly?

"Just how long do you think he's going to stick around anyway?" Donna was saying, echoing Casey's earlier thoughts. "Soon as he realizes she's not going to get any better. . . ."

"Ssh. Don't say that," Patsy admonished.

"What? She can't hear me."

"You don't know that for sure. She opened her eyes, didn't she?"

"That doesn't mean anything. I heard one of the doctors talking. He said that when they open their eyes, it's often a bad sign. It could signify the beginning of a profound vegetative state."

"Well, let's hope they're wrong."

Casey wondered what Donna and Patsy looked like, picturing one tall and fair, the other short and dark. Or maybe tall and dark, she theorized, her mind exchanging one set of features for another, alternating different heads on different body types. One minute, she pictured Nurse Patsy with Dolly Partonesque breasts, and Donna as flat as the proverbial pancake. Or maybe Patsy was a redhead. Maybe Donna's skin was a soft, velvety black. Whatever they looked like, they were right about one thing: Warren Marshall was one handsome man.

Casey laughed, knowing they couldn't hear her. To them she was an inanimate object. No more, no less. A body to be rotated regularly so that it didn't develop bedsores, and washed, so that it didn't start to smell. An uninteresting piece of still life. That's what I've become, she thought, her laugh drying up, dissolving in her throat.

"Oh, look at her face," Patsy said suddenly.

"What's the matter with it?" Donna questioned.

"She just looks so sad all of a sudden."

"What are you talking about?" Donna asked.

"You don't think her eyes look sad?"

"I think her eyes look open. Period. Okay, I'm done with her front. You want to help me turn her on her side?"

Casey felt her body being manipulated, her head placed at a different angle, although she couldn't be sure if this was really happening or just part of her imagination.

"Okay, I'm finished," Donna said after several more minutes passed. "What about you?"

"I think I'll stick around a little while, brush her hair, make her look nice. You don't have to stay."

"Suit yourself."

"We'll just get you all prettied up for that handsome, devoted husband of yours," Patsy said as Donna left the room. Casey imagined her gently running a brush through her hair. "Although, you gotta wonder," she continued, her voice shedding its softness with the closing of the door, like a snake shedding its skin. "I mean, he *is* a man, after all. A drop-dead gorgeous man at that. Not to mention a very rich, drop-dead gorgeous man. You gotta figure the girls are already lining up around the block. And he has an eye for the women, your handsome hubby does." Casey imagined Patsy putting down the brush and leaning forward to whisper in her ear. "I know 'cause I caught him checking out my ass." She laughed. "How long do you think it'll take me to get him into bed?" She laughed again. "What? You don't believe I can do it? Wanna bet? How much? Ten bucks? A hundred? Hell, let's make it a thousand. You can afford it."

The door opened. "Patsy," Donna called from the doorway. "They need us in 307."

"Sure thing," Patsy responded cheerily. "I'm done here."

4

SHE WAS THREE YEARS old when she found out that the beautiful lady with the waist-length rush of natural blond hair that smelled of bubble gum and cotton candy was her mother and not just a mysterious woman named Alana who always had a glass in her hand, and who slept in her father's bed.

"Here, Casey, sweetheart. Can you take this drink upstairs to your mama? I'm on the phone with the cable company, and they've got me on hold."

"My mama?" the child asked. Who was Maya talking about? Maya hadn't been living with them very long. It was possible she still didn't know everyone.

"The pretty blond lady who's married to your father?" Maya said, as if Casey should know. "The one who stays in bed all day?" she added with a laugh. Then immediately, her normally pale complexion reddening: "Don't you dare tell your mother I said that."

Casey took the glass of clear liquid from Maya's outstretched hand and raised it to her nose. "What is it?"

"Water."

Casey lifted the glass to her mouth.

Maya quickly snatched the glass back. At just under six feet tall, she was an imposing young woman whose dark eyes brooked no argument. "What are you doing?"

"I'm thirsty."

"I'll get you your own drink." Maya was instantly at the sink, the phone pressed between her shoulder and her ear as she poured Casey a small glass of tepid water.

"Why can't I have some of *that* water?" Casey pointed with her chin to the other glass Maya was holding. It was nice and cold and even had a few ice cubes floating across its surface.

"Because it's not good to drink from anybody else's glass," Maya said firmly.

Even at the tender age of three, Casey knew she was being lied to. Just as she knew Maya was making up what she'd said about the beautiful woman upstairs in her father's bed being her mother. Not that Casey knew what a mother was exactly. Her only experience with mothers had come at the park a few weeks earlier, when a woman with messy brown hair and faded, baggy jeans had perched herself on one corner of the sandbox and begun playing with a little boy whose nose was covered with a series of big orange spots that Maya had later identified as freckles.

"You're new around here," Maya had said to the woman, leading Casey over to the sandbox and sitting down, then striking up a conversation as easily as if she'd known the woman all her life.

"Yes. We just moved in last week. Still discovering the neighborhood." The woman reached out her hand for Maya to shake. "I'm Ellen Thomas. And this is Jimmy."

"Nice to meet you. And you, too, Jimmy," Maya said to the little boy, who was too busy digging in the sand to acknowledge her greeting. "I'm Maya, and this is Casey. She was named after Casey Stengel."

Ellen Thomas smiled, exposing a top row of uneven teeth. "Her father is obviously a baseball fan."

"Oh, you just name a sport. Mr. Lerner is into it. So who do you work for?" Maya asked in the next breath.

Ellen Thompson looked puzzled. "Oh, I'm not Jimmy's nanny. I'm his mother."

"Really?" Maya sounded very surprised. "That's very unusual in this neck of the woods."

Casey's eyes immediately shot toward the trees surrounding the acres of parkland, trying to figure out where their necks were located, when Maya dropped another bombshell.

"I think you're the first actual mother I've ever seen in this park," she said.

"What's an 'actual mother'?" Casey asked later, struggling to keep up with her nanny as they made their way up the rolling hill toward her home. Maya laughed and said nothing, so Casey let the question die, having already decided from watching Ellen Thomas for the better part of an hour that actual mothers were women with messy brown hair and crooked teeth, who played with little boys in sandboxes.

The woman who slept in her father's bed couldn't be an actual mother. She had sweet-smelling yellow hair she was always combing, and perfectly straight, white teeth. Casey was quite certain she'd never set foot in a sandbox because she rarely left her room, and when she did, it was at night, when the park was closed. "Come kiss Alana good night," her father would instruct as they prepared to go out for the evening, and Casey would happily oblige.

"You look pretty," she'd say to the woman offering up her smooth cheek to be pecked. Once Casey had made the mistake of throwing her arms around the woman's neck and burrowing her nose into her soft, candy-scented hair, and the woman had gasped and quickly pushed her aside.

"Watch the hair," she'd cautioned, and Casey had spent the next minute studiously observing the woman's hair, waiting to see what it would do. "What's the matter with that child?" the woman named Alana had demanded of Casey's father as they were walking out the door. "Why is she always looking at me like that?"

"What are you waiting for?" Maya was asking now. "Take this upstairs." Once again, she deposited the cold glass in Casey's hand. "Careful you don't spill any of it. And don't take a sip. You understand?"

Casey nodded, walking slowly toward the giant circular staircase in the middle of the main foyer. It was very quiet in the house that day. She'd heard Maya complaining on the phone earlier that the housekeeper had called in sick that morning, and so she was being forced to pull down double duty as chief cook and bottle washer—although Casey hadn't seen Maya washing any bottles, she thought as she slowly made her way up the green-and-beige-carpeted stairway. A drop of clear liquid tumbled out of the glass and onto the back of Casey's hand, and she quickly licked it up before it could fall to the floor. It tasted bitter, like medicine, and Casey made a face, wondering if Alana was sick and that was why she wasn't supposed to drink from her glass.

She knocked gently on the bedroom door.

"It's about time," the woman inside snapped. "What the hell have you been doing all morning?"

Casey stepped inside. The woman named Alana was sitting up in her dark oak four-poster bed, surrounded by white lace pillows. The heavy brocade curtains were open at one end of the room and closed at the other, making the large bedroom appear vaguely lopsided. Alana was wearing a pink negligee and her hair, secured by a wide, pink headband, fell past her shoulders to graze the exposed tops of her breasts.

"Oh," she said. "It's you."

"I have your water." Casey extended the glass toward her.

"Well, bring it over here. Do you think my arms are eight feet long?"

"Are you sick?" Casey handed the glass to Alana, watching her take a long sip.

Alana peered at Casey over the top of her glass and continued drinking. She said nothing, not even "Thank you."

"Are you my mother?"

"What?"

"Are you my mother?"

"Of course I'm your mother. What's the matter with you?"

Casey and her mother exchanged worried looks.

"Don't ever call me that in public," Alana instructed.

Casey didn't know what "in public" meant, but she was afraid to say so. "What should I call you?" she asked instead.

Her mother finished the remaining liquid in her glass in one long swallow. Then she pushed away her blankets and swung her feet off the bed, leaving Casey's question unanswered. "Help me to the bathroom," she said.

"You're fat!" Casey exclaimed with a giggle, noting her mother's expanded, round belly as she climbed out of bed.

"Don't be a smart-ass."

Casey took her mother's hand and led her toward the en suite pink marble bathroom. "What's a smart-ass?"

"It's little girls who say stupid things."

Casey wasn't sure what she'd said that was so stupid, but she felt stung by her mother's rebuke, so she said nothing further.

Alana proceeded to throw up in the toilet, then she returned to her bed. "Send Maya up with another drink," she said, before pulling the rose-pink blankets up over her head.

"Your mother's going to have a baby," Maya explained later. "I don't think she's too happy about it."

"Why not?"

"I don't think motherhood's exactly her thing."

"What's her thing?" Casey asked, not sure what they were talking about, as was often the case when she talked to Maya. Still, Maya was the only adult in the house who regularly paid her any attention at all, so Casey hoped the question wasn't too stupid. She didn't want Maya to think she was a smart-ass.

"Your mother is a very complicated woman," Maya said, refusing to elaborate.

"I wish you were my mother," Casey told her.

And then suddenly, Maya was gone, replaced soon after by the not-so-dynamic duo of Shauna and Leslie, the former a dark-haired teenager from Ireland, whose job it was to tend to Casey, and the latter a bosomy ex-barmaid from London who was supposed to be looking after the new baby, but who spent more time looking after Casey's father. Leslie was quickly replaced by Rosie, the daughter of their Portuguese gardener. She, too, spent more time ministering to Casey's father than she did to Casey's baby sister, and she, too, soon disappeared, to be replaced by Kelly, then Misha, and finally Daniela.

"Your father's a lot older than your mother," Shauna remarked one day as she was walking Casey to her pricey private preschool three blocks away.

"Seventeen years," Casey elaborated. She wasn't sure how she knew this, but she did. Probably she'd overheard grown-ups whispering none-too-quietly above her head, as if she weren't there. That was how she learned most of the things she knew. For example, that was how she knew her father had been disappointed his second child had turned out to be "another stinking girl," to quote the short-lived Leslie, and how she knew her mother had undergone an operation to make sure she didn't have any more. It was from Kelly she'd found out her father was a "scoundrel" who "screwed anything that moved," and from Misha that her mother was something called a "trophy wife," and that they were "filthy rich," despite the fact they bathed every day.

"You wouldn't think someone in a coma could get so dirty," Casey heard someone say now, the remark jolting her out of her reveries. How long had she been asleep?

"It's just dead skin," another voice said, and Casey recognized the voices as belonging to Donna and Patsy. Hadn't they just bathed her? How long ago was that? Hadn't they just left?

"Where's your handsome husband today?" Donna asked her, almost as if she expected an answer.

"I haven't seen him in two days," Patsy said, answering for her.

Two days? Casey repeated silently. *Two days?* She'd lost two days?

Better than lying here day after endless day, she acknowledged. Although her days were better than her nights, she thought. At least the days were filled with activity—people coming in and out, fussing over her, discussing her condition, adjusting her tubing, gossiping about assorted friends and celebrities. Nights, on the other hand, were mostly silent, punctuated only by the occasional laugh from the nurses' station or a cry from a nearby room.

Dead air mostly, she thought, a wave of depression washing over her as the hopelessness of her condition reasserted itself, and her panic returned. "This can't be happening," she screamed silently. "It can't be real. Please, somebody help me. Get me out of here. I can't live this way. I don't *want* to live this way. Just pull the plug. Disconnect the machines. Do something to end this torment. Please. You have to help me."

"Careful of the tube in her neck," Patsy said.

"What's that for?"

"Something they put in to help her breathe."

Okay, calm down. Calm down, Casey told herself, realizing the doctors must have performed the tracheostomy, and finding it almost comic that even now, a quarter of a century removed from her childhood, she was still getting most of her information from adults talking above her head, as if she weren't there.

"It's not the most attractive thing in the world," Donna said.

"I don't think anybody's too concerned with the way it looks," Patsy admonished, managing to sound as if she really cared.

Was it possible, Casey wondered, that she'd imagined the earlier scene with Patsy, that the young woman hadn't said any of those hateful things?

"She's in pretty good shape, considering what she's been through," Donna remarked. "Look at these biceps."

"Very impressive."

"She must lift weights."

"Wish I had the time to work out," Patsy said.

"You don't need to work out. You have a great body."

"I have a great body?" Patsy repeated, a smile in her voice. "You really think so?"

"You look fantastic, and you know it."

Casey imagined Patsy spinning around in a small circle beside her bed. "Thanks."

"No thanks necessary. Okay, I'm almost done on my side. How are you coming along?"

A door opened.

"I'm sorry, but you can't come in here right now," Donna said sharply.

"Can I help you?" Patsy asked in the next beat.

"I'm looking for Warren Marshall," a man answered, as Casey tried—and failed—to place the voice. "I was told I might be able to find him in here."

"I haven't seen him today," Donna said.

"I can leave him a message," Patsy volunteered.

"No thanks," the man said brusquely. "I'll wait a while. See if he shows up."

Who was it? Casey wondered. What was so urgent?

"Visitors' lounge is down the hall," Patsy instructed.

"Nice dimples," Donna commented after he was gone.

"Tell me," Patsy said. "Is there any man on earth you don't find attractive?"

"Not too many, no."

Patsy laughed. "Wonder what he wants with Mr. Marshall."

"None of our business."

"He just looks like trouble. You know what I mean?"

"Can't say that I do."

"I wouldn't want to see him upsetting Mr. Marshall."

"You're too sensitive."

"Nurses are supposed to be sensitive," Patsy reminded her.

"We're not nurses," Donna corrected. "We're nurses' aides."

"Same difference."

"Tell that to the man signing our paychecks. Okay, I'm finished here. What about you?"

"Give me another few minutes."

Was Patsy preparing to whisper more poisonous confidences in her ear? Casey wondered, counting down the seconds. She stopped at eighty-five.

"Okay. All through," Patsy said as someone knocked on the door. "You can come in," she called out. "We're done."

Casey wondered if it was the man with the nice dimples, and what he wanted with her husband, why he'd come to the hospital. What did Patsy mean when she said he looked like trouble?

"Oh, hi, Mr. Marshall," Patsy said, her voice suddenly soft and low. "How're you doing today?"

"I'm fine, thank you," Warren replied, approaching the bed. "How's my wife?"

"About the same."

"She seems more comfortable," Donna said, "since they put that tube in her throat."

"Yeah. Hopefully, she'll start breathing on her own soon, and they can take it out."

"We're rooting for her," Patsy said.

Yeah, sure.

"Thank you."

Casey felt the women gathering up their things and heading for the door.

"Oh, there was a man here looking for you a few minutes ago," Donna said. "We sent him to the visitors' lounge."

"I can tell him you're here, if you'd like," Patsy offered.

"I wouldn't want to put you to any trouble."

"It's no trouble at all. Oh, and Mr. Marshall," she continued, and then paused. "If there's anything you need, anything at all . . ."

"Thank you. You're very kind."

"I'd be happy to volunteer my services if you require any help once your wife leaves the hospital."

Oh, you're good. You're good.

"What about your job here?"

"It's just temporary."

"Then thank you. I'll certainly consider your offer . . ."

"Patsy," she told him.

"Patsy," he repeated.

You're the only patsy here, Casey all but screamed.

"Well," Patsy demurred, as Casey pictured her lowering her chin and lifting her eyes coquettishly. "I can only imagine what you're going through. . . ."

"Thank you. I know how much Casey would appreciate the kindness you've shown her."

I wouldn't be too sure about that.

"I'll see if I can locate that gentleman."

Warren thanked her again as Patsy left the room.

Don't even think about hiring that woman, Casey warned. *I don't want her anywhere near me. Can't you see the only thing she wants to do is you? Even I can see that much, and I'm in a coma, for God's sake!*

What was it with men? Were they really so blind when it came to women? "Men are basically very simple creatures," Janine had once remarked, and Casey had dismissed it as the cynicism of someone who'd had her hopes dashed one too many times. Was it possible she was right?

"We marry our fathers," Janine had also pronounced, a remark that had given Casey pause when she felt herself falling in love with Warren. Casey knew that women had been coming on to Warren ever since they'd met. They made no secret of their attraction to him, brushing up against him on the street, or smiling at him from the bar of a crowded restaurant. She'd actually seen one particularly brazen young woman slip a piece of paper into the palm of his hand as he walked past her on his way to the washroom, and she'd held her breath, thinking of her father and all the scented scraps of paper with unidentified phone numbers she'd regularly found hidden about the house. But seconds later, Casey had watched as Warren tossed that piece of paper into a nearby wastepaper basket without even bothering to glance at it. So Warren Marshall was nothing like Ronald Lerner. Nothing like her father at all.

Which meant women like Patsy were of no consequence; they posed no threat to her whatsoever.

"Let's put the TV on, shall we?" Warren said, clicking it on.

Immediately, other voices filled the room.

"You never loved me," a woman was saying. "You've been lying to me from the very beginning."

"Maybe not from the *very* beginning," a man answered, a cruel laugh in his voice.

"How're you doing, sweetheart?" Warren asked, back at her side. She wondered if he was patting her hand, or maybe caressing her hair. She recalled the gentleness of his touch and wondered if she'd ever be able to feel it again. "The nurse said you seem more comfortable since they put the tube in."

They're not nurses. They're nurses' aides. And that one named Patsy. Watch out for her.

"She seems very nice," he said with a sigh.

He sounds exhausted, Casey thought, as if someone had reached inside his chest and pulled out his heart. How different from the first time he'd walked into the small downtown offices of Lerner, Pegabo, wearing a dark gray suit with a pale pink shirt and a silk burgundy tie, looking tan and lean, and exuding confidence and energy. "I have an appointment with Janine Pegabo at eleven o'clock," he'd announced, peeking his head into her room.

"You're Warren Marshall?" Casey asked, trying to ignore the quickening of her pulse, and swallowing the catch in her throat. "I'm sorry, but Janine had to leave rather suddenly. She broke a tooth on a bagel, of all things, and the only time the dentist could squeeze her in was . . ." Why was she rambling on this way? "I'm Casey Lerner, her partner. She asked me to fill in for her. I hope that's all right."

"More than all right," Warren said, making himself comfortable in the red velvet chair across from her desk. "Interesting room," he said, penetrating brown eyes casually absorbing the leopard-print carpeting, the dark walnut desk, and the taupe-colored walls lined with black-and-white photographs of fruit and floral arrangements. "It's . . . quirky."

"Quirky?"

"That's a compliment. I've always liked quirky. Who did you use?"

"I'm sorry?"

"The decorator," he explained with a smile.

"Oh. No decorator. Just me. I did the whole office, actually. Janine's room, too. She's not really interested in that sort of thing, and it's always been kind of a hobby of mine. . . ." She was rambling again, Casey realized, and stopped. "How can I help you, Mr. Marshall?"

"Well, as I explained to Ms. Pegabo on the phone the other day, I've been with Miller, Sheridan for the last five years and I'm looking to make a move. I faxed over a copy of my résumé. . . ."

"Yes, it's very impressive. Bachelor in finance from Princeton, law degree from Columbia. I don't imagine we'll have much trouble finding you a new position. Do you mind my asking you why you want to leave Miller, Sheridan?"

"I'm looking for a firm with more vision, more guts," he said easily. "Miller, Sheridan is a good, capable firm, but they're also a little old-fashioned, and I prefer . . ."

"Quirkier?"

He smiled. "I don't want to wait the requisite ten years before being made a full partner."

"A man in a hurry," Casey observed.

"I prefer to think of myself as a man who knows his own worth."

Casey glanced back at his résumé, although she'd already committed all the relevant facts to memory: Warren Marshall had attended Princeton on a full scholarship and graduated Columbia in the top third of his class; his area of expertise was corporate and commercial law; he was already pulling in a salary of several hundred thousand dollars a year. "I'm not sure I can get you more money than you're getting now, at least to start out."

"Sure you can," he said with a smile.

He was a little arrogant, Casey decided. But that was all right. In the right hands, arrogant could be very attractive. Providing there was something to be arrogant about. Her father had been arrogant. She found herself checking out the ring finger of Warren Marshall's left hand and was happy to see it was empty, although that didn't necessarily mean anything. What was she doing? This wasn't like her.

"Look. Nobody becomes a lawyer to get rich," Warren was saying. "You make a decent living, yes. Okay, more than a decent living. But factor in expenses and taxes and overhead, you're certainly not retiring at forty."

"Is that what you want to do? Retire at forty?"

"No, that's not me. But sixty doesn't sound so unreasonable. Old," he continued with a laugh. "But not unreasonable."

Casey laughed as well. They spent the next half hour talking about his preferences and his politics, his likes and dislikes, his goals and his dreams, all of which were compatible with hers. More than once, they finished each other's sentences. Casey was surprised at their easy camaraderie, as if they'd known each other for years. *He gets me,* she thought, wishing she could think of a way to prolong the interview further.

"So, you think you can do something for me?" he asked, pushing back his chair and standing up.

"I can't imagine I'll have too much trouble," Casey answered honestly. Warren Marshall was a gift, she was thinking, the easiest commission she'd ever earn.

"By the way, will you marry me?" he asked in the next breath.

"What?"

"Sorry. That's the man in a hurry talking. We can start with dinner, if you'd prefer."

"What?" Casey said again.

"I don't believe it," Janine had wailed when she returned to the office half an hour later. "I get a broken tooth; *you* get a date."

She got more than that, Casey was thinking now. She got her knight in shining armor, her Prince Charming, the man of her dreams. Ten months later, she and Warren were married.

The door to her hospital room suddenly swung open.

"I found him," Patsy announced, an irritating chirp to her voice.

"Mr. Marshall," a male voice said. "I'm Detective Spinetti, with the Philadelphia police department."

"Have you found the person responsible for my wife's accident?" Warren asked immediately.

"No," the detective answered quickly. "But there *is* something we need to discuss."

"Thank you, Patsy," Warren said, dismissing the nurse's aide.

"Just ring if you need anything."

The door closed behind her.

Casey didn't know why, but she was certain that had she not been connected to a respirator, she would be holding her breath.

5

"How is your wife doing?" the detective asked.

"About the same," Warren answered. "You have some news regarding her accident?"

"I'd like to ask you a few questions, if you wouldn't mind."

"What sort of questions?"

"Do you know what your wife was doing in South Philly the day of the accident, Mr. Marshall?" Detective Spinetti asked immediately.

"What was she doing in South Philly?" Warren repeated, as if trying to make sense of the question. "She was meeting friends for lunch. Why?"

"Do you recall the name of the restaurant?"

Why do you want to know that?

"I think it was Southwark, over on South Street. How is this relevant?"

"If you'd just bear with me for a few minutes."

There was a slight pause. Casey pictured Warren giving the officer his silent assent.

"You said she was meeting friends for lunch," the detective continued. "Do you know who those friends were?"

"Of course I do."

"Can I have their names?"

"Janine Pegabo and Gail MacDonald."

"That's P-e-g . . ."

". . . a-b-o," Warren finished quickly, as Casey listened to the scribbling of a pen. "MacDonald, spelled M-a-c," he added, without further prompting. "They're her best friends. Again, I have to ask, how is this relevant to my wife's accident?"

A longer pause. Then, "Actually, we're no longer convinced it *was* an accident."

What?

"What?"

What do you mean?

"What are you saying?"

"We have reason to believe that your wife might have been deliberately targeted."

I don't understand.

"What reason?"

"In reviewing the garage's surveillance tapes again—"

Surveillance tapes? There were surveillance tapes?

"Were you able to get a better look at the driver's face?" Warren interrupted. "Was it someone you recognize?"

"No, I'm afraid not. The driver wore a hoodie and dark glasses, and kept his head down. Combined with the poor quality of the tape, there was no way to make any kind of positive identification."

"Then I don't understand. What makes you think someone would have deliberately targeted my wife?" Warren's voice cracked, and he coughed to mask the sound.

Someone deliberately ran me down?

"Maybe you should sit down, Mr. Marshall," Detective Spinetti said. "You're looking a little pale."

"I don't want to sit down. I want to know why you no longer think this was an accident."

"Please, Mr. Marshall. I understand this is upsetting . . ."

"You're telling me somebody tried to murder my wife, for God's sake. Of course I'm upset."

Hold on a minute. You're saying someone tried to murder me? Is that what you're saying?

"If you'll let me explain," the detective began.

There must be some mistake. Who would possibly want to kill me?

"I'm sorry. Of course. Go ahead. I'm sorry," Warren apologized again.

Casey heard the sound of chairs being adjusted and occupied, Warren in one, the police officer right beside him. She pictured the detective as tall and swarthy, with thinning, wavy dark hair and a deeply lined face. His voice, strong and matter-of-fact, indicated he was used to being in charge. She decided he was probably around forty, although she could easily have been off by a decade in either direction. Voices were so deceiving, she thought.

"As I was saying, we reviewed the surveillance tapes." Detective Spinetti paused, as if he expected to be interrupted again, then continued when no such interruption was forthcoming. "Unfortunately, the parking garage has been around forever, and the security cameras are on their last legs. So all we knew for certain was that the vehicle that hit your wife was a late-model Ford SUV, probably silver in color. We enhanced the images and were able to get a partial plate. But you already know this."

"Clearly there's something I don't know."

"After we ran the plates, we discovered they were phony. That, plus the fact your wife is Ronald Lerner's daughter, and Ronald

Lerner was a man who'd ruffled more than a few feathers in his day. . . ."

"That day is long past. The man's been dead for years," Warren scoffed. "Why would someone go after his daughter now?"

"I'm not saying that's what happened. I'm simply saying it got us thinking that this might not have been the simple case of hit-and-run we first assumed it was. So we went back and looked at the tapes again, both at the exit *and* the entrance to the garage, starting first thing that morning, to see if we could spot the SUV when it arrived. Unfortunately, the cameras on the individual levels of the garage contained no film, so they weren't of any help."

"And what did you find out?"

"We saw your wife drive in at just before noon . . ."

Another pause. Was he straining for dramatic effect? Casey wondered impatiently. *Just spit it out.*

"Go on," Warren said.

". . . and the car that hit her drive in soon after."

"How soon?"

"Within seconds."

Within seconds. What does that mean?

"You're saying you think she was being followed?"

"It's an awfully big coincidence if she wasn't. Think about it, Mr. Marshall. Your wife enters the parking garage at just before noon, followed immediately by the same SUV that runs her down several hours later."

"But it *could* be a coincidence," Warren said, clearly struggling to understand what was becoming obvious even to Casey.

Someone had followed her into the garage, waited there until she returned, then tried to kill her.

"It could be," the detective agreed unconvincingly.

"Good God," Warren whispered, as Casey pictured him burying his face in his hands.

"Can you think of anyone who might have wanted to hurt your wife, Mr. Marshall?"

"No one," Warren answered without pause. "Casey is a wonderful woman. Everybody loves her."

"Perhaps a jealous former boyfriend. . . ."

Casey felt Warren shaking his head, imagined several strands of soft brown hair falling across his forehead.

"Does your wife have a job, Mr. Marshall?"

"She's an interior decorator. Why?"

"Any unhappy customers?"

"You fire your decorator if you're unhappy, Detective. You don't run them down."

"Still, I'd appreciate a list of all her clients."

"I'll have it for you first thing in the morning."

"What about the people who work for her? Any disgruntled employees, someone she had to let go recently . . . ?"

"Casey worked alone. The business was relatively new. She used to . . ." He broke off.

"She used to . . . ?" Detective Spinetti repeated.

"She used to run a lawyer placement service with her friend Janine."

"That would be Janine Pegabo?"

Casey pictured him consulting his notes.

"Yes."

"They were partners?"

"Yes."

"But they no longer work together." The observation was part statement, part question.

"No. They went their separate ways about a year ago."

"Why was that?"

"Casey just wanted to try other things. She'd always been interested in design. . . ."

"And how did Ms. Pegabo feel about that?"

"She was understandably upset, at least initially. But she came around. She'd made peace with it. She certainly wouldn't have tried to kill Casey because of it."

"Do you know what kind of car she drives, Mr. Marshall?"

"Uh, a Toyota, I think."

It's a Nissan. And it's red, not silver.

"And it's red," Warren said. "Janine always drives a red car."

"What about Gail MacDonald?"

"I have no idea what kind of car she drives."

It's a Ford Malibu, and it's white.

"Gail is the gentlest person on earth," Warren said. "I've actually seen her scoop up an ant in a tissue and carry it outside rather than kill it. There's no way she'd hurt Casey."

This is ridiculous. Neither Gail nor Janine had anything to do with what happened to me.

"You can't think either of these women had anything to do with this," Warren said, echoing her thoughts.

"I'm just covering all the bases," the detective replied obliquely. "You said that up until about a year ago, your wife ran a lawyer placement service."

"Yes."

"Any lawyers she might have angered?"

"Lawyers are, by nature, always angry about something," Warren answered. "But Casey had a way about her. . . ."

Wait a minute. There was *this one lawyer. . . . The little twerp, Janine had called him at lunch.*

"I honestly can't think of anyone who'd have been angry enough to try to kill her."

Dammit, what was his name? Moody? Money? No. Mooney. That's it. Richard Mooney.

"Maybe you should talk to Janine about that."

But would Richard Mooney really try to kill me because his job placement hadn't worked out?

"Tell me," Detective Spinetti said, "is there anyone who would profit by your wife's death?"

What do you mean?

"Profit?"

"It's no secret that your wife is a very wealthy woman, Mr. Marshall. In the event of her death, who inherits her estate?"

"Probably her sister," Warren answered after a moment's thought. "To tell you the truth, I'm not sure."

"You're not sure? You're a lawyer. . . ."

"I'm not Casey's lawyer, Detective."

"You mentioned a sister. . . ."

"Casey's younger sister, Drew."

"Were they close?"

"Not especially."

"Mind my asking why?"

Another moment's thought, then, "Even though she was extremely well-provided-for," Warren said carefully, "Drew always resented the fact her father named Casey as executor of his estate."

"Effectively giving Casey control over her finances?"

"Drew isn't the most responsible person on the planet," Warren explained. "She's had her share of problems with drugs and alcohol."

"Do you know what kind of car she drives?"

"I have no idea. She trades them in almost as often as she changes boyfriends."

Casey could almost see Detective Spinetti's eyebrows arch. "I see," he noted.

"You don't see anything," Warren said adamantly. "Drew may be a flake. And she definitely has issues. But there's no way she'd hurt Casey."

"Any idea who she's seeing now?" the detective asked, ignoring Warren's protestation.

"I think his name is Sean. Sorry, his last name escapes me."

"So you wouldn't know what kind of car this Sean drives."

"Sorry, no. You'd have to ask Drew. But again, you can't think . . ."

"I'm just gathering information, Mr. Marshall."

Warren took an audible breath and released it slowly. "In that case, I imagine you'll want to know *my* whereabouts on the afternoon my wife was run down," he said.

What? No!

"You understand I have to ask."

I understand no such thing.

"I know the drill, Detective. I also understand the husband is always the prime suspect in cases like this. But *you* have to understand that I'm on the verge of being made a full partner with one of the city's premier law firms, and that I make a very substantial living of my own. I've never been interested in my wife's fortune. And I was in my office, conferring with a client, at the time she was being run down. I'll be happy to provide you with a list of at least a dozen people you can talk to who will verify that I didn't leave my desk all day, not even for lunch. I was there when the hospital called. . . ." Again his voice cracked. Again he coughed in an effort to disguise it.

"Do you hold any life insurance policies on your wife, Mr. Marshall?"

"No."

"That doesn't sound very lawyerly," Detective Spinetti observed.

"Lawyers are notoriously lax when it comes to their own personal affairs. Besides, Casey is young, she was in excellent health, and we don't have any children. I guess we both assumed there was lots of time to talk about those things." His voice drifted into the air, where it hung suspended for several seconds before evaporating. "I didn't marry my wife for her money, Detective. I married her because I love her. I love her so much."

Oh, Warren. I love you, too. More than you'll ever know.

"If I could change places with her, I would." His voice cracked a third time. This time he made no effort to hide the sound.

The door suddenly swung open.

"Oh, I'm sorry," someone said. "I guess I should have knocked."

"Dr. Ein," Warren acknowledged, pushing back his chair. It scraped against the floor, knocked against the side of the bed. "This is Detective Spinetti with the Philadelphia police."

"Did they catch the person who . . . ?"

"Not yet," Detective Spinetti answered. "But we will."

"Awful business," the doctor said.

"Yes," the detective agreed. "Look, why don't I get out of here, let you have some privacy."

No. You can't just walk in here, announce someone tried to kill me, point the finger of suspicion at virtually everyone I know, and then leave.

The sound of another chair being pushed back.

"You'll keep me informed?" Warren said.

"Count on it."

"Everything all right?" the doctor asked as soon as the detective was gone.

"You tell me," Warren countered.

Casey felt the doctor approach the bed, imagined him staring down at her.

"Well, all things considered, your wife's doing very well. She came through the tracheostomy with flying colors. The trach tube looks good. It shouldn't leave too much of a scar. And her breathing is stable at fourteen breaths a minute."

"Which means what exactly?"

"Which means that we can hopefully start weaning her off the ventilator pretty soon."

"Is that wise?"

"I assure you we won't do anything until the time is right."

"And once the ventilator is removed? Once Casey is breathing on her own, what then?"

"Then we remove the trach tube."

"And after that?"

"I don't know," the doctor admitted after a lengthy pause. "Look, I wish I could give you something more concrete to go on. But we'll just have to take it one day at a time."

One day at a time, Casey thought after everyone was gone. One day at a time, she repeated wordlessly as the noises of the day dimmed into the whimpers of the night.

Someone deliberately ran me down, she was thinking as sleep began circling her brain, like a helicopter looking for a place to land. Someone is trying to kill me.

Somebody wants me dead.

Who?

"Where were you on the night in question?" a man asked suddenly.

Detective Spinetti?

"I was home all night," another man answered.

Who's that? Is someone here?

"Was anyone with you?"

"No. I was alone."

I don't understand. Who are you? What are you talking about?

And then suddenly she did understand. There was no one in the room. She was alone, just like the man being questioned on her TV, the night his wife had been cruelly gunned down.

She'd imagined everything.

The entire episode had been nothing but a combination of dreams and television reruns, a little something her mind had cooked up to pass the time and keep her from going crazy with boredom. No one had tried to kill her. There was no one named Detective Spinetti. Her brain had been rocked! That's what the doctors had said. Hadn't they? Maybe that was something else her imagination had invented. How could she tell?

How could she be sure of anything?

Wake up. Wake up. Wake up. This dream is no longer even vaguely amusing. It stopped making sense a long time ago.

A car didn't run me down. I'm not lying, broken and comatose, in some narrow hospital bed. My breathing isn't dependent on a machine; there is no tube in my trachea. I did not hear a nurse's aide confide she intended to seduce my husband. I most assuredly did not hear a police detective speculate that my condition is the result of a deliberate act, and that everyone I hold dear, my friends and associates, my sister, even the husband I adore, are suspects.

I did not. I did not. I did not.

Wake up. Wake up. Wake up.

Casey lay in her bed, unseeing eyes open toward the ceiling. The sky is falling, she thought, recalling the classic children's story of Chicken Little, and struggling to remember its outcome. Had the sky really come crashing down, or had it just been a case of some stupid chicken running around, flapping his wings, stirring things up for no reason other than his own growing hysteria? Whatever happened to that crazy chicken? Casey was still wondering when she finally succumbed to sleep.

6

"OKAY, SO YOU MISSED the film festival this year," Janine was saying, jolting Casey back into consciousness.

How long had she been asleep? When had Janine arrived? What was she talking about?

"But not to worry. You picked a good time to be brain-dead. The movies were shit. I saw one last night, and you would not believe how bad it was. I think if it didn't have subtitles, it would have been laughed right out of the theater. But people always assume that just because it's French . . ." Janine took a deep breath.

Casey tried to focus. The city's modest attempt at a film festival had just ended, which meant it was still April. How much time had she lost since Janine's last visit?

"Anyway, I brought a newspaper. The doctors said it would be a good idea for us to read to you, that it might help stimulate your brain, or something. But there doesn't seem to be a whole lot going on that's very stimulating."

Don't worry about that. My brain seems to be working overtime as it is. I've been having the most extraordinary hallucinations.

"Let's see. Did you know that since the 1960s, Philadelphia has lost approximately six hundred thousand residents, due to something called urban blight, which sounds suspiciously like an STD, if you ask me, and that there are about sixty thousand derelict or abandoned buildings throughout the city, despite all the new development? Is this stimulating enough? Blink twice if the answer is yes."

I'm blinking. Once. Twice. Did you see that?

"Okay, not seeing any blinks, so not very stimulating."

Dammit, I'm blinking. Look again, I'm blinking. I'm blinking. Why can't I make you see?

"Let's see what else is here. What amazing things are you going to miss during the upcoming month of May if you don't snap out of this ridiculous coma?"

Casey heard the rustling of papers. Or was her imagination just providing the appropriate sound effects? Was Janine even there?

"Okay, so there's the Dad Vail Regatta, which, as you know, is the largest collegiate regatta in the United States, one that draws thousands of rowers and spectators to the Schuylkill River every year. Something I'm sure you wouldn't want to miss. And there's Philadanco! which sounds like another STD but is actually a dance troupe from West Philly, who'll be performing at the Kimmel Center for one week only, good seats still available. I'll be sure to call for tickets. And last but not least, May is the month that Philadelphia opens up its historic old homes for public viewing. Your house is pretty historic, wouldn't you say? Ever consider opening it up for the public to trample through? No, I guess not. Although I think you'd draw quite a crowd. All those people wanting to see exactly where and how Ronald Lerner lived. Although the truth is never as exciting as one's imagination, is it?"

Believe me, Janine. You have no idea.

"Anyway, I spoke to that police detective again yesterday."

What?

"How come the policemen on TV all look like Chris Noth, and in real life they look like Detective Spinetti?"

He's real? I didn't dream him?

"Anyway, he told me he questioned Richard Mooney after I told him about our encounter, and that Mooney claims he was visiting his mother at the time of your accident. Although Spinetti clearly doesn't think it *was* an accident."

Okay, it's time for a new dream. This one's turning into something of a nightmare.

"Apparently Mooney's mother backs him up, although Spinetti says the police don't exactly trust mothers when it comes to providing alibis."

Can't say I trust mothers when it comes to much of anything.

"Anyway, they still haven't eliminated him as a suspect, especially since—get this—the guy owns a silver SUV. Although frankly, who doesn't? Besides, you'd think if he was going to try to kill anyone, it would have been me. I'm the one he had the fight with that morning. But then, you always were the chosen one, weren't you?"

Casey pictured the dazzling smile that accompanied Janine's question.

"Anyway, it would appear Mooney's not the only suspect. Spinetti asked a million questions about Drew. Apparently he's left at least a dozen messages on her voice mail, but she hasn't answered any of them. I said welcome to the club, Drew's notorious for not returning calls. He asked how well I knew her, if I thought she was capable of trying to kill you. I told him I honestly didn't know. I mean, who knows anything with Drew? And, of course, he asked a shitload of questions about Warren."

"Are you talking about that police detective?" Gail asked from the doorway.

"Oh, hi," Janine said, her voice receding as she swiveled around in her chair. "How long have you been standing there?"

"Just a few seconds. How's Casey doing today?"

"Not much change."

The sound of footsteps approaching, the air growing heavy above Casey's head, a gentle laugh, like a soft breeze, wafting toward her face.

"Her color's good."

"If you like the color of skim milk," Janine said dryly. "Has he been talking to you, too?"

"Who?"

"That police detective. Spinetti."

"I assume he's talking to everyone close to Casey."

"He ask you about Warren?"

"I told him he was way off base," Gail insisted. "I said Warren adored Casey, that there was no way on earth he had anything to do with this."

"Do you really believe that?"

"Don't you?"

"I guess."

What do you mean, you guess?

"What do you mean, you guess?" Gail said in Casey's stead.

"Well, isn't it always the husband in cases like this?"

"Not in *this* case," Gail said adamantly.

"He could have hired someone."

"You've been watching too much TV."

"You're right," Janine said.

"Warren's a wonderful man."

"Yes, he is."

"He adores Casey."

"Yes, he does."

"Then why would you say something like that?"

"I don't know. Blame it on that detective and his stupid questions."

"He asked quite a few questions about you, as a matter of fact," Gail said.

"About me? What do you mean? What kind of questions?"

"About your relationship with Casey, how upset you were when she opted out of your partnership, if you were jealous or resentful of her success. . . ."

"That moron. What'd you tell him?"

"The same thing I told him about Warren—that he was completely off base."

Casey could feel Janine shaking her head in anger and realized she was almost enjoying Janine's discomfort. It served her right for the reservations she'd expressed about Warren.

"What a jerk. Did you happen to remind him I was with you at the time Casey was run down?"

"He said you had plenty of time to drop me off and get back to the parking garage."

"Did he also have an explanation for how I was able to turn my little red Nissan into a silver Ford SUV? Does he think I'm David Copperfield, for Christ's sake?"

"You could have hired someone," Gail said, echoing Janine's earlier remark.

"Very funny. Anyway, let's talk about something more pleasant. How was your date last night?"

Gail had had a date? With whom?

"It was nice," Gail said shyly, soft giggles bracketing her reply.

"Define the word 'nice.' "

"It was just nice. You know."

"I don't know. 'Nice' is not part of my vocabulary."

"It was okay."

"Just okay? Did you have a good time?"

"Yes, I had a good time. You're worse than Detective Spinetti."

"How good a time?" Janine pressed.

"It was really nice." Gail sighed. "God, I feel like such a traitor."

"Why would you feel like a traitor?"

"Because our best friend is lying here in a coma. . . ."

"You think Casey would want us to stay at home and do nothing?"

"No, I guess not."

"You don't have to guess. I'm telling you," Janine said, as if she were privy to Casey's most secret thoughts. "The last thing Casey would want is for us to sit around moping. If nothing else, what happened to Casey proves that we never know how long we've got on this earth, and that we have a duty to enjoy ourselves when we have the chance."

Is that what it proved? Casey wondered, before deciding Janine was probably right.

"So, tell me about this guy. What's he like?"

"He's just a guy."

"Does he have a name?"

"Does it matter? You don't know him."

"I know everybody."

"You don't know him," Gail repeated, without any accompanying laughter.

"You're being very opaque."

Janine was right, Casey thought, her own curiosity piqued. It was unlike Gail to be so circumspect.

"Did you meet him at work?"

"No."

"How *did* you meet?"

Casey felt Gail shrug, her nervous giggle returning.

"Why won't you tell me who he is?"

"Because . . ."

"Because you *like* him, don't you?" Janine pounced.

Casey felt the burn in Gail's cheeks as if she herself were the one blushing. "I don't know. It's way too early. We've only been on one date. He probably won't even call me again."

"Why wouldn't he call you again? Were you too easy? Did you sleep with him already?"

"Of course not. Honestly, Janine. Can we talk about something else?"

"You're such a prude sometimes," Janine said.

"I'm not a prude."

"Are too," Janine said.

"Am not."

Both women laughed, the tension in the room immediately dissipating.

"Anyway, I should get going," Janine said, jumping to her feet. "Maybe next time I come, I'll bring a book so I can read to Casey."

"That's a good idea."

"Well, it'll be better than that damn TV all the time. Think I'll bring *Middlemarch*. She hated that book in college."

"Then why on earth would you bring it?" Gail asked logically.

"Because maybe if she has to listen to it again, she'll wake up, just so she can tell me to shut up."

"You're crazy."

"No argument there. Anyway, I'm off. I'll see you tomorrow, Casey."

"I'll walk you to the elevator," Gail offered, following Janine out of the room.

Casey listened to their footsteps as they retreated down the hall, replaying the details of their visit over in her mind. How strange it was to be a passive observer to their discussions, to be right there . . . and yet, not there at all. It made her sad, she realized, suddenly recalling an incident from when she was in college. Two students had been found going at it on the floor of the rare book section of the library. They were immediately hauled into the dean's office. "Wouldn't you just love to be a fly on that wall?" Janine had asked as they'd filed past, a wicked smile filling her face. And Casey had enthusiastically nodded her agreement. What could be better? she'd thought then, than to be invisible? To be able to come and go as you pleased, without anyone being the wiser, or indeed even knowing you were present. To be able to eavesdrop, to listen in on private conversations, to find out what people were really thinking, to discover their deepest secrets, witness what they did when they assumed they were alone.

Be careful what you wish for, Casey thought now.

Because invisible was exactly what she'd become. Despite all the wires and tubes and ventilators and casts and nuts and bolts that were holding her together, despite the doctors and nurses and hospital staff who hovered over her bed, despite all the machinery that was keeping her alive, nobody really saw her. Nobody knew she was there.

She was invisible.

And it wasn't fun. It wasn't fun at all. Not even for a second.

It was hell.

"Hi, sweetheart. How are you feeling today? Did you have a good sleep?"

Casey felt Warren's velvety voice curling up against her eardrum, like a kitten in a basket. How long had she been asleep this time? she wondered, coming fully awake, her heart pounding wildly inside her chest as the familiar panic overtook her, although she remained outwardly still. She heard him moving restlessly about the room for several seconds before pulling up a chair beside the bed, clearly trying to get comfortable in a place that afforded no such luxury.

She tried picturing the room in an effort to calm herself down, deciding it was likely small and a sickly shade of green, with clunky Venetian blinds that hung precariously from a lone side window, and maybe one or two straight-backed, vinyl-upholstered chairs shoved into a corner. Perhaps a fading pastel sketch of a nondescript, bucolic landscape decorated the wall above her hospital bed, the bed itself overwhelmed by the latest in medical technology. There was undoubtedly a metal nightstand beside her, as well as the small television suspended from the ceiling.

"The doctors think you might be ready to start breathing on your own," Warren said, his voice soft and reassuring. "They're going to start trying to wean you off the ventilator this afternoon, which is really wonderful news."

Is it? Casey wondered, settling uneasily into consciousness and trying to make sense of everything that was happening. But how could she make sense of anything when she didn't *know* anything, when she didn't know if it was night or day, dark or light, May or June, this year or next, when she had no idea how much time had passed since the last time she was conscious? And what difference did it make if she was breathing on her own or with the help of a machine, if she still couldn't see or move or communicate?

"Everybody keeps calling. Friends, neighbors, business associates. You really have no idea how much everybody loves you."

Except for one rather glaring exception.

"I think you're single-handedly keeping the florists in this city in business."

I have flowers?

"Janine and Gail send a fresh arrangement every week, of course," Warren continued. "This week it's a bunch of white and pink tulips. And there's a vase of spectacular spring flowers from the partners at my firm. Unfortunately, the only flowers I know by name are the daffodils and irises, so I can't be much help in that department, but there are a bunch of puffy white things I think you'd get a kick out of. Oh, and some pussywillows. I think that's what they're called. Not to mention a dozen red roses from yours truly, which are very beautiful, even if they don't smell. Remember how roses used to smell? And now they don't anymore," he said sadly.

Casey vaguely recalled having read something about why roses no longer had any aroma, but she couldn't remember what it was. Besides, what difference did it make if she had no sense of smell? No difference at all, she decided, her mind arranging the spring flowers along the windowsill and placing the odorless roses on the nightstand beside her bed.

There was a gentle knock on the door.

"Sorry for interrupting," Patsy apologized sweetly. "I saw you come in, and I thought I'd stop by and see how you were doing."

"I'm okay, thanks," Warren said.

And now that you know, you can leave.

"You look a little tired."

"Not getting much sleep these days."

"I guess you're not used to sleeping alone."

Oh, that's nice. Good one, Patsy. Nice and subtle.

"I guess not."

"I'm sorry. I didn't mean that the way it sounded."

Yeah, right.

"It's okay. I know what you meant."

"It doesn't get any easier, does it? Seeing her this way," Patsy continued, as Casey felt the nurse's aide edging her way into the room, the scent of lavender following her.

Did she really smell lavender? Casey wondered, sniffing madly at the air. Was it possible? Or was it just all that talk about flowers triggering her already overactive imagination?

"That Detective Spinetti was back again," Patsy said, "asking a lot of questions."

"Such as?"

"Who comes to visit, how long they stay, if we've observed anything unusual or suspicious."

"And have you?"

"I'll tell you exactly what I told the detective, that the only thing I've seen is a lot of really sad people with a lot of love in their hearts. Casey must have been a very special woman."

"She still is," Warren corrected.

"Of course. I'm so sorry. I didn't mean . . ."

"I know you didn't. I'm sorry. I didn't mean to snap at you. It's just that this whole thing was bad enough when we thought it was an accident. To think that someone might have done it deliberately . . ."

"I can't imagine. . . ."

"It's just so unbelievable, seeing her so still. Casey was always so animated, so full of life."

"Tell me about her," Patsy said, managing to sound as if she really cared.

No. Don't tell her anything. This is just foreplay as far as she's concerned.

Warren laughed softly, a tender sound radiating warmth and love. It encircled Casey like a pair of strong, comforting arms. "Well, she's beautiful. You can see that, even in her condition. And I don't mean just on the outside. On the inside, too. And she's funny. We used to laugh so much."

It's true, Casey thought. We used to laugh all the time.

"And she's sensitive," Warren continued, as if a tap had been turned on in his brain, releasing a flood of adjectives. "Strong, smart, sexy. I miss her so much," Warren whispered.

Casey felt Patsy approach, pictured her laying a gentle hand on Warren's shoulder. "If she's half as strong and smart as you think she is, she'll find her way back to you."

"Thank you," Warren said.

"Any time. Can I get you anything? A cup of coffee? Something to eat?"

"Coffee would be wonderful. Here, let me give you some money."

"No, don't be silly. It's my treat. Be right back."

Casey pictured Patsy walking toward the door, an exaggerated sway to her hips. She wondered what kind of uniform Patsy was wearing, if the fabric flattered her figure, whether her hips were wide or narrow. She wondered how old she was, and if Warren thought she was pretty.

"Nice girl," Warren said after she was gone. "Not bad-looking," he continued, as if he understood what she was thinking. "Although I think you'd find her rather common. Maybe five feet four, a hundred and fifteen pounds, at least fifteen pounds of which is makeup. Reddish blond hair, brown eyes, and clearly, her mother never taught her the fine art of applying mascara, which she has an unfortunate tendency to lather on, like shaving cream. I would guess her age as mid- to late twenties. Oh, and I don't think she wears underwear."

Casey heard him swivel around in his chair.

"Let's see. What else can I tell you? You're missing a beautiful day. Sunshine, about seventy-four degrees. Everyone keeps trying to talk me into playing some golf. The course is open, and from what I hear, it's in great shape. I haven't been up there to see for myself. I can't quite bring myself to go, what with you lying here like this. 'You can't stay at the hospital all day,' everyone keeps telling me. But what am I supposed to do? Everything just seems so . . . frivolous. 'You have to get out, live your life,' they say. I keep telling them that my life is here, in this hospital."

Casey felt her eyes fill with tears, although she doubted any tears actually formed. *I keep telling them that my life is here, in this hospital,* she repeated, trying to hold on to his exact inflection.

"Anyway, Ted Bates—you remember him, he's a lawyer, we had dinner with him and his wife a few months back—he's called a couple of times, trying to get me out to play a few holes, keeps telling me it'll be a good distraction, that I have to do something to relax. Life goes on, that kind of crap. I said I'd think about it. God knows I could use the exercise. I haven't been to the gym since . . . Shit. What am I talking about? I'm not going near a golf course until you can go with me. Although this would probably be a good time for me to practice," he said, and tried to laugh. "That way when you wake up, I can surprise you with my newfound prowess." The laugh scraped against his throat before emerging as a strangled cry. "God, Casey. I miss you so much."

I miss you, too.

Another gentle knock on the door.

"I'm sorry," Warren said, sniffing back his tears. "I didn't realize you were standing there."

"Sorry to interrupt. I didn't want your coffee to get cold," Patsy said.

So now even her most intimate moments with her husband were no longer hers alone, Casey thought, her mind absorbing this latest loss, her heart sinking with its weight.

I *will* find my way back to you, she cried silently.

I will. I will.

7

"I CAN'T BELIEVE YOU TOLD that cop you think I tried to kill my sister!" Drew cried loudly.

"I told him no such thing," Warren protested.

"I get home from my holiday to find half the damn police force camped out in the lobby of my condominium. You'd think I was Osama bin Laden, for God's sake. And then to be practically accused of trying to kill my own sister! My sister! How do you suppose that made me feel?"

"I'm really sorry. . . ."

"How could you accuse me of such a thing?"

"Believe me, Drew. I didn't accuse you of anything."

Casey heard the resignation in her husband's voice. You could never win an argument with Drew, she understood, thinking back to that day, three months shy of her fourth birthday, when her sister was born.

"What kind of name is Drew anyway?" Leslie had scoffed when they brought her home from the hospital. Leslie was the new baby's recently hired nanny, a young woman with a strong English accent, round, ruddy cheeks, and spiky brown hair that was constantly falling into her eyes, so she always appeared to be peering at you from under a scrim.

"She was supposed to be Andrew," came the knowing response from Shauna, the young Irish girl hired to take care of Casey after Maya's abrupt departure. Casey wasn't overly fond of Shauna, whose face was always vaguely pinched, as if she was in perpetual pain, and whose legs were heavy beneath her too-short skirts.

"Instead they got another stinking girl," Leslie remarked carelessly, as if Casey weren't in the room.

Shauna made a weird clucking sound with her mouth and nodded her agreement. "Boys are much better," she said.

Casey stood between the two young women in front of the change table in Drew's blue-and-white nursery, the baby fussing before them, waiting for a fresh diaper. "She isn't stinky," Casey protested.

"No? Then you can change her." Leslie thrust the used diaper into Casey's reluctant hands.

Casey quickly disposed of the diaper in the nearby wastebasket. "She smells better than you do."

Leslie laughed. "You saying you don't like my perfume?"

"It smells yucky."

"It smells *musky*," the nanny corrected. "And your father likes it just fine." She giggled, winking toward Shauna as she maneuvered a fresh Pampers around Drew's wriggling little bottom.

"Careful," Shauna warned. "That kind of talk's been known to get a girl fired."

Leslie shrugged dismissively, lifting Drew into the air and carrying the squirming bundle to her crib, then laying her on her back. Casey watched two tiny arms and legs immediately shoot into the air, as if her sister were an insect someone had callously tipped over. The baby's face contorted into a series of angry folds and furrows, and her mouth opened in a silent scream that quickly filled with rage, her shrill screams suddenly piercing the air, like shards of flying glass. "God, what an awful sound," Leslie said.

"Maybe she's hungry," Casey volunteered.

"I just gave her a bottle."

"Maybe you didn't give her enough."

"Maybe it's time for your nap."

"I don't take naps anymore."

"Too bad for you," Leslie said to Shauna as the baby's cries escalated. "God, what is the matter with this child? She cries all the damn time."

"I was speaking to Marilyn," Shauna said, referring to a nanny down the street, "and she thinks Drew might be suffering from fetal alcohol syndrome."

"What's that?" Leslie asked as Casey was about to.

"It's something babies get when they're still in the womb. From their mother's drinking," she whispered, although Casey had no trouble hearing every word.

"Yeah, that mother's a real piece of work, isn't she? No wonder her husband plays around."

"Shh," Shauna warned, eyes lowering toward Casey. "Little pitchers have big ears."

Casey quickly scanned the room. She didn't see any pitchers.

"Besides," Shauna continued over the baby's growing hysterics, "it's hard to know which came first—the drinking or the playing around."

"I think she wants to be held," Casey said, pulling on the pocket of Leslie's denim skirt.

"Oh, you do, do you? Do you want to hold her, then?" She lifted the screaming infant from her crib and handed her to Casey without further ado.

Casey carried her baby sister, whose wet face was now a furious red ball, into a corner of the room, and gingerly lowered herself onto the soft blue carpeting, Drew's loud wails rising, like steam, toward the ceiling. "It's okay, baby," she said softly. "I'm here. You don't have to cry."

In response, Drew cried even louder.

"Way to go, kid," Leslie said, and she and Shauna laughed, an irritating sound that scratched at the walls like fingernails. "You've got the magic touch."

"Think you can manage in here for a few minutes while we go out for a cig?" Shauna asked.

Casey watched the two girls leave the room without waiting for her response. As soon as they were gone, Drew's crying abated. "I don't like them either," Casey confided, rocking Drew back and forth until the baby's roar dropped to a steady whimper. "That's a good girl," she whispered. "You feel better now, don't you? Me too. My name is Casey. I'm your big sister, and I'll take care of you. You won't have to cry anymore."

Except she did cry. Constantly. "Morning, noon, and night," Leslie proclaimed wearily. And then suddenly Leslie was gone, and it was a dark-haired girl named Rosie who was doing the complaining.

"I don't think I've ever heard a baby cry so much," Rosie said, large hands resting on wide hips. "Colic is colic, but this, this is . . ."

"It's a syndrome," Casey explained.

And Rosie had laughed, a loud guffaw that made Casey laugh with her. Casey felt happy that Rosie had come to live with them because Rosie had a kind face and big, dark eyes that Casey had overheard her father telling her were like two large pools of chocolate syrup. Rosie had laughed when he'd said that, and whenever Rosie laughed that wonderful, infectious laugh, Casey felt a brief surge of reassurance and well-being.

"What the hell is going on down there?" her mother yelled from the top of the stairs, Rosie's laughter coming to an abrupt halt. "Can't anybody do something about that damn caterwauling? Where is . . . whatever her name is?"

"I'm right here, Mrs. Lerner," Rosie called back from the nursery door. "I'm just about to feed her."

The response was the sound of a bedroom door slamming.

"I'd say somebody got up on the wrong side of the bed if . . ." Rosie began.

If she *got* out of bed, Casey finished silently for her.

"What's her problem anyway?"

"It's because she's popular," Casey explained, trying to recall what her father had once told Leslie. His wife was bipopular, he'd said, and that's why she acted the way she did.

"How can somebody be popular when they never leave their room?" Rosie asked.

A few nights later, Casey heard strange noises in the middle of the night, and she got out of bed to see what was going on. Her room was in the west wing of the house, on the main floor, next to the nursery. ("So we don't disturb your mother," her father had explained.) Rosie's room was farther down the hall, next to Shauna's. Casey followed the succession of squeals and giggles to Rosie's doorway, then pushed it open.

It took her eyes a few seconds to adjust to the darkness, and even then it was hard to figure out exactly what Rosie was doing. She appeared to be sitting on something, and rocking violently back and forth as if she was having some sort of fit. The next second, she was bouncing up and down, and a pair of large hands were wrapping themselves around her naked hips. She seemed to be laughing and crying at the same time.

And then suddenly the room filled with light, and rough hands were pushing Casey out of the way, and her mother was behind her, screaming, and Rosie was jumping out of bed, struggling to cover up her nakedness and screaming every bit as loud as Casey's mother, and her father was sitting up in bed, begging everyone to please stay calm. Just as Casey was wondering what her father was doing in Rosie's bed, and why he, too, appeared to be naked, her mother was flying across the room toward him, crying and scratching at his face. And suddenly, Drew was screaming from the next room, and Shauna was lifting Casey into her arms and running with her down the hall, and the next morning both Rosie and her mother were gone.

"Rosie got another job," Shauna said over breakfast. "Your mother will be away for a little while." Nothing further was offered.

Two days later, a new nanny for Drew appeared. Her name was Kelly, and she was fired as soon as Alana Lerner returned from wherever she'd been, took one look at the girl's long legs, seductive smile, and wavy brown hair, and sent her packing. Casey breathed a sigh of relief when the employment agency sent over Misha, who was older, shapeless, and "as mousy as they come," according to Shauna. "There shouldn't be any more changes for a while," she'd proclaimed. Mistakenly, as it turned out, because Shauna herself was let go only a few weeks later for ringing up over three hundred dollars in overseas phone charges. Enter Daniela, who was fat, forty, and unflappable. She lasted the better part of two years and was the last of the Lerner family nannies.

"Whatever happened to Daniela?" Drew had asked many years later.

"They let her go when I started kindergarten," Casey answered.

"I liked her."

"How do you even remember her? You were what, two years old when she left?"

"I remember her," Drew insisted. "She's part of the first memory I have."

Casey knew exactly the memory her sister was referring to: Drew running into her mother's bedroom, eager to show her the new stuffed bear she'd received for her birthday, her mother angrily hurling the bear across the room and shouting, "Somebody get this child away from me." And Daniela rushing in and scooping Drew into her arms, carrying her downstairs to Casey's room, Drew crying loudly.

"I can't believe you told that cop I tried to kill my sister," Drew was crying now.

What?

"I specifically told Detective Spinetti that I didn't believe you had anything to do with what happened to Casey."

"Then what's he doing snooping around, asking questions, insinuating that I skipped town . . . ?"

"You didn't return any of his calls. Nobody knew where you were."

"I was in the Bahamas for a few weeks. Sue me."

"You were in the Bahamas," Warren repeated dully.

"I needed a break. Is that a crime?"

"Your sister's in a coma, Drew."

"Yeah, and she's been in a coma for almost two months," Drew reminded him testily.

"During which you've been here how many times?"

"I already told you, it's very hard on me, seeing her like this."

"It's hard on all of us."

"I thought the doctors said she was improving."

"She *is* improving. As you can see, her casts are off. Her injuries have pretty much healed. They're weaning her off the ventilator. They've even started her on physical therapy."

"Physical therapy? Why, for Pete's sake? It's not like she's going anywhere."

Silence.

"I'm sorry," Drew apologized. "I'm just upset. It's that damned detective. I mean, what's he talking about anyway? Who would want to kill Casey?"

"I don't know. Do you have any idea?"

"Me? No. Why would I?"

"You've known her longer than anyone, Drew. Is there anyone from her past, anyone you can think of who . . . ?"

"We didn't exactly run in the same circles."

"Is there anyone from *your* circle . . . ?"

"What's that supposed to mean?"

"One of your friends, perhaps an acquaintance . . ."

"Perhaps an acquaintance?" Drew repeated mockingly. "You wouldn't be referring to one of my scumbag, drug-dealing acquaintances, would you?"

"I'm just trying to figure things out, Drew."

"Well, you figured wrong."

"Look. I don't want to argue. Especially in front of your sister."

"Why? You think she can hear us?"

"No, of course not."

"Can you hear us, Casey?" Drew asked, drawing closer, looming over her, her breath brushing against the side of Casey's cheek like the prickly tongue of a cat. Was she imagining it? "Do you understand what we're saying?"

Yes. Yes, I understand everything.

"Ain't nobody home," Drew pronounced, backing away.

"Watch your elbow," Warren warned. "She's bruised enough."

Drew made a dismissive sound. "So, what happens now?"

"Well, hopefully, she'll keep improving. Now that she's started therapy, her muscles will get stronger. And the doctors will keep reducing the number of breaths the ventilator is providing. They're optimistic that in another week or two, she might be able to start breathing on her own."

"You're saying she'll regain consciousness?"

"No. Nobody's saying that."

"What *are* they saying? That she could be this way forever?"

No, no. That's not going to happen. Warren, tell her that's not going to happen.

Silence.

"So, I repeat, what happens now?" Drew pressed.

A long sigh escaped Warren's lips. "Once Casey is able to breathe without the respirator, I can start thinking about taking her home, hiring the right people—"

"I mean, what happens to me?" Drew interrupted.

Casey might have laughed had she been able to. She found it strangely comforting that some things never changed, no matter what the circumstances. A rose is a rose is a rose, she thought. And Drew was Drew was Drew. She always would be.

Could she blame her?

Her sister had learned from a very early age that the only person who would be there to take care of her was herself. Occasionally, Casey had tried to fill the parental role, but Drew had reminded her vehemently, "You're not my mother." And so she'd backed off.

Casey was, however, the trustee of their parents' estate, the one who made the decisions, the one who signed the checks.

"What happens to *you*?" Warren repeated.

"Yes. It's a reasonable question, under the circumstances."

"One I'm afraid I can't answer."

"Why not?"

"Because I don't *have* any answers."

"You're a lawyer. I thought lawyers were supposed to know these things."

"I'm not an estate lawyer." Casey could hear the struggle to remain calm in her husband's voice.

"I'm sure you've been speaking to one."

"Actually I haven't, no."

"You haven't spoken to anyone about what happens to your wife's fortune should she remain in a persistent vegetative state?"

I am not in a vegetative state. I am not. I am not.

"I find that very hard to believe," Drew continued.

"I've had a few other things on my mind, Drew."

Casey could feel her sister pacing around the bed. She could hear the click of her heels and tried to imagine what she was wearing. Probably a pair of black leggings and a loose-fitting jersey. Her long, dark blond hair was likely pulled into a high ponytail, a pair of her signature large silver hoops dangling from her ears. No doubt, her dark green eyes were flashing daggers in Warren's direction.

"I thought that if anything happened to Casey, my father's estate would automatically transfer to me."

"Casey isn't dead, Drew," Warren reminded her.

"She might as well be."

Oh, God.

"Okay, that's enough," Warren said, as the clicking of Drew's shoes came to a halt at the foot of the bed. "I'm afraid you'll just have to be patient."

"Easy for you to say. You don't have to worry about money."

"Maybe if you got a job," Warren suggested.

"Do I have to remind you I have a child to look after?"

Casey felt a knot beginning to form in the pit of her stomach at the mention of her five-year-old niece, who was her mother's tiny clone in almost every respect. Casey wondered if Lola would be the beauty her sister predicted she'd be when she got older. She remembered the same predictions having been made about Drew. But while Drew had matured—if the words "mature" and "Drew" could be used in the same sentence—into an undeniably pretty young woman, she stopped short of being beautiful, her features a touch too conventional, her eyes too unfocused, bereft of the essential mystery true beauty requires.

"Where *is* Lola?" Warren asked.

"Sean took her to the cafeteria for some ice cream."

"Who is this guy anyway?" Warren asked. "How long have you known him, exactly?"

"What's that supposed to mean—*exactly*?"

"It doesn't mean anything. I was just wondering."

"What are you wondering, Warren? You wonder if Sean had something to do with this? You wonder if I asked my boyfriend to run over my sister? Is that what you're wondering?"

Of course he isn't. You don't think that. Do you, Warren?

"Mommy!" a little voice called out, excited footsteps dashing into the room.

"Oh, God. Get her out of here. No. Go on. I thought you were taking her for ice cream," Drew said all in one breath.

"She *had* ice cream," a male voice protested.

"Then get her some more."

"What's the matter with Auntie Casey?" the little girl asked. "Is she sleeping?"

"She's not feeling well," Drew answered impatiently.

"Is she sick?"

"She was in a car accident," Warren explained.

"Will she be okay?"

"I hope so. We're keeping our fingers crossed."

"Can I cross mine, too?"

"I think that would be very helpful."

"Good. See, Mommy? My fingers are crossed."

"Great," Drew said. "Now, Sean, if you don't mind. A hospital room is no place for a child."

"I can read to her, Mommy."

"Maybe some other time. Sean . . ."

"Okay, okay. Come on, Lola. You can have that piece of cake you had your eye on."

"I'm not hungry anymore."

"Sean, for God's sake—"

"You know what?" Warren interrupted. "I think they have a kids' playroom downstairs. Would you like to see it?"

"Can I, Mommy?"

"By all means."

"How about I show you where it is?" Warren said.

"I'm sure Sean can manage on his own," Drew told him. "There are still some things we need to discuss."

"I think we've discussed enough for one afternoon."

Casey could tell from the way Warren's voice was receding that he was already at the door.

"You can go, too, Sean," Drew said dismissively. "Warren, I'll wait here till you get back."

"Suit yourself."

The door closed, leaving Casey alone with her sister. "I always do," Drew said.

8

"SO, HERE WE ARE again," Drew continued, as Casey pictured her sister walking over to the window. "Just like old times. Except in those days, I was the one pretty much in a coma, and you were the one pacing back and forth, trying to figure out what to do with me."

True enough, Casey thought, her mind racing back through all the years they'd shared the same house, the nights she'd spent waiting anxiously for her sister to come home, the days she'd spent watching her sleeping off a drunken bender, the unmistakable aroma of stale sex and soft drugs still clinging to her clothes.

"You kept telling me if I didn't straighten out, I wouldn't live to see my thirtieth birthday." Drew laughed, although the sound was hollow. "And now look at us." Casey felt her plop down on the side of the bed. "I guess that's what they mean by 'irony.' " She took a deep breath, then exhaled slowly through her mouth. "God, I really can't bear to look at you."

I'm so sorry you have to see me this way, Casey thought, recalling her sister's aversion to anything even vaguely unpleasant.

"Not that you look so awful. You don't. You actually look pretty good for a member of the undead. Your color's great, the bruises are gone, and the doctors stitched you up pretty good. Look, Casey," Drew said angrily. "Enough is enough. You've made your point. I'm a total fuckup who can't manage without you. I get it. Now snap out of this ridiculous coma and come back to us. Come on. I know you're in there."

Do you? Do you really?

"You have to wake up. It's not fair. What you're doing just isn't right. And don't give me this bullshit about not having any choice in the matter, because how many times have you told me that we *always* have a choice? So don't tell me you can't . . . what was it you once said? 'Start effecting some positive changes'? Yeah, that's it. So, start effecting. I need you to get better. And I need you to get better by Friday because I've written a bunch of checks, and they're going to start bouncing all over town if you don't wake up and transfer some money—which is rightfully mine anyway, in case you've forgotten—into my account."

Oh, Drew.

"I mean, I'm sorry to have to lay this on you in your condition, but I'm in a bit of a bind here—a bind, I point out, that could easily have been avoided if Dad hadn't named you sole executor of his estate, or if you hadn't gone along with it."

Please stop.

"The current problem being," her sister continued, bouncing none-too-gently along the side of the bed, "that I haven't received my monthly stipend since you went into hibernation, and what with taking Sean to the Bahamas and shopping for my new spring wardrobe, I've maxed out all my credit cards, and pretty soon, I'm not going to be able to feed my kid. And I know how you feel about Lola, that you love her to pieces, even if you weren't very happy about my pregnancy. And yes, in case you're wondering, I *do* know who the father is. Or at least, I've narrowed it down to three suspects. Just kidding," Drew added quickly. "Two," she said under her breath. "So, what am I supposed to do, huh? I need money, your husband says I have to be patient, and this is all your fault because you're the one who controls the purse strings. So, you tell me. How do we get out of this mess?"

I wish I knew.

"I hate to say it, but this whole situation would have been a lot easier if you'd just died."

What?

"Then I'd have my money. The cops wouldn't be riding my ass. I wouldn't have to come begging to Warren. . . ."

Oh, Drew. Do you really hate me so much?

Casey felt Drew push herself off the bed. She'd never been able to sit still for more than a minute, Casey thought, picturing her sister at the window. What does she see? Casey wondered, imagining a bright, orange sun being swallowed by a malevolent grouping of ominous black clouds.

Drew's current financial situation *was* her fault, Casey was forced to acknowledge. As trustee of her father's estate, it had been her decision to put Drew on a monthly allowance. Her sister had chafed under the imposed restrictions, railing against the unfairness of the arrangement, despite the generosity of the amount, even threatening to sue, then backing off when she learned that any challenge to her father's will could lead to her being disinherited altogether. She'd then tried reasoning with her older sister, arguing persuasively that by putting her on an allowance, Casey was, in effect, not allowing her to grow up. She was *infantilizing* her, Drew had said, and Casey had been impressed enough by both the word and the argument to transfer several hundred thousand dollars to her account.

The money was gone within a year, spent on an ill-advised

franchise that went quickly bankrupt, a yellow Ferrari, a few island vacations, and a lot of addictive white powder. After that, Casey had put her sister on a strict allowance. Drew subsequently sold the Ferrari, the proceeds quickly disappearing up her nose. It was around this time that Drew found herself pregnant and decided to keep the baby, although she refused to name the father. She did, however, agree to go into rehab, and she'd managed to stay clean and sober until after Lola's birth.

The last five years had been more of the same. Casey had moved her sister into a larger apartment in Society Hill, hired a responsible older woman to look after Lola, and paid for Drew's repeated attempts at rehab. Occasionally it looked as if Drew was about to turn a corner, only to disappear around it altogether, sometimes for weeks at a time. Just before her accident, Casey thought, refusing for the moment to think of it as anything else, she hadn't spoken to her sister in almost a month.

Drew was right, she thought again, feeling her sister return to her bedside. She shouldn't have put her in this position, shouldn't have forced her to be dependent on her for what was rightfully hers. She should have divided the estate into two equal halves and let the chips fall where they may. What Drew chose to do with her share of the family money was her business. Casey had no right to dictate to her younger sister, or to try to impose her own moral code on her.

"You can't protect someone who keeps deliberately putting herself in harm's way," Warren had told her more than once. He'd argued vehemently that the best thing Casey could do for her sister was to keep her on a tight rein financially, at least until she'd proven she could handle the responsibility of all that money.

Maybe Drew had realized that time would never come.

"My feet are killing me," Drew said now, and Casey heard her dragging a chair along the floor toward the bed. "Don't let anybody tell you Manolos are so comfortable they're like walking in bare feet. Who said that anyway? Probably Carrie from *Sex and the City*. Did you ever watch that show? I used to love it. I still watch it in reruns. They're on all the time. I probably know all the episodes by heart, I've seen them so many times. Hey, maybe it's on now." She clicked on the remote and began flipping through the channels, continuing to talk over the parade of ever-shifting voices emanating from the TV. "Anyway, you have to admit these are pretty great-looking shoes." Casey pictured her sister lifting her feet into the air to show off her footwear. "Yes, I realize that seven hundred dollars is an outrageous amount to pay for a strap of brown leather and a three-inch heel, but they're really a work of art, and when was the last time you paid only seven hundred dollars for a genuine work of art?" She took another deep breath. "Too bad you can't see them," she continued. "Too bad you can't see how good they look on my feet. Too bad you can't see how good I look, period." She laughed, again with no real mirth. "I actually *am* looking pretty great these days. I'm nice and tanned, and I started exercising. Not running. That's your thing. No, I've been taking dance classes, and I've even started spinning. I'm now officially one of those loony ladies sweating up a storm on those bicycles that go nowhere, which you'd probably say is a metaphor for the way I live my life."

Would she? Casey wondered, feeling instantly guilty. Would she say that? Was she really so judgmental?

"Anyway, I really am looking pretty good. Not as good as Sleeping Beauty here, of course. Even in a coma, you're still the sister to beat. Although I'm seeing a few lines around the mouth I never noticed before. You might want to consider Botox when you wake up, even if the whole idea of deliberately injecting a poison into your system kind of freaks me out. And I know what you're thinking, even if, technically, you're *not* thinking. But you're wrong. That's one thing I've never done. I've never used needles. You know I've always hated needles. Remember that time they were scheduled to give us those shots at school, and we all had to line up, and I started screaming and ran away, and they had to drag you out of class to help find me. Remember that? You were, what—twelve? I was eight or nine." She chuckled. "Those were the days, huh?"

The good old days.

"Anyway, don't do it. Botox scares me, even though I know it's FDA approved, and everybody uses it. But it paralyzes the muscle, and that's kind of scary. I mean, what if something goes wrong, and your whole body gets paralyzed? Shit," Drew muttered immediately. "What the hell am I saying? I'm sorry. That wasn't too swift. I'm pretty sure it isn't what the doctors had in mind when they said to talk to you as much as possible. Anyway, I really am sorry. I didn't mean . . . What am I doing apologizing? It's not like you can hear me. Can you? Can you hear me? I get this feeling sometimes like you can."

Yes. You're right. You're right.

"No. I guess it's too ridiculous," Drew said with a sigh. "So, what do you think of Sean?" she asked in the next breath.

Sean?

"The guy who was just in here," she answered, as if they were having an actual conversation.

Had Drew heard her? Casey wondered. Could she have spoken his name out loud?

"I can't remember if you two ever met. Wavy blond hair, little pug nose, nice brown eyes. Shorter than I normally like them, but what he lacks in length, he makes up for in width, if you know what I mean." She giggled. "Yeah, I know. I'm talking trash. Daddy wouldn't approve. Although he had a taste for trash himself, our daddy did," she mused aloud. "Anyway, Sean's okay. Not too bright. I kind of like that. But he's definitely not a keeper, so you don't have to worry. You have more than enough to worry about right now."

Casey felt Drew lean in closer. "Casey?" she heard her ask, her voice lowering, filling with concern. "Casey, what's going on in there? Why do I think you can hear me?"

Because you know me better than anyone. Because you're my sister, and despite everything, there's a connection between us, an unbreakable bond.

"She can't hear you," a male voice said gently.

Who's that?

"I know," Drew concurred. "There was just something about her expression all of a sudden. I thought for a minute that maybe . . . I don't know. Are you her doctor?"

"No. I'm her physical therapist. Jeremy Ross."

Casey tried to imagine what he looked like. She pictured him tall and fair-haired, with a square jaw and deep-set eyes. Maybe a nose that had been broken in his youth. He was probably in his midthirties, she thought, wondering if he was offering Drew his hand to shake.

"Drew Lerner," Drew said. "Casey's sister."

"Yes, I can see the family resemblance. Nice to meet you, Drew. How's our patient doing today?"

Casey felt Drew shrug.

"She's coming along very well," the therapist remarked, approaching the bed and taking Casey's hand in his, squeezing it gently.

Was he? Or was she just imagining it? Could she actually feel him manipulating her fingers up and down?

"I can definitely feel an improvement."

"You can?"

"She's getting a lot stronger. I can feel a difference in her fingers from even a few days ago. And once the doctors get rid of this thing," he said, obviously referring to the ventilator that was controlling Casey's breathing, "we can start moving her around a lot more."

"What if she's not able to breathe on her own?"

"The doctors won't remove the ventilator until they're sure it's safe."

"Do you think she'll regain consciousness?"

"Hard to say." Jeremy let go of one hand, then lifted the other one into the air. "Some do. Some don't."

"What are the odds?"

"Don't know." He began manipulating Casey's wrist, rotating it in tiny circles. "Generally, the longer the coma, the worse the chances for a complete recovery. But you never know. You can't give up hope."

Casey felt the strength in his fingers as they applied gentle pressure to her own. She felt a pleasant tingle working its way up her arm and experienced a surge of excitement. Were her senses coming back to her, a little at a time? Or was her brain simply projecting her desire to feel these things? She had to be careful not to get her hopes up before she knew for sure.

Although, why not? she wondered. What difference would it make if her hopes were raised only to be dashed? Could things be any worse than they were now?

"Thatta girl, Casey. You're doing great," Jeremy told her.

"Do you want me to leave?" Drew asked.

"No, that's all right. I don't mind you being here. What are you watching?"

"Huh? Oh, nothing. There's nothing worth watching anymore."

The voices on the television were abruptly silenced.

"In that case, you can watch me," Jeremy said. "Learn how to do some of these things yourself, so you can do them with her the next time you come to visit."

"Oh, no. I'd be too afraid. I wouldn't want to hurt her."

"You won't hurt her. Here, let me show you. Go on, take her hand."

"No, I can't. Really."

"Sure you can. Go on. I promise you won't hurt her."

Casey felt her right hand being passed from Jeremy's sure grip to Drew's less steady palm. I can feel that, she thought giddily. I can feel that.

"That's good. Now, slowly and carefully, start moving her fingers up and down, one at a time, real slow, real gentle. That's right. See? You got it. And now rotate the wrist, just like I'm doing. Good. Good. See? You're a natural."

Drew scoffed. "I don't think so."

"I *know* so. Don't sell yourself short. Casey needs you right now."

"Trust me. I'm the last thing she needs." She quickly returned Casey's hand to the therapist.

"And why is that?" Jeremy's hands began massaging Casey's forearms.

This isn't my imagination. I can really feel that.

"Does the phrase 'black sheep of the family' ring any bells?" Drew asked.

Jeremy chuckled. "I understand there are quite a few black sheep in this particular family."

Drew laughed along with him. "You've been doing your homework."

"I like to acquaint myself as best I can with my patients' histories."

"Yeah, well, good luck with this family. We're a pretty screwed-up bunch. Except for Casey. She was always perfect."

"I guess it's hard trying to compete with perfection," Jeremy stated, manipulating Casey's arm at the elbow.

"Oh, I stopped competing early."

"Probably a good idea."

"What about you?" Drew asked. "Any brothers and sisters?"

"Two of each."

"Wow. Big family. Any children of your own?"

"No. My wife and I were thinking about it, then she thought she'd rather have them with somebody else, so we're divorced now. You?"

"I have a daughter. No husband," Drew added quickly.

"Hello, Jeremy," Warren said from the doorway. "Drew, maybe you should leave and let the therapist do his job."

"That's all right. She's not bothering—"

"Sean and Lola are waiting for you downstairs."

"We need to talk," Drew protested.

"Not now."

"That's all right," Jeremy interjected. "I can come back in a few minutes. Nice meeting you, Drew."

"You too."

"Please tell me you weren't flirting with your sister's therapist," Warren said as soon as Jeremy was gone.

"What's the big deal? It's not like she can see me."

"I'm not having this discussion."

"He looks a bit like Tiger Woods, don't you think?"

"I'm not having that discussion either. Look, your boyfriend's downstairs with Lola. You probably shouldn't keep them waiting any longer. Here's some money to tide you over."

"What am I supposed to do with five hundred lousy dollars?"

"It's all the money I have on me."

"I don't want *your* money. I want *my* money."

"It's the best I can do for the time being."

"How long does this go on?"

"I don't know, Drew. It's a complicated situation."

"Then simplify it."

"My hands are tied."

"Untie them."

"Don't you understand? It's not up to me."

Please. I can't listen to any more of this.

"Oh, God, look at her," Drew said suddenly. "Look at her face."

"What's wrong with her face?"

"She can hear us."

"What are you talking about?"

"She can hear us, Warren. I know she can."

Casey felt Warren inch closer, his breath brushing against her lips as his eyes scanned hers.

"You're crazy, Drew," he said after a long pause. "Now please. Do us all a favor and go home." There was another pause, followed by a deep, weary sigh. When Warren spoke again, his voice was softer, more conciliatory. "Look. I'll talk to someone in my firm about your situation. Hopefully, we'll be able to work something out."

"I'd appreciate that."

"Sorry if I said anything to upset you," Warren said.

"Apology accepted. So you'll call me after you speak to your associate?"

"I'll call."

Casey listened to the click of her sister's Manolos as she walked briskly from the room without saying good-bye.

9

"OKAY, ARE YOU READY, Casey?" Dr. Ein asked.

What? Did you say something?

"This is a pretty big step we're taking."

What are you talking about? What big step?

Casey felt herself slipping back and forth between the cracks of consciousness and sleep. She'd been dreaming about Janine, the years they'd spent rooming together at college. She wasn't ready to wake up, to leave her younger, more carefree—care*less*?—self behind. She wasn't ready for any big steps.

"Once we disconnect this last wire, you'll be officially breathing on your own," the doctor announced.

I'm sorry. Did you say something?

Casey saw herself sitting on Janine's bed in the small two-bedroom apartment they once shared. The apartment was on the top floor of a three-story brownstone, located half a mile off the Brown University campus, on a tree-lined street full of once-stately old homes that now functioned as extended university residences, housing a steady succession of undergraduate and graduate students.

"What's he saying?" Janine was asking impatiently from beside her. "Casey, what's he saying?"

I think he said something about breathing on my own.

"Casey, come on," Janine urged, as Casey surrendered to the pull of the past. "You're not doing it right. Let me try."

"What do you mean I'm not doing it right? How can I be doing it wrong?" Casey watched the young woman she used to be surrender the glass she'd been holding between her ear and the wall to Janine's eager hands. "He's not saying anything."

"Impossible," Janine said. "They're talking about me. I can feel it."

Casey had met Janine three months earlier, when she'd answered an ad for a roommate Janine had placed in the campus newspaper. "I don't know," Janine had said when she opened her door, looking Casey up and down and skipping such pleasantries as "Hello. How are you?" She'd stepped back to allow Casey inside, not even trying to hide the once and then twice-over she was giving Casey. "You're way too pretty. Don't even try to tell me you weren't prom queen."

Casey hadn't been sure what to say, so she'd said nothing, deciding it was probably best to let the tall girl with the piercing blue eyes do most of the talking. She'd already decided she wanted the apartment—it was bright and inviting, despite its small size, although it could use a touch of color, she'd thought, mentally adding a couple of chartreuse pillows to the bland beige sofa, and throwing a zebra-striped rug across the light hardwood floor. A vase of fresh-cut flowers would also be nice, she'd thought as Janine motioned for her to sit down. "Okay, so here's the story," Janine had begun without bothering to introduce herself. "I'm loud, bossy, and opinionated. I hate animals, and that includes goldfish, so pets are out of the question, and I'll throw up if you start waxing rhapsodic about the puppy you had when you were three. I'm looking for someone who's neat, quiet, and smart, because I hate stupid."

"I'm not stupid."

"Not so quiet, either," came the instant retort, immediately followed by a brilliant smile. "You're not some sort of weird psycho-killer, are you?"

"What?"

"Didn't you ever see *Single White Female*?"

Casey shook her head.

"You're lucky. It was terrible. So, what are you studying?"

"I'm doing a double major in psychology and English."

"Yeah? English was enough for me. Switched from prelaw, when I decided I hate lawyers. Except the cute ones, of course."

"Of course," Casey agreed, although what she was thinking was that Janine had a lot of hates. Three in as many minutes.

The interview had progressed relatively smoothly from there, Casey careful to say as little as possible, letting Janine expound on whatever subject she chose. Half an hour later, Janine was handing over the second set of keys to the apartment. "Okay. We'll give it a shot. At the very least, you might help attract a better class of men."

"So, okay, do you hear anything?" Casey was saying later as Janine slid the glass slowly along the wall, looking for the perfect spot.

"Just a lot of moving around."

Janine adjusted her position on her double bed, hunching down on her knees and reangling the glass at her ear.

"What are we listening for anyway? Who is this guy?"

"I don't know his name. I just know he's gorgeous. My type exactly. He was outside talking to Peter, who is *so* not my type, even though he practically drools every time he sees me. Anyway, gorgeous guy gave me this look when I was walking up the front steps, like he liked what he saw. You know the look." Janine lowered her eyes and pursed her lips to illustrate. "You know what I mean. And we all ended up coming inside together, although Peter, the dumb-ass, didn't think to introduce us. Or maybe he did, but didn't want to. Anyway, I overheard Peter telling him my name as we were going up the stairs, so as soon as I got to the top, I ran inside and told you to get a glass. I can't believe these walls are so damn soundproof. I thought the walls in these old buildings were supposed to be paper-thin."

"Let me try again."

There was a knock on the door. "You expecting company?" Janine asked accusingly.

Casey shook her head.

"Get rid of them, whoever it is," Janine barked as Casey left the room and approached the front door.

"Who is it?"

"It's Peter, from next door."

Casey swiveled around to find Janine at her back. "What are you waiting for?" Janine whispered hoarsely, pulling her black T-shirt tight across her breasts and fluffing out her hair as she signaled for Casey to open the door.

Casey took a deep breath and pulled open the door to the apartment. Peter, their stick-thin, twenty-year-old neighbor, stood before her with a lopsided grin on his narrow, unlined face, a bottle of red wine in his right hand, and a slyly handsome young man with pale blue eyes and a knowing smile to his left.

"My friend and I thought you might be interested in sharing a bottle of wine," Peter ventured shyly.

"Your friend have a name?" Janine asked, walking around Casey and assuming control.

"Eric," said the handsome young man beside Peter, stepping inside without waiting to be asked. "And you are?" he asked, look-ing directly at Casey.

"She's Casey. I'm Janine," Janine answered. "What have you got there?"

"It's a merlot," Peter answered.

"A merlot," Janine repeated, as if she knew what that meant. "Casey, could you get us some glasses?"

Casey wondered if there were any clean glasses available, since it had been Janine's turn last night to wash the dishes, and she hadn't quite gotten around to it. The one clean glass they had was in Janine's bedroom. "I'll see what I can do."

"I'll help you," offered Eric.

"No need," Casey said quickly, catching the look from Janine.

"Make yourself comfortable," Janine instructed, following Casey into the tiny kitchen at the back of the apartment. "Damn that Peter," she whispered. "He probably told Eric he likes me, so Eric's hands are pretty much tied."

Casey rinsed out four glasses while Janine watched and fretted. "How am I going to do this?"

"Do what?"

"Maybe you could distract Peter for a while, get him talking— if I remember correctly, he's a real movie buff—and that way, I could have a few minutes with Eric, let him know it's just not happening with his friend."

Casey tried. She sat down on the tan chair across from the sofa, allowing Janine to occupy the middle of the couch between Peter and Eric, and she gamely sought to engage Peter in a conversation about movies, even though she disliked both the science-fiction and horror genres he seemed to favor.

"You're kidding me. You never saw *The Vanishing*?" Peter asked incredulously. "How could you miss that one? It's a classic."

"What is?" Eric asked, breaking away from whatever Janine had been telling him, abandoning her, openmouthed, in the middle of a sentence.

"She's never seen *The Vanishing*," Peter said with a shake of his head.

"Oh, you've got to see *The Vanishing*," Eric repeated.

"Isn't that the one with Kiefer Sutherland and Sandra Bullock?" Janine asked, leaning forward and feigning interest.

"Jeff Bridges plays this creepy serial killer who kidnaps people and buries them alive in his backyard," Peter said, as if Janine hadn't spoken.

"Except you should really see the original Dutch version," Eric interrupted. "It's even better."

"If you can find it," Peter said. "Not all video stores carry it."

"I might be able to find you a copy," Eric offered, lowering his eyes and pursing his lips, an exact duplication of the look Janine had shown Casey earlier, the look that said he was interested. Casey pretended not to notice.

"I'm not really into horror," she said.

"This is more suspense than horror. There's not a lot of blood and guts. Nobody slicing people up with a chainsaw."

"Just burying them alive," Casey said, and both boys laughed more than was necessary.

"Anybody here see *Halloween*?" Janine asked. "Or *Friday the Thirteenth*? The first one, of course."

"Who hasn't seen those?" Peter said dismissively.

"I haven't," Casey said.

"Really?" Eric asked. "I have a copy. I could bring it over one night. Hold your hand, in case you get scared."

Casey jumped to her feet. "Anybody for some cheese and crackers? Peter, why don't you give me a hand," she said in the same breath.

"I'll help you," Eric offered, already at Casey's side before Peter had a chance to respond.

"I don't think we *have* any cheese and crackers," Janine said with a smile.

"I'm sure we can find something," Eric said, taking Casey's elbow and leading her from the room. As soon as they reached the kitchen, he surrounded her with his arms and kissed her.

"What are you doing?" Casey asked, pulling away, although her entire body was tingling.

"Kissing you," he said, kissing her again. "And I believe that time, you might have kissed me back."

"Find anything cheesy?" Janine's voice was pleasant enough, although Casey could feel it leaking acid.

Casey immediately broke free of Eric's embrace. She knew that anything she said at this point would be wrong, so she said nothing.

"Like I said, I think we're all out of snack food," Janine continued, followed by a glorious smile.

The impromptu gathering broke up minutes later, when Janine announced she had an assignment she had to complete by morning.

"How about dinner next Saturday?" Eric whispered to Casey on his way out. "I'll call you," he said before she could answer.

"So," Janine said, smiling as she closed the apartment door. "That went well."

"I'm really sorry," Casey apologized immediately. "Of course I won't have dinner with him."

"What are you talking about? Of course you will. Are you crazy? He's gorgeous. And you like him. Why wouldn't you go?"

"Because *you* like him, and you saw him first."

Janine pushed her dark hair away from her face. "Don't be such a dork. Just because I saw him first doesn't mean I own him. Clearly, he's not interested in me. He wants you. And just as clearly, you want him."

"I'm not sure *what* I want."

"Hey, I'm not blind. I saw that kiss you planted on him in the kitchen."

"He kissed *me*. I was caught completely by surprise," Casey protested.

"Maybe the first time," Janine corrected. "Not the second."

Casey said nothing. Janine had witnessed both kisses? Did she have X-ray vision? Or was she just taking an educated guess?

"Close your mouth," Janine told her, clearly enjoying Casey's discomfort. "A fly will get in."

"You really wouldn't mind if I went out with him?"

"Would it matter if I did?"

"Yes," Casey insisted. "Of course it would matter."

"Then you're being stupid. And you know I hate stupid. God, what awful wine." She picked up the bottle. "Guess we could stick a candle in it and pretend it's the sixties."

There was a knock on the door.

"Don't tell me they want it back."

"Who is it?" Casey asked, holding her breath and not moving.

"Casey," the familiar voice sobbed.

"Drew?" Casey asked incredulously. She ran to the door and opened it. Her sixteen-year-old sister stood in the hallway, her eyes swollen almost shut from crying, her face wet with tears. "What are you doing here?"

"I didn't know where else to go. Can I come in?"

"What? Of course you can come in. My God, look at you. You're a mess." Casey led her sister toward the living room sofa, tossing the bright green pillows to the floor and sitting down beside her, her fingers reaching out to smooth the tangle of hair away from her face. "What's going on? I thought you were in New York."

"I was. I went home for the weekend." She looked up at Janine. "You must be Janine. Sorry to barge in on you this way."

Janine joined them on the sofa. "That's all right. Are you okay?"

Drew shook her head back and forth. "No."

"What happened?"

Drew wiped away some stubborn tears. "I hate that stupid school Dad and Alana have me at."

"But it's supposed to be so good," Casey said. "Much nicer than the one I went to."

"I know. It's 'the best private school in the country.' I know, I know. But I hate it there. It's awful. Everybody's so damn . . . studious." She glanced at the bottle of wine in Janine's hand. "Can I have some of that?"

"No," Casey said. "In case anybody hasn't told you, sixteen isn't the legal drinking age in Rhode Island."

"Come on, Casey."

"Tell me what happened."

A slight pause, then, "I got into a little trouble at school."

"What kind of trouble?"

"Nothing serious. They caught me smoking dope in the teachers' parking lot."

"Smoking dope? Drew!"

"Casey, please. Spare me the lecture. I'm tired. I've been traveling all day." She glanced down at her dirt-streaked Windbreaker. "God, I'm a mess."

"What do you mean, you've been traveling all day? How did you get here?"

"I hitchhiked."

"You hitchhiked? Are you nuts? Don't you know the number of crazies out there? Do you have any idea what could have happened to you?"

"Casey," Janine warned under her breath. "Lighten up."

Casey took a deep breath. "Okay. Sorry. No more lectures. Just tell me what happened."

"I got suspended."

Casey bit down on her lower lip to keep from yelling "Suspended!"

"Just for a week. It's no big deal. Anyway, I decided I might as well go home."

"And what? Dad and Alana gave you a hard time?"

"Hardly."

"They weren't upset?"

"They weren't there."

Casey tried to remember her parents' travel schedule. As far as she knew, they were in Philadelphia. "Wouldn't the housekeeper let you in?"

"She wasn't there either."

"Nobody was there?"

"Oh, somebody was there, all right," Drew said. "A very nice couple named Lyle and Susan McDermott. Apparently they bought the house several months ago."

Casey was confused. "You went to the house on Brynmaur Avenue?"

"Of course I went to the house on Brynmaur Avenue. That's where we were living last time I checked."

"But Dad sold that house months ago."

"You knew?"

"You didn't?"

"How would I know? Nobody ever tells me anything. I just get shuffled off to boarding school, and when I decide to come home, I discover my parents have sold the fucking house right out from under me, and moved away without saying a word. Who does that sort of thing? Who moves and doesn't tell their kids? Oh, I forgot," she cried. "They told you."

"I'm sure they thought they told you, too."

"Where the hell are they anyway?"

"They bought a smaller house close to the golf course. Smaller being a relative term," Casey added, picturing the ten-thousand-square-foot showcase her parents had moved into on Old Gulph Road. "I'm really sorry, Drew. I just assumed you knew."

"Yeah, well, next time, don't assume. I could really use a hit of that wine."

"No."

"Come on, Casey," Janine urged, handing Drew the bottle. "One sip won't kill anyone."

Drew took a long swallow before Casey could object. "Okay, Drew, that's enough," she said finally, when it looked as if Drew might chugalug the whole thing down.

"Can you believe people like that?" Drew asked Janine, kicking off her sneakers and bringing her knees up around her chest, then rocking back and forth. "Would your parents do something like that?"

"My parents divorced when I was seven," Janine replied evenly. "My father never paid a dime in child support, despite the fact he had a good job and a steady income. My mother kept taking him to court, but it never did any good. Then he got married again and had another family, and the court forgave what he owed us and reduced the amount he was supposed to pay my mother every month, which of course he didn't pay anyway. So my mother was forced to work three jobs, which meant I hardly ever saw her, and then she got too sick to work, and she died of cancer three months before her forty-seventh birthday." Janine downed what was left of the wine in the bottle.

"You never told me any of that," Casey said to Janine later, Drew snoring peacefully on the sofa. "That must have been so hard for you."

"You know what they say, don't you? Life's a bitch." Janine flashed her most beatific smile. "And then you die."

"So, what happens now?" one of the doctors asked as Janine

literally vanished into thin air, leaving only her smile behind, like the Cheshire cat in *Alice in Wonderland*.

"Well, she seems to be breathing quite nicely on her own," Dr. Ein said with obvious relief as Casey returned to the present, "so I guess we'll just have to wait and see." Casey pictured the doctor shaking his head. "Your guess is as good as mine."

10

" . . . MIRACLE SHE DIDN'T DIE," a voice was saying. "If I were a betting man, I'd have wagered her chance of survival at less than ten percent."

"She's a fighter, all right," a second voice confirmed.

Casey fought back the wave of panic she always felt upon awakening to total darkness. Would she ever get used to it? Would she ever get used to waking up to strange voices talking above her head, commenting on her appearance and condition as if she were an inanimate object? As if she were nothing more than a piece of still life, she thought. Decorative, undemanding, consigned to an appropriate place, to be glanced at and dusted regularly.

Except that someone had wanted her life stilled altogether.

"When they first asked me to consult, I took one look at her and thought, 'Consult about what? This poor woman's a goner,' " the first voice continued. "The extent of her injuries was just so horrific."

"Nobody thought she'd make it through that first night," the second voice concurred. Warren, Casey realized, his voice seeping into her subconscious.

"But she surprised everyone," the first man said, his deep voice filled with admiration. "And now she's breathing on her own—"

"Still . . ." Warren interrupted, obviously wrestling with his thoughts. "Her quality of life . . ." He cleared his throat. "I know there's no way she'd want to spend the rest of her life in this condition."

"I know how hard this must be for you, Mr. Marshall. . . ."

"It's not me I'm thinking about," Warren protested vehemently. "It's Casey. We'd actually had this conversation. You remember that woman, I forget her name, the one who'd been in a coma for years, whose husband wanted to disconnect her feeding tube and put her out of her misery, but her parents were desperate to keep her alive, and they went to court, and it was such a mess, a real media circus, and I remember Casey said that if, God forbid, anything like that ever happened to her, I had to promise I'd put an end to her suffering. . . ."

Yes, I remember saying that.

"You're saying you want to disconnect her feeding tube?"

No, you mustn't do that. Not now. At least not until we find out who's responsible for what happened to me.

"No, of course I'm not saying that."

I need to know who's responsible.

"To be honest, I don't know what I'm saying anymore, Dr. Keith. I know that Casey wouldn't want to spend the rest of her life this way, and I just want to do what's right. I don't want her to suffer anymore. I feel like such a traitor because I know I'm being selfish, that I'm not ready to let her go."

What would she do if their situations were reversed, Casey suddenly wondered, if it was Warren lying comatose in this hospital bed, unseeing and unmoving, week after week, and she was the one standing watch over him? Would she not be saying the exact things he was saying now? Would she not at least be considering them?

"The situation is very different here," Dr. Keith explained gently. "The woman you're referring to was in a profound vegetative state. She was never going to regain consciousness. We still don't know that's the case with your wife."

"When *will* you know? A year from now? Five years? Fifteen?"

Fifteen years? Dear God, no. He's right, Dr. Keith. There's no way I want to live like this for another fifteen years. Or even five. Five months is more than I can bear to think about. I'll go mad. Warren's right, Dr. Keith. I'd rather be dead than go on living like this.

But not yet. Not until I know who did this to me.

It was this mystery, she realized, as much as the various tubes to which she was connected, that was keeping her alive. It was more engrossing than anything she'd been listening to on TV, more stimulating than the conversations of her friends, more riveting than her myriad doctors' reports. The fact that someone had tried to kill her filled her waking thoughts and occupied her brain, like a stubborn squatter. How bitterly ironic, Casey thought, that her main reason for living had come down to finding out who wanted her dead.

"I know this is difficult," Dr. Keith said. "But there's every reason to be optimistic. Your wife has already beaten the odds. She survived an accident that would have killed most people. Her bones are healing nicely. Her heart is strong. Her condition is improving daily. She's off the respirator and breathing normally. Her brain is functioning, albeit at a slowed, decreased rate of activity."

"What about doing an EEG to determine the exact level of brain function?"

"We only perform an EEG if we think the brain is dead. Because your wife's body is functioning, we know that's not the case. We just have to give it more time, Mr. Marshall. We don't know anything for sure. . . ."

"This assessment coming from the top neurologist in the city," Warren said with bitter resignation.

"The brain is such a complicated organ. Here, let me draw you a picture."

Casey heard the accompanying rustling of paper, the clicking of a ballpoint pen.

"This is the brain," Dr. Keith began, as Casey imagined him drawing a large circle on the back of her chart, "and this area at the bottom is the cerebellum."

She fought to remember such details from her high school biology class, berating herself for not having paid closer attention. She imagined a smaller circle trespassing into the bottom right half of the first.

"The brain is connected to the spinal cord by the brain stem, which is full of nerves, twelve to be exact, that control the various senses, as well as—"

"Is there any chance my wife is more aware than we think?" Warren interrupted. "That she can see or hear?"

Casey felt herself holding her breath. Could they tell?

"Highly unlikely," the doctor responded. "But that's relatively easy to find out. We could do an opticokinetic nystagmus, commonly referred to as an OKN test. . . ."

"Which does what, exactly?"

"We use a cone-shaped instrument with alternating squares of light and dark, and we spin it slowly in front of the patient's eyes. A normal person will blink with the change from light to dark."

"Surely the attending physicians have already performed that test."

"They have. Several times," the doctor agreed. "Once, after your wife was admitted, and again later, after her surgeries. But we can certainly order the test again, if you wish, although . . ."

"Although . . . ?"

"Well, I would think that if your wife could see, she'd be doing everything in her power to let us know." Casey heard a deep intake of air. "Are you suggesting your wife could be deliberately faking her condition?"

"What? No. Of course not," Warren said quickly. "Why? Is that even possible?"

"Well, there *is* such a thing as a neurotic reaction to stress. Conversion hysteria whereby high anxiety turns physical. It's not voluntary, so the patient isn't deliberately malingering. But I'd say we could rule that out in this case. We could test for corneal sensation, I suppose," he added after a brief pause.

"Meaning what?"

"We put a wisp of cotton on the cornea. It will produce a very powerful blink, tell us whether sensation to the eye is being received. It's very hard to suppress a blink."

"But she *does* blink."

"A purely reflexive act. What I'm talking about is blinking in response to a direct stimulus." Casey felt the doctor leaning over her. She heard a click. "You see," Dr. Keith continued, "I'm shining this light directly into your wife's eyes. A normal person would blink. A person in a coma doesn't."

"Which means she can't see anything," Warren stated.

"Which doesn't mean that might not change tomorrow."

"And to find out if she can hear? I read about something called 'ice water calorics'?"

"I see somebody's been surfing the Net," the doctor remarked, an indulgent smile in his voice.

"Dr. Keith, the idea that my wife could be conscious but unable to communicate, that she could be a prisoner of her own body, trapped inside her head, desperate to let us know . . ."

"I understand your frustration, Mr. Marshall, but the test you're talking about is more than a little drastic. It involves squirting ice water directly into the eardrum with a syringe in order to stimulate the vestibular system. The patient will react by throwing up, possibly even convulsing. . . ."

I don't care. Do it. Do it.

"But if it meant we'd find out for certain whether she could hear or not . . ."

"Believe me, ice water calorics will raise you from the dead."

"Then maybe we should do it."

We should definitely do it.

"I'd prefer to start with something a lot less invasive."

Like what? Yelling in my ear?

"I'll order a BSAEP," the doctor said. "That stands for brain stem auditory evoked potential."

"How does that work?"

"We put earphones over the patient's ears," Dr. Keith explained. "Then we present a series of tones—clicks mostly—given at different rates, frequencies, and levels of intensity. We record the brain's response with electrodes, and the results go into a computer. We can actually see waveforms responding to the stimuli. This can be a bit tricky because we also have to separate the microvolts the brain is producing from the ones being put out simultaneously by the heart, lungs, and other organs. The computer has to remove these external noises and register only the ones from the brain. If the picture we get on the screen is flat, that means the brain cell is dead. If there are waves, it means she can hear."

"Fine. Do it."

Do it.

"Again, Mr. Marshall, I have to remind you we've already performed this test. . . ."

"But not lately," Warren stated.

"No, not lately. Tell me, has something happened to make you think your wife's condition has changed?"

"No. Not really. It's just something my wife's sister said last week that I can't get out of my head. She said that sometimes Casey gets this look on her face, almost like she's been listening, as if she understands. . . ."

Casey felt the doctor move in again to examine her more closely. "Frankly, I don't see anything in her expression to indicate that. But then I'm not family. You know her much better than I do. And anything's possible. So why don't I schedule the auditory evoked potential test and we'll take it from there."

"How soon can you do it?" Warren asked.

"I would think we could get it attended to pretty quickly. Tomorrow or the next day."

The sooner the better.

"You have to be prepared that even if the test indicates your wife *can* hear," Dr. Keith added, "that doesn't mean she necessarily understands what she's hearing."

"I understand. I just have to know."

"Try not to make yourself too crazy, Mr. Marshall. If your wife *can* hear, which we know she couldn't even a month ago, then that means her condition is improving. It could even mean she's on the road to a complete recovery."

A complete recovery, Casey repeated. Was it possible?

"Have you thought about where you'll be sending her for rehab?"

"I'm taking Casey home," Warren said forcefully.

"You might want to reconsider that," Dr. Keith advised. "Casey is going to require round-the-clock care for at least another two to three months. She'll still be connected to an IV; she'll have the feeding tube; she'll need to be moved every few hours so she doesn't develop bedsores. Taking care of her will be a full-time job. It's much too much for you to handle. If you'd like, my secretary can give you a list of places. . . ."

"I've already arranged for a nurse and a physical therapist," Warren told him, "and I've ordered one of those special beds to rotate her electronically."

"Well, then, I see you've thought of everything."

"I think my wife would prefer to be at home, Doctor."

"I'm sure she would. Good luck, Mr. Marshall."

Casey listened as Dr. Keith walked from the room.

"Well, did you hear that, Casey?" Warren pulled a chair close to her head and sat down. "We're going to find out if Drew was right, if maybe you *can* hear. Wouldn't that be something?"

It would be a start.

"If you *can* hear," he continued, hesitating briefly before going on, "if you *are* listening, I want you to know how much these last two years with you have meant to me. You've been such a great wife, Casey, the best lover and companion any man could hope for. Our time together has been the happiest time of my life. It's very important to me that you know that."

I do know that. I feel the same way.

"Mr. Marshall," a voice interrupted from the doorway.

Oh, for God's sake, Patsy. Scram.

"I'm sorry to intrude. I saw Dr. Keith in the hall. Is everything all right?"

"Everything's fine."

You don't stand a chance here. Go away.

"You're sure? You look so sad."

"I'm fine. And please, call me Warren."

"Warren," Patsy repeated softly. Casey could almost hear her purr. "How's Mrs. Marshall today?"

"No real change."

Casey felt a shift in the air as Patsy approached. The smell of lavender suddenly swirled around her head, danced beneath her nostrils, and sunk into her pores. Casey grasped at the scent as if it were the air itself. Was it real? And if it was, what did it mean? That another of her senses was returning? And if her sense of smell was coming back, how soon before her other senses returned as well? How long before she could see and move and speak, before she was a human being again, before she could hold her husband in her eager arms and whisper soothing words of love into his ear, just as he'd been doing before Patsy's well-timed interruption? How long until she had the pleasure of telling Patsy exactly what she could do with her fake words of sympathy, and just where she could shove her good wishes?

"I see her hair's growing back nicely where they had to shave it," Patsy remarked, propping up the pillows behind Casey's head. Then, "Is something the matter with your neck?"

It took Casey a second to realize Patsy was addressing Warren.

"Oh, it's just a little stiff," Warren replied. "I must have slept on it funny."

"Here, let me have a look. I took a course last year in massage therapy."

Of course you did, Casey thought.

"A woman of many talents."

"I like to think so. Where is it bothering you?"

"Right here. Yeah, that's the spot."

"You're really tight," Patsy said. "This shoulder, too."

"I didn't realize I was so tense."

"Are you kidding? What do you expect? You're here every day, sitting in this uncomfortable chair, worrying yourself sick over your wife. I bet you're not getting enough sleep. Your whole back's probably a mess."

Warren groaned.

"Just relax into my fingers. That's right. Now take a deep breath."

Warren inhaled.

"Now release it slowly. That's good. And again."

Another deep breath, followed by a prolonged exhalation.

"What you need is a proper massage to get rid of all these kinks."

"What I need is for my wife to get well," Warren said.

"You getting sick isn't going to make her any better. You have to take care of yourself, Mr. Mar— Warren. Otherwise, how are you going to manage when she comes home?"

"Well, I'm counting on you to help me there. That is, if that offer you made earlier is still open."

Oh, no. This is not a good idea.

Casey didn't need eyes to see the smile that spread across Patsy's face. "Of course it is. My bags are all packed and ready to go. As soon as you know Mrs. Marshall's release date, you tell me. I'll be there."

"It's a big house. You'll have a very nice room, right next to Casey's."

What do you mean? Where will you be sleeping?

"Do you think it's safe?" Patsy asked sheepishly.

"Safe?"

"You don't think that whoever tried to kill Casey might try again, do you?"

Warren's sigh trembled into the surrounding air. "I think that Casey's accident was just that," he said sadly. "The rest is nothing more than coincidence and conjecture."

Was Warren right? Casey wondered. Could it be just a coincidence that the person who'd run her down had entered the parking garage immediately after she had, that Detective Spinetti had fashioned his theory out of pure conjecture?

"God, that feels good," Warren was saying. "Anybody ever tell you that you have magic hands?"

"What's going on here?" a voice interrupted. "I was under the impression the one in the bed was supposed to be the patient."

"Janine," Warren stated, his voice filling the room. "I had a bit of a stiff neck. Patsy was just—"

"Patsy can go," Janine said pointedly.

A hurried movement. The scent of lavender retreating.

"Sure it's just your neck that's stiff?" Janine asked dryly.

"I could use some coffee," Warren said tersely. "You want me to bring you anything back?"

"No, thank you." Janine sat down in the chair formerly occupied by Warren, brushed her long fingernails soothingly across Casey's forehead. "What was that all about?" she said.

11

"WHAT'S THIS ALL ABOUT?" Casey heard herself cry, a tearful sixteen-year-old waving the morning newspaper in front of her father's bemused face. "I don't understand. How can you let them write these things? Why don't you sue?"

Her father laughed off Casey's outrage. "Let them say whatever they want. Sticks and stones. They have no proof of anything illegal."

"Illegal?" Drew repeated from her place between them at the kitchen table. "You did something illegal?"

Ronald Lerner ignored his younger child, as if she wasn't there.

Casey groaned silently in her sleep, distant memories of her father brushing up against her hospital bed. She'd always thought that if there was one word to best describe Ronald Lerner, it would be "too." He was too handsome, too rich, too charming, too athletic, too successful. His hair was too soft, his hands too big, his voice too smooth, his smile too seductive. Everything—women, money, accolades, power—had always been his for the taking. His exploits—and they extended as far back as high school—were leg-endary: the time he'd seduced the principal's secretary into letting him have a peek at the final chemistry exam; the time he'd not only talked his way out of a parking ticket but ended up in bed with the meter maid; the time he'd dated the most popular girl in school only to ditch her for her mother.

Casey's paternal grandfather had been a successful trader in the stock market and had left his only child an inheritance of sev-eral million dollars, which the son had parlayed into a serious for-tune approaching almost a billion. Along the way, Ronald Lerner had acquired the well-earned reputation of being shrewd, savvy, and not averse to cutting corners. There were constant rumors of his womanizing, which he never denied, and the occasional whis-pers of somewhat shadier shenanigans, which he always dis-missed as the grumblings of jealous, small minds.

"You notice he didn't deny it," Drew pointed out after their father had finished his coffee and left the house.

"Shut up, Drew."

"You shut up."

"You really think he knew that company was about to go under?" Casey demanded of her twelve-year-old sister. "How could he possibly know that?"

"How should I know?"

"You don't know anything," Casey insisted forcefully.

"Neither do you."

"I know our father."

"Yeah, right." Gulping down the last of her orange juice, Drew stomped from the room.

Casey sat there for several seconds, not moving, then lowered her head to the glass tabletop and burst into tears. It wasn't the fight with her sister that was making her cry. Fights with Drew had become a daily ritual, like brushing her teeth and combing her hair. No, Casey cried because she knew Drew was right: despite their father's feigned indifference and his too-easy smile, he'd never denied doing anything illegal.

Something else Casey realized Drew was right about: she didn't know her father at all. She'd given her fantasies power over her instincts. A difficult habit to break, she thought now, opening her eyes.

It took a few seconds for Casey to realize the darkness she was seeing wasn't quite as black as it had been before she'd fallen asleep. It took even less time to realize that she could make out shapes—the end of the bed, the chair in the corner, the dim light of the moon sneaking in between the slats of the thick Venetian blinds, casting an eerie spotlight on the tiny TV suspended overhead.

She could see.

Slowly, Casey worked her eyes from side to side. There was a chair at the side of her bed, and another one against the far wall. A small bathroom was located to the right of the door to her room, its toilet half visible. The door to the hallway was closed, although a thin band of fluorescent light was visible at the bottom. Outside the door, she could hear the familiar sounds of the hospital at night—patients groaning, nurses scurrying across the corridor, clocks ticking down the minutes till morning.

Casey heard footsteps approaching and saw a shadow interrupt the line of light along the bottom of the door. Was someone standing there? Were they about to come inside? Who was it? What did they want with her in the middle of the night?

The door opened. Casey flinched from the sudden flash of blinding light, as if the sun itself had exploded in front of her eyes. A figure entered the room and approached the bed, letting the door swing shut behind him. Was it one of her doctors? Had one of the monitors to which she was connected somehow alerted the staff to the fact she could see?

"Well, well, aren't you a mess," a voice said, a vaguely familiar whine to its cadence.

Who was here? Casey wondered, a wave of panic washing over her as the figure drew closer.

"All these tubes and wires. Not exactly flattering. But then, what goes around comes around, I guess."

What are you talking about? Who are you?

"You put me through hell, you know."

Would somebody please tell me what's going on? Who is this man?

"Did you know the police have questioned me three times since you got yourself run over?"

I got myself run over!

"Apparently, a mother's word isn't enough for our esteemed men in blue. Apparently, mothers lie for their sons all the time, an officer actually had the gall to tell me, as if I might not be familiar with the concept. I'm only a lawyer, after all. Albeit, currently unemployed."

Dear God—Richard Mooney.

"For which I have you to thank."

What are you doing here? What do you want?

"I thought I'd see for myself what sort of shape you were in. Normal visiting hours didn't seem like a very good idea, what with the police still hovering. And I see you're still breathing."

Still breathing, Casey repeated, wondering if he could actually hear the rapid beating of her heart.

"I guess we'll just have to take care of that."

What? No!

"My mother always said to finish what you start." He pulled the pillow out from behind Casey's head and quickly lowered it to her face, forcefully pressing it down against her eyes and nose and mouth.

And suddenly Casey was screaming, screaming as loud and as long as she could, screaming until there was no air left in her lungs, and no strength in her broken body. "Somebody help me!" she shouted, feeling the last of her breath seep from her body even as she heard Warren's footsteps racing down the corridor, and knew he would be too late to save her.

Casey lay in her bed, unseeing eyes staring at the ceiling, and understood she'd been dreaming. Richard Mooney wasn't there. Warren wasn't rushing to her rescue.

There was nothing but darkness.

Nights were the worst.

That's when the dreams came, the nightmares surfaced, and the ghosts visited. How many times had she dreamed she could see, only to wake up in the same black hole into which she tumbled that late March afternoon? How many times had she dreamed she could speak, only to awaken to silence? How many times had she fantasized she could move, walk, run, dance, only to find herself strapped to her bed by invisible chains, her once strong, vibrant body a dungeon from which there was no escape?

How long before she went crazy, before she willingly sacrificed her sanity in order to escape this hell on earth? Who had done this to her, and why—what difference did any of it make? Hadn't her father always insisted that results were all that mattered?

"That's the way, Casey," she heard her father say now, his voice filtering through the night air. "Shift your weight. Get that right hip dropping before you swing the club."

How easy it had been for her—the effortless shifting of her weight from one foot to the other, the instinctive dropping of her right hip, the graceful swinging of the 5-wood, as if her arms and the club were one, the gentle arching of her back as her hands brought the club up and over her left shoulder.

"It's a stupid game," Drew had complained, watching Casey on the practice range. Casey had just completed her first year at Brown and had returned home for summer vacation. Ronald and Alana Lerner had taken off three days later for Spain, leaving the girls with the housekeeper.

"Dad always says golf isn't a game—"

"Oh, please," Drew groaned, cutting Casey off midsentence. "If I have to listen to any more crap about golf being a symbol for life, I think I'll throw up."

"It's true. You can tell a lot about a person's character from the way they play golf."

"Dad cheats," Drew said matter-of-factly.

"Dad's a scratch golfer. He's been club champion for five years in a row. He doesn't have to cheat."

"Nobody said he *had* to. He does it 'cause he wants to."

"That's ridiculous. You don't know what you're talking about."

"I know what they say about him," Drew said smugly. "I overheard these guys talking at the club. They said that whenever Dad loses a ball in the woods, he just drops another one and says he found it."

"They're just jealous. . . ."

"They said that one time he hit a ball on a par three, and nobody saw where it landed, and Dad said he saw it sail over the green and went off to find it. While he's looking for it, this guy finds Dad's ball in the hole. He got a hole in one! And just as this guy's about to shout out the news, Dad yells 'I found it!' and holds up another ball. So, this guy just pockets Dad's ball and doesn't say a word."

"Dad got a hole in one, and this guy didn't tell him?"

"Cheaters never prosper."

"It was probably an honest mistake."

"Why are you always defending him?" Drew asked.

"Why are you always attacking him?" Casey countered.

"You're so blind," Drew said, leaving Casey alone on the practice range.

Casey could still see Drew slumping toward the clubhouse, her fifteen-year-old body just starting to fill out and take shape. Soon the oversize sweatshirts and ratty jeans would be replaced by low-cut, tight-fitting T-shirts and shorts so short they attracted the ire of some of the older women members, resulting in such clothing being deemed inappropriate and banned from the clubhouse. As was one of the junior pros, who was subsequently caught with Drew in a decidedly nongolfing position.

Ronald Lerner was duly embarrassed. "Remember," he'd chastised his younger daughter. "Boys will be boys, but girls will be sluts, if they're not careful." Drew wasn't careful, but she *was* happy. She'd finally found a way to get her father's attention.

Not that it lasted. Nothing held Ronald Lerner's attention for very long.

"Where's your father?" Casey heard her mother ask, Alana's voice coming at her from the far corner of her hospital room.

"I think he went out." Casey stopped packing up her things and turned toward her mother, who was standing in the doorway. It was unusual for her mother to leave her room, although the drink in her hand was as constant as ever.

"What are you doing?" her mother asked. "Are you going somewhere?"

"I'm moving into town," Casey reminded her. "Into my own apartment." She didn't elaborate. There was no point. Her mother wouldn't remember. She'd already told her several times that the business she and Janine had started together was beginning to take off, and she wanted to live in the city. "I told you."

"Everyone always leaves me," Alana said, managing to sound like the injured party.

"I'm sure Dad will be home soon."

"How come we never do things together?" There was more than a hint of recrimination in the slur of her mother's words.

Because you never ask, Casey replied silently. Because you're always drunk or asleep or out of town. Because you've never shown the slightest interest in me. Ever. In all these years.

Because . . .

Because . . .

Because.

"You hate me," her mother said.

Casey said nothing. She was thinking that it was the longest conversation she'd ever had with her mother.

It was also the last.

Three months later, Alana Lerner was dead, perishing beside her husband when the small plane he was piloting crashed into the bay one heavily overcast afternoon. The autopsy revealed high levels of alcohol in both their bloodstreams.

"So what now?" Drew asked, pulling up a chair beside Casey's hospital bed and resting her hands behind her head. "We divvy up the spoils?"

"Not exactly." Casey braced herself for the explosion she knew would follow.

"Why don't I like the sound of that?" Drew brought her hands down, leaned forward in the chair. She was almost four months pregnant with Lola and not yet starting to show, although her breasts were noticeably fuller beneath her white sweater. "You're saying he left everything to you?"

"No, of course not. The estate's pretty evenly divided."

"But?"

"There are conditions," Casey began.

"What sort of conditions?"

"They're for your own protection. . . ."

"Skip the bullshit. Get to the point."

"The point is that Dad appointed me executor of the estate."

"He appointed *you*," Drew acknowledged, her foot tapping restlessly on the floor.

"I wish he hadn't."

"I'll just bet you do." Drew jumped up, began pacing back and forth. "So, you can just release my money, right?"

"Dad wanted you put on a monthly allowance," Casey side-stepped.

"An allowance?"

"It's a pretty substantial amount."

"An allowance," Drew repeated. "Like a child."

"You're only twenty-one, Drew."

"And you're barely twenty-five. What kind of allowance did he put you on?" Her eyes filled with bitter tears. "I thought so. This stinks, and you know it."

"Why don't we sit back, take a few deep breaths . . . ?"

"This whole situation would be a lot easier if you'd just died," Drew said.

"Whoa," Janine said, coming out of the bathroom, a fresh coat of blood-red lipstick on her lips. "What kind of thing is that to say to your sister?"

"She has every right to be angry," Casey said as Drew melted into the far wall.

"Why don't you just give her the money?" Gail suggested, materializing by the windowsill to deadhead a pot of bright orange geraniums.

"I tried that," Casey reminded her friend. "I gave her over a hundred thousand dollars to buy into that gym franchise she was so desperate to have. It went belly-up in less than a year."

"If I remember, you also gave her another fifty thousand . . ." Janine began.

"Which went straight up her nose," Gail said.

"Maybe you could make her a partner in your new business," Janine suggested, a residue of bitterness clinging to her bright smile.

"Come on, Janine. I thought we were past this."

"And I thought we were friends."

"We *are* friends."

"Don't be so sure."

No, no, no. I don't want to hear this.

"The patient is a thirty-two-year-old woman who was the victim of a hit-and-run accident approximately three weeks ago," Dr. Peabody announced suddenly, reading from his clipboard as he entered the room trailed by Warren and Drew, both wearing hospital uniforms.

"How is the patient doing today?" Warren asked, looking over her chart.

"This whole situation would be a lot easier if she'd just died," Drew told him.

Wake up. Please, wake up.

"We should clear out," Gail said. "Let the doctors do their job."

"This test could take a while," the doctor explained.

"We'll grab some coffee. Can we get you anything, Warren?" Janine asked.

Casey heard her husband release a deep breath of nervous air. "No, nothing, thank you."

"Try not to worry," Gail urged. "Like the doctor said, if she can hear, it could mean she's on the road to a full recovery."

"Let's hope so," Warren said.

Wait. What are you talking about?

Seconds later, Casey heard equipment being wheeled into the room. She listened to the drone of doctors' voices, the scribbling of notes. Minutes after that, she felt hands at her head, and earphones being fitted over her ears.

In that instant, she understood that it was no longer night, and the ghosts had all gone home. It was morning, and she was fully awake.

This was really happening.

12

" '*WHO THAT CARES MUCH to know the history of man, and how
the mysterious mixture behaves under the varying experiments of
Time, has not dwelt, at least briefly, on the life of Saint Theresa,
has not smiled with some gentleness at the thought of the little girl
walking forth one morning hand-in-hand with her still smaller
brother, to go and seek martyrdom in the country of the Moors?*'
Huh? Could you say that again?" Janine asked. "Okay. One more
time. *'Who that cares much to know the history of man, and how
the mysterious mixture behaves under the varying experiments of
Time. . . .'* No wonder you always hated this book. I've only read
the first sentence and already I'm totally confused. Is it even in
English? I thought George Eliot was supposed to be from England."

The sound of pages being turned.

"Yes. It says right here in the introduction that Eliot was born
on November 22, 1819, in Nuneaton, Warwickshire, England, and
is considered the best of the English Victorian novelists. Even
better than Henry Fielding, at least according to Henry James, who

reviewed the book in 1873. There are a bunch of comparisons to *War and Peace* and *The Brothers Karamazov*, and some professor named Geoffrey Tillotson says *Middlemarch* is 'easily the best of the half-dozen best novels in the world.' Of course he said that in 1951, when *Valley of the Dolls* had yet to be written. Anyway, to continue: '*Out they toddled from rugged Avila, wide-eyed and helpless-looking as two fawns, but with human hearts, already beating to a national idea.*' Oh, dear. I don't know about this. National ideas have never been my strong suit."

More pages being turned.

"Did you know that George Eliot was actually a woman whose real name was Mary Anne Evans—of course you did—and that her aim in writing *Middlemarch* was to illustrate every aspect of provincial life on the eve of the Reform Bill? Apparently, she wanted to show 'the effects of actions and opinions on individuals widely separated in rank.' Which I guess could be interesting, if only Mary Anne Evans had a touch more Jacqueline Susann in her. Let's see. Where was I? '. . . *already beating to a national idea.*' Yada, yada, yada. Really, this part isn't very interesting. I think we can skip it. '*Some have felt that these blundering lives are due to the inconvenient indefiniteness with which the Supreme Power has fashioned the natures of women: if there were one level of feminine incompetence as strict as the ability to count three and no more, the social lot of women might be treated with scientific certitude.*' I have absolutely no idea what she's talking about. You better wake up soon, or I'll be in a coma right beside you. Come on, Casey. You don't really want to have to listen to another six hundred pages of this stuff, do you?"

A laugh, followed by footsteps. Someone approaching the bed.

A giggle. "What are you doing?" Gail asked. Another giggle.

"Making good on my threat."

"You're going to read her that whole thing?"

"I'm hoping I won't have to. I'm hoping she gets so irritated, she wakes up and hits me over the head with it."

"Do you think she understands what you're reading?"

"If she does, she's one up on me," Janine admitted. Deep sigh. The sound of a book slapping shut. "But now that the tests indicate Casey can definitely hear, her doctors think we should be doing even more to try to stimulate her brain, and what could be more stimulating, I ask, than *Middlemarch*? Dammit, I don't know if this is good news or bad."

"What do you mean?"

Janine lowered her voice. "I know the fact Casey can hear means her condition has definitely improved, and she could be coming back to us. But at the same time"—her voice became a whisper—"I can't help but think how awful for her to have been lying here all this time, unable to see or talk or move, but able to hear everything. What if she *can* understand everything she hears? What if she knows someone might have tried to kill her?"

"What are you getting at?"

The whisper assumed a certain urgency. "Do you think there's any chance she'd think it's me?"

"Don't be ridiculous."

"We both know Casey and I haven't always seen eye to eye on everything. Things were pretty tense when she decided to dissolve our partnership, and I admit to some pretty evil thoughts."

"Such as?"

"I actively prayed her new business would go under, that she'd lose all her money, even that her hair would fall out."

"You prayed her hair would fall out?" Gail's voice was almost as loud as it was incredulous.

"Shh! I didn't mean it."

"Still . . ."

"I wouldn't have wished this on my worst enemy," Janine said.

Is it possible that's exactly what you are? That this past year has been all an act? That you hate me enough to want me dead? That you've simply been biding your time, pretending to be my friend? That you're somehow responsible for this hell I'm living in?

"You know I love you," Janine said plaintively. "Don't you, Casey?"

Do I?

"I think we have to stay positive," Gail was saying. "We have to believe the fact she can hear is a good thing, that it means Casey's on the road to recovery. And Casey, if you *can* understand what you're hearing, as scary and as frustrating as that must be, then at least you know how much we all care about you, and how much Warren adores you, and how much everyone is rooting for you, so hurry up and get well."

Oh, Gail. Sweet, generous, naive, trusting Gail. Forever seeing the good in everyone. At least I can always count on you.

"But what if years go by," Janine broached quietly, "and there's no further change, and she's trapped like this, possibly forever . . . ?"

"She won't be. Casey's strong. She's been through a lot in her life. . . ."

"Oh, please," Janine interrupted, her tone shifting quickly and noticeably. "Yes, Casey didn't have the best parents in the world, but at least hers had the decency to die and leave her an obscenely wealthy young woman. Plus, she wasn't exactly dealt a bad hand in the looks department. Not to mention, she's smart and educated and—"

"In a coma."

"Yes, she's in a coma." Janine drew an audible intake of breath.

"I'm sorry, Casey. If you *do* understand any of this, I'm really sorry. I didn't mean it the way it came out. I know it probably sounds like a bunch of sour grapes, and that's not how I really feel."

Isn't it?

"She knows that," Gail said.

It sounded pretty convincing to me.

"Do you remember the first time we met?" Janine asked, and Casey wondered for an instant if she was talking to her.

"Of course," Gail answered. "It was hate at first sight."

"You hated me?"

"*You* hated *me*," Gail corrected.

"Was it that obvious?"

"Only to those of us who were breathing."

"Yeah, well, I guess I felt threatened," Janine admitted. "I mean, you and Casey had been friends forever. I was the new kid in town."

"You were her roommate, her college buddy. I was the child-hood friend who chose marriage over university, who could never hope to compete with you on an intellectual level—"

"Few can," Janine interjected, and had the good grace to laugh.

Gail giggled. "I guess everyone who meets Casey wants her all to themselves."

"So, how did you and I ever end up as friends?"

"I don't think Casey gave us much choice. She was so persistent. Weren't you, Casey? *'She's a really nice person,'*" Gail mimicked. "*'It just takes a little while to get to know her.'*"

"*'Don't underestimate her. She's really smart. You have to give her a chance,'*" Janine followed.

"All those lunches. . . ."

"Painful."

"And those girls' nights out."

"Excruciating."

"So, when did your feelings change?" Gail asked.

"Who says they have? I still don't like you." Janine laughed. "You do know I'm kidding, don't you?"

"I know."

Don't be so sure.

"I guess it was during Mike's final stay in the hospice," Janine continued, unprompted. "You were so loving and strong that it was kind of hard not to admire you. The way you just accepted what was happening, how you never got angry or cursed your lot in life. Unlike me, who's spent most of her life cursing one thing or another. I thought that was pretty amazing. And I guess that morphed into thinking *you* were pretty amazing."

"I'm not," Gail demurred.

You are.

"Eventually I realized Casey was right, that I *had* underestimated you, that under the frizzy hair and the shy smile, you were a real powerhouse, and I had to admire you. But enough about you," Janine continued, laughing again. "When did you realize you'd been wrong about me?"

Gail laughed. "Around the same time," she admitted. "I was running around like a chicken with its head cut off, trying to make all the necessary arrangements, to be there for Mike's mom, who was a real basket case, and to hold myself together when I was pretty much falling apart. And of course, Casey was there, being her usual supportive self, which was no less than I would have expected. But what I didn't expect was *you*. You were right there beside her. Every time I turned around, there you were, helping with this, organizing that. And after the funeral, you were the one in my kitchen, putting together a plate of sandwiches, and then quietly stacking the dishes in the dishwasher and putting things away, while I talked to guests in the living room."

"I just didn't want Casey to get all the credit."

"Why are you so afraid of letting people see the real you?"

Who is the real you, Janine?

"Maybe because they'll discover there isn't that much to see."

Or too much.

The sound of pages turning. "As George Eliot so wisely observes, *'Who that cares much to know the history of man, and how the mysterious mixture behaves under the varying experiments of Time, has not dwelt, at least briefly, on the life of Saint Theresa . . . ?'* "

"What?"

" *'That Spanish woman who lived three hundred years ago, was certainly not the last of her kind,'* " Janine continued reading. " *'Many Theresas have been born who found for themselves no epic life wherein there was a constant unfolding of far-resonant action . . .'* "

"You're comparing yourself to Saint Theresa?"

" *'. . . perhaps only a life of mistakes, the offspring of a certain spiritual grandeur ill-matched with the meanness of opportunity.'* "

"That's really quite lovely," Gail remarked. "I think."

"And I think I've had enough great literature for one day. I should get going."

The sound of a chair pushing back. A whiff of expensive French perfume. The feel of Janine's lips on Casey's cheek.

It's all coming back, Casey thought, almost bursting with excitement, although she remained motionless. She could hear. She could smell. She could feel. Surely any day now, her body would no longer be able to contain her emotions and she'd be able to move, to talk, to shout from the rooftops.

"Call me later?" Janine asked.

"Sure thing."

A muffled embrace, high heels clicking against the hard floor, a door opening and then closing, the chair being reoccupied, pulled closer to the bed.

"I hope you didn't take any of that to heart, Casey," Gail said. "Janine talks tough, but underneath, she's a real softie. Did you know she's been here every day since your accident?"

According to Detective Spinetti, it wasn't an accident.

"Why would she come every day if she didn't love you?"

Maybe to monitor my progress, look for an opportunity to finish the job she started?

Casey felt a soft hand brush across her forehead. She inhaled the clean scent of Ivory soap. Could there be a more glorious aroma?

"Anyway, we're all so excited about the news. Warren called everybody last night. He was so thrilled. 'She can hear,' he shouted when I picked up the phone. Even before I said hello. 'The test showed she can hear.' We still don't know if that means you can understand anything, but he says the doctors are very hopeful, and that there's reason to be guardedly optimistic. That's the doctor's phrase—guardedly optimistic. But it's better than being guardedly pessimistic, right? I think so. Anyway . . ."

Her voice drifted to a halt.

"I'm not going to read to you. I'll let that be Janine's thing. I'll just sit here and talk to you, if that's okay, tell you what's been going on in my life these last few weeks. And trust me, you won't want to miss a word of this, I promise. It's pretty juicy stuff. Well," she qualified, "juicy for me."

She took a deep breath before continuing. The breath floated across the room in ripples, like a gentle wave.

"I met this guy."

Another pause. The chair inched closer to the bed. A thrilling combination of strawberries and lime floated under Casey's nose.

Probably Gail's shampoo, Casey thought, luxuriating in its wondrous scent.

A soft giggle, then, "His name is Stan. You might have heard me mention him to Janine. Anyway, I really haven't told her very much. You know Janine—she'd want to know everything, and she'd pepper me with questions, and it's still so early, I'm afraid to jinx it. Am I making any sense?" Another giggle. "Okay, so here goes. His name is Stan Leonard, and he's thirty-eight. His wife died of breast cancer three years ago, and he has two children, William, who's ten, and Angela, who's seven. He's a computer programmer, owns a house—mortgage-free—in Chestnut Hill, and he likes movies and theater and traveling, although he hasn't been able to do much of that since his wife died. And what else?

"Let's see. He's not all that tall, maybe an inch taller than I am, which is fine by me. Mike wasn't very tall either. And he could probably stand to lose a few pounds, although not too many. Actually, I kind of like him the way he is—not so perfect. It's just that I know Janine would say he could lose a few pounds, which maybe is one of the reasons I haven't said too much to her about him. I don't want her judging him. Or maybe it's me I don't want her to judge. I don't know. I just know I think he's really cute. Yes, he has a bit of a paunch, and his hair is thinning a little on top, but he has the most beautiful gray-green eyes you've ever seen; they're really unusual. And when he smiles, the corners of his lips turn down instead of up, and I find that strangely endearing, don't ask me why." She laughed again, the soft sound tinkling through the remainder of her description. "But surprisingly, he's quite muscular. He works out with weights, so he's got these really amazing biceps. Not like Arnold Schwarzenegger or anything. But certainly more than you'd expect from a computer nerd. That's how he describes himself, a computer nerd, although I don't think he's at all nerdy, and I don't think you would either.

"I think you'd think he's really cute.

"And he's really nice, Casey. I know you'd like him. He has this way of leaning forward on his elbows when he's listening to you, like you're the only person in the room. But it's not a con. He's genuinely interested. And I find I can tell him things, things I haven't told anyone other than you, you know, stuff about Mike, and he understands, because his wife died so young, too, so we have that sadness in common. Does that sound maudlin? Because it isn't. It's not like we sit around crying and commiserating all the time, because we don't. In fact, we laugh constantly. Does that make me sound callous? I hope not."

You could never sound callous.

"At first I felt really guilty. You know, in the beginning. It was like I felt I was being disloyal to Mike, even after all this time. You know I've only dated a few times since Mike died, and even then, it was only guys I never felt any real attraction to. So I never felt guilty. But with Stan, it's different. Did I tell you how we met?"

Tell me.

"It was at Rittenhouse Square, by that sculpture of the lion crushing a serpent. It was the end of last month, lunchtime. I was finishing this tuna sandwich I'd brought from home, trying not to make too much of a mess, and this guy—Stan—he comes over, studies the sculpture for a few minutes, then sits down on the bench beside me. And he asks if I know what it's supposed to represent. So I tell him: It was made by this French guy over a hundred years ago, and it symbolizes the triumph of monarchy over the rabble of democracy. Which sounds like a line straight out of *Middlemarch,* when you think about it. Anyway, we start having this long conversation about art, and he asks me if I'd like to go to the new exhibit at the Art Institute, and I hear myself saying yes.

"I still can't believe it. I let this total stranger pick me up. In a public square, of all places. I mean, I never do things like that.

"So, a few nights later, we go to the exhibit—it was on the German Expressionists, and it was really good—and then he takes me to this Mexican restaurant over on Lancaster. Warren's gym is on Lancaster, right?

"Anyway, we ended up talking all night. Or at least until eleven o'clock, because that's the time his babysitter had to leave. But before he says good-bye—and he doesn't try to kiss me or anything—he asks me out again, and I hear myself saying yes. And before I know it, he's calling every day, and we're going out again, and on the third date, he finally kissed me good night. And it was great. Casey, it was so great. Just the right amount of tongue. Oh God, I can't believe I'm actually saying this out loud. Do I sound really pathetic?"

You sound like a woman falling in love.

"But now he's talking about maybe going away for the weekend, which means he's probably expecting me to sleep with him. I mean, I don't imagine he's thinking of separate bedrooms, do you? Not that I don't want to sleep with him. Don't get me wrong. I do. I think about almost nothing else. But it's been years since I've been with a man. Since Mike, for God's sake. And even though they say it's like riding a bicycle, I was never very good at riding bicycles. Remember when we were kids, how I was forever losing my balance and falling off? And the thought of taking my clothes off in front of this man, well, I just don't know if I can do it. What if he takes one look at me naked and jumps into the Schuylkill River?

"So I need you, my best friend on earth, to tell me what to do, because I really don't know. And I can't believe I'm sitting here going on and on about this, because I know it's all so trivial compared to what you're going through. And I feel kind of like I did with Mike. I keep thinking, how can I go out and have a good time while you're lying here in a coma? How can I laugh? How can I allow myself the luxury of a good time?"

Because you deserve it. Because life goes on. Because we only get one chance, and we never know what fate holds in store for us.

"Just know that I love you, and I need you, and I miss you more than words can ever say."

Oh, Gail. I love you, too.

"Please come back to us, Casey. Please come back."

The sounds of sniffling.

"Everything all right in here?" a voice asked from the doorway.

"Yes. I'm sorry. Are you Casey's doctor?"

"No. I'm Jeremy, her physical therapist."

"Nice to meet you, Jeremy. I'm Gail, her friend."

"Nice to meet you, Gail."

"How's she doing?"

"Getting a little stronger every day."

"That's great. Did you hear that, Casey? You're getting stronger every day."

I'm getting stronger.

"We'll just keep working on getting those muscles active again."

"I guess I should go," Gail said. "Let you get busy."

"I can give you another couple of minutes, if you'd like."

"Thank you." A slight pause, a shy giggle. "Now, that is one handsome man. You've really got to wake up soon, Casey. He's definitely worth a look. Kind of a cross between Denzel and Brad. Almost as perfect as Warren." She leaned forward, kissed Casey on the cheek. "I'll see you tomorrow."

"I'll see you," Casey repeated silently, the words echoing in the cavern of her mind until they became a prayer.

13

"LESTER WHITMORE, COME ON down!" the announcer brayed. "You're the next contestant on *The Price Is Right*."

"Oh, God, would you just look at that guy," Drew squealed from beside Casey's head. "Oh, sorry. I keep forgetting you can't see. Shit, I smeared my nails."

The pungent smell of fresh polish told Casey her sister was likely giving herself a manicure. She wondered how long Drew had been in the room.

"You should see this guy," Drew continued. "He looks like he's going to have a heart attack, he's so excited. He's sweating right through this ugly Hawaiian shirt he's wearing, and jumping up and down like a lunatic, and hugging the other contestants, none of whom look exactly thrilled to be on the receiving end."

The Price Is Right, Casey thought. She'd grown up with that show. That it was still on the air was strangely—and immensely—comforting to her.

"Oh, look. They have to guess the price of a set of golf clubs, including the bag."

"Four hundred dollars," the first contestant offered.

"Four hundred dollars?" Drew echoed. "Are you crazy? Even I know they're worth way more than that."

"Seven hundred and fifty dollars," came the second bid.

"One thousand," came the third.

"A thousand and one," said Lester Whitmore.

"What do you say, Casey? I bet you know the answer."

Assuming they're good clubs and it's a half-decent bag, I'd guess sixteen hundred dollars.

"The answer is one thousand, six hundred and twenty dollars!" the host announced. "Lester Whitmore, you're the winner on *The Price Is Right*."

"So how close were you?" Drew asked. "Pretty damn close, I bet. There's just no beating you when it comes to anything golf, is there?"

"Wow, that's some shot," Casey heard Warren marvel from a distant recess of her brain, his voice full of unbridled admiration. She watched him emerge from the darkness in her head and step into the bright sun of a brilliant spring day. "Where'd you learn to hit a golf ball like that?"

"My father taught me," Casey said, assuming her place in the sun beside him.

"Who's your father—Arnold Palmer?"

Casey laughed and started walking up the fairway, pulling her golf cart after her.

"I think you might actually have outdriven me," Warren said as they approached the two dimpled white balls, sitting only inches from each other, approximately two hundred yards from the tee box.

Casey had, in fact, outdriven her handsome date.

"What—you aren't even going to tell me it was just a lucky shot? Soothe my wounded male ego?"

"Does it need soothing?"

"Perhaps a few kind words."

"You're so cute when you're insecure," Casey said in response, and was relieved when Warren laughed. She didn't want to come off as either mean-spirited or smug. When Warren had called several days earlier to ask her out, and inquired timidly whether she played golf, she'd refrained from telling him she belonged to the toniest course in the city, and that she had a nine handicap. She'd said simply that she'd love to play. As early as that morning, she'd been debating with herself whether to perform at well below her natural level, thereby allowing Warren to feel appropriately masculine and superior.

She'd decided against it.

Casey watched as Warren prepared for his next shot with a series of laborious half swings and waggles, then watched him slice the ball into the pretty creek that wound its way through the front nine of Cobb's Creek, the public golf course that *Golfweek* magazine had recently named the sixth best municipal course in the country. She thought of her father. "Always kick ass when you've got the chance," he used to say. Still, she had no desire to kick ass, at least where Warren's lovely backside was concerned. What would be the harm in letting him win? It would be so easy to sway, collapse her left elbow, or take her eye off the ball, thereby joining him in the water. Instead, she assumed her proper stance over the ball, made sure she was lined up correctly, banished her father's voice along with all other conscious thought, and swung at the ball. Seconds later, she watched as it flew effortlessly across the creek to land in the middle of the green, approximately ten feet from the pin.

"Why do I get the feeling you've done this before?" Warren asked, his third shot landing just outside hers.

"Actually I'm a pretty good golfer," she admitted, putting in for birdie.

"No kidding."

"I turned down a golf scholarship at Duke," she told him two holes—and two pars—later.

"Because . . . ?"

"Because I think sports should be fun, not work."

"So, let me see if I have this straight: instead of spending your days golfing in the glorious outdoors, you'd rather spend them inside, finding jobs for disgruntled lawyers."

"I'd rather be decorating their offices," Casey replied.

"Then why aren't you?"

Casey retrieved her ball from the cup and dropped it into her pocket, then walked briskly toward the next hole, Warren struggling to catch up. "My father considered things like interior decorating to be frivolous and unworthy of my time. He insisted that if I wasn't going to accept the scholarship at Duke, then the least I could do was get a more rounded education, which is how I ended up majoring in psychology and English at Brown, despite the fact I understand zilch about human behavior, and George Eliot literally makes me want to tear my hair out at the roots."

"That still doesn't explain how you ended up running a lawyer placement service."

"To be honest, I'm still not entirely sure how that happened myself. You'd have to ask Janine. It was her idea."

"Janine?"

"My partner, Janine Pegabo. The woman you were supposed to be seeing the morning we met."

"The one who broke her tooth on a bagel," Warren said, remembering.

"That's the one."

"How is she?"

"She needs a new crown."

"Ouch."

"She's not happy."

"What about you?" Warren asked.

"I don't need a new crown."

"Are you happy?"

Casey gave the question a moment's thought. "Reasonably, I guess."

"Just reasonably, or beyond a reasonable doubt?"

"Is there such a thing?" Casey waited for the foursome in front of them to leave the green of the tricky par three before teeing up. Warren's question was still echoing in her ears as she swung, and as a result, her swing was a touch too quick, and the ball sailed low and to the left, winding up in the sand trap at the back of the green.

"Aha. Now's my chance." Warren grabbed his seven-iron and swung, his ball shooting high into the air and landing delicately on the green. "Yes!" he shouted, only to watch the ball trickle off to the right and bury itself in a clump of leaves. "Damn. That hardly seems fair."

"A lawyer who expects life to be fair. Interesting," Casey said as they walked down the center of the narrow fairway. "Actually I've been taking a number of night courses in interior design for the last few years. I hope to get my diploma in the very near future."

"And what does your father think about that?"

"My father's dead." Was it possible he didn't know who her father was?

"I'm sorry."

"He and my mother were killed in a private-plane crash five years ago." Surely that was hint enough.

"I'm sorry," Warren said again, as if he still had no idea. "That must have been awful for you."

"It was hard. Especially with the press hounding us the way they did."

"Why would the press hound you?"

"Because my father was Ronald Lerner," Casey said, watching for Warren's reaction. There was none. "You never heard of Ronald Lerner?"

"Should I have?"

Casey made a face that said he probably should have.

"I grew up in New Jersey and went to law school in New York," he reminded her. "I just moved to Philly when I joined Miller, Sheridan. Maybe you could fill me in on what I missed."

"Maybe later," Casey said, stepping into the vaguely heart-shaped sand trap as Warren crossed to the other side of the green. She burrowed her heels into the soft sand and secured her footing before looking up to check her line. Out of the corner of her eye she saw Warren waiting to hit his ball, which was sitting nicely on top of a small pile of leaves. Had it always been so visible? she wondered, replaying his tee shot in her mind. "Damn," she heard him say as the ball disappeared from sight. "That's hardly fair." Clearly his ball hadn't sunk as deeply into the leaves as they'd first thought. She was seeing it from a different angle after all. "Worry about your own game," she scolded herself, talking into her chin as she swung at the ball and missed completely, something she hadn't done since she was a child first learning the game.

She ended up shooting 85, very respectable, but still four shots higher than her handicap would indicate. Warren shot 92, although according to Casey's silent calculations, it was actually 93. (She hadn't deliberately been keeping track of his score; it was just something she did automatically.) Still, she could have been wrong. Or it could have been an honest mistake on Warren's part. There'd been an awful lot of chatter, and it would have been easy to forget a stroke. Or maybe he just wanted to impress her.

"He cheats at golf," she heard her sister say.

"Be quiet, Drew," Casey muttered.

"Sorry," Warren said. "Did you say something?"

"I said, do you know why they call it golf?"

"No. Why?"

Casey smiled at the old joke she was sure Warren must have heard at least a dozen times but was too polite to admit. "Because all the other four-letter words were taken."

"Shit," Drew swore again, snapping Casey from her reveries. "This is what happens when you have to resort to doing your own nails. Normally, Amy does them for me. You remember Amy—the one with the diamond stud in the middle of her tongue? She works in that place over on Pine Street—You've Got Nails! Anyway, she's the best manicurist in the city, bar none, and I've been going there once a week since forever, until of course, you ended up in here, and it seems I can no longer afford to spend twenty-five dollars a week, a measly *twenty-five fucking dollars a week*," Drew repeated for emphasis, "on keeping my hands presentable. Anyway, no more manicures for me, unless I want my daughter to go hungry, which wouldn't be such a horrible thing, if you ask me, because little Lola is starting to get a little lardy. And yes, I know she's only five, and there's plenty of time for her to start worrying about diets and stuff, but a girl can't be too careful." Drew made a snort of derision. "Guess I don't have to tell you that. If only you'd looked both ways, we wouldn't be in this mess."

"Angela Campbell, come on down! You're the next contestant on *The Price Is Right*!"

Drew continued prattling on, her voice competing with the shrieks of the latest lucky contestant, and after a few minutes, Casey found herself tuning out. She was exhausted from the steady stream of chatter that had been pressing against her ears, like a hot iron, ever since the doctors had announced she could hear, and that it would be beneficial if everyone talked to her as much as possible. Since then, voices had been coming at her nonstop, in a well-intentioned, if unnecessary, effort to stimulate her brain into further activity. The noise started first thing in the morning, when the interns arrived for morning rounds, continued all day, with the arrival of doctors and nurses, then family and friends, and even extended into the wee hours of the night, when the orderlies came in to mop up. If they weren't talking *at* her, they were reading *to* her: the nurses read the front page of the morning paper; her niece proudly recited the story of Little Red Riding Hood; Janine continued her excruciating trek through the nineteenth-century streets of *Middlemarch*.

And then there was the television, with its parade of moronic morning talk shows, hysteria-filled game shows, and sex-crazed afternoon soaps. Then came Montel and Dr. Phil and Oprah and Ellen, followed by the forensic experts at *CSI* or the libidinous doctors of *Grey's Anatomy* or the bizarre lawyers of *Boston Legal*. Everybody vying for her full, undivided attention.

And, of course, there was Warren.

He came every day. Always, he'd kiss her forehead and stroke her hand. Then he'd pull up the chair next to her bed and sit down, talking softly to her, telling her about his day, reporting his conversations with her various doctors. He said he was hoping there were other tests they could perform, tests that could tell them how much, if anything, she understood of what she was hearing. Surely there was a way of gauging her brain capacity, she'd heard him arguing with Dr. Zarb. How long before she regained the use of her arms and legs? he'd questioned Jeremy. How long before he could take her home?

She imagined him staring longingly into her open, unseeing eyes. Anyone watching would likely turn away, not wanting to intrude on such a private moment. Anyone except Janine, that is, who thought nothing of barging in on them regularly, or Drew, who was oblivious to everything that didn't directly concern her.

Was it possible that Drew was less oblivious than she let on?

Was it possible her sister had tried to kill her, in order to lay claim to the fortune she believed was rightfully hers?

" 'I thought it right to tell you, because you went on as you always do, never looking just where you are, and treading in the wrong place,' " Janine had read. " 'You always see what nobody else sees; yet you never see what is quite plain.' "

Had she missed the obvious where her sister was concerned? Had she been treading in the wrong place, refusing to acknowledge what was quite plain?

This much was plain, Casey was forced to acknowledge: Drew had had both motive and opportunity to kill her.

No, I won't do this. I won't allow Detective Spinetti's suspicions to poison my mind. Warren is still convinced it was an accident. Trust his instincts. Concentrate on something more pleasant. Listen to the damn TV. Find out how much that king-size tube of toothpaste is really worth.

"So, tell me something about yourself," the TV host prompted the newest shrieking contestant.

"So, tell me more about Casey Lerner," she heard Warren say, his soft voice caressing the nape of her neck, beckoning her back into their not-so-distant past, to that time when their relationship was unfolding, when each encounter was a source of wondrous new discoveries and love lurked behind each sigh, wafting tantalizingly through each lull in the conversation.

"What would you like to know?"

They were spending the morning at the farmers' market in Lancaster, a pleasant little town approximately sixty miles west of Philadelphia, with a population of just under sixty thousand people. Originally called Gibson's Pasture, it was first settled by Swiss Mennonites around 1700 and was now a pedestrian-friendly urban center, where historic old buildings competed with a host of new outlet stores. The farmers' market, where many local Amish farmers brought their meat, fruit, vegetables, baked goods, and crafts to be sold, had been in operation since the early eighteenth century, and the redbrick building housing it was one of the oldest covered markets in America.

"I want to know everything," Warren said.

"That's all?"

"I'm not very demanding."

Casey smiled. "I'm not very complicated."

"Somehow I doubt that."

"It's true. I'm pretty straightforward. What you see is generally what you get." She paused, tilted her head to one side, her long blond hair falling across her right shoulder. "So, you tell me—what do you see?"

Another pause. Warren inched closer so that his face was only inches from hers. "I see a beautiful woman with sad blue eyes."

"What?"

"And I can't help but wonder what makes her so sad," he continued, ignoring her interruption.

"You're wrong," Casey demurred. "I'm not—"

"And I want to take her in my arms and hold her, and tell her everything's going to be okay. . . ."

"—sad."

"And I want to kiss her and make it all better."

"Well, maybe just a little sad." Casey lifted her chin as his lips moved toward hers, landing like a soft feather on her mouth. "Come to think of it, I'm actually quite distraught," she whispered, wrapping her arms around him as he kissed her again.

They spent the night—their first night together—at King's Cottage, a Spanish-style mansion that had been converted into one of the area's two B and B's. Built in 1913, it had eight rooms, with private baths, antique furniture, and large, comfortable beds. "It's lovely," Casey said as the flame-haired proprietor handed over the key.

"*You're* lovely," Warren said, once again surrounding her with his arms. They made love, the first of many times they made love over the course of that night and the weeks that followed, and each time was "magical," as Casey later confided to Janine and Gail.

"It's like he can read my mind," she told them.

"It's so romantic," Gail said.

"Excuse me while I go throw up," Janine said.

The subject of children came up during another of their weekend getaways, this time to historic Gettysburg. They were just nearing the end of the mile-long hike along the Big Round Top Loop Trail when three adolescent boys raced past them, almost knocking Casey over. "So, how many children would you like?" Warren asked, grabbing her elbow to keep her from falling.

"I don't know. I've never really thought about it," Casey lied. In fact, having children was something she'd thought about a lot. She often wondered what sort of mother she'd be—absent and indifferent, as her own mother had been, needy and clueless, as Drew was, or possibly, hopefully, more like the "actual" mother she remembered seeing at the sandbox when she herself was a child, a woman who enjoyed her children and wanted to nurture and care for them. "I guess two would be nice. What about you?"

"Well, I'm an only child, remember, so I've always pictured a house full of kids, but two sounds good." He smiled, as if they'd just compromised on an important point and come to a decision.

Casey pretended not to notice. "What were your parents like?"

"Well, I never really knew my dad," Warren said easily. "He died when I was a kid. My mother, on the other hand . . ." He laughed. "She was fierce. A force to be reckoned with."

"In what way?"

"Well, to start with, she was married five times."

"You're kidding!"

"No, I kid you not. According to family legend, she divorced husband number one after he threw her down a flight of stairs, and number two when he went to prison for embezzlement. Husband number three, my dad, the only good one in the lot, according to my mother, died of a heart attack at age forty-nine. I don't really remember much about either number four or five, since I was away at school during both those fiascoes. However, my mother managed to come away from those last two outings with enough money to keep her in the style to which she'd always aspired. Speaking of which, I'm afraid I'm going to have to insist on a prenup."

"What?"

"Before we go any further with this marriage talk . . ."

"What marriage talk?"

"In your office, the day we met. You've forgotten my proposal already?"

"You weren't serious," Casey said, although she knew—had always known—that he was.

"I want you to see a lawyer, and have him draw up a foolproof prenup," he told her. "In the event of a divorce, which, trust me, is never going to happen, because I intend to make you the most deliriously happy woman on the planet, I want to make sure all your assets are completely protected. Nobody—and I mean nobody—is ever going to question my motives where you're concerned, or accuse me of having married you for your money."

"So, do you have my money?" Drew was asking now.

Instantly, Casey snapped back into the present. Who was Drew talking to?

"As I've already explained, this is a very complicated situation," Warren began.

"How complicated can it be? It's *my* money."

"Yes, it is. But it was under Casey's control, and now Casey is—"

"Napping with the fishes. Tell me something I don't know."

"I'm trying."

Casey pictured her sister crossing one arm over the other, fingers extended so as not to smear her freshly polished nails, and leaning back in her chair, her jaw clenched in anticipation. "I'm listening, Counselor," she said. "Give it your best shot."

14

"As I was saying, this is a very complicated situation." Warren paused, as if waiting for Drew to interrupt again. She didn't, so after several seconds, he continued. "I spoke to William Billy, one of my partners . . ."

"That's his real name?"

"William Billy, yes."

"His name is Willy Billy?" Drew laughed.

"You find that funny?"

"Don't you?"

"Not particularly."

It is, kind of, Casey thought, picturing the man. Standing more than six feet five inches tall, he had massive shoulders and a thick tree stump of a neck, both undermined by the almost girlish timbre of his voice. He had thinning red hair, and his ghostly white skin would flush a matching crimson whenever he was agitated or upset, which unfortunately was most of the time, due in large measure to his name. William Billy. Billy Billy. Willy Billy. Willy Nilly.

"William Billy happens to be one of the best estate and trust lawyers in the city."

"He'd have to be."

"Can I continue? I thought you were in a hurry for this information."

"I am. Please proceed." She laughed again.

"Are you high?"

"What?"

"You're stoned, aren't you?"

"Am not."

"*Am not*?" Warren repeated. "What are you, five years old?"

"No, that would be Lola, your niece, who you seem to be intent on starving to death."

"What are you on? Coke? Ecstasy?"

"Oh, please. I wish."

"You're certainly high on something."

"I'm not on trial here, Warren. Don't treat me like I'm one of those witnesses. . . . What are they called?"

"Jehovah's?" Warren deadpanned.

More laughter. "Now, see, that was funny. I knew you had a sense of humor. But no, that's not what I'm talking about."

"Do you *know* what you're talking about?"

"Hostile," Drew said. "That's the word I'm looking for. I'm not a hostile witness. Well, maybe I *am* hostile. A hostile Jehovah's Witness." She laughed again.

"I'm not even going to try to talk to you when you're in this condition."

"I'm not stoned, Warren," Drew insisted. "And do you think you could lower your voice a few decibels? The whole floor doesn't have to be in on this. So I might have smoked a little weed before I got here," she admitted, whispering now. "Can you blame me for wanting to take the edge off things? It's not exactly pleasant, coming down here, seeing my sister in this condition. . . ."

"Who are you kidding?" Warren demanded, finally losing his patience. "You can't see past your own nose."

"Can you?" Drew asked pointedly. "I mean, let me take a guess at what you're going to tell me. Can I do that?"

Casey imagined Warren turning both palms up, as if handing the floor over to Drew.

"You spoke to the esteemed William Billy, one of Philadelphia's top trust and estate lawyers—Philly's Willy Billy! How perfect is that?" She laughed again. "Sorry. Sorry. I couldn't resist. Besides, Casey thinks it's funny, too."

"What?"

"Look at her face," Drew said. "She's laughing. I can tell."

She was right, Casey realized. "Philly's Willy Billy" had done the trick. Despite everything, her sister had managed to make her laugh, even if Drew was the only person who could see it.

"You don't know what you're talking about," Warren said dismissively.

"I was right about Casey being able to hear," Drew reminded him. "And I'm right about this. Casey's laughing. She understands. So, you better be nice to me, because when she regains consciousness, she's going to be plenty pissed if you don't treat me well."

"I'm trying to help you, you little twit."

"How? By stealing my money?"

"I'm not . . . Look, I don't want to argue. I spoke to my partner. . . ."

"And you're the new executor of my parents' estate," Drew exclaimed triumphantly. "Am I right?"

"It's not quite as simple as that."

"Then by all means, simplify it."

"In Casey's . . . *absence*, I've been made temporary executor of the estate. It's just temporary," he stressed, as if expecting Drew to object, "until we have a clearer understanding of what's happening with Casey, at which time a court will have to decide—"

"So we could be talking years," Drew interrupted.

"We could be, yes."

"Years with you *temporarily* in charge of *my* money."

"You'll get your money, Drew. I intend to follow your sister's wishes to the letter. You'll continue to get your monthly allowance."

"This sucks, and you know it."

"Nothing has changed."

"*Everything's* changed. My sister is in a coma. You're the one calling the shots."

"What do you want from me, Drew?"

"I want what's mine. Why do you get to have any part in the decision-making process?"

"Because I'm Casey's husband."

"You've been her husband for what . . . all of two years? I've been her sister my whole life. And even though my father might not have trusted me with his precious estate, he sure as hell wouldn't have wanted you in charge of it."

"This is just temporary, until—"

"Until the courts decide. Which could take years. I get it. And Casey gets it. Don't you, Casey?"

If you're insinuating that Warren is after my money, you're wrong.

"Look, this is getting us nowhere," Warren said. "It's a moot point anyway."

"Meaning it's subject to argument or debate."

"Meaning it's academic, of no practical value or consequence."

"Meaning you're full of shit. I'm going to talk to this Willy Billy myself. . . ."

"By all means. I'd be more than happy to make an appointment for you."

"I don't need you to do anything for me. You've done more than enough already. I'm going to hire my own Silly Billy, and then I'm going to sue your ass. Do you hear me?"

"You do that, Drew. And while you're busy suing my ass, remember that it's very expensive to go to court, and that it takes a long time for these cases to come to trial. You also might want to think about the eventual outcome of such a suit, considering the fact I'm not only Casey's husband and legal guardian, but a damn good lawyer as well. And *you* are an unwed single mother with a long history of drug abuse and promiscuity."

"Whoa. That's some closing argument, Counselor. Casey ever see this side of you?"

"You obviously bring out the best in me."

"Sorry, did you say 'best' or 'beast'?"

"Look, you do whatever you feel you have to do," Warren continued, ignoring the question. "By all means, hire a lawyer and take me to court. If that's how you want to waste your money, that's entirely your choice. I guess it beats shoving it up your nose."

Silence, except for the sound of ragged breathing.

Casey couldn't tell who was breathing harder, Warren or Drew. She found herself actually feeling sorry for her younger sister. She was no match for Warren. He wouldn't allow himself to be steamrolled the way Casey had so often been by her younger sister.

"Who are you to tell me what I can or can't do?" Casey remembered Drew shouting at her one afternoon from across the L-shaped living room of Drew's dark one-bedroom apartment in Penn's Landing, overlooking the Delaware River. Heavy, mustard-colored drapes, the stale odor of marijuana buried inside their deep folds, kept the late-day sun from casting too bright a spotlight on the crowded, unkempt space, although Casey had no trouble making out the assorted drug paraphernalia—an old black pipe, some loose squares of thin white paper, a crumpled twenty-dollar bill, a dusting of fine white powder—spread across the top of the oblong glass coffee table.

"You're using again," Casey stated plainly. "How can you even think of having a baby?"

"You're gonna try to stop me from thinking now, too?"

"I'm your sister. I just want what's best for you."

"You mean you want what's best for *you*."

"You're in no position to have a baby."

"On the contrary," Drew countered. "I was in the perfect position—flat on my back."

"This is hardly the time for bad jokes."

"I didn't think it was so bad. Anyway, this baby is certainly no joke. It's real. And I'm going to have it, whether you like it or not."

"Do you even know who the father is?"

"Does it matter? I'll be the one raising this child."

"How? With what? You think it'll be easy raising a child all by yourself?"

"When has my life ever been easy?"

"Oh, stop with the 'poor me' routine already. It's getting a little tired."

"Sorry if I'm boring you."

"This isn't about me. It's about bringing a helpless little baby into the middle of this"—Casey's arms made wide circles in the air, stirring up the sickly sweet odor of hashish—"mess."

"You think I'll be such a horrible mother?"

"I think you'll be a great mother," Casey said sincerely, "when the time is right. When you're clean and sober and ready to settle down."

"Maybe I'm ready now."

"I don't think you are."

"Maybe you don't know everything."

"I know you had all sorts of problems when you were a baby because of all the alcohol Alana drank when she was pregnant. . . ."

"You're comparing me to our mother? Not nice, Casey. Not nice at all."

"For God's sake, Drew, this baby won't stand a chance. It'll be born addicted to drugs."

"Not if I check into rehab. Not if I get clean."

"Are you willing to do that?"

"I'll do whatever it takes." Drew wiped the tears away from her cheeks, swiped at her nose with the back of her hand. "I really want this baby, Casey. Can you understand that? I want something of my own, something that nobody can take away from me, something I can love, that will love me back. Unconditionally." She wrapped her arms around her chest and began rocking back and forth, as if she were cradling an infant.

"There are always conditions," Casey told her sister. "And it's not a *thing*, Drew. It's a human being."

"I know that. You think I don't know that?"

"What are you going to do when the baby's up all night crying?"

"I'll sing it back to sleep."

"And if it won't go back to sleep, if it's colicky and cranky and—"

"I'll love it all the more. I'm gonna be so good to that baby, Casey. I'll give it so much love. I don't care if it's a boy or a girl. I'll love it no matter what. And I'll take such good care of it. I know you don't think I can do it. . . ."

"I think you can do anything you set your mind to," Casey argued, hearing the obvious lack of conviction in her voice, and knowing Drew could hear it, too. "I just don't think now is the best time to be making this kind of decision."

"I'm not interested in what you think," Drew shouted. "You know what *I* think? I think you should go to hell. Did you hear me? Go to hell!"

And then predictably, less than a year later, her sister was pacing back and forth across that same room, a squalling baby in her arms. "What am I going to do, Casey? She hates me."

"She doesn't hate you."

"She cries all the time."

"She's a baby. That's what they do."

"I try so hard, Casey. I hold her. I sing to her. I change her diapers. I feed her. Nothing I do makes any difference. She cries all day. She cries all night. She cries when I put her down. She cries even louder when I pick her up."

"She probably has gas."

"I should have nursed her," Drew said, crying now herself. "The doctors at the hospital tried to convince me I should—they said it would be better for her—but I was worried there might still be drugs in my system, even though I've been clean for months. I swear I have. I was just being cautious, because I didn't want to do anything that might hurt her. And now it's too late. My milk has dried up."

"Lola's fine with the bottle, Drew. She's gaining weight. She's beautiful."

"She *is* beautiful, isn't she?"

"Just like her mother."

"I love her so much."

"I know you do."

"Why does she hate me?" Drew asked plaintively.

"She doesn't hate you."

"You should see the look she gets on her face sometimes, like she's totally disgusted with me."

"Oh, Drew. She's not disgusted. . . ."

"You haven't seen the look, Casey. She scrunches up her face and gets all red, like a wrinkly old balloon. And these big, dark eyes glare up at me, like she can see right through me. Like she's judging me."

"Babies can't think, Drew. They can't make value judgments."

"All I wanted was for her to love me."

"She does love you."

"No," Drew insisted. "She knows I'm a fraud."

"You're not a fraud. You're her mother."

"I'm a horrible mother."

"No, you aren't."

"Yes, I am. Sometimes when she cries, I get so mad, I just want to smother her with a pillow. Not that I would ever do anything like that," she added hastily.

"I know that."

"But even to have such thoughts . . ."

"You're exhausted," Casey offered.

"I haven't slept in days," Drew confirmed. "Maybe more than a week. Every time I lie down, every time I close my eyes, she starts to cry. It's like she knows, like she's doing it on purpose."

"She isn't."

"I'm so tired."

"How about hiring a baby nurse?" Casey broached carefully. She'd made this offer several times already, only to be turned down soundly each time.

"You mean a nanny?" Drew spat out the word as if it were a curse.

"I mean someone to give you a hand, so that you can catch up on your sleep. Everybody needs a break now and then."

"I won't have my child raised by strangers."

"Nobody's saying it has to be forever."

"I can't afford a nanny."

Casey shook her head. They'd been through this before, too. "I'll pay for it."

"I don't want your charity."

"It's not charity."

"Only because it'll come out of the estate. Because it's *my* money," Drew shouted above the baby's increasingly desperate cries.

"This is ridiculous, Drew. Can't you see I'm just trying to help? Why do you always have to make it about money?"

"Because that's what it's always about! Are you really so blind, or are you just stupid?"

"Oh, for God's sake," Casey said in total exasperation. "Why don't you just shut up?"

"Why don't you go to hell?" Drew snapped in return.

"So, when can I have my money?" Drew was asking now, her voice low and muffled, as if her chin were pressed against her throat.

"I can write you a check right now, if you'd like," Warren said.

Casey heard the scribbling of a ballpoint pen.

"Check it. Make sure it's the right amount," Warren advised.

"It's fine." A second's pause. "Guess I'll get out of your hair. Take care of yourself, Casey," Drew said.

And then she was gone.

15

"Nice to see you haven't lost your touch with the ladies," a voice said from the doorway only seconds later.

Warren jumped to his feet. "What the hell are you doing here?" he demanded, clearly flustered.

Who is it?

"Just thought I'd check on how the patient is coming along."

"Are you crazy?"

"Relax. Take a few deep breaths. You're overreacting."

"I'm overreacting? What if Drew comes back? What if someone walks in?"

"Then I'm just a friend from the gym, paying my respects."

What's wrong? Why is Warren so upset? Who is this man?

"You need to leave right now."

"I'm not going anywhere," the man said calmly, walking toward the bed as the door swung shut behind him. "It's been more than two months, Warren. You don't phone. You don't return my calls. You haven't stopped by the gym."

"I've been a little busy these days."

"The dutiful, loving husband." The man's voice dripped sarcasm, like ice water from the fridge. Casey suddenly felt chilled to her very core, although she wasn't sure why.

"You didn't leave me a whole lot of choice," Warren said.

What does that mean? What kind of choice?

"So how's Sleeping Beauty doing?" the man asked.

"I would think that's pretty self-evident."

"She actually looks better than I expected. Are the police any closer to finding out what happened?"

Warren scoffed. "No. They're clueless. Look, can we talk about this later? This is neither the time nor the place. . . ."

"What is?"

The time and place for what?

"You know this isn't my fault," the man continued after a pause.

"It isn't?" Warren asked.

"No."

"My wife is in a coma, connected to a feeding tube. She might be this way for the rest of her life. And you don't think it's your fault?"

I don't understand. What are you talking about? Are you saying this man is somehow connected to what happened to me?

"Hey," the man protested. "I'm really sorry for the way things turned out. But I plowed into her at almost fifty miles an hour. A normal person would be dead after a hit like that."

What? What! WHAT?!

"For Christ's sake, would you shut up!"

What's happening? Is this real or did I drift off to sleep again? Is it a dream, or maybe another TV movie?

"Look," Warren whispered hoarsely. "You have to keep your voice down. They've done tests. The tests indicate Casey can hear. . . ."

"She can?" Casey felt the man's weight as he leaned across her bed, his arm brushing against the side of her own, his minty breath warm against her face. "Can you hear me, Sleeping Beauty?" She felt him retreat. "You're saying she understands what we're saying?"

"Probably not. But it's possible."

A cluck of reluctant admiration. "Hats off to you, Beauty," the man said. "You're a tough one."

No, this can't be happening. I'm dreaming. Either that or I'm delusional.

How many times had she wondered the same thing in the last several months?

"Look," Warren implored. "You've got to get out of here."

"Not until we come to an understanding."

"An understanding about what?"

"Don't play dumb, Warren. It doesn't suit you."

"If this is about money . . ."

"Of course it's about money. I'm no different than you are. It's always about money. Fifty thousand dollars, to be precise."

Fifty thousand dollars? For what?

"I don't give fifty thousand dollars to people who screw up."

"I didn't screw up."

"Then what are we doing here?"

What *are* we doing here? Casey repeated, her thoughts spinning wildly around in her head, like clothes in a dryer. What were they saying?

"I guess we're waiting," the man answered, his voice a shrug. "It's obviously just a matter of time."

"A matter of time," Warren repeated wearily. "According to the doctors, she could outlive us all."

A long pause.

"Then I guess we'll just have to speed things up a bit."

What things? What are you talking about?

"How do you propose we do that?"

"Hey, man, I'm just a personal trainer. You're the one with the expensive degrees."

"Yeah, well, when we talked at the gym, you gave me the distinct impression you'd done this kind of thing before. I thought I was dealing with an expert."

The man laughed. "Ever think of unplugging a couple of these tubes, maybe injecting an air bubble into her IV? I saw that on TV once. It was pretty effective."

Oh, God. Somebody help me! Drew! Patsy! Somebody!

"Yeah, right. Nobody would suspect anything untoward there."

"Untoward? Pretty impressive word there, Counselor."

"Only for a moron."

"Hey, man, go easy. I know you're upset, but there's no need to get testy."

"I tend to get *testy*, as you say, when the people I hire don't do their jobs."

Warren hired this man to kill me? He offered him fifty thousand dollars to run me down? No, it can't be. It can't be.

"It'll get done."

"Which is when you'll get your money."

A sigh of resignation. "So, what's the story? She in here for good?"

"No. I should be able to take her home pretty soon."

"And anything could happen after that."

No. This is not happening. They've given me some new drug. It's causing me to hallucinate.

"It won't be easy," Warren said. "The police already suspect it wasn't an accident. I have to be very careful."

"Don't worry, man. There's nothing that ties you to any of this."

"Except Casey. If she *does* understand. If she *does* regain consciousness."

Casey felt two sets of eyes burn into her flesh like acid.

"Then we'll just have to make sure that doesn't happen."

Dear God.

"And how exactly do we do that?"

"You're a smart guy," the man said. "I'm sure you'll think of something." Once again, Casey felt the man's mouth stop mere inches from her own, his breath brushing teasingly against her lips, as if he was about to kiss her. "Bye, bye, Beauty. You take care of yourself." He chuckled, the sound gurgling deep in his throat, like oil beneath the earth's surface.

"Would you get the hell out of here!"

"You'll call me when you come up with something?"

"Count on it."

"Try not to wait too long." Footsteps receding, followed by the sound of a door opening and closing.

This can't be happening, Casey thought again. It *isn't* happening. She hadn't really overheard her husband and another man discussing their failed attempt to murder her, and their plan to try again. It was ridiculous. *It hadn't happened.*

There was no way Warren would do anything to hurt her, let alone hire someone to kill her. It was ridiculous. Totally, absolutely, absurdly ridiculous. What was the matter with her? First she'd been suspicious of Janine. Then it was Drew's turn. And now . . . Warren? How could she even be thinking such insane thoughts?

What's the matter with me? Warren is a good man, a man whose job it is to uphold the law, not break it. Not shatter it, for God's sake.

It was that damn TV. How could she be expected to think straight with that constant jabbering going on?

Warren loves me.

She felt motion, a body moving toward her. Who? Was Warren still here? Was anybody?

"That was Nick," Warren said casually. "I'm sure you've heard me mention him. Great trainer. Lousy human being. Mean streak a mile wide. The kind of guy who likes pulling the wings off butterflies. I was joking around with him one day, told him he was wasting his time torturing jerks like me, said he should consider a career as a contract killer. He told me to name the time and place." Warren scoffed. "I probably shouldn't be talking about this, but what the hell? The cat's out of the bag now." He moved even closer to whisper in her ear. "Why couldn't you just have died when you were supposed to?"

And then everything was still. It was as if the air in the room had suddenly ceased to circulate, and she was poised to stop breathing altogether. A wave of panic surged through Casey's veins, like a shot of adrenaline. Was it possible he'd injected an air bubble into her IV, as his accomplice had suggested?

Why couldn't you just have died when you were supposed to?

"I'm gonna get a cup of coffee," Warren said, his voice fading as he walked toward the door. "Don't suppose you want anything," he called back.

So the mystery was solved.

How could it be? They'd been so happy. They never fought, rarely even argued. The only time they'd even disagreed was when she'd wanted to leave the mansion she'd inherited from her parents and move to a condo in the city, and Warren had been reluctant to abandon their quiet, affluent neighborhood. Ultimately they'd compromised and agreed to start looking for a smaller home, but to stay on the Main Line. It was soon after that they'd talked about starting a family.

And all the while, he was planning her death.

Had these murderous impulses only lately popped into his head, or had he been plotting since the very beginning to kill her? Could the man in a hurry have been patient enough to wait two full years before translating his plan into action?

But why? Why would he want her dead?

Why do you think? she asked herself.

Money.

"It's always about money," Nick had said.

But Warren's never been interested in my fortune, Casey argued. He was the one who'd insisted on a prenup. And there are no insurance policies on my life. . . .

He doesn't need any of that, she realized. As her husband, he stood to inherit a good portion of her estate, even without a will. At the very least, he'd probably walk away with more than a hundred million dollars. As a lawyer, he surely knew that.

"Nobody becomes a lawyer to get rich," she heard him say. "Factor in expenses and taxes and overhead, you're certainly not retiring at forty."

Was that what he wanted after all? To retire at forty? No. No way. Warren had a thriving career that he loved. He had everything he needed. They had a terrific life together. There was no way he would do this.

He loves me.

A hundred million dollars could buy an awful lot of love.

"So how's our patient doing today?" someone asked.

What? Who said that?

"I see you're watching Gaslight. Great old movie."

"I don't think I ever saw that one," a second voice said. "What's it about?"

"The usual—unscrupulous husband tries to convince his wife she's losing her mind. That Ingrid Bergman was some beauty, wasn't she?"

Bye, bye, Beauty.

"Her blood pressure's a little higher than normal. What's going on, Mrs. Marshall? Are you in pain?"

You have to help me. I'm having these wild, horrible thoughts.

"Let's increase her meds."

No. Please don't increase anything. I'm dopey enough, believe me. You should only know the weird things that have been going on in my rocked brain. If I weren't in a coma, I'd recommend I be committed.

"I have a favor to ask you," one doctor said to the other as they walked toward the door.

"What's that?"

"If I ever get wheeled in here in that condition, you'll just put a pillow over my face and end it right then and there, okay?"

"Only if you promise to do the same for me."

"It's a deal."

They left the room.

No. Don't go. Don't go. Somebody please help me before I lose my mind.

What was she talking about? Her mind was already lost. As if she wasn't in dire enough straits, now she was imagining that the person who loved her more than anything else in the world, the person she loved more than she'd ever thought it possible to love anyone, was a cold-blooded sociopath who'd hired a man to run her down, and who was, even now, enjoying a cup of coffee and trying to think of ways to finish the job.

Was it possible she *wasn't* hallucinating?

I trusted you, Warren, she thought, unable to ignore what was "quite plain" any longer.

I trusted you with my life.

16

" '*He had been left* an orphan when he was fresh from a public school,' " Janine read. " '*His father, a military man, had made but little provision for three children, and when the boy Tertius asked to have a medical education, it seemed easier to his guardians to grant his request by apprenticing him to a country practitioner than to make any objections on the score of family dignity. He was one of the rarer lads who early get a decided bent and make up their minds that there is something particular in life which they would like to do for its own sake, and not because their fathers did it.*' "

"What's that you're reading her?" Patsy asked, adjusting Casey's head on the pillow. The scent of lavender buzzed around Casey's face, like a stubborn fly.

"*Middlemarch.*"

Go away, Patsy. I was actually starting to enjoy the stupid book.

"*Middlemarch*? What's that mean?"

"It's the name of the town where the story is set."

"What's it about?"

"Life."

It helps me take my mind off my sorry excuse for one.

Patsy made a sound halfway between a snort and a laugh. "Any good?"

"It's considered a masterpiece."

"It looks long," Patsy said.

The sound of pages flipping. "Six hundred and thirteen pages."

"Six hundred and thirteen! Oh, no, that's way too long for me. And look at the size of that print. I'd go blind."

"You like big print, do you?"

Casey pictured a generous smile filling Janine's slender cheeks.

"I don't read all that much," Patsy confessed.

"Well, there's only so much time. I'm sure you're very busy."

Casey imagined Janine's smile spreading into her eyes, causing her shapely brows to arch.

"I do like murder mysteries," Patsy said. "They're always good for a laugh."

"You find murder funny?"

"Well, not funny, no," she backtracked quickly. "But at least it's entertaining."

"Entertaining?"

"Well, interesting then. Like what's going on with Mrs. Marshall." Patsy drew an audible breath. "Do you think somebody really tried to kill her?"

There was a pause of several seconds before Janine spoke. "Well, the police have pretty much eliminated all their major suspects. Apparently, none of their leads panned out. So it's looking like it might have been a hit-and-run accident after all."

What do you mean, the police have eliminated all their

major suspects? Are you saying they've closed their investigation?

"Anyway, sorry to interrupt. Go on. Read some more."

Casey pictured Janine's back stiffening as she straightened her shoulders and lifted the book from her lap. She'd always hated anyone telling her what to do.

" *'Most of us who turn to any subject with love,'* " Janine continued, after a prolonged pause in which Casey thought she was probably weighing the consequences of throwing the heavy tome at Patsy's head, " *'remember some morning or evening hour when we got on a high stool to reach down an untried volume, or sat with parted lips listening to a new talker, or for very lack of books began to listen to the voices within, as the first traceable beginning of our love.'* "

"What's that mean?" Patsy asked.

"I guess it's about remembering the first time we realized we loved something. Or someone."

"Why doesn't he just say that, then?"

"She," Janine corrected.

"Huh?"

"Never mind."

I knew I was in love with Warren the minute I laid eyes on him, Casey thought. Although the experts would no doubt insist that was just physical attraction. The love, they would argue, came later, after she got to know him.

Except she hadn't gotten to know him. Not really.

Who was this man she'd married? Was Warren Marshall even his real name? How much, if anything, of what he'd told her about himself was real? Had his mother really been married five times? Had his father died when he was a boy? Had his mother's last two marriages existed for the prime purpose of keeping her in the manner in which she'd longed to be accustomed? Was it from her that Warren had inherited his taste for the finer things in life?

And now he was seeking an inheritance of his own.

There was no doubt he was a lawyer, and a good one. "Smarter than God" had been William Billy's admiring assessment. Certainly smart enough to know how to play her. Smart enough not to overplay his hand. Smart enough to outwit the police.

The police have pretty much eliminated all their major suspects.

"You know how all these poor bastards get caught?" she remembered him saying one morning not so very long ago, as they read the morning paper in their spacious kitchen. He was referring to an article about a man who'd murdered his wife the day after taking out a million-dollar insurance policy on her life. "Not because they're greedy. That's a given. It's that they're so bloody stupid. Who takes out a million-dollar life insurance policy on his wife the day before he kills her? They don't think that might raise a few alarm bells? Christ, they might as well take an ad out in the paper saying 'I did it!' Use your brains, fellas," he'd said, and she'd laughed her agreement.

She'd laughed a lot during their time together.

"I love to hear you laugh," he'd told her on more than one occasion.

Of course you did, Casey thought now. It meant she was a sucker for his charm.

"I love you," he'd told her every day of their married life.

"I love *you*," she'd answered without fail or prompting.

"God, Casey, I miss you so much," he'd said not so very long ago, sitting at her bedside.

"You have to get out," his friends had purportedly told him. "You have to live your life."

"I keep telling them that my life is here," he'd replied. "In this hospital."

All those wonderful things he'd told Patsy about her. Had he meant any of them? Or had he merely been setting the stage, acting the bereaved and loving husband for her benefit? And, of course, his own. Like any true sociopath, Casey thought, giving the people what they needed to hear.

The police have pretty much eliminated all their major suspects.

"I want you to know how much these last two years have meant to me," he'd told her. "You've been such a great wife, Casey, the best lover and companion any man could hope for."

Had he meant any of it? Casey wondered now. Had he been confessing his true feelings or merely grandstanding for Patsy's benefit?

"I'm sorry. I didn't realize you were standing there," she'd heard him say—how many times?—to the nurse's aide watching from the doorway.

"Our time together has been the happiest time of my life," he'd said. "It's very important to me that you know that."

Why? Was this his way of telling her she shouldn't take his attempt on her life too personally, that she shouldn't consider his wanting her dead to be indicative of his dissatisfaction with her performance as a wife?

How disappointed he must have been to learn she'd actually survived the hit-and-run, how stunned to discover that she could grow old in her coma, that she could, in his own words, "outlive them all." And then, to find out she was not only improving daily but also getting stronger—what a bitter pill to swallow, especially when further tests determined she could actually hear.

Did this information keep him up at night? Did he lie in bed wondering, as she did, what his next move would be, and when would be the best time to make it?

"So, I guess you and Mrs. Marshall have been friends for a long time, huh?" Patsy's voice interrupted her thoughts.

"Since college."

And yet I doubted you, too. What kind of friend does that make me?

"Mr. Marshall said you used to be in business together."

"Really? When did he tell you that?"

"After your last visit. I was saying how you and that other woman . . . what's her name?"

"Gail?"

"Gail, right. Nice to have such good friends."

My *only* friends, really, Casey acknowledged. She had lots of acquaintances, to be sure, but her circle of close friends had grown smaller over the years, especially since her marriage to Warren. There was only so much time, as Janine had remarked earlier, and Warren had filled so much of it.

"So what else did Mr. Marshall say about me?" Janine was asking.

"That was pretty much it."

"Pretty much it," Janine repeated absently. "So how does he seem to you?"

"What do you mean?"

"How is he holding up?"

"I think he's amazing."

"Amazing, no less."

"I guess they were really crazy about each other, huh?"

"What makes you say that?"

"Oh, you can just tell. The way he looks at her. The way he's always holding her hand and whispering to her. It's got to be so hard, don't you think? I mean, one minute, you're a happily married man, and the next minute, well . . ."

"Life's just full of unpleasant little surprises," Janine said.

Tell me about it.

Poor Patsy, Casey thought, almost feeling sorry for the girl. Warren's playing you, just like he played me. Of course, you've been playing him as well. Maybe the two of you deserve each other.

"So, what kind of lawyer is he?" Patsy asked.

"Why? You in some sort of trouble?"

"Me? No. Of course not. I was just making conversation."

"Not really necessary," Janine said.

Patsy cleared her throat. "I guess I should go."

Casey felt Janine smile brightly in response. "Don't let me keep you."

"Well," Patsy said, lingering nonetheless. "It was nice talking to you."

"Have a good day," came the quick retort.

"Oh, hello, Mr. Marshall," Patsy exclaimed suddenly, her voice lifting at least half an octave. "You're late today."

So that's why you've been hanging around.

"I had a meeting with Casey's doctors," Warren said, approaching the bed and kissing Casey's forehead. "Hi, sweetheart. How are you feeling this morning?"

Improving a little bit every day. Isn't that what you're afraid of?

"Hi, Janine. How are things in Middlemarch?"

"Marching steadily toward the middle," Janine quipped.

Patsy laughed. "Your friend's very funny."

Casey felt every muscle in Janine's body tense.

"Yes, she is," Warren said, a playful twinkle in his voice. "Casey looks pretty good today, don't you think?"

"Her trach's healing up real nicely," Patsy said. "Now that the ventilator's gone and the tubes are all out, I'd say it's just a matter of time."

And time is exactly what you don't have, isn't it, Warren? At least, not if I'm really on the road to a full recovery.

"Time for what?" Janine asked.

"I'm planning to take Casey home," Warren answered.

"Really? You think that's a good idea?"

"I think it's a great idea. I can't think of anything better than Casey in her own home, in her own room, surrounded by the things she loves."

If it's all the same to you, I'd just as soon stay where I am.

"What do her doctors say?"

"They agree that now that Casey's injuries have healed and she's able to breathe on her own, there's no real reason to keep her here."

Except that once they release me, I'm as good as dead.

"She still has a feeding tube," Janine reminded him.

"That won't be a problem."

"She's still unconscious," she pressed.

"And could be for some time." A trace of impatience whisked through Warren's voice. "But that's irrelevant at this point."

Irrelevant?

"Irrelevant?"

"The doctors have done all they can here, and they desperately need the bed. It becomes a question of whether Casey goes into a rehab clinic or whether she comes home."

Don't let him take me home. Please, Janine. He only wants to get me home so he can finish what he started.

"But how are you going to take care of her? She'll need nurses around the clock."

"She'll have them," Warren said. "I've also hired a full-time housekeeper and arranged for Jeremy, her physical therapist, to come to the house three times a week."

Not to mention the hit man he hired to kill me.

"And I'll be there," Patsy chirped.

"You?" Janine asked.

"Casey's going to need all the love and care she can get," Warren said.

"Well," Janine said. "You seem to have thought of everything."

Not quite. He still hasn't worked out the final details. He knows he can't move too quickly, yet he can't afford to wait too long. He can't do anything that might arouse police suspicion, yet he can't chance my waking up, not if I've understood anything of what I've heard. It's a tricky situation, a delicate balancing act. He has to proceed very carefully.

With malice aforethought.

"So when is the big move scheduled to take place?"

"As soon as all the necessary paperwork can be processed." Warren leaned closer, brushed tender fingers across Casey's cheek. "God willing, I might be able to take my wife home as early as tomorrow."

Casey felt his eyes boring into hers.

"Isn't that wonderful, Casey? You're going home."

17

THEY CAME FOR HER at ten o'clock the next morning.

"Well, this is a very big day for you," one of the interns said, radiating the fake cheer they all seemed to adopt when talking to her, as if she were a not very bright three-year-old.

Casey thought the voice belonged to Dr. Slotnick, but she couldn't be sure. A new batch of interns had arrived only last week, and she hadn't had time to attach the names to their respective voices. I need more time, she thought.

"I bet you can't wait to get out of here."

No, you're wrong. I don't want to go. Please, don't let them take me. I need more time.

But Casey knew it was too late for any last-minute reprieve. The arrangements had all been made. The finances had been dealt with, the releases signed. All morning, nurses and orderlies had been filing in to say good-bye and wish her well. Interns, residents, surgeons, and specialists alike had all dropped by to pay their respects.

As if I've already died, Casey thought.

"Good luck, Casey," another intern offered, touching her arm.

"Well, I think that's everything," Warren suddenly announced, bounding into the room. "Everything is signed, sealed, and ready to go. They should be here any minute with the stretcher, and then we can be off."

"You'll keep us apprised of her progress?" Dr. Keith asked.

Has anybody called the police? Does Detective Spinetti know I'm about to be released?

"Of course," Warren answered. "Every little improvement, you'll be the first to hear about it."

"If there are any problems at all, if at any point you feel you've taken on too much . . ."

"I'll get in touch with your office immediately."

"Lankenau Hospital in Wynnewood has a wonderful rehab center, or there's Moss Rehab over on—"

"I'm sure that won't be necessary, but thank you. Thank you all," Warren said, his voice cracking. "You've been so kind to Casey, and to me, and words can never adequately express how grateful I am for everything Pennsylvania Hospital has done for us during this extremely difficult time."

Casey heard sniffling and realized people were fighting back tears.

"But now it's my turn to take care of Casey," Warren continued. "Here's hoping that next time I see any of you, my wife will be standing beside me, and she'll be able to thank each and every one of you in person."

"Here's hoping," several voices agreed.

"Amen," someone added.

Sounds like a full house, Casey thought, picturing the small crowd gathered around her bed. Was Patsy among the visitors? she wondered, the squeal of a stretcher racing down the hall, then banging up against the door to her room. The vibrations reverberated throughout Casey's body, traveling up her spine and settling, like a dull cramp, in the pit of her stomach.

"Well, here we are," Warren said.

"Make room, people," Dr. Keith advised.

Casey felt the air in the room stir as people moved out of the way, jockeying for new positions. She felt bodies hovering above her head, and sheets being pushed aside.

"Be careful with her head," someone cautioned, as strong hands gripped her ankles, hips, and shoulders.

No. Don't move me. Please, you don't know what you're doing.

"On three. One . . . two . . . three."

Casey's body slid effortlessly from the narrow bed that had been her home for the last three months onto the even narrower stretcher. In the next second, she was being strapped in and wheeled from the room.

Maybe this is all a dream. Soon I'll wake up and Drew will be sitting beside me watching The Price Is Right.

"Good-bye, Casey," she heard several of the nurses call out as her stretcher was pushed down the hall, the smell of the sick and the dying assaulting her nose, accompanying her to the elevator.

"Good luck, Casey," more voices offered.

No, I don't want to go. Please don't let them take me.

And suddenly everything stopped. Had they heard her? Had she actually spoken those words out loud?

"These elevators take forever," someone remarked.

So, they were simply waiting for the elevator to arrive, she realized. No one had heard her. Casey listened to the sound of distant wires being pulled and tugged and knew an elevator was on its way. Her hearing had become so acute in the last weeks, and her sense of smell was getting stronger every day. She knew when she was being touched. She felt pain and discomfort, could tell the difference between hot and cold. She recognized when her head ached and her muscles needed massaging.

Slowly, everything was coming back.

She just needed more time.

How much longer before her vision returned, before she regained the use of her arms and legs, before she was able to speak, before she could tell everyone what had really happened to her—that her beloved husband had hired a man to kill her, and that it was only a matter of time before he tried again?

And this time, Casey understood with sickening certainty, he'd succeed.

Unless she could find a way to get through to someone.

Please. There has to be a way.

"Here it is."

"Finally," Warren said as the elevator doors opened and several people filed out.

A man and a woman, Casey thought, judging by the cloying combination of aftershave and perfume she smelled as they brushed past. Had either of them noticed she was there, or had they instinctively turned their heads and averted their gaze, as most people did when confronted with their own tenuous hold on mortality? Were they even now whispering a little prayer—"Please let me stay healthy, don't let anything like that ever happen to me"—as they hurried down the hall? Did they have any idea how lucky they were?

Because in the end it was all about luck, Casey decided as the elevator doors closed behind her. Some people were lucky; some weren't. It was that simple. Some people enjoyed a lifetime of good fortune, others were merely afforded a few fleeting moments. Still others . . . how did that song go—if it weren't for bad luck, I'd have no luck at all?

She knew most people considered her one of the very fortunate few. Born into a life of great privilege, possessing both beauty and brains, she'd succeeded at everything she'd set her mind to. She had the Midas touch, as Janine had remarked on more than one occasion.

Until one afternoon on an unseasonably warm day in late March when her luck had suddenly run out, and the gold reverted to sawdust, and the sky went from radiant blue to hopeless black.

The elevator bounced to a tenuous halt on every floor, letting people in and out. "Sorry," a man said as he lost his balance and fell against her stretcher. The apology was followed by a cough and a clearing of his throat. Casey imagined the man quickly righting his position and facing forward, gazing resolutely at the numbers above the doors, until the elevator came to its final, bumpy stop. He can't bear to look at me, she thought, recalling Drew's earlier remark. Where *was* her sister? Was she off on another mindless cruise? Or was she lying in some stranger's bed, stoned out of her mind? Was she taking care of herself, of her daughter?

"Okay, clear some room, please, everybody," the orderly instructed as he pushed the stretcher out of the elevator and down the long corridor toward the exit. "Will you be riding with your wife in the ambulance, Mr. Marshall?"

"Absolutely," Warren replied, as a heavy blanket of heat and humidity descended on Casey's head like a shroud.

"Whew," the orderly remarked. "It's a hot one today."

"Over ninety," another voice agreed.

"We can take it from here," yet another voice announced.

Who were all these people? Casey wondered as her stretcher was transferred into the back of the ambulance. Warren was right beside her, his hand on top of hers.

"Good luck with everything, Mr. Marshall," the orderly said as he closed the ambulance door.

"Thank you," Warren said, settling in beside Casey.

A minute later, the ambulance was on its way.

"We're going up to the Main Line, is that correct?" the driver asked.

The same voice that had commented on the temperature, Casey realized.

"Nineteen twenty-three Old Gulph Road," Warren elaborated. "The town of Rosemont. Just past Haverford. About a half-hour drive. It's probably best to go north on Ninth Street, then make a left on Vine till you get to the Schuylkill Expressway."

"Let's just hope it's not the Schuylkill Parking Lot," the second voice added, the one who'd told the orderly they could take it from here.

So there were two men in the front seat, Casey concluded.

"It shouldn't be too bad this time of day," Warren told them. "I'm Warren Marshall, by the way."

"Ricardo," the driver said. "And this here's Tyrone."

"Thanks for doing this, guys."

"No problem. It's what we do. Sorry about your wife, man."

"Thanks."

"How long's she been in a coma?" Ricardo asked.

"Since the end of March."

"Jeez. How'd it happen?"

"Hit-and-run."

"Yeah? They catch the guy?"

"Not yet."

"You know what I think, man? I think guys like that should be shot."

"You think everybody should be shot," Tyrone said.

"Yeah, well, you start shooting a few of these people, I'm talking now about people who drive drunk, and people who leave the scene of an accident, you start hauling them out of their cars and shooting them on the spot, you're gonna see a lot less people drinking and doing bad stuff before they get behind the wheel. They're gonna think twice. You know what I'm saying?"

"You really think people are thinking that clearly after they've had a few drinks?" Tyrone argued.

"I'm saying they're going to think twice before having that drink in the first place. If they know there's a good chance they're gonna get shot, they just might call a cab instead of deciding to drive home themselves. All it takes is a little careful planning."

A little careful planning.

"You give people too much credit."

"Hell, man, if people are that stupid, they deserve to get shot. Of course, then half of Hollywood would be dead."

They drove for several minutes in silence, Casey absorbing each bump in the road. She was amazed to discover she was actually enjoying the sensation, enjoying the fact she was out of the hospital, out of her bed, and speeding down the street. She felt her body take flight and soar above the traffic, at one with the air. For several minutes, she wallowed in the illusion of freedom. For several minutes, she surrendered to the possibility of happiness.

"Instead, what happens is that innocent people, like Mrs. Marshall here, are the ones getting hurt," Ricardo continued. "Bet that guy who hit her is doing just fine. No injuries there. No, it's always the innocent who suffer. How are you doing back there, Mr. Marshall?"

"I'm fine, thank you, Ricardo."

"Somebody said you're a lawyer. Is that right?"

"Guilty as charged," Warren said. "Who told you that?"

"One of the nurse's aides. Patsy something. Lukas, I think her name is."

"The one with the big—" Tyrone began, then broke off, either because he realized such comments might be considered inappropriate, or because he felt no further words were necessary.

"That's the one," Ricardo said.

"She's pretty hot," Tyrone said.

"If you like that type."

"What's not to like?"

"Actually," Warren broke in. "I've hired Patsy to help take care of my wife."

"No kidding," Tyrone said sheepishly.

Casey pictured Tyrone hunkering down in his seat, burying his chin inside his jacket.

"She's been wonderful to my wife."

You mean she's been wonderful to you.

"She'll be waiting for us at the house," Warren said.

Oh, great. Something to look forward to.

The rest of the drive was relatively quiet, the men in the front seat obviously having concluded that silence, along with discretion, was the better part of valor. The ambulance transferred onto the expressway without incident, and Casey found herself mentally ticking off the exits. Montgomery Drive . . . City Avenue . . . Belmont Avenue . . . They passed the town of Gladwynne and continued on through Haverford to Rosemont, eventually approaching the exit onto Old Gulph Road.

Old Gulph Road was a wide, winding street lined with lots of tall, leafy trees, where stately mansions sat on several acres well back from the road, and meandering horse trails took the place of sidewalks. Between 1775 and 1783, Revolutionary soldiers had been lodged in many of the older homes, as they'd been in houses all along the Main Line. Later, Old Gulph Road became home to soldiers of an entirely different sort: soldiers of fortune, men of money.

Men like Ronald Lerner.

Casey's father had purchased the house on Old Gulph Road over his wife's strenuous objections. Alana Lerner had had no desire to leave her larger, even more palatial estate on Brynnmaur for the somewhat smaller residence on Old Gulph Road, and their arguments leading up to the eventual purchase were both numerous and heated.

"We're not selling this house," Casey remembered her mother shouting as Casey blocked her ears and tried to study for an upcoming exam. She'd come home for the weekend only at her father's insistence. He'd entered them in the parent-child golf tournament at the club, where they were last year's defending champions. Drew was away at boarding school.

"What's your problem?" her father shouted back. "The girls are away at school. We spend more time traveling than we do here. We don't need such a big house anymore. And I'd like to be closer to Merion."

"You expect me to move so that you can be closer to your girl-friend?" Alana's outrage all but shook the crystal chandelier in the main foyer.

"Merion Golf Course, you idiot," her father roared, and Casey had to put her hand over her mouth to keep from laughing out loud.

"I'm not moving," her mother insisted, slamming the bedroom door behind her.

"It's a done deal," came her father's final word.

He'd taken Casey to see the house right after they'd won the tournament. It sat in the middle of three well-manicured acres, contained fourteen large rooms, seven full bathrooms and one powder room, and boasted ceilings that were almost twenty feet high. Casey knew that no amount of furniture would ever make this house feel like a home.

"What do you think?" Ronald Lerner asked his daughter.

"It's pretty formidable."

"It's almost three thousand square feet smaller than the house we're in now."

"Still pretty big."

"How would you decorate it?" There was a mysterious twinkle in her father's eyes.

"I'd put a Biedermeier table over by that wall," she'd said immediately, "and a couple of overstuffed sofas over there, another sofa over there, and maybe a grand piano in that corner."

"Sounds good. Knock yourself out."

"Really? You're saying I can decorate? The whole house? Not just my room?"

"That's what I'm saying."

Casey was so excited she would have hugged her father had he not already been walking away.

Of course, it hadn't worked out that way. The next time Casey returned home, with a binder full of ideas and magazine clippings, the new house was already in the hands of professional decorators. She had no say in anything.

After her parents died, her father's will stipulated that the house be retained until Drew reached the age of thirty, at which point it was to be sold and the profits divided. In the meantime, one or both daughters could live in it, and the estate would pay for its taxes and general upkeep.

Initially, neither girl had wanted to live in that awful "mausoleum," as Drew had christened it, and it was only after Casey's marriage that Warren was able to convince her they should give it a try. "Now's your chance to decorate it exactly the way you always wanted," he told her. "Consider it your grand experiment."

Casey had agreed to the challenge, but once they'd actually moved in, she found herself strangely reluctant to change much of anything. This wasn't really her house, she'd quickly decided, trying to persuade Warren to relocate back to the city. But he loved living in Rosemont, and so she'd agreed to stay in the area. They could take their time looking for the perfect family house. After all, Warren had reminded her, they didn't have to move out until Drew turned thirty.

Which was little more than a year from now, Casey realized, as the ambulance began to slow down.

"It's just two houses past this bend in the road," Warren instructed.

"Yup. There's Patsy waiting at the front door," Ricardo said as he turned the ambulance up the long, circular driveway.

"Lookin' good," Tyrone added quietly.

Warren squeezed Casey's fingers. "We're here, sweetheart," he said. "Home, sweet home."

18

"CAN I GET YOU anything, Mr. Marshall?" Patsy was asking. "I can have the housekeeper put on a fresh pot of coffee before she leaves."

"How about something a little stronger?"

"You name it."

"A gin and tonic sounds pretty good right about now."

"Then a gin and tonic it shall be."

"Why don't you fix yourself a glass as well?"

"Really?"

"It's been a hectic day. I think we both deserve a break."

"Thank you, Mr. Marshall. I'll be right back."

"Patsy . . ."

"Yes, Mr. Marshall?"

"Didn't we agree to dispense with the formalities? I insist you call me Warren."

A satisfied sigh. "I'll be right back, Warren."

"The gin's in the cabinet beside the bar," Warren called after her. "And there should be lots of tonic in the fridge."

"I'll find it," Patsy called back, her footsteps retreating down the stairs.

"How about you, sweetheart?" Warren asked, a solicitous hand brushing across Casey's forehead. "I wish there was something I could get for you. Are you okay? Do you even know where you are?"

Casey felt her heart quicken at her husband's touch, the way it always had. Except before, it had been desire that had fueled its pace. Now it was fear.

"You must be exhausted," he continued. "All that moving. All that jostling around. Quite a busy day for you. But you're as snug as a bug in a rug now. Isn't that what they say? I hope you like your new bed. It looks comfortable enough. It certainly should be—it cost a small fortune. I let the delivery guys take away the old bed. I figured we wouldn't need it anymore. It was always a little girly for my taste anyway. And once you're all better, we can start house hunting again. Then we'll just buy everything new. You'll be able to have everything exactly the way you want it. Lots of bright colors and animal prints. How does that sound?"

Sounds wonderful, Casey thought, wondering why her husband was being so nice to her. Was someone else there?

"I've moved into the master bedroom," he continued. "I know you never liked that room, but it obviously doesn't have the same memories for me that it has for you, so I just transferred my stuff into there, temporarily."

You've moved into my parents' bedroom?

"I don't think your dad would mind too much. And I thought you should have your own space. I'd just be in the way in here. I've positioned your bed so that it looks out the back window, and if you stretch your neck just a bit, you can actually see the creek behind the weeping willow. Well, maybe I'm exaggerating a little. Probably if you want to see the creek, you might actually have to get out of bed. So that's something to aspire to. Can you hear me, Casey? Do you understand what I'm saying to you?"

I hear you. I don't understand anything.

She was home. That much she understood. In the lilac-and-white bedroom that had been hers since she was in her late teens, the same room she and Warren had been sharing since the day they'd moved back here.

Except he'd gotten rid of their queen-size bed and moved into the master bedroom. She'd be sleeping in this new bed alone.

Where would Patsy be sleeping? she wondered.

The phone rang. Casey felt Warren rise from his chair beside the bed. Which chair? she wondered. The mauve-and-cream-striped armchair that normally sat against the far wall, next to the gas fireplace, or one of the two floral tub chairs that normally sat in front of the large bay window?

"Hello?" Warren said. "Oh, hello, Gail. Yes, Casey's fine. We got home about lunchtime, and I'm sorry, I know I said I'd call, but it's been very hectic."

It has?

Actually, it had been pretty quiet, Casey thought. Once the ambulance attendants had maneuvered her stretcher up the stairs and settled her in her new bed, she'd been left pretty much on her own for the rest of the afternoon. Patsy had checked in on her regularly, turning on the large flat-screen TV on the opposite wall, monitoring her blood pressure, and setting up the intravenous hookup to her feeding tube. Warren had stuck his head in the door occasionally to check on her and say hello, but other than the constant drone of the television, it had been very quiet. Of course, she'd fallen asleep in the middle of *Guiding Light* and only awakened to the sound of sirens from the five o'clock news, so maybe it had been more hectic than she'd realized.

"Yes, she seems to be resting comfortably. Her blood pressure spiked a little bit when we first got her home, but it's pretty much back to normal now, and hopefully, it'll stay that way. That's why I'd like to hold off on her having any visitors for at least a few days, if you don't mind. I know how anxious you are to see her, and the flowers you and Janine sent are lovely, of course, as always. I have them sitting on the table beside Casey's bed."

Casey sniffed at the air, detected the subtle fragrance of lilies of the valley.

"I'd just like to give Casey some time to adjust to the change," Warren continued. "You know, to make sure she's getting the proper nourishment, all that stuff. If you could just hold off for another day or two . . . Thanks. I knew you'd understand. Of course I will. And if you wouldn't mind calling Janine . . . Thanks. Okay. Great. I'll tell her. Of course. Good-bye." He hung up the phone. "Gail sends you all her love, says she can't wait to see you, that she has *lots* to tell you. Whatever that means. She also asked me to give you a kiss." Warren leaned closer, planted a delicate kiss on the side of her cheek. "Any excuse to kiss my girl," he said, as the sound of ice cubes tinkling in a glass echoed through the room.

"Everything okay?" Patsy asked, approaching.

"Everything's fine," Warren answered. "Casey seems to be resting comfortably."

"How about you?"

"Me? I'll be fine once I have a sip of this. Thank you."

"I hope it's not too strong."

"There is no such thing." Casey heard him take a sip. "Absolutely perfect."

"Mrs. Singer says dinner's in the warming oven. I told her she could go home."

"Thank you. I didn't realize it was so late. She usually leaves by five."

Who's Mrs. Singer?

"Has she been with you long?" Patsy asked.

"Just since Casey's accident. I was having trouble managing on my own."

"I don't doubt it. This is an enormous house. You didn't have full-time help before?"

"Casey never wanted it. She grew up with a houseful of servants. It conjures up bad memories for her."

"I see," Patsy said, although clearly, she didn't.

"We were managing very well actually. We had a cleaning lady come in twice a week. It was enough. We were doing fine," he said, the ice in his glass clinking.

"Who did the cooking?"

"Well, we ate out a lot, especially when we were both working in the city. Other times, we'd improvise. If Casey was home, she'd whip up some pasta. If I got off work early, I'd throw a few steaks on the barbecue."

"And how do you like your steaks?" Patsy asked.

"Rare," Warren said. "Almost blue."

"Yikes."

"Yikes?" Warren repeated with a laugh.

"I'm afraid I'm one of those Philistines who likes their meat well-done."

"No!" Mock horror filled Warren's voice. "You cook all the flavor out of it that way."

"So I've been told."

"You'll have to try one of my steaks."

"Any time."

"But only on condition that you have it rare."

"Oh, dear. Could we compromise on medium?"

"How about medium rare?" he countered.

"It's a date," Patsy said.

Well, isn't this nice and cozy.

"Sorry," Patsy apologized immediately. "I didn't mean that the way it came out."

"I know that."

You know nothing of the sort.

"I hope you like garlic," Warren said.

"I love it."

"Good. Because my steaks are loaded with it. I'm not kidding. It'll be days before you can kiss your boyfriend."

"Then I guess it's a good thing I don't have one."

Oh, this just keeps getting better and better. It sure beats the hell out of Guiding Light.

"Why do I find that hard to believe?" Warren asked.

"It's not that easy to meet people in this city. Trust me."

Yeah, right.

"Yeah. I guess you have to be lucky."

"Like you were," Patsy said.

Casey felt two sets of eyes travel in her direction.

"Yeah," Warren agreed. "Like I was."

"I was married once," Patsy volunteered after a pause. "It was annulled," she added quickly.

"Really? What happened?"

"Nothing." Patsy laughed. "Nothing happened at all. And I mean that quite literally. The marriage was never consummated."

"Now I know you're pulling my leg."

"I thought he was shy," Patsy said, a touch of wistfulness in her voice. "Turns out he was gay."

"Honestly? And you had no idea?"

"I was very young. Barely eighteen. What did I know? I mean, you think you know everything at that age, but . . . Stupid me, I thought the fact he never tried to get past first base meant he respected me. Can you beat that?"

"Where is he now?"

"I don't know. We lost touch. I think he moved to L.A. He was real good-looking. Everyone was always saying how he should be an actor or something."

"Well, obviously he was a very good actor if he fooled you."

"I don't know. I can be pretty gullible sometimes."

The phone rang again.

"Excuse me," Warren said, answering it. "Hello?" A slight pause. "Janine, hi. How are you?"

Casey pictured him rolling his eyes toward the high ceiling.

"Would you like me to refresh your drink?" Patsy whispered.

"That would be great, thank you," Warren said. "Yes, Janine, that was indeed Patsy. She just offered to get me a cup of tea. Is that all right with you? Okay, okay. Sorry for the tone. It's been a long day. . . . Yes, I know I said I'd call. Gail phoned here earlier. I asked her to tell you. . . . Yes, that's right. . . . Because I think Casey needs time to acclimatize herself to her new surroundings. She was in the hospital a long time. The move was bound to be a jolt to her system. Her blood pressure was a little high. . . . Yes, it's almost back to normal now, but I think she could benefit with a few days' rest, and then the *Middlemarch* marathon can resume. . . . Yes, Saturday would be perfect. . . . Sounds good. Okay. Yes, I promise I'll call if anything changes between now and then. Oh, and thanks for the flowers. They're lovely. As usual. Okay, good. We'll see you and Gail on Saturday. Bye." He hung up the phone.

"That was Janine," he told Casey. "I don't think she's Patsy's biggest fan." A slow release of breath. "Oh, well. Can't please everybody. So, how are you doing, sweetheart? Are you hungry? I think Patsy will be getting you your dinner soon. It's very interesting how she does it, incidentally. I watched her earlier. She opens the clamp on your feeding tube—the clamp is called a stopcock, believe it or not—and then she connects the tube in your stomach to the intravenous hookup. It's all quite easy. The wonders of modern science and all that. Anyway, as soon as you start swallowing on your own, we can remove the feeding tube altogether, which will be a big relief, I'm sure. Then we can start getting some real food into you, put some fat back on those bones. Maybe you could even join Patsy and me for one of my famous steaks." He took Casey's hand and raised it to his lips as Patsy reentered the room.

"Here you go," Patsy said, and Casey pictured her handing Warren his drink. Again, the sound of ice cubes clinking against glass.

"Mmm. Even better than the first."

"Thank you. How's Janine?"

"She's indestructible. Come Armageddon, all that will be left are the cockroaches and Janine."

"It doesn't sound as if you like her very much."

"Let's just say that a little of her goes a long way."

Patsy laughed as the phone rang again.

"Dear God," Warren said. "It's like Grand Central Station in here tonight."

"Would you like me to get it?" Patsy offered.

"No, that's all right. I'll take it. Hello," he barked into the receiver. A long pause, then, "Oh, yes, Steve. Sorry. I forgot all about the meeting. It's my office," he whispered to Patsy. "Yes. If you'll just give me half a minute to locate that file . . ."

"Can I help?" Patsy volunteered.

"My briefcase is in my office downstairs," he instructed her. "The room with the large oak desk and the burgundy leather furniture."

"I'll be right back."

"Sorry to make you keep running up and down the stairs."

"No problem. I can use the exercise."

Casey listened to Patsy's footsteps scurrying down the hallway.

"Yes, someone's just gone to get my briefcase. . . . What the hell do you think you're doing, calling here?" Warren suddenly snapped, his voice a stage whisper that shook the room.

What just happened?

"No, I won't calm down. How dare you call me at home! What's the matter with you? Don't you know calls can be traced?"

What's going on? Who is it?

"Yes, she's here," Warren continued. "I'm with her right now, as a matter of fact. She's getting stronger every day."

The sound of feet running back up the stairs. "Here it is," Patsy exclaimed, noticeably out of breath as she reentered the room. Casey pictured her handing Warren his briefcase. "It's pretty heavy."

"Thank you."

"Would you like me to leave?"

"Sorry, yes. This is highly confidential."

"Of course."

"If you wouldn't mind closing the door . . . Yes, sorry about that, Steve. Thanks for your patience. If you'll allow me a minute to look over the contract . . ."

The door closed. Patsy's footsteps retreated back down the hall.

Warren's tone changed instantly. "Look, I can't talk to you now. No, I don't know when or where. I'll have to get back to you. It won't be long, I promise you that. That's all I can say right now. In the meantime, don't call here again. And don't even think of dropping by. Do you understand? I'll call you in a few days." He slammed down the receiver. "Jesus!" he exclaimed, and Casey pictured him running his hand through his hair. "God, people are so stupid."

That was the man who visited you at the hospital, wasn't it?

The man you hired to kill me. You're not going to waste any time, are you? You're going to finish the job as soon as possible.

She listened to Warren pace back and forth in front of the bed, understanding her time was almost up.

Somebody help me. Get me out of here. Janine, Gail, Drew! Somebody, please. Don't let him get away with this. Because he will, you know. He's smarter than Detective Spinetti, smarter than the whole damn police force.

Smarter than God, Willy Billy had proclaimed.

"Her blood pressure's spiking again," Casey heard Patsy say.

What? When had Patsy come back?

"How high is it?" Warren asked.

"One-seventy over a hundred."

"Is she running a fever?"

"No."

"Should we call the doctor?"

"I don't think that's necessary. Dr. Keith said this was to be expected. I'll check her pressure again in a little while. If it goes any higher, I'll call the hospital. But I'm sure this is just a temporary blip. It should sort itself out by morning."

"I feel so useless," Warren said.

"You're doing everything humanly possible to help Casey. No one could be more supportive."

"I really thought that by moving her back home, it would help her get better."

"It will."

"You honestly believe that?"

"You just have to give it time."

I don't have time.

"Thank you. You're very sweet."

"No thanks necessary."

The phone rang.

"Let voice mail take it," Warren said wearily. "It's probably Drew again. Must be that time of the month. Her allowance," he qualified. The phone stopped after three rings.

"Why don't you get something to eat," Patsy said. "I'll stay here with Casey."

Casey felt Warren's hesitation. "That's probably a good idea. I'll be back soon, sweetheart," he said reassuringly. A pause, then, "Do you think she has any idea how much I love her?"

"I'm sure she knows," came Patsy's unequivocal response.

19

"GOD, MORE FLOWERS," PATSY said, sweeping into the room.

What day is it? Casey wondered, snapping awake. Where am I?

"It's like a funeral parlor in here." The sound of a heavy vase being deposited on a table. "Which I guess it is, in a way," Patsy continued cheerily. "Don't tell your husband I said that." She giggled. "Anyway, this latest batch is from the good doctors and nurses at Pennsylvania Hospital. I guess they miss you."

So she was home, Casey realized. She hadn't dreamed the move. She was really here.

"That was very thoughtful of them to send you flowers, if you ask me. Not that anybody ever does. You notice there was no mention of nurse's aides on the card. Nobody ever thinks to include us. Guess I should have stayed in school, gotten my nurse's diploma, but I thought . . . Hell, who knows what I was thinking? Probably wasn't thinking at all. That's what my mother would say. That's what she says about everything where I'm concerned." The sound of drapes being pulled back. "Let's say we get some light in here. There. That's much better. Such a pretty view you've got."

Casey agreed. She'd always loved the view from this window. It was the reason she'd selected this bedroom over any of the seven others. Drew had wanted this room, too, but Casey had gotten here first. She always did, Casey recognized, feeling the sharp stab of guilt she always experienced when she thought of her younger sister.

"I guess I can't really fault her," Patsy continued, obviously quite content with the one-sided conversation. "My mom, I mean. I've made some pretty stupid decisions in my time. Losing my virginity at thirteen to that creep, Marty Price. Dropping out of school at sixteen. Marrying Jeff at eighteen. Not getting my nursing diploma. Wasting two whole years waiting for Johnny Tuttle to leave his wife, which, of course, he never intended to do. And in case we forget—and believe me, my mother's never gonna let me forget this one—turning down a date with David Frey, who was this nerd with acne and bad teeth who lived at the end of our street, and who invented some stupid board game that—wouldn't you know it?—became this monster success and made him a gazillion dollars. And of course, his skin cleared up, and he had veneers put on all his teeth, and he actually looks pretty damn hot. Of course, now he only dates starlets and heiresses. He was actually in *Us Weekly* a couple of weeks ago, on the arm of that bimbo from that TV show where they're all shipwrecked off the coast of Africa. My mother was thoughtful enough to send me a copy." Patsy laughed. "Mothers—there ain't nothing like them."

You'll get no argument from me there.

Visions of Alana Lerner circled her head like buzzing flies: Alana with a crystal champagne glass in her hand; Alana absently running a brush through her long, blond hair; Alana impatiently pushing Casey aside when she tried to snuggle up against her; Alana all dolled up and ready to go out; Alana's bloated corpse when they pulled her from the waters of Chesapeake Bay.

Casey had wanted to love her mother; she'd tried repeatedly, only to be repeatedly rebuffed. Still, she'd cried when she'd been called on to identify her mother's body.

Unlike Drew.

"Oh, come on, Casey. You expect me to be a hypocrite?" Drew had said.

"I expect you to show a little respect."

"Then you expect too much."

Had she? Casey wondered now. Had she expected too much of Drew? Was she still expecting too much? Or maybe the opposite was true. Maybe she didn't expect enough. Maybe she never had.

"Your mother was quite the beauty," Patsy was saying, roughly lifting Casey's head in order to fluff out her pillow, then letting it drop. "Warren showed me some old pictures of her. There's this one photo where she's wearing a long, beaded gown, with a diamond tiara on her head. A tiara, for Pete's sake. Like she's the goddamn queen of England." She laughed again. "A drama queen is more like it, from what I understand."

Another image suddenly flashed across the dark screen of Casey's eyes: Alana Lerner, her long, beaded gown stained with spilled champagne, her tiara slightly askew, tilted toward her right ear, streaks of blue-black mascara wobbling across her cheeks as she stumbled toward her bed, Ronald Lerner behind her, the child Casey following only steps behind them, silent and unnoticed.

"For God's sake, would you just listen to yourself?" her father was saying.

"Don't you dare try to tell me I'm imagining things. Don't you dare. I did not imagine seeing you with your tongue halfway down Sheryl Weston's ear. The whole goddamn room saw it."

"There was no tongue, for Christ's sake. I was telling her a joke."

"Yeah? Well, I guess the joke's on me, then." Alana laughed, a sharp cackle that caused Casey to clutch at her ears. "Damn you, anyway. Do you have to be so obvious? Does everyone in Rosemont have to know about your latest conquest? Do you always have to humiliate me in front of all my friends?"

"There's no need," Ronald Lerner said evenly. "You do a good job of that all by yourself."

"You're so damn smug."

"You're so damn drunk."

"Miserable bastard."

"Pathetic bitch."

Casey watched her mother lurch toward the night table beside her bed, tripping over her silver stilettos and banging her hip as she struggled to open the top drawer.

"What the hell are you doing now?" her father demanded.

"So I'm pathetic, am I?" her mother countered, finally succeeding in opening the drawer, her right hand rifling blindly through its contents. "I'm pathetic? How pathetic is this?"

What was her mother holding? Casey wondered, inching closer. It looked like the water pistol that Kenny Yaeger had brought to school last week for show-and-tell.

"For God's sake, Alana. Put that damn thing away before you hurt someone."

"I'll show you who's pathetic."

"Put the gun away, Alana."

A gun? Her mother had a gun?

"I'll kill us. I'll kill us both."

What? No!

"You'll do no such thing."

And suddenly Casey's father was knocking the gun from her mother's hand with the back of his own, and then slapping her, slapping her hard across the face. And then again, and again.

"Pathetic bitch," he kept saying, kicking the gun toward the window and pushing Alana toward the bed. And then he was on top of her and they were wrestling, her mother punching at the sides of his head with her fists as he fought to secure her hands above her head. And then he was fumbling with her gown, and she was tugging on his jacket, and soon their angry shouts had turned to grunts and squeals, and even laughter.

"Bastard," her mother purred, as Casey backed slowly out of the room.

When she woke up the next morning, Casey passed by her parents' bedroom and saw them having breakfast together in bed. Her father waved with his free arm, his other arm draped across her mother's shoulder, falling toward her breast. They were smiling and whispering. A quick scan of the floor revealed no weapon. Casey concluded the entire episode had been a bad dream and erased it from her mind.

Until now.

How much of her life had she spent denying what was right before her eyes? Casey wondered.

" 'I thought it right to tell you, because you went on as you always do, never looking just where you are, and treading in the wrong place,' " she heard Janine read. " 'You always see what nobody else sees; it is impossible to satisfy you; yet you never see what is quite plain.' "

Had she really seen a gun in her mother's hand? Casey wondered.

And if she had, where was that gun now? Had they taken it with them when they moved? Was it possible the gun was here, in this house?

"Not that I'm not a bit of a drama queen myself," Patsy was saying. "I have my moments, that's for sure. Just not the wardrobe." She made an exaggerated sigh. "Bet you have a pretty nice wardrobe, don't you? Bet your closet is just stuffed with expensive designer clothes, like the kind your friend—What's her name? The bitchy one . . . Janine? I don't think she likes me—anyway, like the clothes she always wears. Can I have a peek?"

Casey heard Patsy clomp toward the large walk-in closet to the right of her bed.

"You don't mind, do you? I've been wanting to have a look in here since I arrived, but I didn't want Warren to think I was being presumptuous. You don't mind me calling your husband Warren, do you? Not that it matters what you mind."

Casey heard the closet door open, followed by the flip of a light switch.

"Well, isn't this a major disappointment. You're not exactly a clotheshorse, are you, Casey? I mean, what's here is all very nice, if a little conservative for my taste, but it's not exactly what I was expecting. I mean, this is a nice little Armani jacket over here, and these are nice enough pants—Prada, okay, that's a pretty good label—but honestly, Casey, what on earth are these? The Gap? What are you doing shopping at the Gap, for heaven's sake? And does everything have to be black or brown? I thought you were this big-shot designer. Don't you know that color is all the rage for spring and summer? Although I guess you missed the change in the seasons this year, didn't you? Didn't have time to switch your closet around before getting mowed down. You probably keep all your summer clothes in one of the other three thousand bedrooms, don't you? I'll just have to do some major exploring next time Warren goes to the gym. That's where he is now, incidentally. At the gym. Said he was restless, and feeling all flabby 'cause he hasn't worked out in months. Not that he looks even remotely flabby. He's in great shape, and I told him so, but I also encouraged him to go work out. I told him that he couldn't stay glued to your side twenty-four hours a day, that it wasn't healthy, that you'd want him to go out and live his life.

"He's thinking of taking a leave of absence from his job, did you know that? He says he can't concentrate, that his heart just isn't in it. I told him that I understand." She sighed. "Yes, that's me—I'm very understanding. Oh, this is nice," she said in the next breath. "A Hermès scarf. Is it real? Of course it is. You'd never buy one of those awful knockoffs, would you? No, you wouldn't have to. Not when you can afford the real thing. How much are these things anyway? Three hundred dollars? More? For a lousy piece of silk. You don't mind if I wear it for a while, do you? Yellow and black aren't exactly my colors, but hey, it doesn't look half bad. What do you think? Oh, sorry. You can't think, can you? But don't you worry your empty little head. I'm thinking enough for both of us. Yes, I am. And I'm thinking I'm making a little bit of headway every day, as far as your husband is concerned.

"I mean, he's always spouting off about how much he loves you and everything, but personally, I think he's just trying to convince himself. I'm not blind. I see the way he looks at me. A girl always knows when a guy thinks she's attractive, and I can tell he's interested. And he's a man, for heaven's sake. He can only go so long without a little . . . comfort. Yeah, that's a good word. He needs comforting, our Warren does. And since you're in no shape to provide it, I'll just have to step in and fill your shoes.

"Speaking of which, you have awfully big feet. What are these—size nine? Way too big for me. I'm a seven, which is very unfortunate because, I have to admit, you have great taste in shoes. Although you have way too many flats in here for my liking. I mean, I know they're comfortable and practical and better for your feet and all that, but don't you know that men prefer high heels? Honestly, how'd you ever snag a man like Warren wearing all these flat shoes? Oh, I forgot—you're rich."

Patsy pulled a chair up close to the bed and sat down, her mouth close to Casey's ear. "Do you think it's true what they say about the size of men's feet corresponding to the size of their . . . you know, more interesting parts? Do you think that's true? Your husband's a what—an eleven? Maybe even a twelve?" She chuckled. "It doesn't really matter. I'm sure he's more than adequate in that department. Just like I'm sure I'm gonna find out firsthand in the not-too-distant future. Do you understand anything I'm saying?" She chuckled again, this time louder. "I kind of hope you do."

The sound of the front door opening and closing.

Thank God, Casey thought. An end to this torture.

"Guess I better put these shoes back where they belong," Patsy said quickly, scurrying back to the closet and closing its door as the sound of angry voices reached Casey's ears.

"What were you doing? Hiding in the bushes all morning, waiting to ambush me?" Warren demanded from downstairs.

"You don't take my phone calls. You won't answer the door."

Who's that? Is that Drew?

"Sounds like your sister's here," Patsy said.

"I told you your check's in the mail."

"Yeah, that's a good one."

"If you'd prefer to pick up the checks in person, I can easily arrange that with my office, starting next month."

"That's very generous of you, Warren. Just how long are you going to drag this out?"

"Oh, the shit is hitting the fan," Patsy whispered, a smile in her voice. "Here, I'll open the door wider so we can hear better."

"Okay, Drew. I think we've more than covered this ground already," Warren was saying. "Now, if you'll excuse me, I'd like to go upstairs and say hello to my wife."

"Which, strangely enough, happens to be why *I'm* here."

"You're here to see Casey?"

"She's my sister. I didn't even know she was out of the hospital, for God's sake."

"Maybe because you haven't visited her in over a month."

"I still have a right to see her. I have a right to be kept informed."

"She's the same as the last time you saw her, Drew. Nothing's changed."

"I'd like to check that out for myself, if you don't mind."

"I do mind. Go home, Drew."

"This *is* my home," Drew told him, standing her ground. "At least half of it."

"Not until your thirtieth birthday."

"Which, in case you've forgotten, isn't that far off. Fourteen months, by my calculations."

"A lot can happen in fourteen months," Warren said.

What does that mean? Casey asked silently.

"What does that mean?" Drew asked out loud.

"Do I really have to spell it out for you?"

"Yes, you do."

You really do.

"Well, let's see. You do drugs; you drink to excess; I'll bet you even drive drunk, not to mention way too fast. I'd say there's a fifty-fifty chance you might not be around for your thirtieth birthday."

"Are you threatening me?"

"I don't have to threaten you, Drew. I don't have to do anything. You're doing a great job of messing up your life all by yourself."

"Are you actually going to physically stop me from going upstairs?" Drew demanded.

"If I have to."

"I'll get a court order."

"Be my guest," Warren said, calling Drew's bluff.

"How about I go to the police instead, tell them you won't let me see my sister?"

Yes. Go to the police.

"Or maybe I'll just go to the newspapers."

No. Go to the police!

"You don't think this family's had enough bad press?" Warren asked.

"What is it they say?" Drew asked in return. "There's no such thing as bad publicity?"

"Is that what this is to you? A grab at the spotlight? Your fifteen minutes?"

"I just want to see my sister."

A brief silence. Casey pictured her husband taking several steps back and motioning toward the staircase in the center of the circular hallway.

"Thank you," Drew said.

The sound of angry footsteps racing up the stairs.

"Brace yourself," Patsy warned, with barely suppressed glee. "Here comes trouble."

20

SECONDS LATER, DREW CAME bursting into the room.

Casey pictured her younger sister, arms waving, long legs striding purposefully across the threshold, dark blond hair flying behind her, her normally pale cheeks glowing with anger, her teeth chewing on her upper lip as she marched toward the bed. *Oh, Drew. I'm so glad you're here. You have to help me. You have to get me out of here.*

"Who are you?" Drew demanded.

What do you mean? I'm Casey. Don't you recognize me?

"I'm Casey's nurse," Patsy replied, and Casey sighed inwardly with relief. "You must be Drew. I'm Patsy Lukas."

"Why are you wearing my sister's scarf?"

"What?"

She's still wearing my scarf!

Casey envisioned Patsy's hand quickly floating toward her neck, an embarrassed flush spreading across her face into her hairline.

"Take it off," Drew instructed.

You tell her, little sister.

Casey imagined Patsy slowly, and reluctantly, sliding the scarf off her neck, her eyes flashing defiance.

"I didn't mean anything by it. I was just . . ."

". . . helping yourself to my sister's belongings?"

"No. Of course not. I was just . . ."

Just what?

"Just what?" Drew repeated out loud.

"What's going on here?" Warren asked from the doorway.

"It seems that while the devil might wear Prada," Drew told him, an audible smirk in her voice, "the hired help wears Hermès. My sister's Hermès, no less."

"I'm so sorry," Patsy said. "I was just trying to find something to brighten Casey up a bit, make her look pretty for when you came home."

"Wow, you're good," Drew exclaimed, genuine admiration replacing the smirk in her voice. "Tell me, are you as good a nurse as you are a liar?"

"That's enough, Drew. . . ." Warren said.

"Although it doesn't quite explain how the scarf ended up around *your* neck and not my sister's," Drew continued, ignoring Warren's interruption.

"I was just about to put it on her when I heard you coming up the stairs," Patsy said, growing more comfortable with the lie. "Honestly, Warren. I wasn't trying to—"

"Warren?" Drew interrupted, pouncing on the name as if it were a mouse and she the cat. "So, we're on a first-name basis, are we?"

"You're being very rude," Warren told her.

"Am I? I'm sorry. I'm just trying to get a feel for what's going on here, *Warren*," Drew said provocatively.

Her sister had always been feisty, Casey thought, relishing

Warren and Drew's exchange, and realizing she was actually enjoying herself.

"This is really none of your business," Warren said.

"My sister is very much my business."

"Really? Since when? Pardon my cynicism, but I don't remember you showing much concern *before* Casey's accident."

"There was no reason to be concerned then."

"Just as there isn't now," Warren told her. "Casey is being very well looked after."

"Is she?"

The scent of lavender suddenly swirled around Casey's head. Sturdy hands gripped the back of her neck as a swatch of silk slithered across her skin, like a long, thin snake, before curling over itself at the base of her throat.

"There," Patsy said. "That's better."

"You think so?" Drew asked. "Personally, I don't think the scarf does a whole lot in terms of 'brightening Casey up a bit.' She still looks awfully pale to me."

"Your sister's fine," Warren said. "We had a bit of a scare the other day, but . . ."

"What kind of scare?"

"Her blood pressure spiked a bit. But it's back to normal now. The doctor said it was likely the move from the hospital."

"Was he here? Did he check her himself?"

"There was no need. Patsy had everything under control."

"Well, aren't you just the greatest thing since sliced bread?"

"Drew . . ."

"Pardon my cynicism," Drew said, throwing Warren's words back at him, "but when I walked in the room, Florence Nightingale here was wearing my sister's scarf as if it was her own, so you'll excuse me if I'm not quite as impressed with her as you seem to be."

"Honestly, Mr. Marshall, the scarf was for Casey. . . ."

"Oh, so now it's Mr. Marshall, is it?" Drew asked. "Nice touch, Patsy. You learn fast."

"You don't have to explain anything," Warren told the nurse's aide.

"I think she does," Drew said.

"I think she already has."

Drew expelled a deep breath. "Okay. If that's the way you want to play it."

"Nobody's playing anything, Drew. This isn't a game."

"No, it isn't. Unfortunately." Drew plopped down in the nearest chair. "You know, I could really use a cup of coffee."

"There's a Starbucks not far from here."

"There's a kitchen even closer. Patsy, dear, would you mind . . . ?"

"Okay, Drew, enough."

"It's all right," Patsy said. "I'm happy to do it."

"No," Warren protested. "That's not your job."

"Really, it's okay," Patsy said. "I'll ask Mrs. Singer to put on a fresh pot."

"Who the hell is Mrs. Singer?"

"I hired a housekeeper to help out with Casey."

"Of course. I'm sure a housekeeper is exactly what Casey needs at the moment."

"How do you take your coffee, Drew?" Patsy asked.

"Hot and black."

"Can I bring you a cup?" she asked Warren.

"No, thanks."

"Oh, and if Mrs. Singer has baked Casey a cake or anything else she has absolutely no use for," Drew said sweetly, "I could really go for something sweet to nibble on."

"Drew . . ." Warren said.

"I'll see what there is," Patsy said quickly.

"Thank you so much."

"You could lose the attitude," Warren cautioned after Patsy had gone.

"The woman was stealing from my sister's closet."

"I'm sure she was doing no such thing."

"Right. Okay. Just what *does* she do?"

"She's a nurse, Drew. What do you think she does?"

"I believe that was my question."

"You want the gory details?"

"I want an answer."

Casey felt Warren begin pacing back and forth in front of her bed. "Fine, then. She monitors your sister's blood pressure, inserts and removes her feeding tube, bathes her, checks her for bedsores, adjusts her catheter . . ."

"Her catheter?"

"Do you really want me to go on?"

No. Please, no more.

"No," Drew said softly.

"It's not exactly anyone's idea of a good time, and I was very lucky—*we* were very lucky—that Patsy agreed to take it on. So maybe you'd be nice enough to offer her an apology. . . ."

"Who takes over when Patsy goes home?"

A pause. A small sigh, followed by a bigger one. "She doesn't go home. She's living here."

"How cozy. And Mrs. Singer? Does she live here as well?"

"No. I have no idea where she lives."

"But Patsy lives *here.*"

"What are you getting at, Drew?"

"I just don't like the kind of vibes I'm getting."

"And what kind of vibes would those be?"

"Those my-sister's-in-a-coma-and-some-tart's-wearing-her-clothes kind of vibes," Drew answered.

Casey laughed silently.

"That would be funny if it weren't so pathetic," Warren said.

"I thought it was pretty funny."

"I love your sister, Drew."

Silence.

No, don't believe him. I know he sounds oh-so-sincere, but please, don't believe him.

"I know you do."

"Then why are we arguing?"

Drew laughed. "You call this arguing? When Casey wakes up, you'll have to ask her about some of the fights we used to have. Now, *those* were arguments."

"When Casey wakes up," Warren repeated, managing to sound almost wistful, "I think we'll find better things to talk about."

"You really believe she's going to get better?"

"I *have* to believe it."

Don't believe anything he tells you. It's all a con. Don't believe any of it.

"Have the police been in touch with you recently?" Drew asked.

"No. You?"

"No. I think they lost interest. Look, I hate to keep bringing this up . . ."

"You want answers about your money," Warren stated.

"I think I've been pretty patient."

"I'm sorry that things are taking so long, but you have to understand that this is a highly unusual situation, and there are no easy answers or quick solutions. It's going to take more time. . . ."

"How much more time? Months? Years?"

Casey could hear the anger edging back into her sister's voice.

"I don't know."

"I don't like this, Warren. I don't like this one bit."

"Look. I know you're upset, but I'm not the person you should be mad at. It wasn't my idea to name your sister executor of the estate. It wasn't my idea that you be kept on a short leash and put on a strict allowance. Those were your father's instructions, and I'm just making sure those wishes are respected, and that Casey is protected."

"A little late for that, wouldn't you say?"

A pause, followed by a heavy sigh. "What do you want from me, Drew? I'm doing everything I can. If you could just be patient a little longer, I might be able to get you a little extra something until everything's resolved."

"That would be nice."

"I'll call my office Monday, see what I can arrange."

No. Don't be placated so easily. Please. Don't make this just about the money.

"But I'm still picking up some peculiar vibes," Drew said.

Way to go, Drew. That's the baby sister I know and love.

Warren sighed again. "Okay. Whatever. Have it your way. Now, if you'll excuse me, I have to get some work done for Monday."

"Could you ask Patsy what's happened to my coffee?"

He laughed again. "Your wish is my command."

"And would you mind if I opened a window in here?" Drew called after him. "The smell of cheap perfume is suffocating."

"Just show yourself out when you're ready to leave," Warren called back.

The sound of a squeaky brass handle being rotated. "There, that's much better. Get rid of that awful smell. I always find lavender so cloying, don't you? I mean, I know it's supposed to make you feel all relaxed and everything, but it just sets my teeth on edge."

Casey felt a gentle hand at her neck, felt the silk scarf sliding from her throat.

"That's better," Drew said. "I'm not a big fan of Hermès. You need something with a little more zip. I know—you can wear this." There was a slight tapping sound, and Casey pictured Drew patting her throat. "I just bought it."

Again, Casey felt Drew supporting the back of her neck as she leaned forward, pressing the side of her breast against Casey's cheek while she maneuvered something over her head. Casey felt the soft cotton of Drew's blouse against her skin and inhaled the fresh, clean scent of baby powder. She remembered how she used to hold Drew in her arms when she was an infant, and cradle her during a thunderstorm when she was afraid, how she used to bury her nose in her sister's soft hair and assure her everything would be all right.

When had those assurances stopped?

"It's a necklace," Drew explained, returning Casey's head to the pillow. "It's nothing much, really. Just a little silver chain with a tiny silver high-heeled shoe dangling from it. It reminded me of my Manolos, so I bought it. It wasn't expensive or anything. I just liked it. Anyway, you can have it. It looks better on you anyway. What do you think?" she asked, almost as if she expected an answer. Casey pictured Drew walking back to the window, eyes drifting toward the enormous weeping willow tree in the backyard. "So, what's up?" she asked after a pause of at least thirty seconds. "Yeah, nothing much happening with me either. Oh, except I got rid of Sean. You remember Sean. He came to the hospital with me one time. Tall, fair, kind of spacey-looking. He had a bit of that Owen Wilson thing going on. Anyway, I dumped him. I'm not really sure why. He was just starting to get on my nerves." She laughed. "Seems like a lot of stuff is getting on my nerves these days." She returned to the bed, perched on its side, and began absently rubbing Casey's toes beneath the sheet. "You ever have that with a guy? Everything he does just suddenly starts to annoy you?

Probably not. You never had that many guys, did you? You were always much more selective in that regard. Unlike certain younger sisters I could mention. Anyway, I gave old Sean his walking papers. To be honest, he didn't seem all that upset. The only one who was sort of sad was Lola. Turns out she liked him. Do you think I'm a terrible mother?" Drew asked suddenly. "I mean, I know I'm not the greatest mother in the world, but am I terrible?" She paused, as if giving Casey a chance to respond. "It's not that I don't love her. I do. It's just that she's always *there*. Do you understand what I'm saying? Every time I turn around, there she is. And I want to say to her, Look, you're a sweet kid and everything, but can I just have a few days to myself? But how can I do that? I can't," Drew said, answering her own question. "And she's always looking at me, like she's expecting me to do something. Only I never know what it is she expects me to do, so I always feel like I'm letting her down. It's an awful feeling when you think you're constantly disappointing everyone. Although I guess I should be used to it by now."

Oh, Drew.

"I guess I thought it would be different, you know? I thought if I had a baby, she'd have to love me."

She does *love you, Drew.*

A sigh trembled in the air between them. "She loves *you*, though. Before your accident—and I think everybody's pretty much decided that's what it was—she was always asking when we could go visit her aunt Casey. And ever since I brought her to the hospital, she keeps bugging me about when she can come see you again. She has all these books she wants to read to you. Well, I'm not sure if she can actually read, or if she's just memorized the stories. Janet has read those fairy tales to her so many times, she knows them all by heart. Janet's her nanny. I had to fire Elise after I caught her helping herself to my stash of weed. Honestly, it's so hard to find good help these days." She laughed. "Just kidding."

The magnificent aroma of freshly brewed coffee wafted toward the doorway. Casey felt her mouth begin to water and tasted the rich, roasted taste of the coffee beans on her tongue.

"And speaking of good help . . ."

The disparate smells of coffee and lavender fought for supremacy as they entered the room together, like a pair of hostile, conjoined twins.

"Here's your coffee," Patsy said.

"Thank you."

"Careful. It's hot."

"Hot and black. Just the way I like it. Thank you," Drew said again.

"Listen, I'm really sorry about the misunderstanding earlier. I appreciate how it must have looked to you."

"Well, I appreciate your appreciation, so let's leave it at that, shall we?"

The doorbell rang.

"Who's that?" Drew asked.

"Probably her therapist."

"Hot and black," Drew said, a wink in her voice. "Just the way I like it."

21

"WELL, HELLO THERE," JEREMY said, striding into Casey's bedroom. "Haven't seen you in a while. How've you been?"

"Fine," Drew answered. "Nice to see you again." Casey recognized the strain in her sister's voice to sound casual.

"You're a little late," Patsy told him. "Everything okay?"

"There was a bad accident on the expressway earlier this morning, and they were still clearing it away when I got there, so I was stuck for a good twenty minutes. Sorry about that. The good news is I'm here now, and that coffee smells great. Think you could spare another cup?"

Casey pictured an overly ingratiating smile light up Patsy's eyes. "How do you take it?"

"Cream, lots of sugar."

"White and sweet," Drew said under her breath, as Jeremy approached her bed and Patsy exited the room.

Casey absorbed the intensity of Jeremy's gaze as he leaned in to have a better look at her. "Hello, Casey. How are you feeling today? Happy to be back home?"

No, I'm not happy. I'm not happy at all. You have to get me out of here.

"Apparently her blood pressure spiked some," Drew told him, "but it's back to normal now."

"Yeah, that's pretty much to be expected."

"So I've been told."

"She does look a little pale."

"That's what I thought."

"Well, we'll see if a little exercise can't bring some color back to her cheeks."

"Do you want me to leave?"

"Not at all."

"I don't want to be in the way."

"You aren't. And I'm sure Casey appreciates the company. I know I do."

Casey felt his hand on her forehead. Could he feel her mind working? *Listen to me,* she thought, as hard as she could. *My husband did this to me. He tried to kill me, and he's going to try again as soon as he thinks he can get away with it. Which will probably be sooner rather than later, now that it looks as if the police have abandoned their investigation. You have to stop him. You have to get me away from here.*

"She doesn't have a fever, does she?" Drew asked, drawing closer.

"No. Her forehead's nice and cool. And speaking of nice and cool, that's a cool little necklace she's wearing. You give her that?"

"Yes. How'd you know?"

" 'Cause it looks like you."

"I look like a shoe?" Drew laughed.

"You know what I mean."

"Well, thank you. I think. I mean, I'll take that as a compliment."

"Good. That's the way it was intended." Jeremy took Casey's hand in his own and started to manipulate her fingers.

"Can I ask you a question?" Drew asked after several seconds had passed.

"Fire away."

A moment's hesitation. "What's your opinion of Patsy?"

"Professionally?"

"Professionally and personally."

A brief pause. "Personally, I don't know her very well. But she's always seemed nice enough. Professionally, I'd say she's competent, knowledgeable, compassionate. Patients like her. She's certainly dedicated to your sister."

"You think so?"

"You don't?"

"I don't know."

"Did something happen?"

"I'm not sure," Drew said, and Casey pictured her sister glancing toward the open bedroom door, in case Patsy might be lingering outside. "When I got here, she was wearing one of Casey's expensive scarves—that one, actually," she continued, no doubt pointing to wherever it lay, "and I got mad and told her to take it off, probably said a few things I shouldn't have. . . ."

"She have an explanation?"

"She said she was just about to put it on Casey when I came in."

"You don't believe her?"

"Would you?"

Jeremy lowered Casey's right hand back to her side, picked up her left. "Well, normally I'd be inclined to give her the benefit of the doubt. But . . ." He began moving Casey's fingers back and forth.

"But . . . ?"

"But something tells me your instincts are pretty good. So if they're telling you she was trying to pull a fast one, then I'd say she was trying to pull a fast one."

Casey could actually feel her sister's grateful smile.

"Thank you," Drew said.

"For what? What does Mr. Marshall think? Does he know?"

"He knows. I'm afraid he doesn't share your faith in my instincts."

"Well, then, let's hope it was an isolated incident."

"Yeah," Drew agreed. "I guess the important thing is that she's a good nurse, right?"

Jeremy began massaging the muscles in the palm of Casey's hand with his thumb. If only she could grab that thumb, Casey thought, trying to squeeze back, to give him some sign she was aware of what was going on. If only there was a way she could let him know. . . .

"Well, technically, she's not actually a nurse," Jeremy said.

"What do you mean she's not a nurse? What is she?"

"She's a nurse's aide."

"I don't understand. Why would Warren hire her to look after my sister if she's not a nurse? It's not like he doesn't have the money. . . ."

Jeremy's fingers began applying pressure to Casey's wrist, rotating it gently from left to right. "Don't go getting all upset. Patsy's more than qualified for what needs to be done here," he explained. "Your sister doesn't really need an RN at this point." He began rotating Casey's wrist in the opposite direction. "And like I said, Patsy is knowledgeable and competent. She tends to go the extra mile, as far as her patients are concerned. Plus, she's very familiar with Casey's condition. She's been actively involved in her care for months. I wasn't surprised when Mr. Marshall hired her. Frankly, I thought he was lucky to get her." He returned Casey's hand to the bed, picked up her other hand again, began manipulating its wrist. "But you don't like her."

"I don't like her," Drew said quietly.

The sound of footsteps on the stairs. The smell of fresh coffee approaching.

"Coffee," Patsy announced cheerily from the doorway. "Cream, lots of sugar."

"If you wouldn't mind putting it on the nightstand for me. Thank you," Jeremy said, moving Casey's arm up and down from the elbow.

Casey felt the bounce in Patsy's steps as she crossed the room to deposit Jeremy's coffee on the small table beside the bed.

"Anything else I can do for you?"

"No, thank you. That's great."

"What about you, Drew? You ready for another cup?"

"I'm fine, thank you. Actually, Jeremy was just showing me some exercises I can do with Casey. Maybe you'd like to stay so he can show you, too."

"How about you show me later? Right now Mr. Marshall needs me to take care of a few things for him."

"I thought your job was taking care of Casey."

"Casey is in very good hands at the moment," Patsy said sweetly, refusing to take the bait. "Just holler when you're done, Jeremy."

Casey assumed from the ensuing silence that Patsy had left the room.

Please. You have to help me. You have to get me out of here.

"So, okay. I'm a total bitch, right?" Drew stated. "I mean, could she be any sweeter?"

"I don't know," Jeremy said. "I tend to be a little suspicious of people who are too sweet."

Again, Casey felt Drew smile. "So, just how *is* Casey doing? Is she improving at all?"

"Well, it's hard to judge levels of improvement when a patient is comatose, but your sister has good flexibility and an excellent muscle base, so we'll just keep plugging away. Here, why don't you start on her other arm. . . . That's right . . . just do what I showed you last time. That's perfect. And I'll get started on her legs."

"How realistic are her chances of being able to walk again?"

"Well, there's no physical reason why she shouldn't be able to. There was no injury to the spinal cord, and her fractures have healed nicely. If we keep working these muscles," he said, lifting the sheet from Casey's legs and starting to massage the bottoms of her feet, "then once she wakes up, once her brain starts sending out the correct messages, I see no reason why she won't eventually regain complete use of her arms and legs."

"But first she has to wake up."

"First she has to wake up."

I am up, dammit. Why isn't my brain sending out the correct messages?

"The patient's brain has been rocked," Casey recalled one of her doctors saying.

How long ago had that been? How many weeks? How many months? How much time before her damn brain stopped rocking? Would she have enough time? *Come on, brain. Concentrate. Start sending out the right signals. Fingers, squeeze my sister's thumb. Feet, kick at Jeremy's hands. Do something. Do anything.*

"So how long have you been doing this sort of work?" Drew asked.

"Not that long," Jeremy replied. "A little over four years."

"And before that?"

"The army."

"The army?"

"Long, sad story." He sighed, as if debating whether or not to tell it. "I was working as a therapist. My wife and I were struggling to make ends meet. I had a shitload of student loans to pay back.

The army offered to repay those loans if I enlisted. The recruiting officer said I'd be stationed stateside, that I likely would never be sent overseas, and that in the very unlikely event that I was, I'd be assigned to the medical unit and probably wouldn't see any direct combat. I was stupid enough to believe him."

"Where'd they send you?"

"Afghanistan."

An audible intake of air. "What was that like?"

"Not exactly my idea of a good time."

"The recruiting officer lied to you about everything?"

"Well, that's the thing. He didn't exactly lie. No, he was very careful in his choice of words. He said I'd be stationed stateside, which I was—for about six months. He said I *likely* wouldn't be sent overseas, that I *probably* wouldn't see any direct combat. . . ."

"But you *were* sent overseas, you *did* see direct combat."

"Yes."

"Were you scared?"

"Yes."

Drew's voice fell to a whisper. "Did you kill anybody?"

A long pause. "Yes."

"That must have been so awful."

"Yes," he said again.

Casey felt him reach across her for his coffee, heard him take a tentative sip.

"I don't think I could ever kill anyone."

"You'd be amazed at what you're capable of doing. Especially when someone's trying to kill you."

"How long were you over there?"

"Twenty-three months, one week, and five days. But who's counting?" He tried to laugh, but the sound caught in his throat and stayed there. He took another sip of coffee. "By the time I got home, my wife had pretty much moved on. She came back for a while. We gave it the old college try, but it didn't work out. I found out later that she'd been pretty much living with another guy while I was away. Anyway, what's done is done. No point moaning about what can't be changed." He returned his attention to Casey's feet. "How about you?"

"Me?"

"How are things working out for you?"

Casey felt Drew shrug. "I guess I'm still a work in progress."

"Haven't quite decided what you want to be when you grow up?" Jeremy asked.

"Is that awful? I mean, I *should* know. I'm almost thirty. I have a child."

"You'll figure it out."

"You think so?"

"I know so."

"Well, I appreciate the vote of confidence. Thank you."

"For what?"

"Do you mind if I ask you another question?" Drew asked.

"Go ahead."

"What's it like to kill somebody?"

Silence. Then, "I'm not sure I can answer that."

"Sorry," Drew apologized quickly. "It's none of my business. I shouldn't have asked."

"No, the problem isn't with the question. The problem is I'm really not sure how to answer it. I'm not sure how it felt, to be honest. I was so scared." He paused, took another sip of coffee. "You're in a strange country, you don't speak the language, you don't know anything about the damn Taliban. All you know is that you're a long way from home, and that you're supposed to be bringing democracy to these people who are trying to blow your brains out. And bombs are going off, and land mines are exploding, and in the end, you don't give a shit about democracy or the

Taliban or anything else except getting out of that hellhole alive. Your adrenaline is constantly pumping and your heart is racing nonstop, and when you fire that weapon and you see that body drop, you don't have time to feel anything, except maybe relief it wasn't you. Maybe in the beginning, you feel a little elated that you actually managed to hit something, or maybe you feel sick to your stomach. I don't know. All that destruction. All that blood. How can it not get to you? But eventually, that's just what happens. Sooner or later, you don't feel anything." Another pause, another sip of coffee. "That's probably the worst part. To kill another human being and not feel anything at all."

Was that how Warren felt? Casey wondered. Had he felt nothing while plotting her death? Nothing at all?

"Sometimes it feels great," Drew was saying, "not feeling anything."

"I think that's what they call a contradiction in terms," Jeremy said.

"I guess. But isn't that why most people do drugs, so that they don't have to feel?"

"Is that why *you* do them?"

"People think you do drugs to get high," Drew answered, talking more to herself now. "But it's not to get high so much as it is to get to that point where you're *so* high that you're floating above all the crap and the pain, so you don't feel anything at all—" She broke off. "Spoken like a junkie in need of a fix," she said, and tried to laugh.

"Are you?" Jeremy asked, letting go of Casey's leg and returning his coffee to the end table beside her bed.

Dear God. Are you?

"Well, I don't shoot up, if that's what you're asking. I've never done heroin. Not because I haven't been tempted, but I have this phobia where needles are concerned. I snorted it once, mixed it with some cocaine, but it made me throw up, and I hate throwing up almost as much as I hate needles. You ever do coke?"

"I tried it a couple of times," Jeremy said. "Loved the getting high, hated the coming down. Decided it just wasn't worth it."

"Yeah, I've decided that a couple of times myself." Drew laughed.

"What about your sister?" Jeremy asked, returning his full attention to Casey, bending her right leg at the knee, then straightening it out again, then repeating the action over and over again.

"Oh, no. Casey would never do drugs. Never. Ever."

Only because I was so afraid of letting down my guard.

"She was always such a straight arrow. Never skipped classes, never got drunk, never slept around, always did the right thing."

Only because I was terrified not to.

"Always in control."

Somebody in the family had to take responsibility.

"She's not in control now," Jeremy stated.

"No, she's not," Drew agreed. "How fair is that?" She squeezed Casey's hand. "She spends her whole life being the good daughter and the perfect wife and the consummate professional, and look how she ends up. You join the army to pay off a few student loans and end up killing people. I spend half my life shoving enough drugs up my nose to kill a small elephant, yet here I sit, alive and relatively healthy. So, what's the point of anything, I ask you?"

The point is that we have no control. The point is that there are no guarantees, that we never know what's going to happen in life, but we can't give up. The point is that, fallible as we all are, we have to keep trying, we have to keep reaching out to others. . . .

"Oh my God!" Drew exclaimed.

"What's the matter?"

"She just squeezed my hand."

"What? Are you sure?"

I did? I squeezed your hand?

"I'm telling you—she just squeezed my hand," Drew repeated, excitement growing in her voice.

Casey felt Jeremy remove her hand from Drew's.

"I'm not feeling anything," he said after several seconds.

"I wasn't imagining things," Drew insisted. "I swear, she squeezed my hand."

"Can you do it again, Casey?" Jeremy squeezed her fingers, as if to show her how.

Yes, I can. I can. There. I'm squeezing. I'm squeezing.

"Anything?" Drew asked.

"I'm not sure."

What do you mean, you're not sure? I'm squeezing your fingers so hard they're going to break off. Pay attention, damn you. I'm squeezing.

"Come on, Casey. You can do it," Drew urged.

"Do what?" Patsy asked from the doorway.

"Casey just squeezed my hand," Drew said.

"What?"

"Can you do it again, Casey? Can you?" Jeremy asked.

I'm trying, dammit, I'm trying.

"Nothing," he said.

"You were probably imagining it," Patsy said.

"I know what I felt," Drew argued.

Patsy approached the bed, grabbed Casey's other hand. "Okay, Casey, if you can understand me, then squeeze my hand."

Dammit, I'd break it if I could.

"I don't feel anything."

"She squeezed my hand," Drew insisted. "She understands."

"Even if she did squeeze your hand," Jeremy said, "that doesn't mean she was reacting to anything specific."

"What *does* it mean?" another voice asked, entering the room.

Warren, Casey realized, a sinking sensation in the pit of her stomach. How long had he been standing there?

"It was most likely an involuntary muscle spasm," Jeremy explained.

"But it could be more than that," Drew said. "It could mean Casey's starting to regain the use of her hands. It could mean she's trying to communicate. Couldn't it?"

"It could," Jeremy conceded. "But we shouldn't get our hopes up just yet."

"Jeremy's right," Warren said, taking Casey's hand from Patsy's and lifting it to his lips, gently kissing the tip of each finger. "We'll just have to wait and see."

22

IT WAS THE MIDDLE of the night, and the house was completely still.

Casey lay motionless in her bed, wide awake despite the lateness of the hour. How much time had elapsed since the episode earlier in the day when she'd squeezed her sister's hand? How many hours had she spent going over every detail of what had transpired? Had she really squeezed Drew's hand, and if so, had it been a deliberate act on her part or merely an involuntary muscle spasm, as Jeremy had suggested?

Warren was certainly curious to know the answer. He hadn't left her side all afternoon. He'd sat by her head, monitoring her for the slightest twitch, eating lunch in his chair and forgoing his dinner, occasionally taking her hand in his and coaxing her in a soft, gentle voice to squeeze his fingers if she understood anything he was saying. "I love you so much," he'd whispered on more than one occasion, loud enough to be heard by whomever else was in the room.

Were they so easily fooled? Casey wondered, then answered

her own question. Of course they were fooled. He'd fooled everyone. And she—the biggest fool of all.

Jeremy had left when he'd concluded his therapy session, telling Warren he was very pleased with Casey's progress and that he'd see her again on Monday. Drew had stayed until the end of *Guiding Light* before kissing Casey's forehead, and after reminding Warren about his pledge to increase her monthly allowance, she promised to return the following afternoon and bring Lola with her. Patsy had been in and out of the room all day, ostensibly looking after Casey but mostly fussing over Warren, until she reluctantly retired for the night at around eleven o'clock. Warren had remained at Casey's bedside until the end of the David Letterman show. Then he'd pressed the power button on the TV's remote control and plunged the room into silence.

It had been that way ever since, Casey thought now, listening to the assorted squeaks and clicks a house makes when everyone is asleep. Everyone except me, she thought, realizing that in the last twenty-four hours she hadn't lost consciousness once, that she'd been awake for every second of every minute of every hour of the day. There'd been no merciful blackouts, no reprieves from the monotony of lying on her back for hours on end, listening to the voices from the television compete with Patsy's inane yapping or Warren's false protestations of love. Only Drew had provided her with a much-needed jolt of adrenaline. That she'd managed to squeeze Drew's hand . . .

Had she? Or had it been wishful thinking on her sister's part?

And was the fact she was no longer losing large chunks of time something to be celebrated or something to be rued? Was she getting better, or was she even worse off than she'd been before?

How could anything be worse? she wondered, sensing a slight shift in the air.

Something was happening.

Someone was coming.

Casey felt her heartbeat quicken. Someone was watching her from the doorway.

"Casey," her husband said after several minutes. "Are you awake?" he asked, as if he expected an answer.

What was he doing here? Casey wondered. Had he come to finish the job he'd started? How? By holding a pillow over her nose and mouth until she stopped breathing? By injecting an air bubble into her veins with a hypodermic? "I don't know what happened," she could almost hear him sobbing to the ambulance attendants who rushed to the scene, the distraught husband trying to come to terms with this latest tragedy. "I came in to check on her, and I knew immediately something was wrong."

Or would he bide his time and wait until Patsy discovered her in the morning?

Wasn't that his usual modus operandi—staying one step removed?

"I couldn't sleep," Warren told her now, his voice steady and calm as he crossed the bedroom floor to stand by the still-open window. "How about you?"

Was he just here to make conversation? Casey wondered. Had he been having trouble sleeping, as he sometimes did, and reflexively turned to her, as he often had, for comfort in the middle of the night?

Why are you here?

"It's really beautiful out. Warm. A little breeze. The sky is full of stars. The moon's almost full. You'd love it."

I loved you. *With all my heart and soul. How could you have done this to me?*

"So, is it true?" he asked, moving slowly toward the bed. "Did you really squeeze Drew's hand?" He took her palm in his. "And if you did, if it wasn't just the product of your sister's overwrought imagination, the question is, was it simply a muscle spasm, or were you trying to communicate?"

So they'd spent the last several hours kept awake by the same gnawing questions, Casey thought, tortured by the same things. They were still in sync, even now.

Except they were never really in sync. It had all been an act.

Foreplay, she scoffed.

To murder.

Warren squeezed Casey's fingers. "You can tell me, Casey," he whispered seductively. "You know you've never been able to keep anything from me."

He's right, Casey thought. She'd always been an open book where he was concerned.

"Tell me, what do you think about, lying here all day and night? Do you understand anything of what's happening?"

No. I don't understand a thing, least of all you.

"I can't imagine how frustrating this must be, assuming you do understand. Not to mention terrifying. And boring. And humiliating. And God only knows what else. I think I'd be as mad as a hatter by now if I were you. Are you as mad as a hatter, Casey?"

Maybe. Maybe I am.

"Are you aware of time? Of the hours of your life slowly passing you by?"

Every hour, every minute, every second.

"So, what do you think about? Do you think about me? Do you think about how happy we were?" He perched on the side of her bed, began absently stroking her thigh through the thin blanket that covered her.

Oh, Warren, she thought, her body tingling at the touch of his hand, despite everything. We *were* happy, weren't we?

"I have to admit, I do miss you. I miss the interesting conversations we used to have. I miss your laugh. I miss how you used to snuggle up against me in bed, the way you'd poke your cute little butt into my stomach. And I miss the way you touched me." He took Casey's hand, moved it slowly to his leg. "Here," he said, guiding her hand beneath his silk robe to his bare thigh. "And here." He pushed her hand toward his groin. "Do you miss this?" he whispered, moving her hand higher still.

What was he doing? Casey wondered. No, this isn't happening. This isn't happening.

"It's been so long," he said. "And I've been such a good boy. You'd be so proud of me. I actually think I've been a better husband since the accident than I was before it. More attentive, more thoughtful. Certainly more faithful."

What are you saying now? That you were unfaithful to me?

"You never had any idea, did you?" Warren asked. "Not the slightest clue, I'll bet. It was always one of your greatest charms— your naïveté. Despite your upbringing, you still believed in marriage and monogamy. You still believed in fairy tales."

Casey realized with an unseen shudder that her husband was talking about her in the past tense.

"Although I have to admit that, unlike your father, I was very discreet."

Why are you telling me this? Are you hoping for some kind of reaction?

Warren leaned in closer, his lips grazing the side of her mouth. How far was he going to take this? Casey wondered, wishing she could turn her head aside, that she could pull her hand away, use it to slap him, hard, across the face. Was that what he was looking for?

She felt his hand suddenly at her throat, felt his fingers sliding down her neck, then stopping in the space between her breasts.

"Your breasts will get bigger," Gail had said during their last lunch together, just after Casey had informed her of her plans to get pregnant. The fact she'd actually been considering having children with this man made her want to gag.

Could he feel her revulsion? Casey wondered, holding her breath as Warren's hand lingered for several seconds over her right nipple, then quietly withdrew.

"Guess you really can't move," he said after a few more seconds had elapsed. He stood up, letting the hand he'd been holding flop down against the mattress, like a dead fish. "Sorry. I had to make sure you weren't—what's that word Dr. Keith used? Malingering? Yeah, that was it. A definite hundred-dollar word. Anyway, that was my own little test, unorthodox though it may have been. And while I admit to finding it disconcertingly more pleasant than I'd anticipated, necrophilia isn't really my thing." Casey felt her husband moving restlessly about the room. "So, what to do, what to do," he muttered. "You're a real conundrum, Casey. You know that? What am I going to do with you?"

Haven't you done enough already?

He suddenly swooped closer, grabbed her chin roughly with his hand, forced her head up. "Can you see this light? Can you?"

What was he doing? Was he shining something in her eyes?

"No blinks, powerful or otherwise," he said with obvious relief. Casey heard fumbling and surmised he was returning a tiny flashlight to the pocket of his robe. "So, we know you still can't see. But it's just a matter of time, isn't it? And timing is everything. Right? *Right?* Dammit, Casey. Are you in there? Can you hear me? Do you have any idea what's going on? Shit," he exclaimed, releasing her chin.

"Is something wrong?" Patsy asked from the doorway.

Casey heard Warren gasp, felt him jump.

"I'm so sorry," Patsy apologized immediately. "I didn't mean to scare you."

Casey pictured the two of them standing on opposite sides of the bed, Warren in his black-and-gold-striped bathrobe, Patsy in a long, probably flimsy nightgown that undoubtedly revealed considerable décolletage.

"How long have you been standing there?" Warren asked.

"Just a few seconds. I thought I heard voices."

"Unfortunately just mine," Warren said, punctuating his sentence with a slight laugh of embarrassment.

Nice touch, Casey thought.

"Is something wrong?" Patsy asked. "Is Casey all right?"

"She's fine. I just couldn't sleep," Warren explained. "I thought I might as well get up and see how she was doing."

So considerate. Always thinking of others.

"Can I make you something to eat? You didn't have any dinner. You must be starving."

"Not really."

"How about some tea?"

"No. Thank you. You should go back to bed. It promises to be pretty hectic tomorrow. I'm sorry if I woke you up."

"Don't be. I'm a light sleeper. You actually saved me from a very unpleasant dream."

"Really? What was it about?"

"Standard nightmare stuff. Faceless, knife-wielding man chasing me down a dark alley, and I'm screaming, but nobody can hear me. And he's getting closer and closer. . . ."

"Does he catch you?"

"Nope. Like I said, you saved me."

Too bad.

"My hero," Patsy said.

"Glad to be of service."

"Do you ever have nightmares?" Patsy asked.

"Not since I was a child. At least none that I can remember."

"You're lucky. I remember all my dreams. I have this one where I'm standing on a stage, about to give a speech—God only knows why because I've never given a speech in my life—and I look down, and I realize I'm completely naked."

Well done, Patsy. Get him focusing on your more tangible assets.

Warren chuckled. "I think that's a fairly common dream."

"What do you think it means?"

Please spare me the sophomoric dream interpretations.

"Sounds like some kind of performance anxiety to me."

"Have you ever had that? I mean, in court, not in . . . You know what I mean."

I'm sure he does.

"I don't go to court."

"You don't?"

"I'm not a litigator."

"What sort of law do you practice?" Patsy asked. "I asked Janine once, but she was a little vague."

"Vague?" Warren repeated with a laugh. "Not a word I'd normally associate with Janine."

Casey groaned. Did she really have to be an unwilling eavesdropper to this grotesque mutual seduction? Was her condition not pitiful enough?

"I do mostly corporate and commercial work," Warren continued. "And lately, a little bit of strategic planning as well."

"What's that?"

"I advise companies on the best way to accomplish their goals and help them draw up a curriculum to realize those objectives."

Not very good at it, are you?

"Sounds very complicated."

"Everything sounds complicated at three o'clock in the morning."

"How about something nice and simple like a cup of hot chocolate?" Patsy offered.

Nice segue, Patsy. I'm impressed.

"It might help you sleep," she added.

"I don't want to put you to any trouble."

"It's no trouble. Honestly."

"Sure, hot chocolate sounds . . ." A sob caught in Warren's throat. "I'm sorry," he said, his voice suddenly awash in tears. "I'm sorry."

Guess he's not a big fan of hot chocolate.

Casey felt Patsy rush to Warren's side and gather him in her arms, his head collapsing against her shoulder as he cried.

"It's all right," she heard Patsy say. "Let it out. Let it out."

"It's just so awful."

"I know."

You have no idea.

"I'm so sorry."

"Don't be."

"I'm trying to stay strong for Casey. . . ."

"Nobody can be strong twenty-four hours a day."

"Sometimes I feel so desperate."

This is beyond desperate. I know it's three o'clock in the morning, Patsy, but wake up, girl. The man's a cold-blooded killer.

Casey felt her frustration beginning to burn a hole in her stomach. She wanted to grab Patsy by the shoulders, shake some common sense into her. *Sure. Like I'm in any position to judge. It took a coma to wake me up.*

"You're doing everything humanly possible," Patsy told him.

"But it's not enough, is it? It's never enough."

"Don't do this to yourself, Warren," Patsy urged.

"I feel like such a failure."

"You're not a failure. You're the best man I know."

And suddenly the room fell silent, and Casey could see even without the benefit of sight that their positions had reversed, that *Patsy* was now the one in *Warren's* arms, and that his lips were pressing down tenderly against hers.

"Oh, God, I'm sorry," Warren apologized immediately, pulling back. "I'm so sorry. Please forgive me."

"It's all right," Patsy rushed to assure him.

"It's *not* all right. I don't know what came over me."

"It's okay. I understand."

"How could I do something like that?"

"Nothing happened, Warren."

"I've put you in an untenable position. I'll understand completely if you want to leave."

"I'm not going anywhere."

"I had no right."

"You were upset. You've been beside yourself with worry."

"That's no excuse."

"It's okay," Patsy said again. "It was my fault as much as yours."

Another silence. Then Warren's voice: "You're so sweet. Casey's lucky to have you. We're both lucky," he added.

Casey felt a slow smile creep along Patsy's moonlit face. "How about I go make that hot chocolate now?"

How about you go jump off a pier and drown?

"I think I should just get some sleep," Warren said, walking to the door. "Clearly, I'm not thinking straight."

"I'll see you in the morning," Patsy said, following after him.

"I'm really so sorry. . . ."

"About what?" Patsy asked, as if she genuinely had no idea.

"Thank you."

"Good night, Warren."

"Good night, Patsy."

Seconds later, Casey heard the doors to Warren's and Patsy's respective rooms close. Seconds after that, she felt a stirring in her fingers and realized her hands were curled into small fists at her sides.

23

" '*Dorothea, feeling very weary, rang and asked Tantripp to bring her some wraps. She had been sitting still for a few minutes, but not in any renewal of the former conflict: she simply felt that she was going to say "Yes" to her own doom: she was too weak, too full of dread at the thought of inflicting a keen-edged blow on her husband, to do anything but submit completely. She sat still and let Tantripp put on her bonnet and shawl, a passivity which was unusual with her. . . .*' "

"Okay," Janine said, interrupting her own reading. "That's all I can take for one day. I'm afraid poor Dorothea's passivity is starting to get on my nerves. So, how about we shift our attention to something a little more forceful, such as the current issue of *Vogue*, which I just happen to have brought along." The shuffling of objects, the turning of pages. "Did you know that the hippie look—God, how awful—is making a comeback for autumn? Autumn! Can you imagine? It's barely summer, and already they're talking about next fall. I can't stand it." She lowered the magazine to the bed, her hand grazing Casey's.

Slowly, carefully, Casey stretched her fingers toward Janine's.

"We have a visitor," Warren announced, coming into the room.

Immediately Casey's fingers retreated. Had he seen them? Had Janine?

"Detective Spinetti," Janine said, her surprise evident in her voice.

Detective Spinetti? Thank God you're here.

"Ms. Pegabo," the detective replied. "Nice to see you again."

Did Drew call you? Is that why you've come?

"Have there been any new developments?"

"No, I'm afraid not."

Oh, but you're wrong. There have been all sorts of developments. There's so much I have to tell you.

"Whatever happened with Richard Mooney?" Janine asked.

"The doorman at his mother's building corroborated his alibi. He remembered seeing him at around the time of Casey's accident, so . . ."

"Casey's *accident*?" Warren stressed.

But it wasn't an accident. It wasn't.

"We're still not completely satisfied . . ."

I'm telling you it was no accident!

". . . but we have no proof it was anything else."

"You never found the SUV that hit her?" Janine asked.

"We're still looking. But realistically, it's probably scrap metal by now."

"And I take it there are no new suspects?" Warren stated.

"I'm afraid not."

What about the old *suspects? What about the man standing right in front of you?*

"We're still keeping our eyes open."

No, you're not. You're staring right at the person who orches-

trated this, and you don't see him at all. Was everyone as blind as
Dorothea? Could no one see what was "quite plain"?

"Please don't get the impression we're dropping the case.
We're not. Sometimes these things just take time, and we have to
be patient, hope for a break."

"So, why *are* you here, Detective?" Warren asked.

"I heard Mrs. Marshall was out of the hospital, and I thought
I'd drop by to see how she was doing."

"Well, that was very thoughtful," Warren said, managing to
sound as if he meant it. "As you can see, there's been no real
change."

On the contrary, there's been plenty of change. Look at me, De-
tective Spinetti. Look at me.

"How are you managing?"

"We're doing okay. We've had a few scares regarding Casey's
blood pressure. She's obviously still very fragile."

I'm not fragile. Grab my hand, Detective Spinetti. I'll show you
how fragile I am.

"But Casey's being well looked after. She has a nurse and a
therapist, plus her friends stop by almost every day."

"And her sister?"

"What about her?"

"Has she been here lately?"

"Yes. Why?"

"Just asking."

You're asking about the wrong person. Drew had nothing to do
with this.

"Well, I just wanted to stop by, pay my respects."

"I appreciate everything you've done, Detective."

No, don't leave. Look at me. Grab my hand.

"I can show Detective Spinetti out," Patsy said.

How long had Patsy been standing there? Casey wondered, the
scent of lavender suddenly tickling her nose.

"Good luck, Casey," Detective Spinetti said.

Grab my hand. Please, grab my hand.

His fingers grazed hers, and she felt her body stir.

"Good-bye, Detective," Janine said.

"Ms. Pegabo, Mr. Marshall," Detective Spinetti said, withdrawing his hand, then quickly exiting the room.

No! Come back. Come back.

"What was that all about?" Janine asked as the downstairs door opened and closed.

"I don't know."

"It sounded like he still considers Drew a suspect."

"It did, didn't it?" Warren agreed, barely able to mask the note of satisfaction in his voice.

"What do you think?"

"I don't know what to think anymore." Warren released a long, deep breath. "So, how are things at work? Doesn't seem as if you've been spending much time there."

"No. I've kind of let things slide."

"Nobody expects you to visit every day, you know."

"I know."

Another sigh, followed by a prolonged pause.

"You have nothing to feel guilty about," he said.

"Who says I feel guilty?"

"Don't you?"

"Do you?"

What are you talking about?

"Life's too short for regrets," Warren said, as the smell of lavender returned.

Regret what? Feel guilty about what?

"Can I get anyone anything?" Patsy asked. "Some coffee or maybe some herbal tea?"

"I thought you had a housekeeper for that sort of thing," Janine remarked.

"She doesn't work weekends."

"But Patsy does?"

"For the time being."

"I'm happy to be of help," Patsy said.

"A regular little Saint Theresa," Janine said.

"Who?"

"Nothing."

The doorbell rang.

"I'll get it," Patsy said.

"Busy morning," Janine remarked.

Seconds later, the front door opened, and a child's high-pitched voice raced up the stairs. "Auntie Casey! I'm here!"

"More fun and games," Warren said.

A loud clumping on the stairs, followed by a series of gleeful shouts. "Auntie Casey, wait till you see what I made for you."

"Easy there, Lola," Warren cautioned as the little girl bounded into the room.

Casey pictured her niece in a frilly white dress with a pink bow in her long, fine hair, although in all likelihood she was wearing shorts and a T-shirt, her hair pulled into a high ponytail, looking just like her mother had at that age.

"I painted a picture for Auntie Casey. Do you want to see it?"

"I sure would," Warren said. "Wow. What is it?"

"It's a zebra."

"I thought zebras were black and white."

"This is a special zebra. It's black and white and orange and red."

"It's very beautiful," Janine said. "I'm sure your aunt Casey will love it."

"Can I show it to her?" Casey felt the child's body bang up against the side of the bed.

"She can't see anything right now, sweetheart," Warren explained. "But how about I tape it to the wall, right here, and that way she'll see it as soon as she wakes up."

"Okay."

"I'll go get the tape."

"Don't leave on my account," Drew told him, entering the room.

"I'll be right back."

"He's getting some tape for my picture," Lola explained as she climbed onto the bed, arranging herself at Casey's feet.

Casey felt a stirring in her toes.

"Hi, Janine," Drew said. "Nice to see you again."

"You just missed Detective Spinetti."

"Really? What was he doing here?"

"Apparently he just wanted to see how Casey was doing."

Drew approached the bed, touched her sister's thigh. "Interesting. And how *is* she doing?" She withdrew her hand just as Casey began flexing her right ankle.

"About the same."

"Still reading her that book?"

"It's the gift that keeps on giving."

Drew laughed. Casey began wiggling her toes beneath her blanket.

Look at my feet, Drew. Please, look at my feet.

"I have a book, too," Lola said. "Where's my book, Mommy?"

"It's in my purse somewhere. Purses are so damn big these days, you can pretty well put your whole life in them. Trouble is, they're so heavy, they kill your shoulders. Omigod. . . ."

Did you see that? Did you see my toes moving?

"Are my eyes deceiving me?" Drew asked. "Is that really the new *Vogue*?"

"Hot off the press."

"I didn't realize it was out yet. Can I see it?"

Look at me, for God's sake.

"Careful. It's almost as heavy as your purse."

"I want my book," Lola demanded.

"Sorry, Lola. It looks like I forgot to bring it. Can't you just wing it?"

"What's 'wing it'?"

"Make something up," Drew advised, plopping down into a nearby chair and starting to flip through the pages of *Vogue*. "Oh, great. The hippie look is coming back again. I love that."

"Okay, I'll wing it." Lola giggled. "Since Auntie Casey's still asleep, I'll tell her the story of Sleeping Beauty."

"How very appropriate," Janine said.

"Once upon a time," Lola began, "there was a king and a queen who loved each other very much. Right, Mommy?"

"What?"

"You aren't listening."

"Mommy's reading her magazine. But Auntie Casey is listening, and that's what's important. Go on. Tell her the story."

"The king and queen just had a baby, so they decided to throw a big celebration," Lola continued, her voice becoming increasingly animated as she recited the story from memory. "And they invited all the people in the kingdom, and all the fairies came. Except the king forgot to invite one of the fairies, and she was so mad, she crashed the party, and when it was her turn to give the baby a blessing, she gave her a curse instead. She said that when the princess was sixteen years old, she would prick her finger on a spinning wheel and die. That was a very mean thing to do, wasn't it, Mommy?"

"It certainly was," Janine answered when Drew failed to respond.

"But luckily," Lola continued, tripping over the big word, "one of the good fairies was able to change the bad fairy's curse, so that the princess wouldn't die. She'd just fall asleep for a hundred years."

"Look what I found," Warren said, reentering the room. "Some magic tape."

"Is it really magic?" Lola asked, her voice full of wonder.

"Well, I guess we'll find out. Let me have your picture."

"Can we put it right next to Auntie Casey's head?"

"We can put it close. How about right here?"

"That's good. Do you think she'll like it?"

"I think she'll love it," Warren said.

"Lola's been entertaining us with the story of Sleeping Beauty," Janine said.

"Mommy forgot to bring my book, so I'm winging it," Lola clarified.

The doorbell rang again.

"I'll get it," Patsy called up the stairs.

"So helpful," Janine said.

"So, in hopes of warding off the evil spell," Lola recited from memory, picking up the threads of her story as if there'd been no interruptions. "What's 'warding off'?"

"Preventing," Janine explained. "Making sure it doesn't happen."

"Oh. Okay. So, in hopes of warding off the evil spell," Lola repeated, "the king had all the spinning wheels in the land destroyed. But he missed one."

"First he forgot to invite one of the fairies, then he missed one of the spinning wheels. That's one careless king," Janine remarked.

"Hi, everyone," Gail said from the doorway.

"Hi, stranger," Janine said pointedly. "She's so busy with her new boyfriend, I don't get to see her anymore."

"That's not true," Gail demurred with a shy giggle. "How's Casey?"

"Pretty good," Warren said. "You remember Casey's sister, don't you?"

"Of course. How are you, Drew?"

"Fine. Catching up on the latest fashion." Casey pictured her lifting up the magazine for Gail's perusal.

"I'm Lola," Drew's daughter announced.

"Very nice to meet you, Lola. You look just like your mother."

"I'm telling Auntie Casey the story of Sleeping Beauty."

"What a good idea."

"I'm at the part where the baby grows into a beautiful princess," Lola elaborated. "And how on her sixteenth birthday, she found a little room hidden at the top of the stairs, and there sat a spinning wheel."

"And then what happened?" Gail asked, managing to sound genuinely curious.

"Well, she didn't know what it was, so she walked closer and closer and held out her hand, and then . . . she touched it."

"Oh, no."

"And sure enough, she pricked her finger and fell to the floor, fast asleep."

Casey felt the toes of both her feet curl under to grip at the bedsheet. She began moving them back and forth.

"And then the king and queen fell fast asleep, and then the servants, and all the people in the kingdom. And vines started growing on the castle walls, until soon there were so many vines that nobody could get through. And a hundred years passed and . . . Hey!"

"What's the matter, sweetheart?" Warren asked.

"Auntie Casey poked me."

Oh my God.

"What?" three voices asked in unison, everyone catapulting toward the bed as Casey held her breath.

"Where did she poke you?" Warren asked.

"On my bum," Lola said.

Lola was quickly lifted off the bed and Casey's blanket pushed aside.

"She grabbed my hand yesterday," Drew said.

"She did?" Janine and Gail asked simultaneously.

"It was probably just a muscle spasm," Warren said.

"Casey," Drew urged, "if you can hear us, wiggle your toes."

Casey didn't know what to do. More important, what would Warren do when he realized she was getting better? She was still weeks, probably months away from recovering full use of her limbs. If Warren knew she was starting to regain control of her muscles, that she was on the verge of being able to communicate, would that speed up his plans, make her a sitting duck? She needed time—time to grow stronger, time to decide what to do.

"Can you hear us, Casey?" Drew asked. "Wiggle your toes."

Sorry, Drew. I can't take that chance. Not yet. Not while he's around.

"Nothing," Warren said after several seconds.

"You sure you didn't just sit on her toes?" Drew asked her daughter accusingly.

"I don't know," Lola admitted, her voice a whine. "Maybe."

"Casey, can you wiggle your toes for us?" Janine asked.

"Still nothing," Gail said after another ten seconds had passed.

"You know what I think?" Warren asked, returning the blanket to Casey's feet. "I think this would be a good time to break for milk and cookies. What do you think, Lola?"

"What kind of cookies?"

"Peanut butter crunch."

"They're my favorite."

"I thought they might be. Why don't we go downstairs and ask Patsy to get you some."

"Why don't you bring a few back up here," Drew suggested, returning to her seat.

"Nice to see your sister's condition hasn't interfered with your appetite," Warren said, leading Lola from the room.

Casey breathed a deep sigh of relief. She had to be more careful. She had to find a way of telling the others about her progress without alerting Warren.

"So, what's going on with you?" Janine asked her friend. "How are things going with Stan the man?"

"Good," Gail said shyly. "Everything's good."

"When am I going to meet him?"

"Soon."

"She's been saying that for weeks now," Janine told Drew. "Wouldn't even tell me his name until a few days ago. I'm not convinced this guy even exists."

"He exists," Gail said, a nervous giggle bracketing her words.

"Prove it."

"I don't have to prove anything."

"Let's all have dinner together next Saturday. You too, Drew."

"I can't," Gail said quickly.

"Why not?"

"I'll be away next weekend."

"What do you mean, you'll be away? You never go anywhere."

"I'm going away next weekend."

"With Stan?"

Gail's breath trembled into the air. "Yes."

"I don't believe it. How long have you been sleeping with him? Is he any good?"

"Will you just listen to her," Gail said, embarrassed laughter replacing the nervous giggle.

"Is he?" Drew asked.

"God, you two . . ."

"Well?"

"I don't know," Gail answered. "I haven't . . . we haven't . . ."

"Oh, I can't stand it," Janine snapped. "What are you waiting for?"

"Next weekend?" came Gail's response.

This time everybody laughed.

Later, after everyone had left, Warren returned to Casey's bedside. "Busy day," he commented, once again pulling back the blanket from her feet. "You must be exhausted. All that excitement. All that exertion."

Casey felt his fingers tickle the underside of her foot, her foot reflexively withdrawing from his touch.

"So, tell me, Sleeping Beauty. Was that just another involuntary muscle spasm?" He squeezed her toes, hard, before replacing her blanket. "Too bad Detective Spinetti missed all the excitement."

He'll be back. You won't fool him forever.

"You aren't fooling me, you know," he said. "I know you're getting better. I know you understand every word I say. Just like I know you aren't really asleep. Beauty never sleeps, does she?" he asked, kissing her forehead.

His words remained in the room long after he'd left.

Beauty never sleeps, the walls whispered. Beauty never sleeps.

24

"WELL, WELL," PATSY TRILLED, entering the room and circling the bed, pulling the covers from Casey's body in one continuous swoop. "How are we feeling today? Did we sleep well?"

We didn't sleep at all, Casey thought, feeling the young woman tugging on her blankets and top sheet, until she succeeded in freeing them from the mattress. Cold, conditioned air immediately wrapped itself around Casey's bare legs, and Casey shivered, although she doubted this was visible, or that Patsy would have noticed even if it were.

"It's Monday," Patsy announced cheerily. "Which means it's laundry day, according to Mrs. Singer. Not that that's my job, but considerate employee that I am, I told the old bag I'd get your sheets for her. Although to get at that bottom sheet, looks like we'll have to get you out of that bed and into this chair." She sighed, as if exhausted by the mere thought. "Think I'll wait for Warren to give me a hand with that." Another sigh, this one decidedly more lusty than tired. "He's just finishing up in the shower right now, getting all nice and clean after his workout. So dedicated, that husband of yours. Up at six o'clock, out of here by seven to go to the gym. Back by eight thirty, ready to start the day. Did I tell you he brought me a cappuccino from Starbucks? So considerate, that husband of yours. Anyway, I'm in a good mood," Patsy continued. "Which is lucky for you because normally I hate Mondays. And I hate doing laundry. Especially somebody else's. Let's get that pillowcase." Without further warning, she pulled the king-size pillow out from behind Casey's head, letting Casey's neck snap back toward the mattress, unsupported. Casey lay prone on the bed, wondering if Patsy was going to try to whip the bottom sheet right out from under her, as if it were a tablecloth and Patsy a magician. Which made Casey . . . what exactly?

A place setting? A bowl of fruit?

Still life, she thought. That's all I am.

Except no longer quite so still, she thought, feeling a renewed surge of excitement, and fighting the impulse to stretch her fingers and curl her toes, lest Patsy was paying closer attention than she suspected. The less Patsy knew the better, Casey had decided in the hours she'd lain awake after Warren had left her bedside, hours she spent taking stock of her situation and trying to figure out what she could do.

Could she do anything?

She had no doubts her senses were returning and growing stronger every day. She could hear; she could smell; she could tell the difference between hot and cold, hard and soft; she could distinguish between Patsy's indifferent touch and Gail's caring caress; she could identify the artful gentleness of Warren's lips as they brushed across her forehead; she could recognize the underlying harshness of his intent behind the superficial kindness of his words.

And now she could stretch her fingers and wiggle her toes. She could form fists and rotate her ankles. In another week, she might be able to lift her hands above her head. A few days after that, she might be able to swing her feet out of bed. She might even be able to walk, and then to see, to speak.

To tell everyone what had really happened.

I am woman, she thought, recalling the words of the old Helen Reddy song. Hear me roar.

Did Patsy know that one?

Casey took a series of invisible deep breaths, trying to calm her growing optimism, to prevent her hopes from getting too far ahead of her reality. It was entirely possible that she had already made whatever progress she was going to, she reminded herself, that she might never walk again, or see, or find her voice, that she would be trapped this way until her dying breath, that no one would ever know the truth.

No, she wouldn't believe that. Couldn't believe it.

Every day brought some improvement, sometimes big, sometimes small, but always significant. She was gradually being returned to the body she'd been so violently torn from, to the woman she'd abandoned, however unwillingly.

To herself.

Would she even recognize her when she found her again?

And would she find her in time to save her?

Casey heard footsteps approaching from down the hall.

"What are you doing?" Warren asked, entering the room, bringing with him an assortment of shower smells—soap, shampoo, talcum powder.

Casey froze. Had her thoughts betrayed her? Had she been clenching her fingers, wiggling her toes? Was her brow even now furrowed in concentration, her mouth open in anticipation, as if about to say "Please. You don't have to do this."

"You don't have to do that," Warren said, usurping her words.

"Oh, it's no problem," Patsy assured him, as Casey breathed an inaudible sigh of relief. "I thought it might be too much for Mrs. Singer. She's not as young as I am."

Not as young as you are. Good one, Patsy. You spry little thing.

"It's really not necessary."

"Nonsense. Casey's my responsibility. I want to do it."

"Thank you."

"Thank *you* for the cappuccino."

"I didn't add too much cinnamon?"

"No way. It was perfect."

"Good. Do you need some help with that?"

Casey wondered if he was referring to her or the bedsheets. Had she become a "that"?

"No, but I will need some help getting your wife into the chair."

"I'll do it."

Casey felt his strong arms immediately reach beneath her torso to grip her waist and the underside of her knees.

"Careful," Patsy cautioned as Warren scooped her into the air. "Don't strain yourself."

"I'm used to lifting much heavier weights than this," Warren said.

So now she was a "this."

A this and a that. Casey laughed, although no sound emerged.

Warren suddenly loosened his grip on her waist, so that her body slipped back toward the bed.

"Something wrong?" Patsy asked. "Did you hurt yourself?"

"I thought I felt Casey . . . No. It's too crazy."

"What is?"

"No," Warren said again.

"What?" Patsy pressed.

A slight pause, then, "There was this slight rumble. It was almost, I don't know, as if Casey was laughing."

"Laughing?"

You felt that? My God, you felt that?

"What could she possibly have to laugh about?" Patsy wondered out loud.

"I said it was crazy."

"It was probably just her stomach," Patsy said.

"Probably." Warren tightened his grip on Casey's waist. "Or my imagination."

What did it mean? Casey wondered. Did the fact that Warren had been able to detect the laughter stirring inside her mean anything? Did it signify she was closer to actually laughing out loud?

"We should probably change her nightgown while we're at it," Patsy said.

She listened as Patsy rifled through the top drawer of her dresser, like a thief in the night. She felt her muscles tense with indignation and wondered if Warren could feel it, too.

She'd have to be so careful. At any second, her body—already a foreign object—could betray her without warning.

"Here's a pretty one. What do you think, Casey? In a 'blue' mood today?"

Warren deposited Casey gently in the chair beside her bed, carefully arranging a series of pillows around her, to make sure her body was fully supported on all sides so that she didn't fall over. It feels like the striped chair, Casey thought, adjusting to its contours as her arms were lifted over her head and whatever nightgown she'd been wearing was pulled up and off.

Leaving her naked, except for her diaper, Casey realized. In front of her husband and his soon-to-be lover.

A wave of revulsion washed over her as she felt Patsy's eyes travel across her body. Was Warren looking at her, too? she wondered, mentally covering her torso with her hands, trying to shield herself from their critical gaze.

"Would you like a sponge bath?" Patsy asked so sweetly that Casey wasn't sure if she was addressing her or her husband.

The thought of this woman's hands touching her while her husband watched, making Casey a part of their perverse, mutual seduction, was just too horrible to contemplate.

"I don't think there's enough time for that now," Warren said. "Jeremy should be here any minute."

"Assuming he isn't late again."

Casey felt a fresh nightgown being quickly lowered over her head, and her arms pushed through its appropriate holes. She felt the silk slither across her breasts and over her stomach and knees, then drop, like a parachute, toward the floor.

"You don't sound like you're overly fond of him," Warren commented.

"He's a little cocky for my taste."

"You don't like cocky?"

Casey tried not to picture the twinkle in Warren's eyes, or the corresponding one in Patsy's.

"Depends," Patsy said with a laugh, the doorbell ringing as she pulled the bottom sheet off Casey's bed. "Speaking of the devil. . . . And what do you know? He's right on time. I'll take these sheets down to Mrs. Singer."

"If you don't mind sending Jeremy up . . ."

"It would be my pleasure."

Casey pictured Patsy's pronounced sway as she sashayed from the room.

"She's a surprisingly good kisser," Warren confided as soon as she was gone. "How long do you think I should wait before I sleep with her? A week? A month? How much time would you consider appropriate for a man in my position?"

Why are you saying these things to me? Are you so convinced of your own invincibility that you no longer worry about voicing such sentiments out loud? Are you so sure I won't be around to expose you?

"I guess I really shouldn't be talking to you about these things," he continued, as if directly addressing her concerns. "Just that I suspect you've already heard the worst, and I've kind of gotten used to using you as a sounding board."

The front door opened and closed.

"Casey?" her sister's voice called up from the foyer.

Drew!

"Crap," Warren said. "What's she doing here?"

"Casey," Drew shouted again, racing up the stairs and into the room. "Omigod, look at you! Sitting up in a chair. Wow. You look great. Look, Jeremy, she's sitting up in the chair."

"Jeremy?" Warren asked as the therapist followed Drew into the room. "Well, isn't this cozy. You two come together?"

"We pulled up at the same time," Jeremy explained.

"How convenient."

"What's that supposed to mean?" Drew asked.

"Just that I'm surprised to see you back so soon, Drew. You're usually not so . . . constant."

"Hmm . . . constant. Don't think I've ever been called that before. I think I like it." Drew dropped to her knees in front of her sister. "Look at you. You look so pretty. Although your hair's a bit of a mess. Doesn't anybody ever comb it? Where's her brush?"

"Patsy can take care of her hair later."

"I'm sure Patsy has lots of other things she'd rather take care of," Drew said. "Besides, I want to do it. Casey used to brush my hair all the time when we were kids, so I know just how she likes it."

"Here's the brush," Jeremy offered.

Casey didn't have to see the expression on her husband's face to know he wasn't happy. She felt the straightening of his shoulders, the stiffening of his spine, the tightening of his jaw from across the room, as Drew positioned herself behind Casey and gathered Casey's long, silky hair into her hands.

"Casey always had such beautiful hair. I'm glad they didn't have to hack it all off. Just that little bit over here," she said, patting the shaved patch on Casey's scalp, "and it's starting to grow back nicely. Although it could use a touch-up," she whispered in Casey's ear. "Maybe next time I come, I'll bring some coloring, fix up these roots. What—you thought she was a natural blond?" she asked, obviously in response to a look Warren was giving her.

"I think there are more pressing concerns than Casey's roots."

"Clearly you have no understanding of women."

"I understand we should get out of here and let Jeremy get to work."

"I'm not in your way. Am I, Jeremy?"

"Drew . . ."

"That's all right. She really isn't," Jeremy said.

"In that case, you don't mind if I stay, too," Warren said.

"Not at all."

"The more the merrier," Drew said, running the brush delicately but firmly through Casey's hair. "She actually is a natural blond," Drew explained, as Jeremy pulled up a chair in front of Casey and began massaging her fingers. "Until she was about twelve, her hair was like spun gold. Daddy's golden girl, he used to call her. Remember that, Casey? Remember how Daddy used to call you his golden girl?"

I remember, Casey thought, breathing in echoes of the past, finding them surprisingly close at hand, and understanding they'd never strayed too far away.

"Even after her hair started getting darker, he still called her his golden girl."

"I'm sure he had a few choice adjectives for you as well," Warren said.

Drew laughed. "Yeah, you're certainly right about that." Her hands continued expertly drawing the brush through Casey's hair.

That feels wonderful, Casey thought, as the soft bristles of the brush gently scraped across her scalp like hundreds of tiny fingers. She felt each hair being stretched and separated, then stretched and separated again, and again, with each successive stroke. At the same time, Jeremy was manipulating her fingers and wrists and massaging the muscles of her forearms. It feels so good, Casey thought, giving herself over to the mixture of pleasant sensations, her eyes closing in relaxation.

"She closed her eyes," Warren said.

What?

"Now they're open again."

Casey felt her husband inch closer until they were practically nose to nose, his breath brushing against her lips, like a lover's first tentative kiss.

"It's just a reflex action," Jeremy said. "It doesn't mean anything."

"So everyone keeps saying."

"Certain bodily functions are automatic. I'm sure her doctors have explained that Casey has no control over—"

"What if she does?" Warren asked, cutting him off.

"What do you mean?" Drew stopped brushing Casey's hair, dropped to her knees at Casey's side, a protective hand on Casey's arm. "You think Casey has control? You think she's trying to tell us something? Is that what you're trying to do, Casey? Are you trying to tell us something? Casey, can you hear me? Blink once for yes."

Casey kept her eyes resolutely still. Could she blink, even if she wanted to?

"Nothing," Drew said, the sadness clearly audible in her voice.

The phone rang. Seconds later, Patsy appeared in the doorway. "It's for you, Mr. Marshall. He says it's very important."

"I'll take it in my office." Warren stood up, walked to the door. "I'll be back in a few minutes."

"Take your time," Drew called after him, taking Casey's hand in hers.

Casey listened as Patsy followed Warren down the stairs.

"Something's a little off with him," Drew said, not quite under her breath.

"What do you mean?" Jeremy asked.

"I can't put my finger on it exactly. He's just gotten a little too comfortable as lord of the manor, if you know what I mean."

"I'm not sure I do."

"I know he's dealing with a lot of things—Casey, his practice, me. And I know I don't always respond well to crises, that I haven't been a whole lot of help. . . ."

"On the contrary. I find you extremely helpful."

"Really?"

"Don't sell yourself short, Drew."

"Thank you," Drew said, then burst into tears.

"Hey, there," Jeremy said. "What's happening?"

"I'm sorry," Drew cried. "I guess I'm just not used to people being so nice to me."

Oh, Drew.

"Wait. I'll get you a tissue." Jeremy got to his feet, crossing quickly over to the en suite bathroom.

"I'm sorry," Drew apologized again, inadvertently squeezing Casey's hand.

Slowly, deliberately, using all the strength she could muster, Casey squeezed back.

25

"OH MY GOD," DREW exclaimed, as Casey felt Drew's head snap toward hers. Drew jumped to her feet, although her hand remained wrapped around her sister's. "Jeremy!"

Casey squeezed her sister's fingers a second time, this time even harder than the first. The squeeze said *No! You can't tell him. You can't tell anyone.*

"Something wrong?" Jeremy asked from the bathroom doorway.

Casey squeezed a third time. *Please don't say anything. He'll tell Warren. This is important, Drew. You mustn't say anything to anyone. Not yet. Not until I find a way to tell you what's happened.*

"Did you find a Kleenex?" Drew asked, as if she somehow understood.

Oh, thank you. Thank you.

"Got a handful right here." Jeremy quickly returned to her side. "What's the matter? You're looking a little pale. Are you okay?"

"I don't know. I got a little dizzy for a few seconds there."

"You better sit down."

"I'm fine now. Really."

"Don't argue. Come on."

Drew reluctantly relinquished her grip on Casey's hand, which immediately slid into her lap. Casey heard Jeremy pull up a chair, pictured Drew sinking down inside it, her eyes never leaving Casey.

"Take a few deep breaths," Jeremy instructed, and Drew complied. "Can I get you anything? Some water? Maybe some tea?"

Yes, let him get you some tea.

"Tea sounds wonderful."

"I'll be right back."

"Thank you." As soon as he was gone, Drew was back at Casey's side. She grabbed her sister's hand, positioned her fingers underneath Casey's. "Okay, that was no accident. You're here, aren't you? You can understand me."

Casey squeezed her sister's fingers. *Yes, I'm here,* the squeeze said. *Yes, I can understand you.*

"Okay, okay, okay," Drew muttered, her breath hitting the air in a series of shallow bursts. "This is amazing. I don't believe this. I don't know what to do."

Casey squeezed Drew's hand again, urging her to calm down.

"Okay, okay. You're in there, and you can hear me, and you understand what's going on, but for some reason, you don't want me to tell Jeremy. Is that right?"

Another squeeze.

"Okay. I'm gonna assume that means yes. Why don't you want me to tell Jeremy? No, way too complicated. That won't work. Do you want me to tell Warren? What am I saying? Of course you want me to tell Warren."

Casey squeezed Drew's fingers as hard as she could. *No, don't tell Warren. Whatever you do, don't tell Warren.*

"Okay, I'm not sure what that means exactly. Are you saying you don't want me to tell him or you do?"

Casey squeezed several times in rapid succession. *No. Don't tell him. Don't tell him.*

"Okay, this isn't working. We need a system. Can you blink? That might be easier. Blink once for yes, twice for no."

Casey transferred all her energy to her eyelids. *Blink,* she told them. *Blink.*

"Nothing's happening."

Blink, damn you.

"Okay, we'll go back to squeezing," Drew said. "Squeeze once for yes, twice for no. Do you want me to tell Warren?"

Casey squeezed once, then tried a second time, but her fingers refused to cooperate.

Oh, God. Oh, God. Would Drew think she meant yes when she meant no?

"Sorry, I couldn't tell whether that was once or twice. Can you try it again?"

Thank God. Yes, I'll try again.

"Can you try what again?" Warren asked suddenly from the door.

Oh, no. How much had he seen?

Instantly, Drew released Casey's hand. "Oh my God, Warren! You scared me half to death. I didn't see you there."

Don't tell him. Please don't tell him.

Warren entered the room. "Where's Jeremy?"

"He went downstairs to get me some tea."

"I didn't realize that was part of his job description."

"I got a little dizzy."

"I see. And that clearly trumps my wife's coma."

"Jeremy was just being kind."

"I believe I'm paying him to be kind to Casey."

"Don't be angry at Jeremy, Warren. He's a nice guy. He didn't do anything wrong."

"Suppose you let me be the judge of that. And if you're dizzy, perhaps you should go home and lie down."

"That's all right. I'm starting to feel better."

"Interesting. Try what again?"

"What?"

"When I got here, you were asking Casey to try something again."

Slow down, Drew. Don't let him bamboozle you.

"I was?" Drew cleared her throat once, then again. "Oh, that. It was nothing. I was just thinking out loud, asking Casey whether or not she thought I should give Sean another chance. You remember Sean? You met him at the hospital. Anyway, he's been calling lately, asking me to give our relationship another try."

"Really? And what was Casey's advice?"

A long pause.

"She thinks I should err on the side of caution."

Bravo, Drew.

"Well, that would certainly be a first for you, wouldn't it?"

Drew laughed. "It just might."

"Although I'm not sure I agree," Warren said.

"What do you mean?"

"I mean that caution might not be the best way to go here. Sean struck me as a pretty nice guy. He might be worth another shot."

"You think so?"

"Well, things have been pretty tense around here since Casey's accident. Not exactly conducive to a successful romance."

"I guess not."

"It might even be a good idea for you and Sean to think about getting away for a couple of weeks. Maybe take a nice, romantic cruise."

"A cruise? Now? With my sister in a coma?"

"It wouldn't be the first time, Drew," he reminded her.

"It's different now."

"How so?"

"I think Casey needs me. I think she wants me here."

"Why would you think that?"

"It's just a feeling I get sometimes."

"Casey wants you to be healthy and happy," Warren told her. "I'm sure she'd understand."

"You really think so?"

"I know so."

Jeremy reentered the room. The aroma of blueberry-flavored tea wafted toward Casey's nose.

"Unless, of course, there's something else keeping you here," Warren said.

"Careful," Jeremy warned. "It's hot."

"Thank you," Drew said.

"Feeling any better?" Jeremy asked.

"Drew's fine," Warren answered in Drew's stead. "My wife, on the other hand, is feeling a tad neglected."

Jeremy immediately sat down, lifting one of Casey's legs into his lap and gently rotating her ankle. "Well, we'll try to rectify that right now." He worked for several seconds in concentrated silence.

"Maybe we should ask Jeremy what he thinks," Warren said.

"Thinks about what?" Jeremy asked.

"One of Drew's ex-boyfriends is after her to give their relationship another shot. I think he's a pretty decent guy. Certainly better than most of the lowlifes she's been involved with. So, I think she should go for it. What do you think?"

Casey felt a sudden tensing in the pressure of Jeremy's hand. "I think Drew is the only person who can make that type of decision," he said evenly.

"Yeah, well, that's the problem. Drew's never been very good at deductive reasoning. She rarely knows what's good for her. Do you, Drew?"

"I'm learning."

Warren laughed. "Anyway, I think it would be a good idea if she got away for a while. She's feeling weak enough that you saw fit to abandon my wife in order to fetch her a cup of tea, and we wouldn't want her coming down with anything, possibly transferring any of those nasty viruses going around to Casey."

"I'm not coming down with anything."

"Lola's at that age where she's in contact with lots of other kids, all of them seething little incubators of disease. Where is your daughter, by the way?"

"At school," Drew told him. "Just one more week of classes."

"And then what? Ship her off to sleepaway camp, like you did last year? Most parents don't like to send their kids off so young. Not Drew. Lola was the youngest camper in the history of Camp Arrowroot," he told Jeremy.

"Arrow*head*," Drew corrected. "And no, she won't be going back there this year. Actually," she continued brightly, "I was thinking the two of us might move in here with you for the summer. How would you like that?"

This time it was Jeremy who laughed.

"Something funny?" Warren asked.

Jeremy said nothing as he switched to Casey's other leg.

"I think that's enough therapy for today," Warren announced abruptly.

"We've just started," Jeremy told him.

"On the contrary, I think your work is finished here."

"I'm not sure I understand."

"I think you understand perfectly."

"You're firing me?" Jeremy asked.

"That's ridiculous," Drew said.

"This is none of your business, Drew."

"You're firing him because he went to get me some tea?"

"I'm firing him because I didn't hire him to fetch you tea. I hired him to take care of my wife, not to use her condition to get into her sister's pants."

"Hey, wait a minute. . . ." Jeremy said.

"No, you wait a minute. I hired you to do a job, and as far as I can see, you haven't been doing it. You've been late, you're neglectful, you're rude. . . ."

"You're out of line."

"You've got attitude. . . ."

"You're full of shit."

"You're out of my house," Warren said, with infuriating calm.

"This is my house, too," Drew reminded him.

"Stay out of this, Drew."

"My sister is making progress. I want Jeremy to stay."

"Your sister will continue to make progress with someone else. Jeremy goes. Unless, of course, you intend to start paying for his services yourself." Drew didn't respond. "I didn't think so."

"Hey, man, lighten up," Jeremy warned.

"What part of 'you're fired' don't you understand? Now please leave before I'm forced to call the police."

"Warren, for God's sake. This is insane."

"I suggest you go with him, Drew."

"I'm staying right here."

"What—you don't want to exchange phone numbers? Or have you already done that?"

"Go to hell," Drew said.

"Believe me, I'm already there." Warren released a deep breath. "Okay, Jeremy. Time to go."

No, please. Stay.

Silence. Then, "I believe you owe me some money," Jeremy said.

"And it's all about the money, isn't it? Well, then, follow me, Jeremy. I'll write you a check for services rendered."

"Wait . . ." Drew called after them.

"Bye, Drew," came Jeremy's response. "Take care of your sister."

Casey listened as their footsteps retreated down the stairs.

"Jesus. What the hell was that all about?" Drew cried in exasperation.

Okay, Drew. Grab my hand. We don't have a lot of time before Warren gets back.

"Oh, God," Drew exclaimed. "You heard all that, didn't you? You heard what just happened." She took Casey's hand.

Casey squeezed Drew's fingers. Once. Hard.

"Once for yes," Drew said. "Okay. So, what do we do now? Tell me what to do. I don't know what to do."

Casey squeezed Drew's hand, held it tightly until she felt her grip start to grow weak. *You have to calm down,* the grip said. *You have to focus.*

"Okay. So I have to think of simple questions. Questions that can be answered yes or no. What questions? I don't know what questions. Okay. Okay. Think. Think." Drew took a succession of deep breaths. "Okay. First question. You don't want me to tell Warren? No, sorry, forget that. Double negative, right? Too complicated. *Do* you want me to tell Warren? That's better. Do you want me to tell Warren?"

Casey squeezed her sister's hand twice. Had Drew felt it?

"That was twice. So you *don't* want Warren to know. Why not? I mean, granted he's acting a little strange, but he's under a lot of stress. And maybe I *was* flirting with Jeremy. I don't know. You're sure you don't want me to tell him?"

Casey squeezed Drew's hand.

"Why not? What's going on? Oh, shit. That was stupid. Okay, how are we going to do this? How are you going to tell me?"

Casey felt Drew's eyes searching the room for answers.

"All right. All right. This is what we're going to do. We're going to try spelling things out. I saw that once on TV. This guy was paralyzed, but he spelled things out by blinking. Except you can't blink. And this squeezing thing is too confusing. Can you tap? With your finger? Can you tap your finger against my hand?" Drew positioned her hand directly under Casey's fingers.

Casey threw all her concentration into her right index finger. Her mind lifted it into the air, brought it down against the back of her sister's hand. Once. Twice. Three times.

Drew literally squealed. "Great. That's great, Casey. That's so great."

It's working. I can do this.

"Okay. Okay. So, one tap is A, two is B, et cetera, et cetera. Okay. This might take a while, and I don't know how long we've got until Warren comes back, but here goes: Why don't you want him to know?"

Casey tapped twice on Drew's hand.

"A . . . B," Drew said. "B."

Casey tapped five times.

"A . . . B . . . C . . . D . . . E. E," Drew repeated. "Okay, so we have B and E. . . . Be . . . because?"

Casey squeezed Drew's hand with her remaining fingers. Then she tapped eight times for the letter H, followed by five more taps for the letter E.

"H . . . E . . . He? Because he . . . ?"

Because he tried to kill me!

Casey squeezed her sister's hand, then began tapping out the letter T.

"Wait," Drew wailed. "I lost count. We have to do it again. Sorry, Casey." She resumed counting the taps out loud. "A . . . B . . . C . . . D . . . E . . ."

It seemed to take forever until they reached the letter *T*.

"T!" Drew exclaimed, dropping Casey's hand with excitement, then quickly scooping it up again.

Casey began tapping out the letter *R*. Why did all the letters have to come so near the end of the alphabet?

"O . . . P . . . Q . . . R . . . S?"

Casey squeezed twice. *No!*

"Not S?"

The sound of the front door closing reverberated up the stairs, followed immediately by Warren's footsteps on the stairs.

"Shit. We don't have enough time. Is there anybody I can tell about this?"

Was there anyone? Casey wondered. Who could she trust not to tell Warren?

The footsteps were getting closer.

"Warren?" Patsy suddenly called out from downstairs.

The footsteps stopped. "Yes?" he called back.

"Mrs. Singer wants to know if you'd like her to prepare anything special for dinner."

Jeremy. Warren had just fired him. She could certainly trust Jeremy not to tell Warren now.

Casey began furiously tapping on Drew's fingers.

"Wait. We have to do this a different way. How about I say the letters, and you squeeze my hand when I say the right one. Okay? Ready? A . . . B . . . C . . . D . . ."

Faster. Faster.

"Tell her anything she wants to make is fine," Warren called down the stairs.

"H . . . I . . . J . . . J?"

Casey squeezed Drew's fingers.

"Jeremy? Oh, wait. Janine? Which is it, Janine or Jeremy?"

Footsteps on the stairs. Drew let Casey's hand drop.

"Looks like Jeremy has left the building," Warren said, his presence filling the room. "And I think it's time for you to do the same."

"I think I'll stay, if you don't mind."

"I'm afraid I have to insist. I think my wife's had enough excitement for one day."

You don't know the half, Casey thought, knowing Drew was thinking the same thing.

"Okay, I'll go," Drew said, pushing herself off her chair. She leaned in, buried her face in Casey's hair. "Don't worry, Casey," she whispered. "I'll be back soon."

26

"ARE YOU OKAY?"

Patsy's voice was warm, solicitous. Casey knew immediately she wasn't talking to her.

"I don't know," came Warren's response from the chair next to Casey's bed. "It's been a very trying day."

"Can I get you anything? A sandwich, maybe? Some brandy?"

"I don't think so."

"You hardly touched your supper."

"I'm not very hungry."

"Casey's sister really gets under your skin," Patsy remarked.

"Drew's been a selfish mess her entire life, and suddenly she turns into sister of the year. I'm not sure what to make of it."

"Maybe it's just a phase, something she'll get tired of in another couple of weeks."

"I don't know. . . ."

"What is it? You look worried."

"You don't think . . ."

"What?" Patsy repeated.

"You don't think she'd do anything to hurt Casey, do you?"

What?

"What do you mean?"

"No, it's too crazy. Forget I said anything."

"You think Drew had something to do with what happened to Casey?"

"No. Of course not. I mean, the police obviously still consider it a possibility, but . . ."

What are you trying to do here, Warren?

"I can't believe I'm thinking these things, let alone saying them out loud."

Are you trying to set my sister up? Is that what this is about, you bastard?

"At the very least, I think her visits upset Casey," Warren said. "You saw how her blood pressure spiked after Drew left."

"You think there's a connection?"

"I don't know what to think anymore."

Casey pictured her husband burying his face in his hands and tried not to see the slow smile spreading behind his fingers.

"Part of me would like to bar Drew from the house altogether," he continued. "To lock the front door and refuse to let her in, no matter what she says or does. And believe me, sometimes I'm *this* close to doing just that. But she's such a loose cannon, there's no telling how she'd respond. She might slink away with her tail between her legs, or she might make good on her threat to go to the press. Which is the last thing this family needs."

The last thing you *need, you mean.*

"Should you talk to Detective Spinetti about her?"

"And say what? That I'm worried because Drew is actually showing signs of sisterly concern?"

"So, what do we do?"

"We'll just have to be extra vigilant when she's around. Don't let her out of your sight. Make sure she's never alone with Casey. Think you can do that?"

"I'll do my best."

"I know you will. You're the one thing in my life right now I can count on."

Casey felt her fingers stir beneath the covers and concentrated on keeping them still, knowing the slightest twitch would arouse Warren's suspicions. He'd barely left her side since returning her to her freshly made bed, and while someone like Patsy might mistake this steadfastness as concern for her welfare, Casey understood that the only welfare he was concerned about was his own.

"Are you going to report Jeremy to the hospital board?" Patsy asked.

"Report him? No. What's the point? I don't want to get him in trouble."

"You're too nice."

Yeah, right. Mr. Nice Guy.

"I'm not out for blood."

Not his, anyway.

"Have you thought about who you'll get to replace him?" Patsy asked.

"Actually I've already hired someone."

"From the hospital?"

"From my gym," Warren said.

Casey felt her entire body go numb.

"He's dropping by this evening."

What?

What was Warren up to? Had she run out of time already? Was he planning to kill her as early as tonight?

"Should I put some coffee on?" Patsy asked.

"I don't think he's much of a coffee drinker."

"How about some ice cream?"

Warren laughed. "God, you're sweet."

"I just want to help."

"I know you do. And you are, just by being here."

Oh, please. If I had a gag reflex, I'd throw up.

"Look, it's still early," Warren said. "Why don't you take the rest of the night off, go to a movie or something?"

No, don't go. Don't go.

"I'm kind of tired. Think I'll just go to my room, watch some TV, maybe go to bed early."

"Sounds good."

"Just shout if you want anything."

"I will."

Patsy made a show of fluffing up Casey's pillow. The fresh scent of Tide burst like firecrackers around her head. "Good night, Casey. See you in the morning." She walked to the bedroom door. "Good night, Warren."

"Sweet dreams."

"You too."

Casey felt Patsy hovering in the doorway for several seconds before making her exit. So, what happens now? she wondered, hearing her husband pull his chair closer to the bed.

"So, what happens now?" he echoed.

It's your call.

He sat there for at least ten minutes, saying nothing, his eyes burning quarter-size holes in her skin. Was he trying to figure out what to do next, or how best to implement what had already been decided? "How did everything get so complicated?" he asked finally.

The doorbell rang.

"Well, what do you know? Looks like your new therapist has arrived. And unlike your old therapist, he's actually a bit early. Clearly he's eager to get started."

"Do you want me to get that?" Patsy called out.

"No, that's okay," Warren called back. "I'll get it." He touched Casey's arm. "Don't get up," he said before leaving her side.

I *have* to get up, Casey thought as her husband descended the stairs. I have to get out of here. There's no time left.

She projected all her energy into her feet. *Move, damn you. Move.* Miraculously, she felt an almost immediate stirring in her legs and thighs. Her arms stretched to their full length, her hands flexed. Her body was responding. It was gathering its strength, garnering all its reserves, readying itself to propel her out of bed.

And then . . . nothing.

Her back lay prone against the mattress. Her head remained still on her pillow.

She wasn't going anywhere.

What had she been thinking? Even if she'd been able to move, she couldn't see. She couldn't speak. She couldn't scream for help. Besides, who would hear her if she did? Patsy?

Did she really think Patsy would come to her rescue?

Casey heard voices talking softly in the downstairs foyer, followed by the sound of several sets of footsteps on the stairs. "Casey," Warren announced seconds later. "Gail is here to see you."

"How's my girl?" she asked, approaching the bed and kissing Casey on the cheek.

"No real change," Warren said.

"I think she's definitely improving," Gail insisted. "Her color's better than it was even the other day."

"You think so?"

"Don't let the delicate features fool you," Gail said. "Casey's tough. She's been through a lot, and trust me, if she can survive her mother, she can survive anything. Even this. This is nothing compared to Alana, is it, Casey?"

This may actually have my mother beat.

"She'll come through this," Gail pronounced. "Casey's not going to let a little thing like a coma stop her for long. Are you, Casey?" Gail took a deep breath. It trembled upon release, breaking up into little fragments before disappearing. "I feel guilty about going away this weekend. Maybe I shouldn't."

"Where are you off to?" Warren asked.

"Martha's Vineyard. Believe it or not, I've never been."

"You'll love it. It's beautiful."

"So Stan keeps telling me, but . . ."

"But nothing. You'll go and have a good time. It's what Casey would want."

"I'm a little nervous," Gail confided.

"About what?"

"You know," Gail said. "Janine talked me into buying a new nightgown. It's black and slinky, and the bodice is lacy and low-cut. It's really pretty, and it cost a fortune. I think it looks okay. Just that it's a little bit out of my comfort zone, and I really wish Casey was here to advise me."

"If I might offer a little advice in Casey's stead," Warren said gently. "Just be yourself."

"You think that'll be enough?"

"If it isn't, he's a fool who doesn't deserve you."

Gail's grateful sigh filled the room. "Thank you." She leaned over and kissed Casey's cheek. "You picked a good one, Casey," she whispered. "I can see why you're so crazy about him. Anyway, I should go. Bye for now, Casey. I'll see you in a couple of days."

"I'll show you out."

So what do I do now? Casey thought as they left the room, her hands curling into fists. Warren had even her closest friend fooled. He was going to murder her, and he was going to get away with it. There wasn't a damn thing she could do about it.

There had to be somebody who could help her.

Except what could anybody do?

Casey tried bending her knees, feeling every muscle in her legs cramp with the effort. But something had moved, she realized, aware of a slight trembling in her thighs. She tried lifting one foot up, feeling it strain against the stiffness of the sheet. She attempted to raise her arms, to bend them at the elbows. She tried turning her head from side to side. Had she moved at all?

"Oh, my," Patsy said from the doorway. "What happened to you?"

How long had Patsy been standing there?

"Looks like your friend got a little too close for comfort. Look what she's done to your poor head." Patsy walked over to the bed and took Casey's head in her hands, readjusting her position. "That can't have been too comfortable. Good thing I thought to look in on you."

I moved my head? I actually moved my head?

Patsy took a step back, as if surveying her handiwork. "That was a pretty quick visit. Although that's what happens, doesn't it? Visits get shorter and shorter, with longer and longer intervals in between. Soon it'll be once a week for five minutes, then once a month for two, then maybe once a year, until you won't even be able to remember the last time anyone dropped by. That's the way it goes." She sighed.

I moved my head, Casey thought.

"Although, personally, I hate when people just drop over. My mother's like that. She's always showing up at my door unexpectedly, and then she gets all upset when I'm not thrilled to see her. I keep telling her she should call first, and she says, 'Why? You have something to hide?' Wonder what she'd make of this place." Patsy laughed. "Oh, well. Maybe one day I'll find out. I could be the new mistress of the manor. You never know. Stranger things have happened."

"Everything all right?" Warren asked from somewhere behind her.

Patsy quickly spun around. Casey imagined her hand flying to her hair in an effort to hide her embarrassment. "Everything's fine. Casey's head was tilted a bit to one side. Probably Gail hugged her when she said good-bye."

"Her head was tilted to one side?"

"It's okay now."

The doorbell rang. Who was here now? Casey wondered.

"You want me to answer that?" Patsy asked.

"If you wouldn't mind."

The front door opened and closed. Then came a man's muffled hello and a muted exchange of pleasantries, followed by footsteps on the stairs.

"Hello, Warren," a man said seconds later.

Dear God.

There was no mistaking that voice.

Help me. Somebody, please help me.

The man drew closer. "Hello, Beauty," he said.

27

"HOW ARE YOU DOING tonight?" the man continued, looming over Casey like a giant king cobra, body swaying and poised to strike.

"Apparently she moved her head," Warren told him.

"What's that mean?"

"Could mean nothing," Warren said. "Could mean Sleeping Beauty's getting ready to wake up."

Casey felt the man's eyes travel down her body as he lowered her blankets to her knees.

"Looks dead to the world to me. Although, I gotta say she's lookin' pretty damn good for a corpse. You ever think of . . . ?"

"Get your mind out of the gutter," Warren told him, managing to sound convincingly indignant.

The man laughed. "Did I ever tell you about the time I did it with this girl who was so drunk she passed out right in the middle of everything? I mean, smack dab in the middle, if you can believe it. I'm humping away, and suddenly her eyes roll back in her head, and she is out of there." He laughed again. "Weird feeling, I gotta tell you."

"You're one sick puppy."

"Good thing for you."

"So, what'd you do?" Warren asked.

"With the girl? What was I supposed to do? Stop midstream? I kept going till I was finished. She was pretty much superfluous at that point anyway."

"Superfluous? Pretty big word for you, isn't it?"

The man laughed off the insult. "She was just lying there anyway. It wasn't that big a change." His laugh became a low rumble. " 'Course then I flipped her over, did a few things she wouldn't let me do when she was awake."

"A regular prince."

"I do my best. Speaking of which, that little nurse downstairs is pretty cute. I hope you don't mind, I took her up on her offer of some espresso. . . ."

"When we're done here."

"Of course. Let's have a look. See exactly what we've got." The man reached over and took Casey's hand in his, moving it up and down, bending her elbow, then rotating her wrist.

"Well?" Warren asked.

"I'm not feeling much of anything, to tell you the truth. Certainly no resistance. It's dead weight, man." He let go of Casey's hand. It flopped to the bed like a dying fish.

The man's fingers slid slowly down Casey's thighs to her legs. Casey had to summon all her strength to keep her body from recoiling at his touch.

He gripped her right ankle, brought her right knee up toward her waist, then twisted her leg from side to side. "She has good range of movement. No question if you keep working these muscles, they'll keep getting stronger. Of course, strong muscles aren't going to take her very far as long as she's in a coma."

"And if she comes out of it?"

"You honestly think there's much chance of that?"

"I think there's a very good chance."

"And we can't let that happen."

"No, we can't."

"So tell me what you want me to do. I'll do it."

"Something simple: you come in, you put a pillow over her face, you leave without anybody seeing you," Warren said calmly, as if he were reading from a recipe book.

You come in, you put a pillow over her face, Casey repeated silently, feeling tears form in the corners of her eyes. Were they real? Would Warren see them?

"Think you can do that?" he was asking.

"When did you have in mind?"

"This weekend."

"So soon?"

The tear escaped Casey's eye to trace a thin line down her cheek.

"Things are happening faster than I expected," Warren said, his attention clearly focused on his murderous thoughts. "I can't afford to waste any more time. I'll make sure everybody's out of the house. While we're gone, you come in, do the deed, and get the hell out."

"Sounds like a plan."

"Don't screw up."

"I won't."

"Hey, everybody," Patsy suddenly called up from the bottom of the stairs. "Espresso's ready. Come on down."

"Wendy Jackson, come on down. You're the next contestant on *The Price Is Right*!"

Casey pictured Wendy Jackson as a forty-year-old woman with bottle-blond hair and a visible roll of loose flesh that jiggled beneath the bottom of her rose-colored sweatshirt with each bounce of excitement.

Where was Drew? Why wasn't she here yet?

"I can't believe it. I can't believe it," Wendy Jackson cried, no doubt jumping up and down.

"Hello, Wendy," the host said.

Hello, Beauty.

"Okay, try to settle down now, Wendy, and pay close attention," the host urged. "Here's the next item coming up for bids."

Where are you, Drew? What's keeping you?

"A new dining room set!" the announcer exclaimed to an escalating chorus of oohs and aahs.

"What a pile of junk!" Patsy pronounced from the chair beside Casey's bed, as the announcer began his hyperbolic description of the items on display. "I can't believe how excited she's getting over that ratty table and chairs. Although I probably would have gotten pretty excited about them myself before I came to live here. Once you see the kind of furniture you guys have—" She broke off. "Don't let anybody ever tell you that money doesn't buy happiness. It buys nice things, and nice things go a long way to making you happy. Believe me."

And we know it's all about the money.

"Twenty-five hundred dollars," came the bid from Wendy Jackson.

"Three thousand," came the second bid.

"You know they have to pay taxes on the stuff they win?" Patsy asked as the bidding continued. "And they have to sign an agreement promising they won't sell it. So if they don't really like it, they're kind of screwed."

Where are you, Drew? I'm running out of time.

A loud buzzer sounded.

"That buzzer means you've all overbid," the host explained cheerily.

"I told you it was junk," Patsy said.

The four contestants quickly offered up new bids, and this time one of them won, although it wasn't Wendy Jackson.

Bye, bye, Beauty.

"Poor Wendy. She's not going to win anything," Patsy said dismissively. "You can tell. She has loser written all over her."

She can see, she can move, she can talk, hell, she can scream. That makes her a winner in my book, Casey thought, wondering again what was keeping her sister.

"I liked Bob Barker better than this new guy. Did he die or something?"

"You come in, you put a pillow over her face, you leave," she heard her husband say. Or words to that effect.

Had she really cried?

And if she had, if tears had not only formed but fallen, had Warren seen them?

Not likely, Casey decided, judging by his subsequent actions.

"Espresso's ready," he'd said with a laugh, then tossed Casey's blankets back up across her body, as if she were already dead.

The doorbell rang.

"Can you get that, Mrs. Singer?" Patsy called down the stairs. "Probably your sister," she said to Casey. Seconds later, Drew hollered up hello. "Told you," Patsy said proudly.

Drew, thank God! Where have you been? I have so much to tell you, and we have so little time.

Seconds later, Drew bounded into the room, then stopped abruptly. "Oh, hi, Patsy. I didn't realize you'd be here."

"Where else would I be?"

"How's Casey doing today?" Drew took Casey's hand, gave it a conspiratorial squeeze. "Sorry I'm late. There was a minor crisis at Lola's school. Seems I forgot to sign this permission slip to let her go on some field trip. And when I showed up at the school, nobody knew who I was. Can you believe it? They're so used to dealing with the nanny. I actually had to show them my driver's license. Which, of course, had expired. Remind me I have to go renew it next week. Anyway, the school was very apologetic. It was actually pretty funny. Do you think I could get a cup of coffee?" she asked Patsy.

"You'll have to go downstairs and ask Mrs. Singer," Patsy said. "I'm under strict instructions not to leave Casey's side until Mr. Marshall gets back."

"Really? Why is that?"

"I think he's just being extra cautious."

"Why? Did something happen?"

"Her blood pressure's been a little erratic. And she's been having these spasms."

"What do you mean, spasms? Since when?"

"Since last night. First her head was tilted off to one side, and then, later, when I looked in on her before I went to bed, I found her slumped over on her side." She laughed. "Mr. Marshall said it almost looked like she was trying to get out of bed."

"Casey was trying to get out of bed?"

"What? No! Of course not. How could she?"

"I don't know. I just . . ."

"Warren called her doctor first thing this morning. He rushed right over and checked her out, said maybe she was experiencing muscle spasms, which can be quite painful, so he gave her a shot and prescribed some painkillers and a muscle relaxant, which is where Warren is now—picking up the medication."

No. I don't want any more drugs. They just make me dopey.

Which was exactly the point, she realized. Warren wasn't taking any chances.

"Well, I can watch Casey now," Drew said. "I'm sure Warren wouldn't mind if you took a half hour break."

"It's time for the final showcase on *The Price Is Right!*" the announcer declared.

"I better not. Besides, it's time for the final showcase. Wouldn't want to miss that."

Please, Drew, get this woman out of here. We have to talk.

Drew pulled up a chair and sat down beside the bed, her arm reaching under the covers to clasp her sister's hand. "Are you okay, Casey? Are you in pain?"

Casey squeezed her sister's thumb twice, as the announcer began his description of the first showcase. "It's a set of encyclopedias!" he said to a chorus of exaggerated appreciation.

"As if anybody is going to get excited about a stupid set of encyclopedias," Patsy scoffed.

"These handsome *Britannica* encyclopedias are bound in genuine leather . . . and you can use these encyclopedias to learn about everything from A to Z, starting with . . . the Acropolis," the announcer continued. "Information that might come in handy on your trip to . . . Greece!"

A prolonged series of oohs and aahs. A burst of applause.

"Yes, you and a companion will fly first-class to Athens, where you'll stay at the fabulous King George II Palace hotel for five nights, and visit the Acropolis and the other many amazing sites of ancient Greece. Then it's off for a spectacular cruise of the Greek Islands."

"You like cruises, don't you?" Patsy asked. "Have you ever been to Greece?"

"I was there a few years ago," Drew answered.

"Is it as spectacular as he's making it sound?"

"It's pretty amazing."

"I've never been anywhere."

"You should go."

You should go right now.

"I can't afford it." Patsy chuckled, as if she knew something they didn't. "But who knows? Maybe one day."

"I'll pass on this showcase," the contestant declared.

"She thinks the next showcase will be better," Patsy said.

There has to be a way to get rid of this woman, Casey thought. There has to be a way to tell Drew what happened last night. There has to be a way to tell her about Warren.

"I tried contacting Jeremy," Drew said, relaying the news to Casey while ostensibly speaking to Patsy. "But the hospital wouldn't give out any of his personal information. So I stopped by there last night and left him a note. They said they'd give it to him, but he hasn't gotten back to me yet."

Yes, you have to find Jeremy.

"Your showcase begins with camping equipment," the television announcer began.

"Why would you want to contact him?" Patsy asked.

"Just to see if he's okay," Drew answered. She squeezed Casey's hand a second time. The squeeze said, *To tell him about Casey.* "Warren was pretty brutal with him yesterday."

"No more than he deserved."

"Anyway, I could do some of the exercises he showed me with Casey," Drew suggested.

"I'm not sure that's such a good idea," Patsy said.

"Why not?"

"Because Casey has a new therapist now, and he probably has his own way of doing things."

"And you can carry all that equipment in your new car!" the TV announcer continued to a thunderous ovation.

"Warren hired a new therapist already?" Drew asked. "Who is he?"

"His name's Nick something-or-other. Margolin . . . Margolis? Something like that. He's pretty cute."

"Well, that's important for a therapist. Where'd he find him?"

"He's a trainer at the gym where Warren works out."

"Warren hired a personal trainer to look after my sister?"

"He's very qualified."

"And you know this because . . . ?"

"Because Mr. Marshall would never hire anyone who wasn't highly qualified to look after his wife."

"He hired you," Drew said.

"And if you get tired of sleeping in the great outdoors," the TV announcer declared, "you can spend the night in your new trailer!"

"I'm taking excellent care of Casey," Patsy bristled. "You have no right to be so judgmental."

"I'm concerned about my sister."

"You have no idea how good that man is to her," Patsy continued, unprompted. "You should get down on your knees every day and thank God for Mr. Marshall, instead of giving him such a hard time."

"I should get down on my knees?"

"Why not? From what I understand, it's a position you're quite familiar with."

"Ouch," Drew said. "Good one, Patsy."

"I'll bid twenty-three thousand, five hundred dollars," the contestant said.

"Way too low," Drew remarked absently.

"Warren is a wonderful man," Patsy persisted. "If Casey were conscious, I bet she'd be pretty pissed at the way you treat him."

"Do you think so?" Drew's fingers wrapped around Casey's under the blankets. "Is Warren a wonderful man, Casey? Is that what you think?"

Casey grasped Drew's fingers.

"Okay, let's see who came closest to the price of their showcase without going over. . . ."

Casey squeezed once.

Then again.

Twice for no.

"That's what I thought," Drew said.

"You thought what?" Patsy asked.

"I thought her bid was too low. Now that other lady has to go all the way to Greece to see some old ruins she couldn't care less about. Look, I owe you an apology," Drew said in the same breath.

"You do?"

You do?

"I've been very rude and I'm sorry." Drew squeezed Casey's fingers, as if to say *Bear with me.* "I know you're doing your best for Casey. It's just so hard seeing her in this condition day after day."

"I'm sure it is."

"And I've been taking out my frustration on you and Warren."

"He deserves better."

"I know he does."

Casey recognized the mock sincerity in her sister's voice, remembered hearing it herself on many occasions. She pictured Drew's downcast eyes, the slight tremble in her lips, the soft fluttering of her hands, as if she was searching for just the right words of contrition.

"Wow. I'm not used to apologizing. That took a lot out of me." Drew laughed, a disarmingly soft sound that floated through the air like a wisp of smoke. "I don't suppose you'd reconsider getting me that cup of coffee."

"Not a chance."

Shit.

"Bitch," Drew muttered under her breath.

The front door opened and closed. "I'm back," Warren called from the foyer. In the next minute, he was up the stairs and inside the room. "Drew, hi. Nice to see you." Casey felt him lean forward to give her sister a kiss on the cheek. Clearly, he was trying a new approach.

"I understand Casey had a bit of a rough night," Drew said.

"The doctor thinks she's experiencing muscle spasms."

"So Patsy was telling me. She seems okay now, though."

"We'll give her a shot later, make sure she has a restful night."

No, I don't want a shot of anything. I need my head to be clear.

"Do you really think drugs are a good idea?" Drew asked. "Won't they just interfere with her progress?"

"I'm really not seeing a lot of progress, Drew. Are you?"

"Well, no. But you never know. . . ."

"I don't want her in any pain."

"Neither do I."

"Then suppose we let the doctor decide. Patsy, I'm dying for a cup of coffee. What about you, Drew?"

"Oh, I wouldn't want to put Patsy to any trouble," Drew said sweetly.

"Would you mind?" Warren asked Patsy.

"Of course not."

"Thank you, Patsy," Drew said. "You're so kind."

"So, how's my niece?" Warren asked Drew as Patsy left the room.

"She's fine."

"I was thinking maybe I could take the two of you to Gettysburg this Sunday. If that works for you."

"You want to take us to Gettysburg?"

He wants an alibi.

"I thought you might enjoy it. I know I would. Casey and I had such a good time when we went there. And it would give me the chance to make up for being such an asshole lately."

No. Don't fall for this.

"I haven't exactly been all sweetness and light myself," Drew said.

"So, how about it?"

Don't do it.

"Think you could give me another chance?"

Several seconds of silence.

No. Please, no.

"Sunday would be great," Drew said.

28

" '*Dorothea seldom left home* without her husband, but she did occasionally drive into Middlemarch alone, on little errands of shopping or charity such as occur to every lady of any wealth when she lives within three miles of a town,' " Janine was reading.

Where am I? What's happening?

" '*Two days after that scene in the Yew-tree Walk, she determined to use such an opportunity in order if possible to see Lydgate, and learn from him whether her husband had really felt any depressing change of symptoms which he was concealing from her, and whether he had insisted on knowing the utmost about himself.'* "

Was she back in the hospital? Had the last week been nothing but a dream?

" '*She felt almost guilty in asking for knowledge about him from another, but the dread of being without it—the dread of that ignorance which would make her unjust or hard—overcame every scruple.'* "

Dread, yes, Casey thought. That was a good word to describe what she was feeling.

" 'That there had been some crisis in her husband's mind she was certain: he had the very next day begun a new method of arranging his notes, and had associated her quite newly in carrying out his plan. Poor Dorothea needed to lay up stores of patience.' Poor Dorothea needs to get a life," Janine said.

What's happening? Would somebody please tell me what's happening?

"Almost finished that book?" Patsy asked, her voice swimming somewhere above Casey's head.

"Page three fifteen."

"Still a long way to go."

"Guess I could say the same thing about Casey," Janine said.

"I guess."

"Gail told me she was making progress."

"I think it was a case of wishful thinking."

"She hasn't opened her eyes since I've been here."

"That doesn't mean anything," Patsy said. "And at least she's not in pain anymore."

When was I in pain?

"I guess that's something to be thankful for."

Casey fought through the fog in her brain to piece together the puzzle of what was happening. It came to her in fits and starts, a series of images exploding across her mind's eye, as if from one of those twirling mirrored disco balls. In one such flash, she saw Patsy standing over her bed, her voice penetrating the darkness, commenting on her raised blood pressure and continuing distress, assuring her she was going to make her more comfortable. And then the prick of a needle in her arm, the subsequent floating in and out of consciousness.

How long had she been floating? What day was it?

"Casey," she heard her sister whisper. "Casey, can you hear me? If you can hear me, squeeze my hand."

How long ago was that? Had she been able to muster the strength required to tell her sister she was still cognizant?

"Casey, listen to me," Drew had said on another occasion.

Or had it been the same occasion?

"Tap once for yes, twice for no."

What day is it? How much time do I have left?

"Warren's taking Lola and me to Gettysburg on Sunday. He's being awfully nice to me all of a sudden. I can't tell if he's really trying to make up for being such a jerk lately, or if he's up to something."

He's going to kill me.

"You come in, you put a pillow over her face, you leave without anybody seeing you," Warren had said.

When had he said that?

"I love your T-shirt," Patsy was saying now. "Who's Ed Hardy anyway?"

Ed Hardy? Who the hell was Ed Hardy?

"The designer," Janine said.

"Designer T-shirts. Wow. Guess it was expensive, huh?"

"Reasonably."

"What's reasonable?"

"Two hundred dollars."

"Two hundred dollars for a T-shirt? Doesn't sound very reasonable to me."

A buzzer sounded.

"That buzzer means you've all overbid."

What?

"What's that?" Patsy asked.

"My BlackBerry. Oh, God. Another message from Richard Mooney."

The little twerp?

"Who?"

"A client. I actually managed to find him another job, and he's still not happy. Look, I'm going to call him back, get rid of him once and for all. Is there a room I can use for a few minutes?"

"Only about eighty of them."

"I'll just be down the hall."

"Take your time."

What time is *it?*

How much time had she lost? Casey wondered. How many days had passed since the last time she was fully conscious? How much time before she was sedated again?

"Your friend sure has expensive taste. Imagine spending two hundred dollars for a T-shirt."

Casey tried moving her fingers beneath the covers, but she felt nothing. She tried wiggling her toes, but they refused to cooperate.

"Squeeze my hand," she heard her sister urge. "Casey, squeeze my hand."

When had she said that? Today? Yesterday? The day before that? When was the last time Drew had been here?

"It's nice that Janine still comes over so often," Patsy was saying. "And on her lunch hour, too."

Her lunch hour? That means it's a weekday.

"Although who knows how often she'll come once she's finished that damn book."

The front door opened and closed. Was it Drew? Again, Casey tried flexing her fingers. If it was Drew, she had to be fully conscious and prepared.

"I'm back," Warren called up the stairs.

Not Drew. Warren. Where had he been?

"Hi," he said from the bedroom doorway moments later. "How's Casey?"

"She seems to be resting peacefully," Patsy said. "How was your workout?"

"Not great. I think I might have pulled something in my shoulder."

"Oh, no. Let me have a look at it."

"No, that's all right."

"Come on," Patsy said. "I'm the one with the magic hands, remember? Now sit your ass down and let me have a look. Sorry," she apologized immediately. "I didn't mean to overstep . . ."

"You haven't," Warren said, chuckling. He plopped down in the nearest chair.

"Where is it sore?" Patsy asked.

"There. And a bit there."

"Okay, take a deep breath and release it into my fingers. That's right."

"God, that feels good. You really *do* have magic hands."

"Those seem to be your trouble spots."

"In more ways than one," Janine said flatly, returning to the room.

"Janine," Warren said.

"I think this is where I came in."

"I didn't realize you were here."

"Clearly. That'll be quite enough, Patsy."

"Thank you, Patsy," Warren said.

"We need to talk," Janine said.

"Certainly. About anything in particular?"

"In private."

"I'll be in my room," Patsy said.

Seconds later, Casey heard the door to Patsy's room close.

"Is there a problem?" Warren asked Janine.

"You tell me."

"You mean other than the fact my wife is in a coma?"

"What's with you and Florence Nightingale?"

"If you're insinuating . . ."

"I'm not insinuating anything. I'm asking flat out. Are you sleeping with her?"

"Don't be ridiculous."

"You haven't answered my question."

"Of course I'm not sleeping with her. I hurt my shoulder, at the gym. Patsy was just being kind. . . ."

"Kind of what? Kind of available?"

"Really, Janine, if you could hear yourself sometimes."

"Really, Warren, if you could *see* yourself sometimes," Janine countered.

"What exactly did you see that was so awful?"

"Whatever it was, it was the second time I saw it. And I don't like it one bit. And more important, Casey wouldn't like it."

"Casey wouldn't have liked my sleeping with you either, but that didn't concern you a whole lot at the time."

What?

Silence. Then, "This is neither the time nor the place to talk about that."

"Maybe it is."

Janine closed the bedroom door, took an audible breath. "What happened between us happened a long time ago."

"Less than a year," Warren corrected.

What? No, this can't be. I'm having a nightmare. It's the drugs the doctor gave me. I'm hallucinating again. None of this is happening.

"It should never have happened," Janine said.

"Maybe not, but it did."

I don't believe it. I won't *believe it.*

What's so hard to believe? Casey asked herself. If she could believe her husband capable of murder, surely he was capable of betraying her with one of her closest friends.

It wasn't Warren's betrayal she was having such a hard time processing, she realized. It was Janine's.

"Look. I'm not proud of what I did," Janine said. "I was going through a hard time, what with Casey opting out of our partnership. I was angry, I was spiteful, I let myself be seduced. . . ."

"As I recall, it was you who did the seducing," Warren corrected again.

"I was flirting. I didn't think you'd take me up on it."

"You're fooling yourself, Janine."

"Maybe. You fooled Casey, that's for sure."

"I love Casey."

"You have an interesting way of showing it."

"I'm showing it now."

"A little late, isn't it?"

"I guess that's a guilt we'll both have to live with."

"You seem to be living with it rather well."

"I can't change the past," Warren said. "What happened happened. It's over. It's time to move on."

"Move on to the next in line?"

"It beats doing penance in Middlemarch."

"It's that simple?"

"It's not that complicated."

"You're unbelievable."

"You're jealous."

"I assure you that jealous is the last thing I am."

"Then why are we having this conversation?"

Janine took a deep breath. "We're having this conversation because what I am is sick at heart. Sick over the fact that I betrayed my best friend on earth with her lowlife scum of a husband, sick that her husband isn't the man she thought he was, sick that she's the one in a coma when I'm the one who deserves to be."

"Oh, please, Janine. Give it up. Nobility doesn't become you."

"And most of all," Janine continued, ignoring Warren's interruption, "I'm sick that you have so little decency that you could carry on with another woman while your wife is lying there right in front of you."

"Bullshit," Warren said coldly. "The only thing bothering you is that that woman is no longer you."

"I want her out of here, Warren. I want her out of here this afternoon."

"What?"

"You heard me. I want Nurse Patsy gone."

"Pardon me, but I don't think that's your decision to make."

"Either she goes, or I swear I'll tell everyone all about us. And that includes Detective Spinetti."

"Now why on earth would you consider doing a stupid thing like that?"

"Because it's all I *can* do for Casey now."

"And you think she'll thank you for it? Assuming, of course, that she wakes up."

"I don't know. Probably not. But I *do* know that if she stands any chance of waking up at all, she needs the very best of care, and frankly, I don't think Patsy is the one to give it to her."

There was a silence of several long seconds. "You might be right about that," Warren said finally.

"I *am* right."

"And I'm not stupid. Or callous. I may not have always been the best husband to Casey, but whether you believe it or not, I do love my wife, and I want what's best for her."

"Meaning?" Janine persisted.

"I'll tell Patsy her services are no longer required."

"When?"

"Right after you leave," he said pointedly. "Oh, and Janine," he continued, as Casey heard Janine gathering up her things and walking to the door.

"Yes?"

"I think we could use a time-out. Call the next time you decide to drop by. I'll arrange to be elsewhere."

Janine said nothing as she closed the bedroom door behind her.

"Look, I'm sorry," Casey imagined Warren saying to Patsy sometime later. "It's just not working out."

"What do you mean?" she heard Patsy answer back.

"It's nothing you've done. You've been wonderful. It's just that I underestimated the amount of care Casey would require."

"We could hire someone to give me a hand. I could call Donna. . . ."

"Casey needs an RN, someone with more experience. . . ."

"I could still help out."

"It won't work."

"I don't understand. I thought we . . ."

"That's just the point," Casey could almost hear Warren whisper. "There is no 'we.' There can't be a 'we.' "

"If this is because of Janine, because of what she thinks she saw . . ."

"Janine's a very astute woman, Patsy. She doesn't see things that aren't there."

"I'm so sorry. . . ."

"You have nothing to be sorry for. *I'm* the one who should be apologizing to you. You're lovely. That's the problem in a nutshell. You're beautiful and sweet and kind and thoughtful, and I find myself being drawn to you in ways I never expected. And I can't afford to let that happen. Not yet," Casey imagined him adding, holding out the carrot, perhaps even allowing a hint of tears to cloud his eyes. "Maybe later. Should circumstances change . . ."

Or something like that, Casey thought now, hearing Patsy sniffling as she carried her suitcase from her room to the top of the stairs. Something to give the young woman hope, a reason not to be angry he was firing her without notice or cause.

"I want you to take this," Warren said from just outside Casey's bedroom door.

"What is it?"

"Just a little something to tide you over until you find another position."

"No, please. I couldn't."

"It's only fair."

"It's *more* than fair. It's way too much money. I can't."

"You can and you will. Please. I want you to have it."

Oh, take it. It's my money anyway. And I'll be dead in a few days.

"Is it all right if I say good-bye to Casey?"

"Of course. Take as long as you like."

Casey pictured Warren picking up Patsy's suitcase and carrying it down the stairs as Patsy entered the room and positioned herself at the foot of Casey's bed. She felt Patsy's eyes burrow into her brain. "Bitch," she said.

And then she was gone.

"Well, that worked out rather well, all things considered," Warren was saying minutes later, pulling up a chair and making himself comfortable. "Mrs. Singer's gone for the weekend, Patsy's out of the picture, Gail's out of town, and I don't have to worry about Janine for at least a few days. So it looks like it's all systems go for Sunday. That's the day after tomorrow, in case you're keeping track."

The day after tomorrow, Casey repeated. Where was Drew? She had one day left to get through to her.

"I've arranged for a private nurse to come in tomorrow, and the doctor's going to drop by later to give you your shot. So you won't get too frisky when Drew comes to visit," Warren said, as if her thoughts were printed across her forehead. "So, let's just try to relax, shall we?" he said, taking her hand in his and lifting it to his lips, kissing the inside of her palm. "It'll all be over soon."

29

SHE DREAMED SHE WAS in the passenger seat of a twin-engine Cessna when it crashed into a wall of turbulence and spun out of control, propelling its passengers into the thin, cold air, as if they'd been shot from a cannon.

"Daddy!" Casey screamed, as she watched her mother somersault through the sky in her pink chiffon gown, a drunken Alice disappearing into the rabbit hole below.

"Try to relax, golden girl," her father's voice urged from behind an ash-colored cloud. "Grab my hand."

Casey stretched her arm as far as it would reach, her fingers waving frantically in the void for her father's reassuring grasp. They touched nothing, latched onto no one. Her father wasn't there, she realized. He never had been.

He couldn't save her.

Nobody could.

Casey lay in her bed, slowly drifting back into consciousness. Even through the wooziness that occupied her head like an expanding sponge, she understood that although she was no longer plummeting through the air to her doom, she was no less at risk. She was going to die, she realized, trying to imagine how her parents must have felt the afternoon their plane had plunged into Chesapeake Bay.

She'd never really thought about it before, she realized, never permitted herself the necessary introspection to board that doomed plane, to feel what her parents must have felt, to think what they surely thought as the plane careened wildly through the sky before disappearing into the sea. Had her mother been flailing about helplessly and crying with fear? Had she been berating her husband, lashing out at him in a panic-fueled fury, or had she tried to embrace him, to hold him in her arms one last time, even as the waves rose up, like a crazed chorus, to welcome them? Had her mother even been conscious? Or had she passed out early in the flight from a surfeit of alcohol and fatigue, her head lolling obliviously from side to side as Casey's father fought frantically with the controls? Had he been too drunk to fully comprehend the danger they were in? In his last seconds, had he thought about his daughters at all? Had either of them?

Did it matter? Casey thought now.

Did anything?

Had she ever really meant anything to anyone?

Her father had loved her only as a reflection of his own accomplishments. Her mother had been too self-absorbed to share that love with anyone else. Her sister's love had always been tempered by equal measures of resentment. And Warren? He loved her money, Casey thought ruefully.

And then there was Janine. Her former roommate and business partner, supposedly one of her closest friends. Yes, they'd had many disagreements over the years. Yes, they'd argued and fought and occasionally said things they'd regretted. But never had Casey imagined the scope of Janine's anger, never had she appreciated the lengths to which Janine would go to get back at her.

And yet, as shocked and disappointed as she was, Casey realized she wasn't angry with Janine. Her friend had simply made the same mistake Casey had: Warren. God knew she was sorry. And anyone who could atone for her sins by reading *Middlemarch* out loud day after day, week after week, deserved not only compassion but a second chance.

Too bad she wouldn't be here to give it, Casey thought, those thoughts transferring to Gail. Gail, the one person who'd always been there, who'd loved her unconditionally since childhood. She was somewhere in Martha's Vineyard with the new man in her life, and she'd be devastated to learn of Casey's death when she returned.

I'm sorry, Gail, she said now.

I'm sorry for everything, she cried silently, trying to project two days ahead, to imagine how it would feel to have someone put a pillow over her nose and mouth until she stopped breathing. Would she gasp for air and fight for breath? Would it take a long time for her to die or would death be mercifully quick? Would there be an angel waiting to greet her? What would death be like?

Could it be any worse than this?

And yet, despite the horror of the past few months, despite the revelations and the lies and the betrayals, despite the loss of her vision and her speech and her mobility and everything that made her who she was, Casey realized she wasn't ready to die.

Not now. Not when she was so close to recovering all she'd lost.

Certainly not without a fight.

Sure, some fight, she thought in the next instant, as a wave of dizziness washed over her, the result of the powerful drugs in her system. Not exactly a fair fight.

"What's the point of fighting if you're going to fight fair?" she heard her father ask, his too-big laugh trailing after him as he strode into the room to peer out the window overlooking the back-yard.

"Daddy, hi," Casey told him, pushing herself up in bed.

"What are you doing still in bed?" He pivoted around on his heels and stared at Casey with disapproval.

"I'm not feeling very well."

"Nonsense. You're just feeling sorry for yourself. Mind over matter, Casey. Just put one foot in front of the other. See where it takes you."

"But I can't see."

"Then open your eyes," her father said simply, before disappearing into the night.

Casey opened her eyes.

The first thing she saw was the light of the moon coming in through the window at which her father had been standing.

She blinked once, twice, a third time.

Each time the light grew stronger.

Okay, try not to get too excited, she warned herself. You're obviously still dreaming.

Except it didn't feel like a dream.

You're hallucinating.

Hallucinations felt more real than dreams.

Except this didn't feel like any of her previous hallucinations.

It's the drugs. They're playing tricks on your mind. You're woozy. You're dizzy.

Not that dizzy. Not that woozy.

I can see, she thought, blinking again.

The powerful blink.

Don't be ridiculous, she told herself. You're getting yourself all worked up over nothing. It's dark. It's the middle of the night. You're just imagining the curve of the moon peeking in the large bay window. You can't really make out the lilac-colored drapery open to either side of it or the floral tub chairs in front of it. You can't see the striped chair beside the bed or the large flat-screen TV on the opposite wall, flanked by paintings of orchids and daffodils. You can't see the fireplace or the bed you're lying in, its crisp white sheets visible even in the dark. You can't see the mauve blanket lying at your feet, can't see the indent of your toes wiggling beneath it.

I can't. It's impossible.

Casey's eyes moved frantically inside their sockets as they shot from side to side, then up and down, then back and forth. I can see, she understood, elation spreading through her body like a fire through dry wood.

Don't get too excited. This has happened before. It's the drugs. Any minute now, you'll wake up.

"Relax, Casey," she heard Warren say. "It'll all be over soon."

No. Not now. Not when I'm so close. She lay in her bed, feeling her breath grow increasingly ragged, and staring up at the round overhead light fixture in the middle of the large expanse of ceiling, trying to calm herself down.

I will get out of this. I will. I will.

She heard Warren's footsteps in the hall and knew he was coming to check on her. She told herself to close her eyes, that even in the dim light, Warren would spot immediately that she could see, and that she couldn't afford to take that chance. And yet, she couldn't close them, so terrified was she that once she did, her sight would vanish again, and that when she reopened them, all would be blackness, as it had been before.

Warren stepped into the room.

Casey took a deep breath, uttered a silent prayer, and closed her eyes.

"Hi, sweetheart. How're you doing?" He perched on the side of the bed, and Casey could smell the liquor on his breath. "I was having trouble sleeping again, so I thought I'd come in and see what you were up to. Seems I'm missing our little chats already." He rubbed her leg. "Your breathing seems a little labored. What's with that? You're not going to die on me, are you?" He laughed. "I mean, wouldn't that be ironic? You up and dying all on your own, after everything you've put me through these last months." Casey felt him shaking his head. "That'd really be something, wouldn't it? Although if that's what's happening, I'd appreciate it if you could hold off till the morning when the nurse gets here. Think you could wait till then? Maybe till I'm out of the house? That way, nobody can harbor any suspicions about me or accuse me of doing anything unseemly." He got up, walked toward the window. "There's almost a full moon. It's pretty spectacular. What is it they say about full moons? That they bring out the beast in people?" This time his laugh was more of a shrug. "Did you know it's a fact that more crimes are committed during a full moon than at any other time of the month? Interesting, isn't it? Nobody's ever been able to explain exactly why that is.

"So, your sister called earlier," he continued after a pause. "She was thinking of stopping by tomorrow with Lola. I told her that would be terrific, that maybe I'd send out for pizza and we'd have a picnic in the backyard. She thought that was great, and you know what? So do I. I mean, why waste time and energy fighting when we all know I'm a lover, not a fighter." He laughed again, a boisterous "hah!" that bounced off the walls to slam against the side of Casey's head like an errant rubber ball. "I've been thinking a lot about the situation with Drew, and I suddenly realized it's very simple, and I don't know why I didn't see it sooner. Probably I was just so pissed off at everything. But now I see that Drew's like this sad little puppy who just wants to be loved, but everybody's always kicking her to the curb. So instead of joining the crowd, instead of treating her like a Gucci-clad piece of shit, the way she's used to being treated by the men in her life, I've decided to treat her like a princess in one of Lola's fairy tales. I'm going to shine up my armor, ride in on my white horse, and sweep her off her feet.

"How, you may ask? Well, I'll tell you, even though prudence dictates I keep my mouth shut. Who is that Prudence anyway, and how dare she tell me what to do?" He laughed. "But what the hell. I'm drunk, and you're not going to be around past Sunday. And once you're dead and gone, it'll be up to me to provide your sister with a sturdy shoulder to cry on. The grieving widower comforting his distraught sister-in-law. So understanding. So compassionate. How will she be able to resist? How will she not fall in love?

"And who would condemn such a love?" he continued, as if delivering a summation in front of a jury. "A love born of grief, of a shared sense of loss. It's perfect, don't you think? We'll take it slow, of course, wait at least a year before announcing our engagement, followed by a quick but tasteful wedding, Lola serving as flower girl. Maybe we'll even ask Gail and Janine to serve as bridesmaids. Well, maybe not Janine.

"Anyway, Drew and I get married, we live happily ever after. Or at least happily ever a year or two. And then another horrifying twist of fate. Mother and child lose their lives when their sailboat capsizes in treacherous waters off the coast of Mexico; distraught husband almost drowns trying to save them. I can see the headlines now.

"Of course there'll probably be some whispers surrounding their deaths. You know how people talk. You're no stranger to gossip and innuendo. Hell, you grew up with it. And what was your father's philosophy? To hell with gossip and innuendo! Show me the cold, hard proof. So while I expect there'll be those who question the likelihood of this kind of lightning striking twice, of two wealthy young sisters dying in separate but equally tragic accidents way before their time, and Detective Spinetti will no doubt come snooping around again, I suspect his investigation will hit the same brick wall his last one did. And I think I can put up with a few months of suspicion in return for a lifetime of luxury. And this time, I won't even have to share. It'll all be mine. Everything your father worked for. And cheated for. And stole for. Because your father really wasn't a very nice man, Casey. In his case, the rumors and innuendos were all true. I know because I followed his career for years. I studied everything about him. I can't tell you how much I admired him, how much I wanted to *be* him. I even wrote a paper on him in law school. I don't think I ever told you about that, did I? No, of course I didn't. As far as you knew, I'd never even heard of Ronald Lerner before I met you."

Casey felt her eyelids flutter with indecision. She wanted to see this man, this man she'd loved and married, who'd tricked and deceived her, who'd played her and used her, and ultimately tried to destroy her. If nothing else, she had to look at his face—to see the grotesque ogre behind the Prince Charming mask—one last time before she died.

It was risky, she knew. What if he was no longer staring at the moon? What if he was looking directly at her? Could she fool him into thinking her eyes saw nothing? Could she manage to fool him for even several seconds as easily as he'd fooled her for more than two years?

Slowly, cautiously, Casey opened her eyes.

He was standing by the window, although he was no longer staring out at the night. Instead, his gaze was focused on the far wall of the bedroom, his handsome profile backlit by the rounded spotlight of the moon.

He looks exactly the same, Casey thought, suppressing a sigh of longing so deep, she almost gasped out loud. Longing for what? she wondered impatiently. Longing for the life she'd had, the life she'd lost? A life built on lies and deceit? How could she long for a man who longed only for her death?

And yet, there it was—longing, albeit mixed with fear and anger and loathing, but longing nonetheless. Was there any doubt at all that Drew would succumb to that same magnetic pull? They were both Ronald Lerner's daughters, after all, and he'd prepared them all too well for men like Warren Marshall.

Warren sighed and ran a hand through his thick brown hair, which was longer than the last time Casey had seen it. He tightened the belt of his silk bathrobe, one of a dozen gifts Casey had given him last Christmas, and then sighed again. "So, what's your opinion of my latest plan, Casey?" he asked, spinning around.

Casey immediately closed her eyes.

"Think it'll work?" He walked to the side of the bed. "Think Drew will fall for my Prince Charming routine the same way you did? Think she'll consent to becoming Mrs. Warren Marshall the second? I think she will," he said without pause. "Okay, then. Think I'll go back to bed now. All this patting myself on the back has proved quite exhausting." He leaned forward, kissed the side of Casey's lips.

Casey wondered if his eyes were closed, and had to fight the urge to open hers.

"I'm really going to miss these little talks of ours," he said.

Casey lay awake for the balance of the night, her eyes open and refusing to succumb to either wooziness or fatigue, as she listened to the chimes of the grandfather clock in the downstairs foyer announce the passing of each quarter hour. She watched the moon grow dimmer, as the sky traded its inky pallor for something more pastel. She watched as the pale blue of the early morning hours turned to steel gray at around seven o'clock when the skies filled with ominous clouds that promised rain. By the time she heard Warren singing in the shower an hour later—*"By the time I get to*

Phoenix, she'll be sleeping. . . ."—lightning was streaking across the sky, as if put there by a cartoonist's hand, and thunder was shaking the room.

A sound-and-light show just for me, Casey thought, enjoying the spectacle in spite of everything. Or maybe because of it. When was the last time she'd derived such pleasure from the sight of rain slamming against the window? She thought of Drew and wondered if she was still asleep, or if the thunder and lightning had woken her up.

Drew had always been terrified of storms. When they were little, she used to come running into Casey's room in the middle of the night and crawl into her bed, burying herself beneath the covers and digging her fingers into the flesh below Casey's ribs as the thunder raged. And Casey would kiss the top of Drew's head and assure her that the storm would soon stop. Invariably Drew would fall asleep in this position, while Casey would remain awake, guarding her younger sister until the storm had, indeed, passed. In the morning, Drew would climb out of bed without a word and return to her own room, her pride refusing to allow even the hint of a thank-you to drift toward her sister. As they grew older and increasingly estranged, Drew had stopped coming into Casey's room altogether. Eventually, she found other arms to comfort her, other beds to share.

The phone rang.

Casey heard Warren answer it in his bedroom. "Yes, this is Warren Marshall. Right. We've been expecting you. Is there a problem?" A slight pause, then, "Well, I can't say I'm surprised, what with this weather. No, I guess you're kind of stuck. Hopefully, the police will have it cleared up before too long. Right. Okay. I should be able to manage with Casey until then. It's unfortunate. You're only one exit away. Yeah, not much we can do. Okay. Get here as fast as you can. Thanks." Moments later, standing in the doorway to Casey's bedroom, he announced, "Accident on the Schuylkill Expressway."

Because of the thunder, Casey hadn't heard him approach, and hadn't had time to close her eyes. Please don't come in, she prayed. Please don't look at me.

"The nurse is stuck a mile from the Rosemont exit. Apparently the police are busy cleaning the mess up now."

Out of the corner of her eye, Casey saw him shake his head.

"I don't know what happens to people when there's the slightest bit of rain," he said, his words accompanied by another loud clap of thunder. "They forget how to drive. Anyway, she should be here in the next half hour. You can wait till then to eat, can't you?"

The phone rang.

"Probably Nurse Friedlander again," he said, crossing to the nightstand as Casey closed her eyes. "Oh, hello, Drew," he said seconds later, his voice as warm as cashmere. "Yes, I can see what's doing out there. It's pretty awful. And according to the weatherman, it's only going to get worse. But the good news is that it's supposed to clear by late tonight, so we should be all right for Gettysburg tomorrow. No, I wouldn't drive today if I were you. Of course. I understand completely. You wouldn't catch me driving in this weather either. Don't worry about it. We'll do pizza tomorrow. Absolutely. I'll call you later with a full report. Okay. Try not to worry, and give Lola a big kiss from me. . . . Well, tell her I'm looking forward to it, too." He hung up the phone.

"That was your sister," he said, sinking into the chair beside Casey's bed and flipping on the TV. "She won't be coming over today."

30

"WELL, WELL," A SOFT female voice was saying. "How are you feeling this beautiful Sunday morning, Mrs. Marshall? Did yesterday's storm upset you? Your blood pressure's still a little high, I see."

Casey recognized Harriet Friedlander's voice from the previous afternoon and welcomed her gentle touch. How different it was from Patsy's, she thought, as Harriet removed the tight blood pressure apparatus from around her arm, then gently brushed the hair from Casey's forehead with the palm of her hand. She continued with her ministrations, running a warm washcloth over Casey's face and hands, and then tending to her feeding tube. "There," she said when she was done with everything. "Now you're all set to face the day."

To face my death, Casey amended, hearing the other woman walk toward the en suite bathroom, and opening her eyes just enough to catch a fleeting glimpse of neat gray hair and a crisp pink uniform.

"How's my wife this morning?" Warren asked, entering the

room and approaching the bed, taking both of Casey's hands, which Mrs. Friedlander had left lying on top of the covers, in his.

"Her blood pressure is still higher than I'd like. You might want to consult with her doctor."

"I'll call him first thing tomorrow morning. Unless you think I should take her to the hospital right now. . . ."

"No, no. I don't think that's necessary. Sunday's never a good day to go to the hospital. All you'll get are interns and residents. Casey's in no immediate danger."

That's where you're wrong, Casey thought.

Dead wrong.

"So, she's all set until tonight?" Warren asked.

"I'll be back to change her feeding tube at five o'clock."

"Perfect. I'll see you then."

"Is there anything else I can do while I'm here?"

"No, thank you. You've been more than generous with your time. It was very kind of you to come in today at all, especially on such short notice."

"I'm glad I could help. Good-bye, Casey. See you later."

Please don't go.

"Let me show you out," Warren offered.

"Thank you."

As soon as they were gone, Casey opened her eyes. A spectacular summer sun was blasting through the bedroom window, causing Casey to blink several times in rapid succession. It was a breathtaking day, the kind they put on the covers of brochures. A shame to waste it by dying, Casey thought, flexing her fingers and toes, and rotating her ankles and wrists. Slowly, with great care, she began turning her head to one side, stopping only when she heard the front door close. Warren would be back up the stairs in seconds, Casey knew, carefully returning her head to its former position.

"Now, that's one nice lady," Warren commented, reappearing in the doorway. "She's going to be very upset when she comes back this afternoon and finds out you passed away. Probably blame herself for not insisting I take you to the hospital. Oh, well. What can you do?" He paused, as if waiting for an answer. "Okay. I'd love to stay and chat, but I have to finish getting ready for my date. Wouldn't want to keep your sister waiting. So, if you'll excuse me."

Casey kept her eyes closed for the ten minutes it took her husband to do whatever he had to do and come back to her. When he reentered the room, he smelled of mouthwash and cologne.

"How do I look?" He perched on the side of the bed, once again taking her hands inside his. "No, I guess you're right. This really isn't the time to be making bad jokes. Nick'll be here in a couple of hours. Hopefully he won't stay very long. Hopefully I'm sending you to a better place. So, take care of yourself on your journey." Warren leaned forward and kissed her full on the mouth.

Casey fought the urge to grab hold of his lips with her teeth. Could she do it? she wondered. Did she have the strength?

"Good-bye, Casey."

She felt him leave her side and pause in the doorway for one last look. Did he have any regrets at all? she wondered. Seconds later, the front door closed. Only then did Casey risk opening her eyes. The room came into immediate, sharp focus.

I have to get out of here.

How? What could she do?

Casey tried turning over on her side. But her body refused to cooperate, allowing her only limited movement as she fought to bring her right arm toward her left side. After several frustrating and fruitless minutes, Casey gave up, tears filling her eyes as she stared up at the ceiling.

If she could just manage to get out of bed, she was thinking. If she could get to the phone, call 911. Even if she couldn't speak, the police would be alerted, then dispatched. Someone would come. Someone would save her.

Except how was she supposed to get out of bed when she couldn't even turn on her side, when her larger muscles had all atrophied from months of inactivity, and she was as powerless as a newborn baby?

There has to be a way.

She couldn't just lie here and wait passively for a coldhearted stranger to smother her to death. Warren had said she had a couple of hours. Surely with enough concentrated effort, she could get out of this bed, get to the phone, and get out of this house.

After what felt like an eternity, Casey succeeded in turning her head several inches to the left. Slowly, she watched the room slide across her line of vision, the intense blue of the sky disappearing into the subtle lilac of the drapery and the soft mauve of the wall. She kept up the effort, her eyes scanning the plasma TV on the opposite wall, falling across the striped chair, and landing on the night table beside her bed as her cheek hit the pillow. I did it, she thought, catching sight of the time on the digital clock that sat on top of the table: 11:15, the large red numbers boldly announced.

I have lots of time, Casey reassured herself, starting the laborious process again, fighting dizziness and nausea as she succeeded in bringing her head back to its original position on the pillow, and then continuing on to the other side, catching sight of the closed door to her walk-in closet and the open door to the hall.

All I have to do is get myself out of this bed and grab the phone, tap in 911.

Her fingers were already tapping at the air as Casey painstakingly brought her head toward the phone on the night table to her left. She pictured the night table beside her mother's bed and wondered if her mother's gun was still in its top drawer, where she'd always kept it.

Was it possible?

No one had used that room until Warren.

Drew had always balked at sifting through their parents' belongings, declaring it ghoulish, and postponing one visit after another, until it lost all sense of urgency. For her part, Casey hadn't been eager to go through her parents' things either. They'd get to it eventually, she'd reasoned. They had lots of time.

And now time was up, she realized, trying to force herself into a sitting position, and feeling every muscle in her body rise up in protest and refuse to cooperate. Besides, even if the gun *was* still there, even if she *could* get to it, would she have the necessary strength to pull the trigger?

Would her conscience allow her to even if she could?

Oh my God, Casey thought as her eyes settled on the clock beside her head—11:52, the numbers read. That couldn't be right. No way had more than half an hour passed since the last time she'd checked. No way could it have taken her this long to do so little.

What am I supposed to do? Would somebody please tell me— what the hell am I supposed to do?

You keep trying, she told herself as the phone started ringing. Once, twice, three times. You reach over and answer the damn phone. Four times. Five. *Hello? Hello?* Except that even as Casey was stretching her hand into the air toward the sound, the ringing stopped.

This isn't fair. This isn't fair.

"Oh, grow up," she heard Janine admonish from a distant corner of her brain. "Who said life was fair?"

"You think I was ready to die?" her father asked.

"You think I liked crashing into the cold waters of Chesapeake Bay?" her mother demanded.

"My husband died of leukemia when he was still a young man," Gail reminded her. "How fair was that?"

You're right, Casey acknowledged silently, bringing her head back to its original position on the pillow. Fairness had never been part of the equation. If you asked "Why me?" when times were bad, you had to ask the same question when times were good. The bottom line was that you had to play the hand you'd been dealt. In her case, she could either raise the stakes or fold. And I'm not ready to fold, she thought.

Not yet.

She started in on the exercises Jeremy had done with her, bending her arms at the elbows and trying to bend her knees. Except that she was tucked in so tightly, her legs had almost no room to maneuver. Still, she continued pressing her toes up against the sheets, determined to loosen the bed's firm grip. After another ten minutes, Casey felt the sheets finally start to give way. She closed her eyes, exhausted.

When she opened them again, it was ten minutes after twelve.

No, it can't be. It can't be.

How could she have fallen asleep, even for a few minutes? She was running out of time. She had to get out of bed. She had to get out of the house.

Again, Casey tried lifting her legs. This time she succeeded in bringing her knees halfway up to her chest before she collapsed with fatigue. Her heart was pounding erratically in her chest. She had little doubt that if Mrs. Friedlander were here right now to check her blood pressure, it would be through the roof.

I have to get up. I have to get out of bed.

"I haaat . . ."

Casey heard the strange sound as if it was emanating from

somewhere across the room. Who was here? Had Warren come home during the minutes she'd been asleep? Was he even now sitting in a chair by the window watching her, and laughing at her futile attempts at escape?

Casey slowly brought her head around to the chairs in front of the window.

No one was there.

A careful scan of the room confirmed she was alone.

"Whaaa . . . ?"

Oh my God. Oh my God.

The sounds were coming from her own mouth, Casey realized, quickly pushing more sounds out. Most shattered instantly upon contact with the air, emerging more as a series of grunts and hoarse whispers.

I can't die now. I can't.

"I caaaaa . . ."

The phone rang again. Casey's head moved toward the sound. Not quickly, but not quite as slowly as it had the last time.

Keep moving. Keep moving.

Who was calling? Was it Nick, the horrible man Warren had hired to kill her? Was he phoning to say he couldn't make it, that he was stuck in traffic on the Schuylkill Expressway? Or maybe that he'd had a change of heart, that it was one thing to plow into someone with a piece of heavy machinery, but quite another to smother that person with your bare hands, to actually feel that person's dying breath as it brushed against your fingers? Surely even hired killers had their limits.

The phone stopped ringing, this time after only four rings.

You don't have time for this, Casey castigated herself, forcing one knee back to her chest, and then the other. But when she tried to lift both legs at the same time, it proved impossible.

That's okay. That's okay. Keep trying. Keep trying.

"Keeeee. . . ."

The next time Casey looked at the clock, it said 12:30.

Keep trying. Keep trying.

12:35. 12:42. 12:47.

The phone rang again.

Maybe someone would get suspicious that no one was answering the phone. Maybe they'd drive out to investigate. Maybe they'd alert the police, ask them to check on the house, make sure everything was all right.

Four more rings, and then the ringing stopped.

Five minutes later, it was the doorbell that was ringing, followed by a loud pounding on the door.

Thank God, Casey thought. Someone was here. Someone had come to rescue her.

Help me. Somebody, please help me.

"Hellll . . ." Casey sighed, the faint sound riding the wave of her breath as the front door opened and closed.

He's here, Casey realized. Her killer was in the house.

Except why would he ring the bell and knock on the door? Clearly Warren had given him a key. Why the charade?

"Hello?" a female voice called out from the downstairs foyer. "Anybody home?"

Patsy?

"Hello?" she called again.

What was Patsy doing here? Was she part of the plan? What was happening?

"Warren? Are you home?" Patsy asked, reaching the top of the stairs and turning toward his bedroom. "Warren?"

Casey brought her legs down as her hands returned to the top of the covers, her head finding its familiar groove in the middle of the pillow. She kept her eyes open and stared straight ahead. Whatever was going to happen, she decided, she wanted to see it.

"Well, well, well," Patsy said, walking into Casey's bedroom and dropping her large canvas purse to the floor. "You *are* here! I thought maybe they'd taken you back to the hospital or something. Where is everybody, anyway? I can't believe everyone went out and left you all alone. That wasn't very nice of them, was it? Although you can't say I didn't warn you." She laughed, leaning over the end of the bed and filling Casey's line of vision.

She looked much as Warren had described, although she was prettier than Casey had expected. Her eyes were a rich shade of brown that was somewhat dulled by the grayness of her eye shadow and the blackness of her lavishly applied mascara. Her skin was pale, her reddish blond hair twisted into a wayward bun at the top of her head. Lush breasts spilled out from between the deep V of her bright purple jersey. Her belly button, pierced by a small gold loop, was visible above the low rise of her tight white jeans.

"Where's Warren? Working out?" Patsy asked. "Couldn't he find anybody to look after you? Maybe he shouldn't have been so quick to let me go. Hard finding someone of my caliber." She laughed again, although the laugh was more bitter than sweet. "You're looking a bit flushed. Are you sweating?" Patsy leaned in closer, then pulled back sharply.

Does she realize I can see her? Casey wondered. Should I let her know?

"What am I doing?" Patsy asked, backing away. "You're not my job anymore." She walked toward the window. "This really is such a pretty view. I'm gonna miss it. Oh, well. Maybe I'll be back." She sighed. "You're probably wondering what I'm doing here *now*."

The thought crossed my mind.

"It seems I *accidentally* left a sweater of mine at the back of a drawer in my room. Accidentally, on purpose, of course. So my original plan was to stop by, ask Warren to help me find it, tempt him with a few kind words and a little bit of cleavage, and hope-fully wind up in his bed. I tried phoning, just to check on how many people were around, but nobody picked up. I even called when I was right outside the front door. And I knocked and knocked, and waited and waited. I almost went home. And then I thought, well, what's the point of coming all this way and leaving empty-handed? So I decided to come in. I still have my key. I *accidentally* forgot to give it back. Anyway, like I said, I figured you must be back in the hospital. It never occurred to me you'd be here all alone.

"But here you are, and here *I* am. And since it doesn't look like I'm gonna get to sleep with that handsome husband of yours any-time soon—which I guess means you win the bet—I might as well leave with a few parting gifts. Like they do on all those game shows we used to watch together on TV."

She walked to Casey's closet, pulled open the door, then stepped inside.

"Like this silk scarf, for example," she said, returning moments later with the yellow-and-black Hermès scarf she'd admired ear-lier. "The one your sister got in such a snit about." Patsy wrapped it loosely around her neck. "I mean, what are you gonna do with it? Besides, it looks much better on me anyway. Don't you think?"

You can have the fucking scarf. Take whatever you want. Just get me out of here.

"Help me," Casey cried softly, the barely audible plea tumbling from her mouth like a leaf from a tree.

Patsy froze. Her eyes opened wide. Her lower lip dropped toward her chin. "What?"

Casey tried to form the words again, but they refused to coop-erate, their letters floundering on her tongue, unable to regroup.

Patsy stared at her for several long seconds, then burst out laughing. "God, you scared the hell out of me. You know that? I actually thought you said something. Christ, I almost wet my pants. What's the matter with me? Shit, I've gotta get out of here."

No. No, wait. Please.

"I'll just grab a few more things," Patsy said, once again disappearing inside the closet. "I mean, these Prada pants are way too small, but I might be able to get something for them on eBay. And I *do* like this Armani jacket, although I'll probably have to let it out a bit at the bust."

You have to help me. You have to take me with you. You can't leave me here.

Casey began frantically kicking her feet beneath the covers, as if through water. She pushed her head off the pillow and lifted her right hand, grabbing at the air as if it were a lifeline.

Help me. You have to help me.

"Okay, I think that's everything," Patsy said, emerging from the closet, her arms filled with Casey's belongings. "Jesus fucking Christ!" she said, dropping everything to the floor as her eyes connected with Casey's.

Casey fell back against her pillow, overwhelmed by the effort of what she'd just accomplished, as Patsy crumpled to the floor.

31

PATSY? PATSY? WHERE ARE you? What the hell happened?

Had she run away? Casey tried to raise her torso off the bed to get a better look, but her body refused to cooperate.

Patsy, for God's sake, where are you? Get back here. You have to help me. You have to get me out of here.

Several more minutes passed before Casey was able to muster sufficient strength to lift her head again. At first, all she saw were her clothes spread, like loosely raked leaves, across the ivory-colored carpet.

And then she saw her.

Patsy was half sitting, half lying on the floor, her back against the open closet door, her head lolling toward her right shoulder, her eyes closed.

Don't you dare faint on me, you thieving little twit. Wake up! Do you hear me? Wake up!

I don't believe this, Casey thought, unable to sustain her position and collapsing back on her pillow.

No, no, no, no, no, no, no.

Patsy groaned.

Yes! Wake up. Wake up, damn you.

The groan became a moan. Was Patsy coming to or going deeper under? What was happening?

"Jesus," Patsy whispered several long seconds later. In the next minute, she was scrambling to her feet, her eyes slowly, and with obvious reluctance, traveling toward Casey. "I don't believe this," she said without moving. "You can see me, can't you? You're conscious." She took two tentative steps toward Casey's bed. "When did this happen? Where's Warren? Has anyone called the hospital?" She walked toward the phone, her hand outstretched.

Oh, thank you. Thank you.

And then the unmistakable click of a key turning in a lock. The front door opening.

"Warren," Patsy gasped, glancing back at the pile of Casey's clothes she'd thrown on the floor.

Not Warren, Casey knew, hearing the door close.

Death.

Casey saw confusion shoot through Patsy's eyes like lightning bolts.

The sound of footsteps as they ascended the staircase.

"Shit," Patsy muttered, running back and scooping up all of Casey's belongings from the floor and hurling them into the closet. "What'll I tell him? How am I going to explain . . . ?"

"Beauty?" the voice purred seductively from the hallway. "Your prince has arrived."

Casey watched Patsy's eyes narrow, her eyebrows crunching toward the bridge of her nose. What's going on? her eyes asked Casey's. That's not Warren. What am I supposed to do now?

Just make your presence known. That will be enough to stop him. He'll be as flustered as you are.

Save me, Casey shouted silently.

Patsy swayed toward her, her hands reaching for Casey and then dropping to her sides as the footsteps drew nearer.

No. What are you doing?

Patsy suddenly turned and ran into the closet, bringing the door closed after her. Almost immediately the door reopened and Patsy bolted out again.

Had she had a change of heart? Had her nurse's training finally triumphed over her baser instincts?

Thank God. Thank God.

But ultimately Patsy's instincts were only to save herself. She grabbed her purse from the floor, then scurried back inside the closet. This time she didn't have time to close the door after her.

Was she watching? Casey wondered. Would she see what was about to happen? Was there still a chance she might come to her rescue?

Out of the corner of her eye, Casey saw Nick's muscular frame appear in the doorway. He stood there for several seconds without moving. Casey prayed he was having second thoughts, that now that he was here, now that he had to actually confront what he'd come here to do, maybe he'd realize he couldn't go through with it.

Please don't come any closer.

But he was already walking toward her. He advanced easily, then stopped at the foot of the bed, his eyes traveling up the length of her body, stopping when they reached her face. "You sure are a pretty thing," he said. "It's a shame I gotta do this."

Casey found herself staring at the man her husband had hired to kill her, assessing him in a detached, almost clinical way. He was of average height, maybe five feet nine or five feet ten inches tall, with a barrel chest and notable biceps that all but over-whelmed his slim hips. His hair was dark and cropped very short, his nose straight and narrow, his eyes brown and flecked with mischievous gold, his lips surprisingly lush and girlish. Under normal circumstances, she might have considered him attractive.

She watched him dig into his pockets and pull out a pair of latex gloves. Her eyes widened in fear, although the man was too preoccupied with putting on the gloves to notice. "Can't go leaving any telltale DNA," he said, coming around the side of the bed to stand next to her head. "Now you just lie still and be a good little girl, and I'll try to make this as quick and painless as I can." Without any further delay, he reached down and gripped the tip of Casey's nose, squeezing her nostrils together with the fingers of his right hand while covering her mouth firmly with his left.

Casey fought desperately for breath as the smell of latex assaulted her nose, and the room began spinning. Her arms shot reflexively from her sides, her feet twitching uselessly beneath the sheets. She heard a loud gasp escape her lips.

Except the gasp hadn't come from her, she realized, as the pressure on her nose and mouth suddenly weakened and the man's hands quickly withdrew.

"What the hell was that?" he asked, leaving Casey's side.

Casey's mouth flew open, sucking the surrounding air into her lungs like a powerful vacuum. She watched the room spiraling out of control, the floor changing places with the ceiling, the tub chairs by the bay window skating from one side of the room to the other, the various paintings sliding across the wall.

Nick walked purposefully toward the closet. He took two steps in, then reemerged, dragging a sobbing Patsy into the center of the room. "What the hell are you doing here?"

"Please," she was crying. "Don't hurt me. Don't hurt me."

His response was to slam her against the end of Casey's bed. "You gotta be kidding me," he snarled, slapping her hard across the face.

Patsy screamed as she tried to evade his murderous grasp.

She grabbed the striped armchair, trying to drag it between them, but Nick was too fast and too strong. He pushed the chair aside as if it were a stuffed toy, then grabbed Patsy by the throat, twisting the Hermès scarf at its base and pulling it tight. Patsy's hands shot up, ripping into the man's latex gloves, then clawing at his face.

"Shit!" he yelped as Patsy's long fingernails found their mark, drawing blood. In an obvious rage, he pulled the scarf so tight around Patsy's neck it disappeared inside the folds of her flesh.

Casey watched in horror as Patsy's feet lifted off the floor to kick frantically at the air, her fingers straining to loosen the deadly silk at her throat, her eyes growing wide at the vision of her own impending doom.

No, please, no.

And then Casey heard something snap, and suddenly Patsy stopped struggling. Her feet stopped kicking; her hands stopped flailing. Casey closed her eyes, understanding Patsy was dead.

When she opened them again, Nick was loosening his hold on the scarf, allowing Patsy's body to slide clumsily to the floor. "Shit," he cursed repeatedly, pacing back and forth while dabbing at his cheek with the back of his hand, wincing at the sight of his blood on the white latex. "Look what you did to my face, bitch. Shit!" He kicked at Patsy's lifeless form. "And you ripped my fucking gloves." He tore the gloves from his hands, throwing them to the floor, and glared at Casey.

Casey forced her face to go blank, her eyes to stare straight ahead.

Nick stood absolutely still for at least two full minutes, clearly weighing his options and trying to decide his next move. "Okay," he said, as if he'd come to a decision. "Looks like you get a reprieve, Beauty. I'm bleeding. My gloves are ripped. The bitch has my DNA under her fucking fingernails. And there's no way in hell

I'm doing two for the price of one. That was definitely not part of the original deal. I'd say we have to renegotiate before we proceed any further."

Casey tried to keep a grateful cry from escaping her throat.

She watched as he began straightening up the room, returning the armchair to its former position and making sure everything else was where it was supposed to be. Then he stopped and looked around, as if searching for something in particular. "She's gotta have a purse around here somewhere," he said, his eyes sweeping across the floor. He stepped over Patsy's body on his way to the closet, then returned seconds later, Patsy's big canvas bag in his hands. He rifled through it, locating her wallet. "I wondered whose piece of shit was parked out front," he commented, pocketing Patsy's car keys. "That makes another car to dispose of. I'd say my bonus just got a little bigger." He returned to the bed, taking a minute to straighten Casey's covers, and even wiping some errant spittle from the side of her mouth. "Catch you later, Beauty." Then he returned to Patsy, scooping her dead body into his arms and tossing it unceremoniously over his shoulder, the scarf still embedded tightly in her neck. Without so much as a backward glance, Death strode from the room.

Only when she heard the door slam behind him and knew for certain he was gone did Casey unleash a low, guttural wail, as primal as life itself.

Two hours later, the front door opened and Lola burst through, followed by Drew and then Warren, the three of them laughing at some shared private joke. Already a happy little family unit, Casey thought, wondering how Warren would react when he saw she was still alive.

"Auntie Casey," Lola called out, running up the stairs. "Auntie Casey, I'm here!"

"Me, too," Drew said, laughing as she followed after her daughter.

Was Warren right behind them? What would he do when he saw her? Casey realized she was actually looking forward to finding out.

Her niece raced toward the bed, clambering up its side and burrowing in against her side. "We've been to Gettysburg," she announced. "It was so fun. Wasn't it, Mommy?"

"It was so fun," Drew agreed. "Oh, good. Your eyes are open."

"Is Auntie Casey awake?"

"I don't know, sweetie. Are you awake, Casey?" Drew grabbed Casey's hand.

Casey squeezed as hard as she could.

"You know what, Lola?" Drew said. "I have an idea. Why don't you go downstairs to the kitchen and paint your aunt a picture of some of the things we saw in Gettysburg."

"We saw a bunch of big, big rocks," Lola said. "What are they called, Mommy?"

"Boulders."

"Can I paint the boulders green and blue?"

"I don't see why not."

Lola jumped down from the bed and ran to the bedroom door, colliding with Warren's legs in the doorway.

"Is something wrong?" he asked.

"I'm going to paint a picture of boulders for Auntie Casey."

Casey could feel Warren's confusion as he advanced slowly into the room. Had they not realized his wife was dead? she could almost hear him thinking.

"How's Casey?" he asked tentatively.

"Her eyes are open again," Drew said. "I mean, I know they say it doesn't mean anything, but . . ."

Warren approached and took Casey's hand away from Drew's,

surreptitiously checking her pulse as he held tight to her wrist, obviously trying to come to grips with what he was seeing. "But you think it's a good sign," he said, finishing Drew's sentence for her.

"Maybe it just makes me feel better."

"Me too." Warren returned Casey's hand to the bed, stared directly into her eyes.

Casey stared back, unblinking.

"Where's Patsy?" Drew asked suddenly.

"I had to let her go." Warren's eyes never wavered from Casey's.

"You fired Patsy?"

"She wasn't working out."

"Wow. First Jeremy, then Patsy. You've been doing some major housekeeping."

"You try to learn from your mistakes."

"And Patsy was a definite mistake," Drew said, scanning the room. "So who's looking after Casey?"

"I hired a temporary nurse."

"Where is she?"

"I told her to come back at five," Warren said, as if he'd just dismissed her. "Would you excuse me for a few minutes? I have to make a phone call."

"Take your time," Drew said, reaching for Casey's hand as Warren left the room. "Okay, are you still there?"

Casey squeezed Drew's hand. "Help me," she managed to whisper, the words glomming together at the base of her tongue like sticky rice.

"Oh my God. Did you just say something?"

"Help me," Casey said again, stronger the second time, although the words remained murky, indecipherable even to her own ears.

"Oh, God. Warren!" Drew cried. "Get back here."

"No!" Casey said. This time the word was crystal clear.

"I don't understand. Why don't you want me to tell Warren? He loves you so much, Casey. He didn't stop talking about you all day. And we had such a wonderful time. He was so great with Lola. I realize how unfair I've been to him."

"No!" Casey said again. *You have to get me out of here. He's going to kill me. Call the police. Call 911. Get me out of here.*

"Why don't you want me to tell Warren?" Drew asked again.

Because he tried to kill me. Because you're next. Because we have to get out of here.

But the words refused to form, tumbling from her lips as a series of disconnected vowels and consonants.

"Is Auntie Casey singing?" Lola asked, skipping back into the room.

"I thought you were going to paint your aunt a picture," Drew said, clearly flustered.

"I couldn't find the paints."

"I think they're in the cupboard under the sink."

"I looked there."

"Look again," Drew said forcefully as Lola climbed back up on the bed.

"I don't want to. I want Auntie Casey to sing me a song."

"She can't sing, sweetheart."

"Yes, she can. I heard her."

"Did you call me?" Warren asked suddenly from the hallway.

"Auntie Casey is singing!"

No!

"Lola . . ."

"What?"

"She wasn't singing," Drew said.

"Yes, she was. I heard her."

No. No.

"What exactly *was* she doing?" Warren crossed to the bed in two giant strides.

"It was really more of a groan than anything else." Drew glanced warily at Casey.

"Why are you looking at her that way?" Warren demanded. "Do you think she can see you?" He suddenly reached over and ripped Lola's zebra painting off the wall, waving the colorful stripes back and forth in front of Casey's eyes. "Can you see this? Can you?"

"You're ruining my picture," Lola cried.

Casey tried closing her eyes, but it was too late.

"You blinked," Warren said. "Dear God, you blinked."

"What does that mean?" Drew said.

"It means she can see."

"Is that true? Casey, can you see?" Drew grabbed Casey's hand. "Squeeze once for yes."

"What are you doing?" Warren's face registered first shock, then amazement. "Are you saying she's responsive? For God's sake, Drew. If you know something about my wife's condition that I don't, tell me. Don't you think I have the right to know?"

There was a long pause.

No. Don't tell him. Please, don't tell him.

"Casey is conscious," Drew said finally.

No. Oh, no.

"What? For how long?"

"I'm not sure. Probably just a few days."

"A few days?" he repeated. "How do you know?"

"She's been squeezing my hand, spelling out words."

"Spelling out words?" Warren repeated dully. "Why on earth didn't you tell me about this?"

"I don't know," Drew said again. "I'm so sorry."

Warren sank into the armchair beside the bed and lowered his head into his hands.

"Please don't be angry," Drew said. "This is such great news. We should be celebrating. Casey can see. She can understand. She's starting to communicate. Soon she'll be walking and talking and as good as new. Isn't that wonderful, Warren? Casey's come back to us."

32

"IS SHE ASLEEP?" WARREN asked from Casey's bedside several hours later.

Drew stepped into the room. "Out like a light. I guess she was pretty exhausted, what with Gettysburg and then all the excitement with Casey."

"It's been quite the day," Warren agreed.

"It certainly has. How's my sister doing?"

"She seems to be resting comfortably. Looks like the Valium the nurse gave her is finally starting to take effect."

"Do you really think it was necessary?" Drew approached her sister's bed. "I mean, it seems a shame to knock her out just when she's starting to come around."

"Casey was awfully agitated, Drew. You saw the way she was carrying on when Mrs. Friedlander was here. She's confused and terrified. I don't want her falling out of bed and hurting herself."

"I guess you're right. Were you able to reach any of her doctors?"

"Not yet. I called the hospital; I've left messages all over the city. So far, nothing. It's Sunday night—what can you expect? I'll keep trying."

"I'm so sorry I didn't tell you earlier."

"How could you keep something like that from me?" Warren asked, his voice incredulous.

"I don't know. I was just so mad at you, I guess. I wasn't thinking straight. And then today, we were having such a good time, and you were so wonderful with Lola, and I wanted to tell you, I was *going* to tell you . . . ."

"It's all right," Warren said after a pause of several seconds. "What's important is that I know now." Another pause. "So, you think a little champagne is in order?"

"Champagne?"

"To celebrate the great news."

Drew hesitated. "I don't know. I really shouldn't . . ."

"Come on. You're sleeping here tonight. You won't be driving. One glass. I won't let you have any more than that."

"You really think it's a good idea?"

"I think Casey deserves a toast in her honor."

Drew laughed happily. "I guess she does."

"Be right back."

As soon as he was gone, Casey reached through the dense fog enveloping her head and grabbed Drew's hand.

Drew gasped with fright. "Casey, my God. You scared me. I thought you were asleep."

"Help me," Casey said, opening her eyes, not sure whether she'd said anything at all.

"What? I don't understand."

He's trying to kill me.

"You're not making any sense. Just try to relax. Do you want me to get Warren?"

Casey twisted from side to side, squeezing Drew's hand with all the strength she could muster. *No!*

"Okay, okay. Please try to calm down. Warren's right. You're going to hurt yourself if you keep thrashing around like this."

Warren didn't call the hospital. He has no intention of trying to reach my doctors. He's going to get you good and drunk, and then he's going to kill me. Tonight. Then he's going to find a way to put the blame on you.

"I'm so sorry. I can't understand what you're trying to tell me."

He's going to kill me! You have to get me out of here.

"Please try to calm down, Casey. I know this is frustrating, but you're not making any sense. Get some sleep, and in the morning when you wake up, I promise you'll be feeling much better."

I won't wake up in the morning. It'll be too late.

"Oh, I think I hear Warren coming with the champagne." Drew looked toward the bedroom door.

Don't have anything to drink. Please, Drew. It's important you stay sober.

"Is there a problem?" Warren asked, entering the room.

Casey closed her eyes, released her sister's hand.

"Casey was groaning a bit, but she seems okay now. Here, let me help you with those glasses."

Please, Drew, Casey thought, refusing to give in to the sleep that was hovering over her head like a plastic bag. Don't have a drink.

"Dom Pérignon," Drew said. "How nice."

"I've been saving this bottle for a special occasion," Warren said.

"Which this definitely is," Drew agreed, as Casey heard a loud pop, followed by the sound of her sister's high-pitched laughter. "Careful. It's spilling on the carpet."

"So we'll buy new carpet," Warren said, laughing now as well. "Hold out your glass."

No. Don't. Please don't take a sip. One sip will lead to another. You know it will. You know what will happen.

"Well? What's the verdict?" Warren asked.

"Absolutely fabulous."

"You hear that, Casey? It's absolutely fabulous," Warren said. "To the love of my life."

"Welcome back, Casey," Drew seconded.

Casey pictured her husband and her sister raising their glasses in her direction.

"Hurry up and get better," Drew urged, "so you can sample some of this incredible champagne." Casey pictured her sister quickly emptying the contents of her glass. "Oh, man, I forgot just how good great champagne can be."

"Let's have another toast," Warren suggested. "Your turn to go first."

"My turn," Drew repeated. "I think I need a little more champagne first. Thank you. Well, let's see. To my sister, whom I love with all my heart, even if I don't always know how to show it."

"Here, here," Warren said. "And to health and wealth and . . ."

". . . the American way."

Warren laughed. "To the American way."

"I don't suppose I could tempt you into topping off my glass again," Drew said moments later.

No, Drew. Please, don't do this.

"I guess I can let you have just a little bit more."

"You're a real sport. Aw, come on, Warren. You can do better than that, can't you? My sister's come back from the dead. We're supposed to be celebrating."

"All right. But this is it."

Casey listened to the sound of liquid being poured into a glass.

"To true love," Drew said.

"True love," Warren echoed.

Casey felt sleep gently massaging her temples, and her eyes rolling back in her head. It took all her concentration to keep from drifting off.

"Think I'll ever find it?" Drew asked wistfully.

"True love? I don't see why not. You're a beautiful girl. . . ."

"A *rich*, beautiful girl," Drew amended.

Warren laughed. "And you're funny and feisty and . . ."

"Fabulous."

"And fabulous."

"Like this champagne," Drew said, giggling. "How about just one more glass? I promise I won't ask for more."

"All right. But absolutely no more."

"It goes down very smoothly for something with so many bubbles."

"That it does."

"I like things that go down smoothly." Drew giggled again.

"And speaking of going down," Warren said, "what happened with you and Sean?"

"Who?"

"Sean? Your old boyfriend? The one who wanted to get back together with you?"

"He did?"

"He didn't?" Warren asked.

"He probably did," Drew said, and laughed again. "I mean, why wouldn't he? I'm funny and feisty and . . . what else am I?"

"You're fabulous."

"I'm fabulous."

"Yes, you are. And you're a very fast drinker. I can't believe your glass is empty already."

"That's because you're a very slow pourer."

"Well, then, let me correct that."

"You're a kind and generous man."

"And you are a sweet and sensitive woman."

"Thank you. Don't let me drink too much."

"I wouldn't dream of it."

"I have a very high tolerance for alcohol, you know."

"I can see that."

"I've been doing this a long time."

"Everybody needs a hobby."

Drew laughed as if this was the most hilarious thing she'd ever heard. "You're very funny. You know that? Funny and feisty."

"What happened to fabulous?"

"You're pretty fabulous, actually."

"Thank you."

Again the sound of liquid filling a glass.

"So, have you heard anything from Jeremy?" Warren asked.

"Who?"

"Jeremy. Casey's former therapist. I was sure he'd get in touch."

"Oh, right. Him. Actually he did call. Yesterday, as a matter of fact."

"He didn't waste much time."

"I guess you had him pegged."

"What did he want?"

"I'd left a note for him at the hospital, asking him to call. You know. Just to see if he was all right."

"And was he?"

"He said he was pretty upset at first, so he took a few days off. He's okay now."

"Good man."

"He *is* a good man."

"Drink up," Warren said.

"You're a good man, too."

Warren laughed. "So where is he taking you on your first date?"

"Who says he's taking me anywhere?"

"I had him pegged, remember?"

Drew laughed again. "We haven't decided yet. He said to think of something unusual. I'm supposed to call him."

"Are you going to?"

"Maybe."

"Have another drink." Warren filled her glass again.

"Don't tell me that bottle's almost empty."

"That's all right. I have another one."

"Why doesn't that surprise me?"

"He's not good enough for you, you know," Warren said.

"What? Who?"

"Jeremy."

"Probably not. But you have to admit he's pretty damn cute."

"Not exactly my type."

Drew laughed.

"You can do better."

"You have anyone in particular in mind?"

"I might."

"Wait—don't tell me. Could his name by any chance be Willy Billy?" Drew shrieked with laughter.

"I can promise you his name is definitely *not* Willy Billy."

"Why not? Is there something wrong with Willy Billy's willy?" Drew collapsed in a series of loud guffaws.

"Something tells me you've had enough champagne."

"Oh, come on, Uncle Warren. We might as well finish the bottle."

"Looks like this is the last of it."

"But you said you had another one."

"I did, didn't I?"

Drew jumped to her feet. "Where is it? I'll go get it."

"I don't know if that's such a good idea."

"It's a great idea. We're celebrating."

"That we are. It's in the fridge. Be careful on the stairs."

"I'm fine. Don't worry about me."

"I won't." Warren sank down into the chair beside Casey's bed. "I have enough to worry about at the moment. Wouldn't you say, Casey? What with old Nick screwing up again." He began stroking her hair. "I called him earlier. He was full of his usual excuses: I hadn't warned him anyone else might be here; what was he supposed to do? he'd had no choice but to kill Patsy." His hand stilled, resting on her forehead. "And now he expects to be paid double. Can you beat that? He screws up, and I end up having to pay for his mistake. What the hell was Patsy doing here anyway? Stupid girl."

Casey opened her eyes, saw Warren staring back at her. Who is this man? she wondered, watching his image split in two, then double up and circle around her head.

" 'You always see what nobody else sees,' " she heard Janine read.

"Stop trying to fight it, Casey," Warren was saying, his voice low and warm as a kitten's fur. "You're only making things harder for everybody." He leaned over, resumed stroking her hair. "This really has to be the last of our little chats, I'm afraid. What was it you said to Janine? That it was time to move on? Well, it seems it's almost that time again."

Casey watched two Warrens kiss the backs of two pairs of hands as her eyelids grew increasingly heavy. " 'Yet you never see what is quite plain,' " she heard Janine read. Seconds later, her will alone no longer enough to sustain them, she gave in to their weight.

"Thatta girl," Warren said as her eyes closed.

Casey fought to remain conscious. Stay awake, she told herself. Don't make it so easy for him. He'll just wait until Drew passes out, and then . . . what? Throw her down the stairs and somehow make it look like an accident? Or would he smother her with a pillow, perhaps even strangle her with his own hands, all the while finding a way to place the blame on Drew?

I'm so tired.

He hadn't realized the extent of Drew's enmity toward her sister, she could hear him tearfully telling Detective Spinetti, all the while berating himself for his stupidity. Drew had obviously gotten tired of waiting for the inheritance she considered rightfully hers, especially now that Casey was showing real signs of improvement. And she'd been drinking—she was so drunk, in fact, he'd insisted she spend the night. How could he have been so careless?

Drew would be too wasted to remember much of anything. And even were she to turn around and throw the accusations back in Warren's face, it would be her word—the word of a drunken party girl with both motive and opportunity—against his, a lawyer with an impeccable reputation and an airtight case of reasonable doubt.

Drew didn't stand a chance against him.

And neither did she.

You have to keep fighting. You can't let him win.

He'd won already, she realized. He'd won the minute Drew took her first sip of champagne.

Warren suddenly jumped from the chair and walked to the door. "Drew," he called out, as if she'd spoken her sister's name out loud. Had she? "What are you doing down there? Drinking the whole bottle yourself?"

"I'm coming," Drew called back. "Ready or not," she sang out from the stairway seconds later. "Here I am."

"What took you so long?"

Drew was chortling as she walked back into the room. "Did you miss me?"

"I missed Mr. Pérignon."

"Then it's a good thing I found him. It wasn't easy either. He was hiding way at the back of the fridge. Here you go."

"Thank you."

"It looks like Casey finally settled down."

"Looks that way. Stand back," Warren said. A loud pop followed, like the pop of a gun.

"What are we toasting now?" Drew asked.

"How about world peace?"

"Always a favorite. To world peace."

"To world peace."

"And Madonna," Drew said.

"Madonna?"

"She's my idol, the way she keeps reinventing herself."

"To Madonna," Warren said, with a laugh.

"And to Angelina Jolie. That woman's a saint."

"To Angelina."

Drew stumbled against the side of Casey's bed, falling into the chair Warren had formerly occupied. "Whoops. Somebody spilled champagne on Casey's blanket."

"Here. Let me pour you some more."

"To Casey."

"To Casey," Warren said. Then, "Drew, what's that on your nose?"

"My nose?"

What? No. Please, no.

"What exactly were you doing downstairs?" There was a smile in Warren's voice.

"You know what I was doing," Drew said defensively. "I was getting the champagne."

"Champagne produces bubbles, not white powder."

Casey felt her sister pull back as her husband reached his hand toward Drew's face. No, Casey thought. *No, no, no.*

"It's just baking soda," Drew said, sniffling loudly. Casey pictured her covering her nose with her fingers.

"Baking soda? You really expect me to believe that?"

"Maybe I was baking a cake."

"What have you been doing, Drew?"

"Nothing."

"I don't believe you."

"You're just getting yourself all worked up over . . ."

"Nothing?"

"Okay, so it's a little something. Just to take the edge off. A lot happened. And what is it they say? Things go better with . . . ?"

Oh, God, Drew. What have you done?

"How much did you do?"

"Just a couple of lines. It's no big deal."

"Drew . . ."

You played right into his hands.

"Honestly, Warren. It's no big deal. Come on. We're supposed to be celebrating. Let's have another glass of champagne."

You signed my death warrant.

"I think maybe you've had enough."

"Are you kidding me? This is nothing. Come on. Don't be a party pooper. Pour me another glass."

Warren sighed. "You're sure this is what you want?"

"I'm sure. And pour yourself another glass while you're at it."

"I'll make you a deal. We finish this bottle, then we go to our respective rooms and try to get a few hours' sleep. How does that sound?"

"Sounds like a plan."

Sometime in the next hour, her sister and her husband still noisily toasting her recovery, Casey gave up the fight, gave in to the inevitable, and surrendered to unconsciousness.

33

WHEN CASEY WOKE UP some time later, she was alone.

What time is it? she wondered groggily, turning her head toward the clock on her nightstand.

2:07, the large red numbers announced.

Two in the morning, she thought, allowing the numbers to sink in and wondering what had woken her up.

And then she heard it—the gentle squeak on the stairs that warned someone was approaching.

Who would it be this time? Casey wondered, stiffening beneath the sheets. Warren, or the man he'd hired to do his dirty work? Was her husband even now asleep in his bed, waiting for Death to pick her up and hurl her down the stairs like so much soiled laundry? Or maybe it was Warren himself, having easily seduced Drew into a drugged and drunken stupor, come to finish the job himself.

Casey strained through the darkness toward her bedroom door, the light of the moon through the window cloaking the room in a gentle mist. A figure appeared in the doorway, filling the frame. He paused for an instant, then crept quickly across the carpet like a large cat. Tears filled Casey's eyes, causing her vision to blur. Would she have enough strength to scream? she wondered as the man reached the bed, his arms extended. Would it do her any good if she could?

"No!" Casey heard herself cry, her heart thumping wildly, threatening to explode in her chest, as a large palm quickly covered her mouth. Her eyes opened wide, unable to comprehend what they were seeing.

"Shh," the man whispered.

Was she dreaming? How was this possible?

"It's okay," the man said soothingly, slowly alleviating the pressure on her mouth. "Don't scream. It's okay."

What was he doing here? How had he gotten inside the house?

The man pulled back her covers and lifted her carefully out of bed.

Jeremy.

"We're going to get you out of here," he said.

We?

It was only then that Casey became aware of a second figure watching from the doorway.

"Hurry," Drew whispered, urging him on.

Drew. My God. It's Drew.

"Hang in there, Casey," Jeremy said, carrying her into the hall.

"I'll get Lola," Drew said, leaving their side as Jeremy headed for the stairs.

And suddenly there was a third figure. He stepped into the hall, blocking their path.

Warren.

"Going somewhere?" he asked, almost casually. He was wearing the same blue-and-white-striped shirt and denim jeans he'd been wearing earlier, and even through the darkness, Casey could plainly make out the gun in his right hand.

Her mother's gun, she recognized. He'd found it.

"Put my wife down," Warren directed Jeremy. "Now."

Slowly, Jeremy lowered Casey to the floor, resting her back against the wall at the top of the stairs. "Easy, man. . . ."

"Shut up," Warren said. "What the hell do you think you're doing?"

"We're taking my sister out of here," Drew said defiantly.

"You're kidnapping my wife?"

"We're getting her away from you."

"Why would you want to do that?"

"Because it's what Casey wants."

"I see. And you know this how?"

"Because I know my sister. And I know you," Drew continued after a pause.

"And what is it you think you know?"

"I know you're up to something. I don't know what it is, but I *do* know you deliberately tried to get me drunk."

"I don't recall twisting your arm."

"You almost had me fooled, you know. I was starting to doubt my own instincts. I was actually feeling guilty about having given such a sweet guy such a hard time. But then you suggested we celebrate, and I thought, why is he offering me champagne when he knows what will happen if I start drinking? Although what you obviously *don't* know is that it takes a whole lot more than a couple of bottles of champagne and some stale baking soda to knock *me* out. And it really *was* baking soda, incidentally. I found it at the back of the fridge when I was looking for the champagne."

"You think you're very clever, don't you?"

"Just trying to be as convincing a fuckup as possible."

"And Jeremy?"

"I phoned him after we went to bed, told him I'd come up with this really unusual idea for a first date."

"Put the gun down," Jeremy urged. "We walk out of here. Nobody gets hurt."

In response, Warren aimed the gun directly at Drew's head. "I don't think so."

"You're going to shoot us all?" Drew asked.

"If I have to."

"You'll never . . ."

"I'll never what? Please tell me you weren't going to say I'll never get away with it. Because aside from being a trite and over-used turn of phrase, I absolutely *will* get away with it. I mean, clearly you haven't called the police, because you knew there'd be no way they'd allow you to remove Casey from the house without any evidence of wrongdoing. So there's no chance of the cavalry riding to your rescue. And just off the top of my head, I can come up with any number of scenarios to offer Detective Spinetti when I call him later. How's this for one? Jealous coke-head enlists the help of a disgruntled former employee to help murder her sister. The brave and selfless husband, still coping with the tragic accident that left his wife in a coma, confronts the two killers as they try to sneak out of the house and is forced to shoot them dead. What do you think? Think the good detective will buy it? It's not perfect, I know, but by the time the cops get here, it will be."

"Oh my God," Drew muttered, her eyes traveling between Warren and her sister. "Detective Spinetti was right—what happened to Casey was no accident."

"On the contrary," Warren corrected. "Your sister's coma was very much an accident. She was supposed to die."

"That's what she's been trying to tell me."

"And damn near succeeded. Not very nice keeping things from your husband, Casey," he said, waving the gun in her direction.

"Come on, man," Jeremy said. "Put the gun away before you hurt somebody."

"That's the general idea, isn't it?" Warren pointed the gun at Jeremy and squeezed the trigger.

"No!" Casey screamed, Drew's cries echoing her own as shots rang out and Jeremy collapsed, bleeding, to the floor. Drew immediately ran to his side as Warren calmly pointed the gun at her head and prepared to shoot again.

"Mommy?" a little voice asked from somewhere behind Warren. "What was that noise?"

Warren swung around. In the next second, Casey watched her sister literally leap off the floor and propel herself toward Warren, her hands and legs thrashing out in all directions at once, her feet kicking at his shins, her fingers clawing at his eyes and throat. The gun flew from his hands and spun down the hallway toward Casey, landing several feet from where she sat propped against the wall.

Slowly, her fingers stretched toward it.

You can do this. You can do this.

After several failed attempts, Casey managed to make contact with the cold metal of the gun's handle, her fingertips dragging the weapon closer, inch by inch, until it was almost within her grasp.

At the same time, Warren succeeded in pinning Drew's hands behind her back. Lifting her into the air, he hurled her against the wall, as easily as if she were a tennis ball. Drew crumpled to the floor in a shapeless heap, gasping for breath.

"Mommy!" Lola cried, rushing to her mother's side.

Warren strode purposefully toward Casey just as her fist closed around the handle of the gun.

"Give me the gun, Casey," he said, lowering himself down and balancing on the balls of his feet.

Casey lifted the gun from her side, pointing it directly at her husband's heart. Does he even have one? she wondered.

"You know you don't have the strength to pull the trigger," Warren said.

Was he right?

"Tap once for yes, twice for no," she heard Drew say.

"Even if you had the strength, you couldn't do it," Warren said, his voice as soothing and hypnotic as a lullaby. "I'm your husband, Casey. I love you. You know that. And you love me. You know you do. I'm so sorry for everything I've put you through. You know that in your heart, don't you? You know how much I love you. It's not too late. We can start over. Please, let me make it up to you."

"Tap once for yes, twice for no," she heard Drew say again.

"You don't really want to shoot me, do you, Casey?"

"I thought it right to tell you, because you went on as you always do, never looking just where you are, and treading in the wrong place. You always see what nobody else sees; it is impossible to satisfy you; yet you never see what is quite plain."

Casey looked into her husband's warm brown eyes, seeing the cold-blooded monster behind them very plainly indeed. As he reached for the gun, she tapped her finger forcefully against the trigger.

Once for yes.

34

" *'She did not move, and he came towards her with more doubt and timidity in his face than she had ever seen before,'* " Janine read. " *'He was in a state of uncertainty which made him afraid lest some look or word of his should condemn him to a new distance from her; and Dorothea was afraid of her own emotion. She looked as if there were a spell upon her, keeping her motionless and hindering her from unclasping her hands, while some intense, grave yearning was imprisoned within her eyes.'* Are you okay?" Janine asked, laying the book across her lap and reaching out to take Casey's hand in hers.

"She's great," Gail said from her chair next to the fireplace. "Aren't you, Casey?"

"She just wants to get the hell out of Middlemarch," Drew said, leaning over to stoke the fire, several errant sparks shooting from the fireplace toward the dark hardwood floor of her living room. Drew immediately stamped them out with the soles of her black high-heeled Manolo boots. "I can't believe you still haven't finished that book."

"Just twenty-three more pages to go. Come on, you want to find out what happens. Admit it."

"You mean something happened in the first six hundred pages?" Drew said. "Okay, I admit it. I'm enjoying it. God, does that mean I'm maturing?"

"It happens to the best of us."

"I'm far from the best."

"And far from the worst," Gail said.

"Thanks for noticing."

"You've come a very long way these last four months," Janine commented.

"So my therapist tells me."

"Casey says she's terrific," Gail said. "That she's really helping the two of you reconnect."

The women turned as one toward Casey, smiles filling their faces.

"We're working things out," Drew said. "Aren't we, Casey?"

"How about some tea?" Gail asked.

"Sounds great," Janine said.

"I'll make it," Drew offered.

"No, I'll do it," Gail said. "Just tell me where you keep everything."

"Tea bags are in the pantry, mugs are in the first cupboard to the right of the stovetop, kettle's on the burner," Drew said. "Can you believe I'm so domestic?"

"What I can't believe is how cold the weather's gotten all of a sudden," Janine said.

"It always gets cold for Halloween." Gail pushed herself off her chair and headed for the kitchen. "Those poor kids freeze their butts off every year. Stan says his kids end up wearing their coats over their costumes, so nobody ever knows what they're supposed to be."

"Are you taking Lola trick-or-treating this year?" Janine asked Drew.

"Yup. She's going as a cat."

"A cat? I would have thought she'd be a fairy princess."

"Fairy princesses are so last year. This year she wants to be a cat." Drew's proud smile filled her face. "Like her mother," she said, beaming. "I always used to dress up as a cat on Halloween. Remember, Casey?"

Casey smiled at the distant memory.

"So when Lola gets home from school, we're going to make cat ears."

"Sounds like fun," Janine deadpanned.

"Gail's coming with us. And Casey. They're going to be cats, too."

Janine turned her attention back to Casey. "Is that the price you have to pay for staying here until you're all better?"

"She loves it here. Don't you, Casey?" Drew said. "She's never leaving."

"Are you sure you're up for so much activity?"

"Jeremy thinks she is," Drew answered in Casey's stead. "We're only going to go a couple of blocks."

"How *is* Jeremy?"

"He's great. His shoulder's almost healed. He hopes to be back working by the first of the year."

"And the two of you?"

"Still going strong," Drew replied, borrowing Gail's girlish giggle.

"That's nice." Janine sounded genuinely pleased. "I'm really happy for you. And for you," she told Gail as she reentered the living room. "Even if all this sex she's been having lately is making her quite unbearable."

"You'll meet someone," Gail said.

"Not high on my list of priorities at the moment," Janine said, squeezing Casey's hand.

"How's your business doing?" Drew asked. She sank down in the coffee-colored sofa across from the large window overlooking the lake.

"Seems to be picking up. Oh—you'll never guess who I ran into the other day. Richard Mooney! Apparently he got a job over at Goodman and Francis."

"Aren't they the guys who represented Warren?" Gail asked.

"That was Goodman, Latimer. They're better than Goodman and Francis. Not that it did Warren any good."

"I guess their hands were kind of tied once Nick Margolis agreed to testify against him in exchange for taking the death penalty off the table."

"I still can't believe he tried to kill Casey, and then strangled that poor nurse's aide," Gail said after a pause, deep sighs replacing her usual soft laughter.

"I don't know," Janine said. "There were times I wanted to wring that girl's neck myself."

"I don't believe you said that." Gail pushed an errant curl behind her right ear, her eyes widening in shock.

"What? What'd I say?"

"At least Warren got what he deserved," Gail said.

"Not really," Drew countered. "He's still alive, isn't he?"

"If you call spending the rest of your life behind bars any kind of life."

"Beats spending it in a coma. Right, Casey?" Drew asked. "Too bad my sister's such a lousy shot. If that bullet had been another two inches to the right, we wouldn't be having this conversation."

The kettle started whistling from the kitchen.

"That's my cue," Gail said, exiting the room.

"I'll help you," Drew said, going with her.

"You're very quiet today," Janine told Casey after a pause of several seconds. "Does it upset you? Listening to us talk about what happened?"

"Not really," Casey said, her words slow and measured. She was still adjusting to the sound of her own voice, just as her body was still adjusting to its growing range of movement.

"I guess I sounded pretty insensitive before."

"I know," Casey said quietly.

"I'm sorry. I didn't mean . . ."

"About you and Warren," Casey qualified. "I know."

There was a moment's silence. Janine nodded, as if she wasn't entirely surprised by the revelation. "Do you hate me?"

"No."

"*I'd* hate *you*," Janine said.

"I know you would."

"Do you want me to leave?"

Casey shook her head. "How can you leave now? You still have twenty-three pages to go."

Janine smiled sadly, a gentle upturn at the sides of her mouth. "You don't need me to read them to you."

"On the contrary," Casey said. "I honestly don't think I could get through them without you."

Janine lowered her head to her chest and burst into tears. "Oh, Casey. I'm so sorry."

"I know you are."

"I was so stupid."

"Yes, you were."

"And I *hate* stupid."

Casey smiled. "Warren fooled everybody, Janine."

"If only I could go back . . ."

"You can't."

"I know."

"We have to move forward."

"If there was something I could do to make it up to you, you know I would."

"You can come trick-or-treating with us tonight," Casey suggested.

"What?"

"I'm sure Lola will be happy to make another set of cat ears."

"You really *do* hate me," Janine said.

Casey laughed out loud.

"Now, that's a beautiful sound," Drew said, returning to the living room, holding an orange enamel tray containing a plate of pumpkin-shaped cookies, four mugs, and a sugar bowl, Gail following right behind with the teapot. Drew deposited the tray on the brown leather ottoman in front of the sofa and knelt on the cream-colored shag carpet. Gail sank down beside her. Casey pushed herself off her overstuffed beige-and-brown velvet chair to join them on the floor.

"Careful," Janine said.

"Watch yourself," Gail echoed.

"I'm okay," Casey told them, crossing one leg over the other.

"I don't know how you do that," Janine said as Gail poured the sweet-smelling herbal tea into each mug. "Whenever I cross my legs, my knees end up around my ears."

"Speaking of ears," Casey said, "Janine's decided to come with us tonight."

"Fantastic," Drew said.

"Good stuff," Gail agreed.

"How could I turn down a chance to join the ever-popular pussy posse?" Janine quipped, and the other women laughed.

"Just don't let me hear you talk like that in front of my daughter," Drew cautioned protectively. "Here. Try one of my cookies. I made them myself."

"God, is there anything worse than a reformed junkie?" Janine asked rhetorically, biting into one of the cookies. "These *are* good," she admitted, taking another bite.

"It's my own recipe," Drew told her. "Peanut butter, sugar, a little hashish. Just kidding," she said to more laughter. "Honestly, Casey. Just kidding."

Casey joined in the women's laughter, feeling the fire from the nearby fireplace warm against her back. "To my sister," she said, securing the mug in her right hand and raising it to her lips, "who saved my life."

"To my sister," Drew echoed softly, "who saved mine."

Casey rubbed the tiny silver shoe dangling from the chain around her neck, wishing she could always feel this safe. She sipped slowly at her tea, her taste buds soaking up the subtle flavor of strawberries and vanilla as the liquid swirled around her tongue, then traveled smoothly down the back of her throat. She took a deep breath, her eyes floating lovingly between her sister and her two closest friends, and breathed again.

© Mark Raynes Roberts

JOY FIELDING is the internationally bestselling author of
All the Wrong Places, *The Bad Daughter*, *She's Not There*,
Someone Is Watching, *Now You See Her*, *Shadow Creek*,
Mad River Road, *See Jane Run*, and other acclaimed novels.
She divides her time between Toronto and Palm Beach, Florida.

joyfielding.com
Twitter: @joyfielding
Instagram: @fieldingjoy
Find Joy Fielding on Facebook